The Essential
Angler

The
Essential
Angler

DAVID FOSTER

**BEING A GENERAL AND INSTRUCTIVE
WORK ON ARTISTIC ANGLING
COMPILED BY HIS SONS**

WORDSWORTH CLASSICS

In loving memory of
MICHAEL TRAYLER
the founder of Wordsworth Editions

I

Readers who are interested in other titles from
Wordsworth Editions are invited to visit our website at
www.wordsworth-editions.com

For our latest list and a full mail-order service, contact
Bibliophile Books, 5 Thomas Road, London E14 7BN
TEL: .44 (0)20 7515 9222 FAX: .44 (0)20 7538 4115
E-MAIL: orders@bibliophilebooks.com

First published in 2006 by Wordsworth Editions Limited
8B East Street, Ware, Hertfordshire SG12 9HJ

ISBN 1 84022 267 0

Typeset in Great Britain by Antony Gray
Printed and bound by Clays Ltd, St Ives plc

Contents

Preface to the Third (English) Edition

The demand for another issue of *The Scientific Angler* [retitled *The Essential Angler* for the 2006 edition] has given the compilers an opportunity for the further improvement of the work. The additions indicated take the shape of delicately coloured [black and white in the 2006 edition] engravings of sixty land and aquatic natural and artificial flies, inclusive of a few 'fancy' artificials of repute.

The art of fly-making has advanced so much of late as to leave little to be desired in point of accuracy of attitude, colour, etc. Angling writers have almost invariably refrained from placing their artificials and the naturals in juxtaposition. The great improvement that has been achieved of late in the development of modern methods of fly-dressing has encouraged the compilers to place the natural and the author's carefully studied copy side by side. The chief distinction is, as a matter of course, the presence of the hook in the artificial. This, it is claimed, however, is practically invisible when placed *horizontally*, with the wings and legs of the fly *perpendicular*. The new double-hooked flies are constructed on this principle.[*] Several illustrations are given (see Plates 4 and 5) of the new 'invisible' hook as being the latest improvement of importance affecting the fly-fisher.

Since the publication our last edition, an American reissue has been published.[†] The renowned production of the venerable Walton,

---

[*] This hook, being lightly brazed, is found to maintain its position when floating. It is thus all but invisible in use, whilst the distended wings and legs are boldly outlined on the water's surface.

[†] Edited by Wm C. Harris, editor of the *American Angler*, the journal devoted exclusively to fishing in the USA.

the *Compleat Angler*, and the present work are the only English books on angling that our transatlantic cousins have deemed worthy of reprinting.

Four years have elapsed since this work was originally published, and since that time four editions have now left the press. We trust this new issue will meet with the appreciation so generously accorded its predecessors.

COMPLIUS
Ashbourn, 1886

CHAPTER ONE

The Habits and Haunts of Fish

Power of Vision, Hearing, etc., Possessed by Fish.
Periodic Movements and Habits of Salmon,
Brown Trout, Charr, Grayling and Pike

The habits of fish depend in no small degree on the power of their senses, and to these we will briefly allude before dealing with the subject in detail. The first faculty to claim our attention is that of sight.

᠅

Sight The clearness with which a grayling, lying at a depth of eight or ten feet of water, can distinguish a small speck of a midge, invisible almost to the human eye, is often a matter of comment and surprise. All fish, however, are not equally well endowed in this respect; but it may be safely affirmed that their organs of sight are quite as well adapted to their native element – water – as are those of birds and respiratory animals generally to the atmosphere. But, on the other hand, experience tends to prove that the more suited the eye of the fish may be to his particular element, the more indistinct is his vision beyond it. We have an instance of this in the grayling, which, although more cautious and timid, and possessed of keener visual organs than the trout, will rise much nearer the angler, and is not so easily disturbed and affrighted. The inferiority of a fish's perception of objects in the air, as compared with what is in or upon the surface of the water, partly arises from the fact that the eye adapts itself to the medium through which the rays of light are transmitted. We have frequently observed the pupil of a fish's eye

contract considerably in the course of a second or two after it has
been taken from the water, from the same principle which causes the
pupil of the eye of the domestic cat to expand or contract as the light
diminishes or increases. Observation shows that it is the *moving object*
that frightens the fish. We have seen trout suddenly cease feeding and
return to their accustomed retreat upon our merely raising an arm;
and when their 'holt' has proved to be near the opposite bank, and we
have been in full view, in clear relief upon a high bank, on keeping
perfectly stationary for fifty to seventy minutes, they have again
ventured into the open to take our fly. From a constant repetition of
convincing experiments we have been led to infer that the crystalline
and various other humours of a fish's eye are capable of reflecting but
a vague and distorted image of any object that may be even a yard
from the water's surface. We have stood over the centre of a stream,
upon a narrow plank, placed within a few inches of the surface of the
water, perfectly motionless, just as the fish have turned out of their
usual haunts to poise near the surface to feed on the flies which have
suddenly become plentiful. So long as our perpendicular position was
maintained the fish rose fearlessly all around to our very feet, but
the least movement had the effect of affrighting all the fish in the
immediate vicinity.

But, notwithstanding all this, it must not be forgotten that the
organ of sight is the most important in their possession, and not
only their food supply, but their very existence is dependent upon
its proper exercise. True it is that constant practice, in a measure,
develops their ocular faculties; and as acuteness of vision increases
the natural timidity of the trout, so surely does he gradually decline
surface feeding, preying upon fry and the smaller yearling fish, as
also upon the larvae of aquatic insects, etc., thus showing reliance on
his greater powers of discernment in his own element. In comparatively clear and still water, the old corpulent denizens of the
limpid depths thus exhibit the most provoking discretion, defying
frequently the rodster's best efforts to allure.

The superior power of vision the fish has in its own element is
partly due to the fact that *light*, like sound, on penetrating water

suffers an alteration both of the rate of progress and the direction of the rays. Refraction enables the fish to see an approaching or moving object, even when a projecting bank or overhanging rock or other substance intervenes. Mr Ronalds illustrates this by a familiar scientific experiment with a coin and vessel of water, by which the former, when placed in the bottom of the latter, is seen at an acute angle, when the side of the vessel intercepts a straight line between the coin and the eye of the spectator. We have known persons who have domesticated trout, being unacquainted with the laws of refraction, who have attributed this to various other causes.

༂

Sense of Hearing That trout are not wholly devoid of this sense is now a well-established axiom. There is nothing about the exterior of the head of a freshwater fish that would indicate that it is provided with an ear. Our leading physiologists and anatomists assert, nevertheless, that fish and other aquatic creatures have the internal organ in a state of perfection. In animals of higher grade the mechanical apparatus of hearing consists of two connected portions, external and internal. Fish appear to have the internal part, which is in direct communication with the brain. The organs of hearing possessed by terrestrial animals are designed for the reception of the more delicate vibrations of the atmosphere, whilst those of the fish are better adapted to the stronger pulsations of a denser element. Thus, though the inhabitants of the waters are insensible to atmospheric sound, they are very susceptible to vibrations of the earth which are communicated to the water, though undistinguishable to us. Who has not observed the terrified agitation of the fish, as far as the eye can penetrate the water, at the least perceptible vibration caused by a stamp of the foot at the bottom of a punt or boat? We have frequently ourselves seen fish clear the water altogether in ponds and lakes at a distance of forty yards from the point or focus of concussion. That sound is not communicated only by the external ear may be seen by the following experiment: take an ordinary tuning fork, strike it, and take the full volume of the sound quite close to the ear, then strike again and place the handle against or between the teeth, when, though at some distance from the ear, the sound will not be found to be diminished. Vibrations vary in intensity according to the degree of solidity and density of the conductive bodies. Thus, we are told that in the atmosphere sound travels at the rate of something like one thousand feet per second on bright, clear days, but 1,100 in murky, dull, and hazy weather. In water, however, sound travels very much quicker, being at the rate of 5,000 feet per second, and where wood is the medium quicker still, 16,000 feet per second being its rate of progress. If, therefore, a solid substance is the conductor of sound, it naturally follows that it will become more distinct. The operator upon the violin has thus a keener perception of the various strains of the instrument than the ordinary listener, since wood is the sole conductive body in his case. The organ of hearing being enclosed in the hard case of the head is, in the case of fishes, susceptible therefore to no slight variation of sounds; no noise that does not occasion a vibration of the element which they inhabit reaches them. Thus the effects of approaching heavy footfalls will be perceived, when a loud acclamation will have no visible effect on them. A learned doctor of divinity, once known to the writer, used to include in his category of angling requisites a gigantic musical-box, which, for bottom-fishing, it was supposed, served the double purpose of being a convenient seat and a charming substitute for ground bait. So far as the latter object was concerned, the effect was purely imaginary, as, to the impartial mind, results amply testified.

We have now dealt with the two chief organs possessed by fish, namely, those of sight and hearing, a knowledge of both of which is highly important to the angler. With regard to the senses of taste and smell, we may briefly state that from what we have been able to ascertain they are very slightly developed; that of taste we do not believe is possessed in the faintest degree by the majority of fish. Roach, grayling, and the smaller species of delicate organism we have found display fastidiousness in this respect, but the mass of voracious fish we believe to be totally devoid of all sense of it. The nostrils are doubtless the medium by which impurities in the water are detected. Certain it is that such impurities are perceived, and whenever possible avoided, as is plainly exemplified in these days of river pollution.

Apart from the above causes the movements of fish, both migratory and non-migratory, are generally determined by one of two causes: first, by the search after suitable places for the deposit of their eggs, a certain temperature of water being necessary to vivify them; and secondly by the quest of food. The movements of all animals which feed on living creatures are greatly influenced by the habits of the creatures preyed upon, and fish offer no exception to this rule. We shall now proceed to lay before our reader a comprehensive view of what has taken us well nigh 50 years of patient application to acquire, namely, the characteristic habits and movements of andamorous and non-migratory fish, a knowledge of which it is incumbent upon every fisherman to possess.*

౫

The Salmon (*Salmo salar*) As is well known, these fish, with other orders of the same family, elsewhere described, pass a portion of each year in salt water, descending to the sea after they have deposited their spawn on the gravelly beds of the higher portions of rivers. The time of migration varies in different waters; thus we hear of early and late rivers. The spawning season ranges from March to November. The majority of mature fish ascend and descend at fixed periods, the time chosen generally being during a flood. The early spring floods bring the first and main instalments to the sources of the rivers; but in the event of these failing, the fish often prolong their stay in salt water bays and in the mouths of rivers until the first rising of water will admit of a passage. There are in most salmon rivers numerous weirs so constructed as to render the passage of fish an impossibility, except

---

* The compilers of this publication deeply regret their inability, from the limit of space at their disposal in the present edition, to publish more than one half of the information given by the author upon the habits of fish, a life history of most of which is given in the original manuscript.

during a heavy flood. In waters where these artificial obstructions do
not exist, migratory fish pass frequently to and fro, these periodic
ascents being doubtless occasioned by the quest of food. For a salmon
to remain in good condition for a protracted period in freshwater
would appear to be an impossibility. Their ova are vivified and their
young flourish in the inland streams, but after attaining a given size
their growth stops, and they sicken and die if the passage to salt water
is obstructed. The cleansing influence of the marine trip is necessary
at least every two years, even when the supply of food in freshwater is
ample, which is seldom the case. The freshly run fish may be said to
be invariably fat, and in the best possible condition, not only in the
substance of the flesh, but in the large quantities of adipose matter
which is found on the pyloric appendages, which secret store serves
as an internal source of sustenance supporting the fish during its
summer stay in freshwater, where food is comparatively scarce.

It is often asserted that andamorous fish will not feed except in salt
water, and that their internal fat sustains them when absent from it.
This is most certainly erroneous, as migratory fish are not more
given to fast than are any other freshwater species when food is
plentiful. The young of both grayling and trout suffer greatly from
the presence of salmon in the tributaries of our rivers, the former
particularly are sought after and taken by them.

A salmon in its young state is commonly called a parr, smolt,
smelt or samlet. When at this stage, they rise boldly at the artificial
trout-fly, but it is unlawful to take them. The terms for the young of
other migratory fish (Salmonidae) are scad, shed, black-tip, blue-
fin, hipper, etc. When the young of these fish attain a length of about
six inches, which they do in from eighteen months to two years from
the time of hatching, they descend to the sea, where their stay is,
generally speaking, about four months. Upon the first return of the
young fish, after a sojourn of about this period, it is commonly
termed a grilse or salmon-peal. The term 'kelt' is applied to male
or female after spawning time, the male being also specially distinguished by the appellation 'kipper'. The fish then assume the
colour and form of the fully developed fish. With regard to the hard

and fast rules usually given for their growth and development, their stay in their native or in salt water, we may state that great variation exists amongst individuals living under the same apparent conditions. The pisciculturist well knows that a portion of every brood or hatch of fish are larger, stronger, and more vigorous than the remainder, and the same thing is exemplified when the fish attain maturity. We cannot endorse the statements of some who affirm, though they never attempted to prove, that the fry mature so quickly and grow so rapidly, when at liberty, as to be able to descend to the sea within twelve months from the hatching period. Of their rapid growth during the marine trip we have had ample proof; this is perfectly rational, the sea being the feeding ground for the whole family of migratory fish, the abundance of small animalculae therein contained forming a never-failing supply to the immigrants.

In ascending rivers, salmon usually keep near one side of the bottom of the water, but when their tributaries are being ascended, they take the middle of the swiftest streams. When a stream forms the outlet of a lake, or any sheet of water known to be the annual resort of migratory fish, it is of the most vital importance that no obstruction be erected to arrest their passage. There has been a considerable falling off in the takes of salmon during the last twenty years or so. This may be attributed to three combined causes: (first) the erection of weirs and flood gates; (second) river pollution; (third) the depredation of the fungoid growth termed 'the salmon disease'.

With regard to the first and second causes here given, we will take the particular case of the Trent. This river was formerly one of the most important for salmon yields in the United Kingdom, and it still ranks next to the Thames for its yields of other fish. The river itself, devoid of tributaries, is of the following extent: in Lincolnshire, 20 miles; in Nottinghamshire, 55 miles; in Derbyshire, 30 miles; and in Staffordshire, 40 miles. The tributaries take their rise at 1,500 to 1,900 feet above the sea level, and are pure. They extend as follows: the Dove and Churnet, 63 miles; Wye and Derwent, 67 miles; the Soar and Wrecke (Leicestershire), 65 miles; the Idle, 45 miles; the Blythe and Anker, 35 miles; the Terme, 25 miles; the Tame, 25 miles;

the Erewash, Sow (Staffordshire) and Devon river, each 20 miles. The whole of the above streams, owing to the rapid fall in most cases, and the purity and cool temperature of their waters, were the annual resort of salmon and other migratory fish in immense numbers a few generations back. What do we find to be the case today? The salmon are debarred from ascending even the main river, except during heavy floods, by senselessly contrived weirs at different points, and with the same exception, the passage up the Derwent is entirely shut off by weirs below Derby. In respect to the Dove, being swift and of excessively rapid fall, it was originally the favourite resort of Trent salmon, many of which would ascend as high as Dovedale. There are some four or five weirs that are rendered passable only when the river is bank-full, after a very heavy shoot of water from the hills, until Rocester is reached, where there is situated a weir that is impassable at all times from its peculiar construction. All this may seem strange to those of our readers who have been led to imagine that the natural buoyancy and strength of andamorous fish enables them to over-come both ordinary and extraordinary difficulties in the way of impediments to their upward course. It is, nevertheless, the fact that salmon are to be annually seen for weeks and even months vainly trying to ascend an obstruction known to be an effectual bar to their upward progress, until finally they deposit their spawn at the point where the passage is arrested, whether suitable or not. Salmon leap to a great height to surmount a cascade or perpendicular fall, but the long slanting weirs are not to be stemmed when they exceed a given length and angle.

But to return. The Tame is now polluted to such an extent that even pike fail of late to flourish in it.[*] The main river, too, is now also polluted so as to admit only of the presence of fresh-run migratory fish when flooded by its tributaries. Thus, out of 575 miles of water only a very few can be accessible to the salmon as spawning ground. It will, therefore, be seen that, taking the noble Trent as a type,

---

[*] This has been corroborated by the evidence given at a recent inquiry instigated by the Trent Fishery Board of Conservators.

salmon in English waters, unless more urgently looked to by the district conservators and other responsible bodies, will soon be a thing of the past.

The fungoid disease, named as the third cause of the falling off of the product of salmon in our largest and most important rivers, is most disastrous in its results, and when it attacks the fish in the spring or early summer months its depredations are great. Owing to the circumstance of its being unknown to salt water, the gradual growth of fungus over the fish is speedily arrested, and finally cleansed away when the fish leave the rivers. This fungoid growth, so detrimental to the well being and life of fish, has been termed the *salmon* disease, which is anything but a correct appellation, seeing that its deadly effects are often even more marked in the case of trout and other fish. This disease is a choleraic disorder, and we are told owes its immediate origin to animal or vegetable substances, one or both, in a state of poisonous decomposition in the water. Effectual remedies there would appear to be none. The only safe and efficient remedial course would appear to be to avoid river pollution, and thus purify instead of putrefy water containing fish. Occasionally, however, this deadly disorder is found to be rife in waters that cannot have been polluted by any of the numerous impurities to which the waters of populated districts are exposed, and in these instances it may be assumed that the presence of decaying vegetable substances is owing to protracted, unhealthy weather.

Salmon frequent only the northern and temperate parts of the earth. It is a noteworthy fact that the inhabitants of the more southern latitudes, when mature, are much inferior both as regards size and gameness of disposition – this at least in the eastern hemisphere – than those of colder regions. In Norway these fish are capable of attaining a prodigious size and weight, 80 to 90 lbs occasionally; whilst in the waters of Britain, the adult fish very rarely attain to one half that weight.

The Common Trout (*Salmo fario*) For variety of size, colour, and disposition, the brown or common trout may be said to eclipse all other species. Every loch and river, and almost every tributary, has its variety. The geological formation of the bed of the river, the aquatic vegetation, and the quality and description of the food obtained by the fish, have much to do with this variation. No fish can be said to be so widely distributed, or so capable of affording more variety of sport, from the lordly Thames fish to the game little denizens of the Devon streams. Trout will flourish in almost all waters capable of sustaining fish, but their chosen resorts are rapid, clear mountain streams; the jostling waters of which, foaming amidst fragments of rock, whirling and surging in their rapid course, form numerous cascades and caverned banks. Such are the favourite haunts of the trout. The merest rill of clear and rapid water will often contain vast quantities of these fish, when from its appearance it would be deemed incapable of sustaining a single fin. Under shelving banks and submerged substances, amongst roots of trees bordering the banks of the streams, trout secrete themselves when not on the feed. A casual observer may ofttimes affirm a length upon a noted trout stream to be wholly devoid of fish after a careful and prolonged inspection along its banks, when the subsequent appearance of surface food will prove the water to be alive with them, and they may as suddenly disappear upon the insects leaving the water's surface to secrete themselves before an impending atmospheric change. In some districts trout spawn in winter, in others in October and November, or in December; and elsewhere in January and in February, or in March.* The precise time depends also in a measure on the prevailing state of the weather and water. In the close season, trout leave the larger streams, ascending the brooks and rivulets, in the gravelly bottoms of which they deposit their spawn.

---

* The close season, as by law established, is from the 2nd of October to the 1st of February following, both inclusive. Bye-laws are, however, framed to meet exceptional cases: 'The close season for salmon ranges from the 1st of September to the 1st of February following, but it is lawful to take salmon up to the 1st of November *with the rod and line.*'

When this operation is effected they disperse to their wonted haunts, the tails of currents, lying for the most part above and below pools and slow running deeps, behind any impediment to the running water, such as thick piles and sunken timber. As they get into condition they move to stronger water, occasionally for this purpose ascending brooks whose waters may be turbulent and strong to their very source. Here they linger by the edges of streams that flow into the throats of the pools, and at this period rise boldly and unsuspectingly for a time, and are then to be allured by the novice in a comparatively easy manner. After the lapse of a few short weeks, as the water and weather become clearer and brighter, the trout grow cautious, where heavily fished over, they having now entirely recovered their customary vigour, and with it their beauty of form and colour. They now take up their old positions, vacated prior to the commencement of the spawning season. These are chosen as vantage ground for food, the largest fish occupying the best feeding ground, and when one of these has been extracted the next best fish in the immediate vicinity takes possession of the vacated post. These fish will often fight desperately for a favourable situation, hence it is that the larger tenant the best positions. Near circulating eddies, behind large stones, in side- and mid-stream, below jutting portions of banks, etc., ever near the main volume of water, and the perpetuated line of bubbles wherever it may tend, the trout lie assiduously observant of passing objects, whether in or on the top of the water.

When a quantity of flies are 'up' in rapid water, the fish poise themselves near the surface, the more readily to close upon their winged prey; but, upon the other hand, when no surface food is presented to their view, they are quick to seize adventurous fry of their own or any other species, without distinction. In the latter half of May their attention is generally attracted and absorbed by the then active grub or pupa of the mayfly or drake, and as these nymphae are, generally speaking, numerous in the waters frequented by trout, the fish are seldom found rising at this particular period. In about a week or ten days from the first signs of activity, the pupae referred to vacate their case and rise to the water's surface, when, after emerging from yet another skin, they appear in their subimago state as green drakes. The fish, not comprehending the change, continue to feed upon the undeveloped worm for a few days, until the now profusely laden surface allures them from the river's bed, and monopolises their whole attention during the stay of the mayfly, which is usually prevalent from 17 to 20 days. By the time the season of the drake terminates, the fish have so regaled themselves upon this lusty ephemeral that for a week or so they find it incumbent upon them to retire to the deep still water, to doze off the effect of the excess, after which they again resort to their accustomed posts, which are not forsaken until the spawning season again comes round, except when forced to retreat in the face of what in Highland phraseology is called a heavy 'spate', when, particularly in hilly districts, the water rises and the stream becomes 'bank-full', to overflow in a few hours; not only is the force of the current too strong, but the water is generally too thick in mid-current to admit of the movement of the fish. In these circumstances the quiet corners and side eddies, no matter if quite out of the usual water-course, are the resort of not only trout, but all other species that may inhabit the water. The whole congregate in places of comparative safety when danger threatens, the minnows with the trout, the pike with the gudgeon. When trout reach a more than ordinary size they disdain surface food. At twilight, and even later in the hot months, however, they will rise at the large moths, but are not to be allured to the surface by small flies. When over two pounds weight the flesh assumes a beautiful red tint, not unlike that of a well-conditioned salmon, but when they much exceed that weight they do incalculable harm to the water they inhabit by greedily devouring the small half-grown fish. They occasionally attain a prodigious size, five and six pounds being not altogether uncommon. But although a trout may reach this weight, he does not long retain it, for within a comparatively brief period all the store fish within a hundred yards of his haunt will have disappeared, and the cannibal who has thus depopulated it will diminish quickly in flesh, showing a gaunt head and rakish-looking frame as the result of the scarcity of food; for, strange as it may appear, the veteran trout seldom forsakes his chosen haunt, even to appease hunger's keen pangs. Fish of this description should be destroyed. At twilight they will frequently come boldly at the minnow. At midday it is of little use angling for them, as the tackle must then necessarily be fine to get them to face it, and when this is the case it is unequal to the task of holding them when hooked. In large rivers the existence of hybrids in certain of the first sub-genus group of Salmonidae is by no means infrequent, the non-migratory fish interbreeding with the migratory, producing tidal or slob trout, and other varieties, which occasionally attain considerable dimensions. The common trout in certain waters sometimes attains a large size, notably in the Irish Loughs, those of Lough Neagh frequently scaling 18 to 20 lbs. Thames fish are occasionally taken weighing in the teens of pounds, but such captures are few, and we regret to have to add, are becoming yearly more infrequent, notwithstanding the instalments from High Wycombe and other sources. Kingston, Shepperton and Chertsey were years ago the best localities for these fish, and, therefore, the chief resorts of the anglers. More recently Sunbury, Weybridge, Maidenhead and Marlow Weir have become the favourite places.

ॐ

The Gillaroo* **Trout** of Ireland is another large variety. In their native lakes they attain frequently four or five pounds weight, but when introduced into other waters they often much exceed that weight. This variety affords much excellent sport when hooked, even when small. It is scarcely advisable, however, to introduce this large variety into ordinary trout streams, as the effects in all probability would be similar to those following the introduction of bass in the American trout rivers, the original stock gradually disappearing. Large fish invariably require an enormous amount of food to enable them to grow and flourish, and should never be introduced into water which will not afford the necessary supply.

---

* So-called from the structural arrangements of the stomach, which is usually as large as a chicken's, in formation resembling the gizzard of the bird known as the gillaroo.

ᕁ

Charr and Pollan (*Coregonus*) Both these fish are extremely local. The first named are found in large lakes, the deepest parts of which they frequent. Like trout, they vary in different waters, chiefly however in colour, which is often most brilliant when they have been freshly taken, the fiery red breast being then marvellously vivid. The torgock, or Welsh charr, is perhaps the most conspicuously coloured. It is found in Llanberis and other lakes in the north of Wales. It is smaller than those of Windermere and other northern lakes, its average length being 13 to 15 inches. The charr is strictly a northern fish, and flourishes much better in lakes fed by underground springs at some elevation than in shallow and low-lying waters. The lakes and lochs chiefly noted for these fish in England, Ireland and Scotland are Windermere, Ennerdale, Buttermere and Wast-Water in the north of England; Lough Enniskillin, Lough Eske, Lough Dan, Lough Melvin, Lough Killin and Lough Corrib in Ireland; Lochs Grannoch, Roy and Awe in Scotland; and Lake Helier in Hoy in the Orkneys. From their habit of seeking the seclusion of the very deepest water during the greater part of the year, they are seldom taken by the sportsman, although bold risers at the fly. Occasionally they are excessively shy, and are not to be approached within a considerable distance when surface feeding. The contents of their stomachs when taken generally consist of aquatic and aerial insects, and the small fish known as the stickleback, which latter form their principal food. This fact failed to attract our notice until the year 1862, when we were fishing upon the Awe, in Argyleshire, at different periods during a visit of four months. We had observed a succession of bubbles appearing upon the water's surface for an instant, and having never succeeded in raising a fish in immediate proximity, we concluded that they were caused by an escape of gas or air from the bottom of the water. After a while there came a day when the momentary bubbles were exceptionally numerous, though they never occurred near the boat. This circumstance did not escape us, and we put up a cast of brown-trout flies, in lieu of the larger salmon fly we had previously been using, and these we succeeded in casting in the midst of a rising of bubbles, and this time not in vain, for the next instant we not only had a rise but a hooked fish, which eventually proved to be a charr of the northern species, and was found to be gorged with small sticklebacks. Subsequent experience proved that the eruption referred to was simply a shoal of these tiny fish clearing the water in their frantic and futile endeavours to elude their enemies. The fish here spoken of was sent to the proprietor, Colin Campbell, Esq., of Loch Nell, as we were informed that the existence of charr in the loch was unknown and unsuspected. We were afterwards assured that such was the case by the proprietor, who wished to know the precise fly that had allured the specimen forwarded. Since then, charr have been regularly taken in their proper season. Charr come into shallow waters to spawn during the autumn, often running into the lake feeders to perform this operation, when nets are frequently illegally used for their destruction. Charr are classed with trout under the new Freshwater Fishery Acts, and the close time is therefore the same. The Pollan, or Powan, are confined to the Irish lakes, Lough Neagh being especially noted for these fish; Lough Erne, and Loch Lomond, too, are stocked with them. They feed, like the charr, upon the fly and other aquatic insects, etc. The prevailing colour is silvery grey, the head and back being bluish brown.

They spawn in December and January, and afford good sport during the genial months to the angler.

The Grayling (*Thymallus vulgaris*) This is a much more fastidious and delicate fish than the trout; and, although it abounds to profusion in some streams, yet it is very local when compared with the trout. Both Scotland (excluding the Tweed, Clyde and the Orkneys) and Ireland are graylingless; neither do they occur in Wales, except in the border streams. They require a peculiar combination of favourable surroundings to enable them to flourish and locate permanently when introduced into strange streams. A moderate temperature of water is requisite for their wellbeing, and a succession of stream and still deeps. They generally frequent the lower portions of trout streams in hilly districts; a fair volume of water, too, is essential, as, when there flows less than two tons or thereabouts per minute, grayling descend to a lower point, where their needs in this respect are satisfied. The bottoms of our best grayling rivers usually consist of an alternate mixture of loam, marl, sand and gravel. The brown trout, in his habits of migration, penetrates still further upstream to more rapid water. The grayling, on the other hand, more generally descends to slower running waters; still, there is little doubt that this fish would thrive in many waters in which it is at present unknown. Grayling are, to a certain extent, gregarious, generally frequenting the stills, even when surface feeding. It is owing to this fact that they are given to rise nearer the rodster than the trout, ascending often from the deepest part of the river to seize a passing insect. Although, when top food is plentiful, these fish rise boldly and continuously, they, especially when the water is slightly discoloured, are very partial to the larvae of water flies, wasps, maggots, cabbage grubs, etc., as they are also to any imitation of these.

Grayling grow rapidly in comparison with other Salmonidae, the young attaining several inches in size in a very few months. They spawn usually in April and May. By October or November, the fry are little larger than a minnow,* and are then termed 'pink' grayling. The summer following they average four to the pound, and are then known as 'shote' fish. About two years from the time of hatching they attain about half a pound, by which time the ova is matured, but not before. The half-pound fish takes the name of grayling. The fish is in the very zenith of health and vigour from October to January. When in perfect condition they are almost black upon the back, which contrasts prettily with the silver-grey and pure white of the

---

* Sir Humphrey Davy affirmed that the ova of a fish hatched in April attains the weight of half a pound, or even 10 ozs, by the following October. This we cannot endorse. Since the days of this eminent modern philosopher infinitely greater facilities for observation have been afforded by the artificial hatching and rearing of fish, pisciculture having afforded reliable testimony as to the times of growth and sexual development.

bosom. The dorsal fin, which is immensely large in this variety of Salmonidae, is faintly tipped with a ruddy hue. In reference to the habits of the grayling much diversity exists in current literature bearing upon this subject, as the following brief quotations will show:

Early in spring grayling ascend the rivers, where they remain till autumn, and then return to their former element. *Donavon*

Grayling are found in the North Sea, Cattegat and Baltic. *Nilsson*

He is a fish that lurks very close all the winter, but is very pleasant and jolly after mid-April, in the hot months. *Walton*

They delight in rivers that glide through mountainous places, and are met with in the clearest and swiftest of those streams. *Mackintosh*

The grayling is the deadest-hearted fish in the world. *Cotton*

The grayling passes its time entirely in freshwater, and I cannot understand how Donavon – whose figure, bad as it is, shows itself to be this fish – says it is migratory. *Haughton*

I have proved that grayling will not bear even a brackish water without dying. *Davy*

Grayling are best in season in autumn and winter; indeed, they should not be taken till August, and all caught before that period should be returned. *Francis*

They cannot stem rapid streams, and are gradually carried lower and lower, and at last disappear. *Shipley* and *Fitzgibbon*

The grayling is an excellent fish for sport. *Ronalds*

The juxtaposition of these extracts shows how many inaccuracies and fallacies are diffused by those who profess to be the teachers of truth.

The quotations are accurate in detail, as grayling fishers of experience will concede. The annual movements of these fish occur in
much the same way as those of the trout, with the exception of the
one being in condition in the cold season and the other in the most
genial part of the year. In the spawning season (April and May) they
repair to the broad shallows, where the watercourse widens, and the
gravelly bottom is plainly apparent. Here they lie in shoals, and,
before the national law prohibited the practice, sacrilegious work
was often perpetrated with the net by the poaching fraternity, who,
unfortunately, are much better acquainted with the habits of their
quarry than is generally credited. After the sexual functions have
been in due course accomplished, they seek the best feeding positions
vacant, near the sides and at the tails of sharp streams, where they
lie at the bottom, ever on the lookout for what the stream may bring
down, such as the larvae of the several orders of large water flies and
other aquatic insects – the water-spider and freshwater shrimps
(*Gammarus aquaticus*). The grayling, though a delicately organised
fish, nevertheless possesses a strong stomach, superior to that of the
trout, which enables it to digest insects inhabiting shell-like cases,
and other molluscous food. After their health has been somewhat
restored by a short location here, the approach of the hot months
drives them to the seclusion of the deepest water, near the bottom
of which they lie, where the heat is less felt. We believe this to be the
main secret as to the suitable water and locality for these fish, as in
these days of artificial propagation and experimental ventures in
the transportation of fish, it has been often observed that when the
water is not adapted for the peculiarities of this fish, *they have
invariably descended* at the approach of warm weather, never to
reascend. There are many waters that do not at present contain
grayling, that are perfectly adapted to their peculiarities. Streams
having lime spring sources are found to be particularly suited to
these delicate fish. In the Canadian lakes the trout lie, whenever the
weather is oppressive, in masses near the cool springs, especially
when these are situated at the bottom of the water. Grayling in this
country are found to flourish in similar situations, but in more

genial climes they cannot be preserved, being a northern fish. In early autumn they leave the still deeps and congregate upon the lower running streams, where the water is from three to four feet deep. Here, in the wake of piles encumbered with sticks, etc., they sport in company, and are to be allured by fancy artificials, even when there are no flies on the water. At this period they afford really excellent sport when fished for by the sunk fly, as well as by the other methods of angling for them, described elsewhere. As the year advances the vitality and vigour of the grayling increases, and by the time the sharp frosts of winter set in, whenever the water is in fit condition, they afford exceptionally good sport. Grayling often attain a large size; they are frequently taken from two to four pounds in the rivers most noted for them, which are as follows: the Avon, Itchen and Test in Hampshire; the Dove, Wye and Derwent in the Midlands; the Aire and Swale in Yorkshire, and the Lugg and Teme. This fish has recently been turned into the Clyde and Tweed, where it appears to flourish.

࿓

Pike frequent the more shallow portions of the water when they are in quest of food, as also for spawning purposes. The smaller fish naturally throng to the thinner waters for better security, and the larger fish of prey lurk in their vicinity, as the vicious dogfish do near the herring shoals, upon the shelving strand. Pike also love to be concealed in weedbeds, amongst the friendly shades of water plants, from which they pounce upon their unsuspecting prey. In rivers and running water, like trout, they generally take up an advantageous position before a jutting portion of the river's bank, or in a deep curl of water at a sudden bend. These places are favourite haunts, and are sure to be tenanted by either large or small fish. In both winter and summer the pike is a solitary and unsocial fish. They spawn in the spring, April and May being the usual months, but the spawning period varies with the locality to a certain extent. As pairing time approaches they repair to creeks, side-ditches, backwaters, etc., and in the case of lakes and ponds to the seclusion afforded by weed and reed beds. In the fall of the year the wanderers congregate in a social sort of way in the still and deepest parts of the water, or in some favourite nook which may have been an annual place of assembly since it was originally formed. The ova of the pike hatch quickly, 32 or 33 days being the period. Their fry are also of rapid growth. In the pickerel and jack stage they devour enormous quantities of food, if favourable. At a very early stage their vicious propensities are exemplified. We once placed three pickerel, scaling from 2 to 3½ lbs, in a small pond, in which had been turned some four score store fish, the majority being carp of small size, the remainder tench and perch. Upon being netted at the end of the year, there was not a single carp in the pond; two-thirds of the perch were left, as were also a few of the tench. The pickerel had meanwhile developed into respectable pike, scaling 5½ to 6½ lbs weight. Belief in the ancient doggerel, anent the natural propagation of pike, eels and other fish, from the pickerel weed, chopped horsehair, etc., it is said is not as yet fully dispelled amongst the lower agricultural orders in some parts of Scotland, and in several English counties.

Walton, who invariably quotes the German naturalist, Gesner, upon the natural history of freshwater fish instead of relying solely upon his own personal investigations, affirms his belief in these and kindred superstitions, characteristic of our forefathers. The same absurd nonsense is credited in the *Piscatory Eculogies*, where we find the following:

> Say, canst thou tell how worms of moisture breed,
> Or pike are gendered of the pickrel weed?
> How carp without the parent seed renew,
> Or slimy eels are form'd of genial dew?

To indulge in day-dreams about the abnormal instincts and habits of animalia would appear to be characteristic of the speculative naturalist of past ages, vague theories being treated as solid facts, and so set forth for the acceptance of credulous readers.

CHAPTER TWO

The Habits and Haunts of Fish – continued

The Barbel, Carp, Tench, Bream, Roach, Dace,
Gudgeon, Chub, Eel, Perch and Pope

The Barbel (*Barbus vulgaris*) is a gregarious fish. It spawns in May and the beginning of June, and is found in the sluggish parts of slow-running streams. It not unfrequently attains a weight of 10 or 12 lbs, and specimens are occasionally taken measuring three feet in length. Its fins, especially the pectoral, are exceptionally large, and by their aid it can breast the most powerful currents, and is, moreover, capable of affording good sport to the angler, owing to its excessive pertinacity of life and strength. The Thames and Trent are the best rivers for this fish. It is rather local in this country, but is occasionally found abundant in the waters of low-lying counties. Large barbel are most prevalent about Shepperton, Walton and Weybridge upon the Thames, where they have been taken scaling 15 or 16 lbs or more. They abound in the Trent for many miles about and below Nottingham. During the hot months, after spawning (which operation is effected amongst weeds, roots, etc., around which substances they entwine the ova in a rope-like form), they seek deep slow-running streams, near the bottom of which they lie. A cold climate does not appear to suit the barbel. In more southern latitudes, as in the Danube and the Rhine, it is said to reach occasionally 50 or even 60 lbs. In Scotland this fish does not appear at all. With the advent of frosty weather in the fall, they leave the still deeps and holes, and may be found at the bends of rivers, near bridges, floodgates, locks and weirs, which form their haunts during the winter season. Here they are often taken, in favourable circumstances, in heavy quantities by practical adepts. The mouth of the barbel is situate much lower than is the case with most fish. It is a flat-stomached fish, with a hog-shaped head and snout. The fore-barbs, or wattles, attached to the end of the latter, and appended to the corners of the mouth, are plentifully encompassed by nerves, which serve as feelers to the fish whilst foraging amongst gravel, etc., in the bed of the water. It belongs to the carp family, and is noted for its subtlety and wiliness. Barbel are in the best condition in August and September.

ᕫ

Carp (*Cyprinus carpio*) do not thrive in northern latitudes. Like the barbel, they attain much greater dimensions in temperate and southern climes. It is supposed by some that the whole carp family are not indigenous to this country, which may be very probable; but nothing is certainly known of the period or source of their original introduction. The naturalist Linnaeus affirms that carp were first brought to England about the year 1600, but this assuredly is erroneous, as in Dame Juliana Berner's book on angling, published in 1496, we have the following mention of the carp: 'It is a dayntious fysshe, but there bene but faue in Englond, and thereforce I wryte the lesse of hym.'

The carp is a vegetarian, feeding upon the more tender parts of aquatic plants, and the growth of algae and fungus with which aquatic vegetation is often overspread. Insects and larvae also are taken by them. Where carp run large they are anything but 'dayntious', as any vegetable garbage and refuse will be eagerly and voraciously devoured by them when cast within their reach.

In the winter season carp lie partially buried in the mud at the bottom of the lakes and ponds in which they delight. Their ova becomes matured about June; they deposit their spawn upon weeds, etc. These fish have the curious habit of emitting but a small part of their eggs at once; thus, they are taken for some months containing more or less mature spawn, the male fish having a similar character-istic. The carp, like most leather-mouthed fish, have teeth in the throat – these, in the instance of the common carp, very much resemble the molar teeth of a quadruped. They are very long lived, and many remarkable instances of this are recorded. There are many varieties of these fish now common in this country. The Crucian and Prussian variety are abundant in many waters. These are much shorter and more plate-like in form than the ordinary carp.

☞

Tench (*Tinca vulgaris*), like carp, flourish best in weedy ponds or deep pits, and though in very sluggish rivers they may take up their quarters upon some quiet reach, they are seldom found abundant in these situations. In the winter months these fish lie dormant in the mud at the bottom of the water, as we have already stated to be the case with the carp; indeed, the main habits and instincts correspond closely with those just ascribed to the carp. The chief points of distinction are that the tench possesses greater powers of suction, is considerably less in size (seldom attaining more than 6 or 7 lbs in our home waters) and is inferior in cunning. The body of the tench is abundantly supplied with mucous, which is generally supposed to have medicinal properties. This would be difficult to prove, and we very much doubt whether it ever has been satisfactorily established. Both carp and tench are eminently tenacious of life, and able to breathe with the most meagre supply of oxygen. The young of both fish are also of marvellously quick growth where food is plentiful and the surroundings are favourable to their wellbeing. The golden variety of tench, now acclimatised here, is being artificially bred and distributed upon an extensive scale.

☞

Bream (*Abramis brama*) abound to profusion in many of our lakes, rivers and canals, as also in small confined sheets of water throughout the land. There are two principal British varieties of these fish, viz., the common or carp bream, and the white bream, or breamflat. There are numerous hybrids among bream, as, indeed, is the case with the whole carp tribe. These are occasionally taken for new varieties, and new species. In early morning, with the first gleam of the sun in the east, the bream, in common with most fish of like order, are to be observed playfully gambolling and turning over, so that their most frequent haunts are easily discernible to the early riser. When a bream suddenly descends from near the surface of the water, unlike any other fish, it causes bubbles to appear upon the water immediately above it. This must be owing to its peculiar formation. It probably emits a certain portion of oxygen by the exertion. The teeth of the bream, as with other aquatic vegetarians, are in the throat, there being, in the case of the common bream, a series of five upon each bone, a double complement of these being possessed by the white variety. Bream spawn in July. They always frequent the deepest parts of the water they inhabit, and are fond of weedy quarters. About the middle of October they are in the height of condition. It is not in every likely looking place upon a river known to contain bream that they are found. They are rather migratory as well as gregarious, and are given to roam, changing their haunts, for no apparent reason, for an indefinite period. These fish seldom attain more than 6 or 7 lbs weight, though specimens are occasionally taken scaling considerably more.

ॐ

Roach (*Leuciscus rutilus*) are also gregarious, congregating and swimming together in shoals. They are generally numerous at the lower portions of trout streams, in water from three to five feet in depth, and of very moderate velocity. They feed upon aquatic insects, worms, the larvae of flies, and also on certain vegetable matter. These fish spawn in May and the early part of June. When thus ill conditioned they are particularly rough to the touch. Their ova is deposited amongst the roots of weeds or upon some pro-jecting or submerged substance there may be in the bottom of the water. The length of a full-sized, well-conditioned roach ranges from ten to twelve inches; but, being a broad and thickset fish, the weight is greater than its length would indicate. Upon some waters, a fish of this description, measuring ten inches, will generally scale about ¾ lb. They are of marvellously slow growth, as compared with other fish of the same order. The roach is not esteemed as an article of diet.

∽

Dace, Dare or Dart These fish are gregarious, and are common in our clear streams, especially in the south. They frequent slow running waters, where they feed upon the larvae of insects, worms, etc., and towards September rise well at the fly, and are to be readily taken. There are other species of what are designated coarse fish that rise at the fly, such as the perch, chub and pike, but these are not nearly so partial to surface feeding as dace. Though these fish generally prefer clear water, they are found plentiful in the polluted portions of large rivers. Their spawning time is April and May. Dace will flourish wherever trout abound, which fish they resemble in their general habits. They seldom attain more than 14 oz weight. Though common to running waters, they will flourish in still pools and ponds. The same observation may be applied with equal truth to the gudgeon.

∽

Gudgeon These little fish, in common with minnows and other small fry, frequent main rivers and tributaries alike in incredible numbers, migrating in shoals. They are extremely prolific. Their chief use to the angler is for bait for the larger species of fish.

∽

Chub (*Leuciscus cephalus*) Chub frequent deep and rapid waters. They rank among the very coarsest of freshwater fish; nevertheless, they are not to be found in stagnant, foul or habitually discoloured water; indeed, it is rarely they flourish except where they have the advantage of a constant supply of food, as is the case in the vicinity of the rapid passage of a volume of water. In lakes, ponds or canals, these fish are rarely found. Their 'holts' in small rivers are usually deep still pools, those sheltered by overhanging trees or bushes being their chosen resort, especially when the stream is powerful just near

the head of the pool. In larger and wider ones the fish lie in the
streams when gently flowing, and near the shelving or well-wooded
bank. Sandy or gravelly bottoms are preferred by the chub. They are
seldom or never found where the bed of the water is of mud or loam;
they, like the grayling, find food in the gravel and sandy bed. They
feed, as is the case with the whole *cyprinus* family, upon aquatic
plants, and have, in common with their order, fully developed throat
teeth. Their food also consists of worms, flies, beetles, grubs and,
indeed, everything that in general forms food for their more aristo-
cratic fellow-tenants of the stream; and they are to be taken with
almost every conceivable bait, from a minnow to a midge. Their
edible qualities are bad, but when rubbed with saltpetre immediately
after being killed and cleansed, they form tolerable fare.

ॐ

Eels There are two distinct varieties of these fish that are indigenous
to this country, viz.: the sharp-nosed species (*Anguilla vulgaris*) which,
as far as can be ascertained, are migratory in their habits, and the
broad-nosed. The former annually descend to the mouths of the rivers
they inhabit to find brackish water. This excursion is made in the
autumn, the main object being to find water of the right temperature
for vivifying their ova, as, unlike all other species of freshwater fish,
they would appear to require a higher rate of temperature for this
purpose. It is well-known that the water in the tidal part of rivers is
several degrees higher in temperature than that nearer the source,
owing, first, to the greater elevation of the sources and, secondly,
to the contact of two fluids of different densities, as salt and freshwater, which causes an increase of temperature of at least two degrees.
The passage of the adult fish, during or immediately after a flood
downstream in the autumn, is well-known to the owners of fisheries
upon our large rivers, who place traps for their capture. The
immense numbers that inhabit some waters is simply incredible.
But if the downward passage of eels is remarkable, it shrinks into
insignificance when compared with the spring ascents.

Many accounts of the marvellous number of young elvers that pass upstream in the spring months, have been given by various writers upon this and kindred subjects.

The broad-nosed species do not ascend the rivers, but locate in holes and crevices in masses of stone. In the winter they lie dormant in the mud. This variety is not esteemed as an article of diet.

The young of the eel are eagerly devoured by all freshwater fish, including the trout and salmon, and even the adult eels themselves, hence it is that so few live to become developed. Eels are vicious devourers of fish spawn, and were they to multiply to any great extent, the effect upon the higher order of fish would be disastrous. Eels were long considered viviparous, but this is now known to be erroneous.

The spawn of the migratory or sharp-nosed variety is usually deposited and buried in sand beds, that of the non-migratory species is deposited in the mud gradually, during a considerable length of time, which accounts for the intermittent passage of the young elvers or fry for months in the spring of the year. Whenever there has been incessant heavy rain eels turn out of their hiding places to feed upon worms, the larvae of insects, *crustacea*, etc., and in the case of the larger specimens upon small fish. Mild winters are favourable for their capture, as in the flushed waters that are then usual, they are always on the forage for food. Poachers often take the best of these fish upon their night-lines, as eels are undeniably nocturnal in disposition.

ᘓ

The Perch (*Perca fluviatilis*) flourishes in both stagnant and running water. In the former they are more commonly numerous; the river perch are, however, larger and far more wily. The perch are to an extent a gregarious fish, moving in shoals. Deep holes and the slower reaches of large rivers are their chosen resorts. They are extremely hardy, flourishing in the foul water of roadside pits, etc. They spawn in April and May. They are extremely prolific, the number of eggs carried by an adult fish being over 200,000. The spawn is deposited in an unbroken band or festoon of eggs, which are generally entwined around weed stems, etc. Moles, ducks, water-fowl and vermin eagerly devour it.

Perch are of slow growth, considering the fact of their being such voracious feeders. In confined places, where the water is over-stocked, they gradually diminish in size, until they range to almost the length of a minnow. To keep a stock of good perch in a confined water, they should be netted every alternate season, the larger only of the fish being returned; the smaller may be distributed elsewhere as store fish. Yearling perch average 2½ inches in length when fed plentifully. In favourable circumstances perch acquire an unusual weight, 5 or 6 lbs being sometimes reached by them when the supply of food has been good, and the surroundings favourable. The remaining member of the *Percidae* species is the Pope.

Pope or Ruffe (Rough) This fish is extremely partial to canals and muddy pools. The more sluggish running waters often contain vast quantities of them. It is inferior to the perch, both as regards size and the quality of its flesh. It is an equally voracious feeder, and affords good sport to the youthful fisherman where it abounds, it being readily taken with the coarsest tackle. Ruffe spawn in April, and, like perch, multiply rapidly. Pike and other large fish feed upon them. Both the form and the habits of this fish are similar to those of the perch. Its average length is four inches, and it very seldom exceeds six. For live bait for pike it is often in great request, on account of its hardiness and attractive colour.

CHAPTER THREE

Bottom-Fishing – General

*Pond-fishing for Perch, etc., Gudgeon, Dace, Roach and
Barbel Fishing*

Under this heading we purpose dealing with each individual fish
sought after by the bottom-fisher. The constant increase in this class
of anglers has of late become so noteworthy that any work on modern
methods of angling would be signally incomplete were this important
branch ignored. Still-water or pond-fishing is associated with the
earliest recollections of the majority of fishermen, whether fly-, mid-
water- or bottom-fishers. We shall, therefore, commence with this
simple phase of the gentle art. Worm-fishing may be practised
successfully for almost every variety of fish in freshwater, not
excluding even the trout and salmon. We have devoted a separate
chapter to worm-fishing for the first named. The usual objects of the
bottom-fisher in still water are what are known as coarse fish, ranging
from the pike down to the perch and gudgeon, and the arrangement of
the tackle employed varies both according to the kind of fish it is
desired to take, and the lay of the water. Float-fishing is the chief
resort of the bottom-fisher in standing water. Almost anything in the
shape of a rod will answer for this purpose, the only essential being
stiffness and strength. Bamboo is the best material for a general
bottom-rod, a variety of top joints of different strength and length
adapting it for both heavy and light work. Before taking the fish in
detail we would enjoin the attention of the tyro to the following hints:

Don't unduly expose either the person or the rod by restless
movements upon the edge of the water.

Avoid disturbing as much as is possible the surface of the fish's element by incessant movements of the float and bait.

Never employ a larger float, and therefore more sinkers, than is *absolutely requisite*.

Always ascertain the precise depth of the water it is intended to fish before commencing, so that the bait may come within the ken of the fish.

See that the lure is placed upon the hook in as natural a manner as is possible, viz., by threading the worm, if a worm is used, up the centre, leaving a portion of each extremity free.

When a fish is hooked, do not suddenly, as Homer has it, 'lift it quivering to the skies'. There is no need for transporting your 'finny prize' in a strictly perpendicular direction. The thing to do is to gently tug the quarry to the bank before leaving the water, as by so doing the pulling power, without the addition of the weight of the capture, is placed upon the tackle. To work out the diagram given, we commence with perch fishing.

ॐ

Perch Fishing The first consideration for the youthful aspirant, after fixing upon a likely spot, *where the water is most discoloured* (which is generally in the vicinity of weeds), is the *depth*. This may be easily ascertained by plumbing, by means of a scrap of sheet lead or lead wire, rolled round the hook, or without this by observing the float when properly weighted, as in standing water it lies on one side when the sinkers touch the bottom. After thus accurately taking the depth, the tackle should be so arranged as to admit of the lure reaching within three inches or so of the bottom. A few pieces of turf, containing worms, may be put in the water before 'rigging up' the tackle. The vigorous action of these, on being suddenly introduced into a strange element, answers admirably in attracting the notice of and collecting the fish. A small, well-scoured dew or lob worm should then be carefully threaded upon the hook. The float should

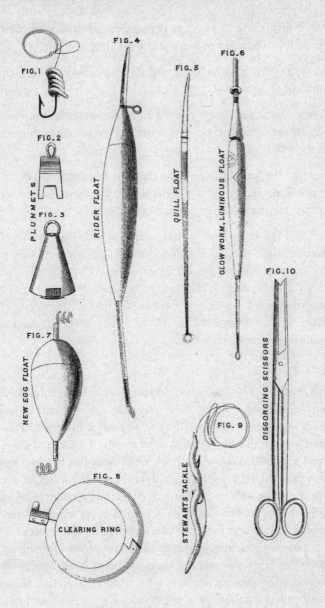

FIG. 1

FIG. 2

PLUMMETS

FIG. 3

FIG. 7

NEW EGG FLOAT

FIG. 8

CLEARING RING

FIG. 4

RIDER FLOAT

FIG. 5

QUILL FLOAT

FIG. 6

GLOW WORM, LUMINOUS FLOAT

FIG. 10

DISGORGING SCISSORS

FIG. 9

STEWARTS TACKLE

PLATE I

be cork, *not coloured*. The brilliantly daubed articles usually offered for sale ought always to be assiduously avoided. A common bottle cork is not to be surpassed, and if the quill that pierces the cork be vermilion-tipped so much the better. By the use of a small forked stick the rod may be suspended upon the bank, whilst the owner looks out and prepares a new place, in case a change may become desirable, or two rods may be used. When fish run large, for better security, a pot-hook-shaped iron inserted in the ground at the full extremity of the rod will render all safe. Large hooks should be used, as by such voracious and bold biters as perch an ordinary worm-hook for trout fishing will be paunched without difficulty.

In rivers, in the early part of the season, perch are generally found in gently flowing water, not very deep. As the season advances, they locate under hollow banks and by whirling eddies, or smooth, gravelly bottomed swims, but towards September and October they frequent the deepest parts of the river, near roots, sunken sticks, or in other fastnesses. Perch are gregarious; care should, therefore, be taken not suddenly to disturb a hole or swim. They will run eagerly at the minnow, especially in the summer months, but the method by which most sport may be derived from them is to cast for them with a trio of artificial red palmers or caterpillars (double-hooked), attached to a moderately strong fly-cast, one at the point and the others mounted upon gut lengths and attached as droppers. These are used as small flies, just as when working them for trout, with this exception – when a fish is hooked no action is taken whatever. The hooked fish will quickly be shown, and will work the remaining palmers infinitely better than the rodster can, and, incredible as it may seem, by this means each lure will have secured its capture in a very short time after the first was hooked, and the difficulty of landing those contributions adds in no small degree to the diversion. It sometimes happens when the casts are full fine, or the fish extra large, that a loss of a portion of the gut, together with its appendage, is experienced; but this is an unusual occurrence, more particularly if sound and strong casts be used.

The best way to land a string of perch is to secure the endmost one in the net first, and when this is done the rest seldom get into mischief, and are generally easily landed. There are numerous methods of extracting perch, and if it be true that the amount of diversion derived from sport is in proportion to the novelty introduced, perch fishing presents important attractions. The artificial spinning bait and spoon, the roving live bait, the fly, both artificial and natural, may be successfully used. The more advanced methods of bottom-fishing may also be resorted to in the case of the perch; indeed, this is a matter of necessity in river-fishing, where the large fish exhibit a degree of wariness akin to that of the acute carp. Whipping with the cad-bait, freshwater shrimp and other aquatic insects in nymphae form also affords capital sport, even in clear water, under the overhanging banks, trees or bushes, amongst well-educated shoals of these fish.

❧

The Gudgeon (*Genus Gobio*) are very prevalent in slowly-running waters, those having gravelly or sandy bottoms being the best adapted for them. They increase wonderfully, and, like most small fish, they spawn twice and often three times in the year. Upon most of our large rivers, as well as upon the majority of our small streams, gudgeon fishing is a popular pastime in its season, which commences with July and ends with September. The following is the system mainly resorted to upon the Thames and Trent. A punt is moored in a moderate flowing stream, four or perhaps five feet in depth. The bottom is disturbed by a large and heavy metal rake, brought for the purpose, when the fish (which are gregarious, going in large shoals) congregate in great numbers in the water thus discoloured to feed upon the grubs and larvae of insects. But little skill is needed to catch this fish. Its excessive gullibility is well known. The meaning expressed by being 'gudgeoned' is, as everybody knows, being easily deceived. Poets, too, adopt the bold little gudgeon as an analogy to convey the same impression, as Gay serenely sings:

> What gudgeons are we men,
> Every woman's easy prey;
> Though we feel the hook, again
> We bite, and they betray!

Notwithstanding all this, the finest tackle is essential to moderate success, and a nine- or ten-foot rod, stiff and light. The telescope Japanese bamboo rods answer well for these fish, though we cannot commend their use for fish of heavier calibre. The finest possible line should be used; as to whether it be twist or plait is immaterial. A light cork, or better still, a small quill float, and small No. 12 hook, complete the equipment. Some fishermen advocate the use of extra strong tackle to meet exceptional emergencies; as for instance, when angling for gudgeon they will employ a hook and line equal to landing a heavy tench, perch or chub. That this is folly is proved by the result of a trial of the two systems in the weight of fish taken. If you wish to take perch or chub, why not angle for them? Do not use unsuitable tackle upon any pretext. We have often known anglers spoil all prospects of sport by their stupidity in this respect, rigging up trout baits with gimp because of the probable presence of a pike, for instance, in which case the result is, generally speaking, simply *nil*.

The best bait for these fish are worms, gentles and the cad-bait grub, the latter found in its sheath at the bottom of the water. The small worm known in the Midlands as the 'cockspur' is the favourite lure, and the brandling, too, often does great execution. In striking even a gudgeon, a little art and aptness tells marvellously in a day's fishing. No slack line should intervene between the rodster and the feeding fish, as, though a bold biter, it is equally energetic in rejecting the bait when the hard substance of the hook is detected. A rapid striker will hook two fish to a dilatory angler's one. The bait, which should be very minute, should be so arranged as just to escape the bottom.

From an edible point of view, the gudgeon is superior to many, we may say the majority, of fishes that inhabit freshwater.

᠅

Dace This fish seldom attains more than ½lb in weight, though occasionally it may reach 1lb. Dace are numerous in most trout streams, more especially in those of Wales and the southern counties of England. They afford excellent sport when feeding in sufficient quantities, though they are occasionally very annoying to the fly-fisher for trout; indeed, they are to be taken in large numbers by a gaudily dressed fly, towards the end of the summer. The small palmers (red, grey and black), bumble, and red tags, etc., are the description that find most favour in the eyes of this fish, though sometimes they are by no means partial in this respect.

To the fly-angler for dace, we would observe that when these fish are fastidious in rising, a gentle or a wasp grub, or even a tiny strip of flannel, when placed so as to hide the hook, will render the thing effective; but the usual mode of angling for these fish is by bottom-fishing. The tackle and hooks hereafter recommended for roach are equally well adapted for dace fishing, and as both are found upon the same swims, the angler frequently extracts a mixed bag. Like the gudgeon, the dace is a bold biter, and is sharp, often incredibly so, in discharging the lure if not struck speedily. It is unlike the roach in the latter characteristic. As regards gameness the dace has considerable repute. Bait-fishing for dace is mostly followed, and is most productive in winter. His flesh is not, however, much appreciated for the table. For live-bait-fishing for pike the dace is valued, and justly so.

᠅

The Roach (*Genus leuciscus*) is rightly awarded no mean position in angling literature. This cannot be said to be on account of its weight and size, or its edible qualities, but purely because of the skill requisite for its capture. The early authors we know write differently, and their statements may then have been justified by their comparatively un-sophisticated fish and are still in the case of underfed pond fish. With river roach, however, the case is widely different; to bag a decent take, the rodster must be a practical hand of no mean attainments and experience. This branch of angling is so popular in these days that upon all the most noted rivers these fish are marvellously well schooled, so much so upon some waters as to rival in wiliness the trout upon some streams; but the accomplished roach fisher will make a respectable bag, even in adverse circumstances, always supposing the fish are there to catch. With regard to the suitable equipage, the rod demands the first attention. This should be stiff, light and of fair length. Some anglers use implements of prodigious dimensions. We recommend an East India cane, of ten or twelve feet, as being well adapted for every useful purpose. Some capital roach rods are made from lancewood, red deal being employed for the butt-piece. When good material is employed, a rod of the following dimensions for a three-part rod will combine lightness with strength. The diameter of the ferrules at the top of the butt joint should be ⅝ inches *inside*, that of the end of the middle piece ⁵⁄₁₆ of an inch, reel fittings and terminating ferrules on the foot of the butt about 1⅛ or 1¼ in diameter. This ratio will be found to form a well-proportioned taper from the hand upwards, the wood, of course, tapering so as to fit the ferrules *without the metal being sunk in the joints*. Incalculable disasters ensue from a non-observance of this all-important provision. The wood of the immense majority of rods manufactured, being robbed at its weakest point to accommodate the ferrules, leads to frequent breakages. We deal more fully with this subject elsewhere. Roach are noted for their excessive shyness and quickness of vision, therefore in clear water it is essential to exhibit as little of the rod and person as possible, as in addition to this they are adepts, when they understand the situation, at abstracting neatly the bait from the hook, and leaving the mere skin or frame behind.

We remember keeping for some years a large roach, amongst other fish, in a tank fed by a small rill of spring water. Upon our casting a score of house flies or gentles in a batch, one only having a small hook concealed carefully, Mr Roach would invariably absorb unhesitatingly all and every insect but the identical specimen containing the hidden hook, nothing of which but the point would be visible, although other and smaller fish would exhibit no such scruples. It is this special caution of the roach that calls into play so much care and tact on the part of the rodster. The line should be of the very finest possible texture* and undressed. Raw silk is the best material for firmness and strength. When angling with fine line, more especially is it requisite to keep proper command over the bait by retaining little slack line from the tip of the rod downwards. Many advantages ensue from the use of an extra-fine line, retaining of course full requisite strength, both in live-bait-, bottom- and surface-fishing. As every angler will allow, the less the surface of the line the less resistance offered by the air, and the greater chances of success and deception. The hook is also a point of the greatest importance, and one to which meagre attention is but usually paid. A bad or defective hook is an abomination to the user; to employ one is as detrimental to sport as the use of pasteboard bullets would be for deer stalking. As we have devoted a separate chapter to the consideration of hooks, we shall merely quote an instance from our own personal experience, anent this subject.

In company with an angling acquaintance, we were fishing upon a once celebrated roach reach on the Trent, not many miles from Burton. Our companion was rather positive in his ideas of hooks. He inherited a notion from his sire, who it was asserted was the best roach fisher of his day, that the weight and dimensions of one's takes ranged in a certain degree according to the weight of metal and dimensions of the hook employed, the heresy of which doctrine will be obvious to any modern disciple of the rod. The descendant of the redoubtable rodster favoured a No. 8 Carlisle hook, and nothing we could advance appeared to convince him of the absurdity of his prejudiced opinions. Finally, we arranged to *fish* the matter out, hence it was that we had repaired to a noted spot upon the noble Trent. Circumstances were

---

* Two-and-a-half drams silk is used in the construction of a new roach-and-live-bait fishing line lately perfected by us, which retains full strength, whilst reducing the substance by one half. It will sustain a dead weight of 9 lbs. This line is sixteen plait, and is, perhaps, the finest plait line ever manufactured. It is equally appreciated by live-bait-fishers for Thames trout as by Nottingham float-fishers.

favourable to sport, and as the swim had been nicely and judiciously baited the day previous, we quickly did some execution. After an hour or two's fishing, we had gained gradually but at an increasing rate on our antagonist; he accounted for this by affirming that we had monopolised the best position, on which we 'swapped' places. The main result, however, was still the same. Our companion now suggested that the secret lay in our bait, on which our reserve was immediately placed at his disposal. Still the same result appeared, though in a much more marked degree, and our friend now became irritable, and his patience collapsed, together with his rod and tackle. 'Luck's dead against me, and it's useless fighting against fate,' was the explanation tendered, while the process of unjointing was being gone through. We now thought it high time to expostulate by delivering ourselves of our view of the affair, which we speedily did, winding up with an offer to so rig up our friend that he would equal if not rival us. This was finally carried out, and the result showed that with an accurately constructed hook five bites amounted upon the average to four fish, whilst with a badly made or deformed one, the bites, or rather nibbles in this case, yielded but a meagre percentage of captures, the precise number ranging, as a matter of course, according to the size and nature of the hook.

The float should be very light. Another consideration is the substance to mount the hooks upon – whether hair or gut – some anglers preferring one, and some the other. There are equally good anglers upon both sides, but the ancient hair, it cannot be denied, is rapidly losing ground before refined gut, which is now imported in such immense quantities from Spain, Sicily, China and elsewhere, and may be said to be thrice the strength and half the substance of the traditional hair. It is or should be the object of the fisherman to reduce his lines and general tackle so as to be as nearly invisible as possible, to which end it is essential that the bulk and surface presentable should be reduced as far as is compatible with strength. It is therefore an advance in the right direction (and one that should have been taken before) to have the gut drawn whilst in its gummy state to as fine proportions as are requisite to meet special cases, for, although we were the originators of the gut-drawing system, we have no hesitation in proclaiming the superiority of the gut drawn accurately, prior to its being set and hard, as then it retains its enamelled surface entire. Had this been done a quarter of a century or so ago, the *necessity* for our oft repeated researches would not have existed. To assert that hair of any description is equal to even gut of equal thickness is absurd. The former is not only *weak*, being hollow, but is given to stretch when strained, and is very susceptible to breakage at knots. It magnifies greatly in the water, and, lastly, absorbs the wet and swells. On the other hand very little can be urged in regard to the use of the gut that is detrimental. It can now be obtained *one third* the thickness of hair, each strand being far superior in point of strength, and when slightly stained the colour of the water where it is intended to be used, it is as near being invisible as anything ever discovered. Hair effectually superseded the Indian weed, and silkworm gut will eventually supersede hair quite as effectually.

To return to our subject. Gentles, pastes, boiled grain, cad or straw bait, and small red worms are most worthy the angler's attention as baits. It is necessary to bait *moderately* the swim fixed upon the evening previous. We emphasise moderately, because it is the custom to sink so much food for the fish under the appellation of ground bait, that by the time the expectant rodster 'turns up' the whole school will have gorged themselves and dispersed to more secluded nooks to doze off the effects; hence it is the enterprising angler so frequently meets with scant sport. This is often attributed to the influence of passing electricity, whether in the earth, or atmosphere, or may be both; failing this, and a thousand and one other abstruse reasons, the weary angler can always comfort himself and explain to his friends and neighbours that as there was scarce anything in the swim in question, it followed in the natural course of things that little could be hauled out of it. After baiting judiciously overnight the fish will have congregated upon the baited spot at daybreak, if not before, when they are on the forage for breakfast. The object in baiting over-night, it must not be forgotten, is merely to produce an appetising effect on the next morning. If the object in view be to collect fish at any given spot from more distant localities, a good store of ground bait should be placed there for a day or two previous, always allowing a whole day and night's interval between the final baiting and the time for angling.

Having first ascertained the depth by the method previously described, and arranged the float so as to admit of the bait ranging three or four inches from the bottom of the water, the hand supporting the rod should be ever ready to knock home the hook nicely and carefully, and not too hastily. The correct motion will be readily acquired by practice. Small fish will often take the float under by a jerk, whilst the corpulent members of the same species will scarcely indicate their presence by a disturbance of the float at all, though when these begin to pay their addresses to your lure after this style, it generally proves a favourable symptom for sport; but frequently this exhibition of tenderness and delicacy is merely the result of their style of mouth-work, if we may be allowed to use the expression, the object of which, as the angler soon finds out, is to abstract the bait *from the hook* neatly and effectively. Now this is just as bad a sign as the other is a good one, and what is worse, as a general thing, the angler cannot help himself. A plan we have found to answer ourselves in these circumstances is to hang a scrap of the finest and best gut one quarter of an inch below the hook, and upon this excessively fine gut to attach a very small hook (though of small size, to retain good strength of metal), upon this one-half of a maggot or gentle is attached, with a full-sized one, or even two, upon the hook above; this will not fail to 'fetch' the most finicking of the finny race in question. Upon hooking a fish, the chief consideration must be how to extract him without damage to the swim, dash and bustle being highly unfavourable to the situation, therefore the capture must be consummated as soon as is compatible with the general weal. A judicious change of situation is the best thing under the circumstances, therefore when this can be carried out effectually, the fish may be quietly landed in some secluded side-spot away from the baited swim.

The persistent voracity of bleak, where they are numerous, is often very annoying to the roach fisher. These small fish, locating near the surface of the water, absorb the lure before it comes within the ken of the portly roach. The effect of this is the more tantalising when fishing with gentles, or grain of any description. When this petty larceny is going on, resort must be had to the following expedients. Get a fair-sized piece of paste or clay, bell shaped, the hollow of which must be filled up with dry bran. This should then be attached to the hook and slowly let down. The bran will gradually escape as it sinks, the bright atoms of which, as they are carried downstream, attract the small fry after them. When clay or paste – the latter is preferable, as it will serve a double purpose in dispersing the bleak and forming ground bait for the roach – is not handy, a handful of bran thrown in the water will have the desired effect, though somewhat temporary in its character. To reach the roach at the bottom of a still deep hole, a few gentles should be pressed in clay, leaving small outlets for escape. A few of these will have the desired effect of attracting the notice and exciting the foraging instincts of the larger fish. Whenever roach fail to approach the bait presented, a change should be made, if practicable. The wisest policy is, however, to examine the stomach of the first capture, as in the case of fly-fishing.

We have frequently found a predominance of beetles, and even flies, in the stomachs of the fish, which accounted for a previous marked indifference to our bottom bait: we are now speaking of roach in our smaller streams, where the variety of food is much greater. In the lowest portions of the majority of our best trout streams, as, for instance, the tributaries of the Thames and Trent, much execution may be done with the sunk house-fly in September, when these and the wood-fly are blind and feeble, and are scattered as the falling leaves by each gust of wind. Whatever may be the contents of the stomach of the fish, the bait should harmonise as much as possible with what is found to be the inclination of the quarry, whether it be worms, grubs, larvae of insects, or even weeds, for the roach is occasionally a vegetarian. In the case of the last named predominancy, paste may be used with advantage, and failing this, silk-weed when procurable. Whatever you do, do not use stale bait, or the sure Nemesis will be stale sport. Roach are excessively nice in their ideas, and the careful panderer to their base desires will reap ample payment for his exertions.

ح

Barbel (*Genus barbus*) is one of the gamest fish the bottom-fisherman essays to allure. He requires considerable tact and aptness, even when hooked, to effect a safe landing. Immediately upon feeling the hook, he will often resort to a variety of expedients to rid himself of it, indeed, he may be said to be only surpassed by the trout in this respect. When in the immediate vicinity of weeds, roots, etc., he displays no mean muscular power to gain their friendly shelter; indeed, so furiously does he fight when hooked, that with a fine tackle none but a practised hand has a chance of netting a full-conditioned fish. We would recommend the uninitiated to fish the more open lengths, comparatively free from cover, with an even bottom, which is desirable, as the bait being taken up by the fish from the river's bed, it is undesirable to render the lure in any way obscure, as between the chinks of large stones, etc.

There are two different systems of float-fishing for barbel, the most artistic of which was originated upon the Trent, and is now rapidly becoming general upon the Thames. We refer to the method styled tight corking. The float employed is large and taper, being capable of sustaining a good lot of shot, the exact weight of which is regulated strictly according to the power of the stream. After plumbing the depth of the swim selected, the line is lengthened below the float at least two feet more, the result of which arrangement is that the shot rests at the bottom, the float being kept stationary, but it indicates the least movement of the bait. The position of this is allowed to be an inclined one, the bites being indicated by a partial or entire depression. This method might be termed ledgering with a float. When used in conjunction with the bran-and-bread- or clay-ball system, it is exceptionally killing at times. The barbel has been referred to as being one of the most cunning fish that swims, and the devices for his allurement are ingenious and various. Before passing on, however, to other systems, we shall offer some hints as to the method just alluded to. The substances used are, as we have already stated, bread, bran, or clay. Of the first two of these an admixture is made, being formed into a stiff paste. A ball of the size of a ripe plum is then formed, the centre being dry bran. This is attached to the line an inch or so above the barbed hook. There it gradually breaks away, thus forming a kind of concentrated ground bait, which brings fish to the morsel. The clay is generally stiffened by bran, and is used in balls from the size of a marble to an orange, the contents being maggots or worms. The hook should be mounted with an exceptionally attractive specimen of what the ball may contain. The barbed hook is allowed to peep forth below the clay and its contents, which latter soon finds a way out, and if not, the barbel, being a rooting fish, soon finds out their retreat. Occasionally, the hook is encased inside the ball, allowing the fish to prog for it. This we think to be as unnecessary as it is foolish, as when the baited hook protrudes it is naturally seized first, and often before the hidden store is discovered, which, therefore, does not require replenishing.

Another style still prevalent, both upon the Thames and Trent, is that of ledgering. This tackle consists of a perforated lead barrel, or a roll of sheet lead, an ounce or so in weight. Through this runs the gut-line, which has free course, an odd shot being fixed two-thirds of a yard from the hook to restrict further supply through the sinker,* which latter should be of fair size for barbel fishing. The worm most suitable is a well-scoured fresh lob, a small portion of each extremity of which should be allowed freedom, after neatly threading the worm upon the hook. The angler should strike at the second or third knock (as a bite is called), the vehemence of which should be regulated according to circumstances, and as to size of bait, hook, tackle, etc. A recent improvement upon the above is to employ two swan shots, one upon the line and one below the movable barrel, this from eight to twelve inches above the hook, and the other twelve to eighteen

---

* It is sometimes advisable in strong waters to attach a very fine piece of stained gimp for the ledger lead to work upon.

inches above this again. This arrangement serves as an automatic check to the line, admitting of the fish hooking themselves instantly. Another plan is to employ a rider float, one that has a ring of wire at both ends for the free passage of the line to and fro. The shot attached, as is usual, a foot or so from the hook serves as a stopper at the bottom, whilst above, a scrap of a small bird's quill, or a bit of india rubber, small enough to enter the rod rings, but too large to pass through those of the float, is attached. At the right depth of the swim to be fished the freedom thus accorded to the float works admirably in fishing deep and difficult reaches, and not only this, but the extra power possessed by the user in fishing at greater distances is no despicable advantage over the old stationary system. In addition to the different methods of fishing for barbel, these fish are to be taken by roach and dace tackle, as also by spinning occasionally.

To handle a barbel artistically, as we have previously stated, requires a certain amount of practice and skill; perfect presence of mind is essential to commence with, and experience will do the rest. Whenever a float is not used (as in ledgering), the line is held between the forefinger and thumb of the left hand, the least movement of the bait at the other extremity being then felt, when the line is preserved straight, and with no loose links, ample time being given to strike at once effectually. The extreme sensitiveness of the touch in this respect, is often a matter of surprise. The larger and more cunning of the fish will often attempt, especially when the hook is plainly visible, to head the bait from the hook, and that, too, without seriously disturbing the line; the rodster, however, if at all on the alert, will not fail to detect this dishonest attempt before the swindling act can be fully effected. When there is circumstantial evidence of an attempt at underhand dealing after this fashion, a very fine tackle, with a strong hook of fair size, should be mounted with a couple of medium-sized worms, one being threaded above the other upon the line, allowing but the least possible freedom to their extremities. This done, the line may be cast in the precise locality before fished, some score or so scraps of worms being thrown in to allay their already aroused suspicions; this done, strike at the second knock and you will seldom fail to hook your quarry. With the finer tackle the chances of effecting a landing are, nevertheless, lessened somewhat, and unless some tact and dexterity is employed, in the event of the hooked fish proving an old 'stager' of some considerable proportions, the safety of the tackle will be seriously imperilled.

With regard to the vexed question of ground baiting, we would again record our firm conviction that the system so generally in vogue of inserting bushels of food upon traditional swims and resorts, tends but to satiate, in many cases, until some time after the subsequent attentions have been discourteously treated. The remarks anent baiting for roach apply also in the case of the barbel. After continued rains, when the water is gradually rising from the influx of surplus surface drainings, those fish invariably turn out in quest of food; but, after the water they may inhabit has been flooded, and is again running down and clearing, they have gorged themselves with the abundance of food, in the shape of worms, etc., brought downstream; therefore the best time to fish for them is in rising water. In the summer months when they first come in season, early and late in the day are their feeding times; the worms are then the best bait, as they are invariably in discoloured water; gentles and paste come more to the fore in the autumn.

The formation of the aquatic quarry of every fisherman ought always to be noticed by him, so as to enable him to strike with some knowledge of the probable effect. The mouth of the barbel is placed well under the head, which therefore enables it to take the bait, and its food generally, from off the ground: hence to strike directly perpendicularly will most likely be to hook effectually. The barbel is so leather-mouthed that the hold of the hook, however meagre, seldom breaks away.

CHAPTER FOUR

Bottom-Fishing – continued

Angling for Carp, Tench, Bream and Chub

The Carp (*Genus Cyprinus*) is a very wily fish; in waters much fished, they come rather as an exceptional prize to the angler, whose attentions and baits were intended for the allurement of other fish. In well-preserved and little fished waters, they are to be occasionally taken of very large size. The smaller fish, under three pounds or so, are far less cunning.

The angler for carp cannot be too careful and quiet in his movements, nor too skilful in the use of the tackle, which latter cannot possibly be *too fine*, so long as a reasonable amount of strength is retained. We put forth the above, notwithstanding the exhortations of the early writers as to the use of strong 'harnessing' and tackle, for if any fish is gifted with reasoning powers it is the carp; as even when hunger-bitten it displays the most tantalising caution in what it absorbs. An all-round inspection is invariably given to the bait before it is cautiously closed upon; sometimes the rodster in clear water plainly discerns a yellow monster, which, after describing a number of circles around the bait, traces the line to the surface, which done, the carping critic waves a courteous or contemptuous farewell flourish with his broad tail, and is gone. Occasionally, however, the programme is varied, for instead of clearing up the problem by a judicious investigation up to the source, he proceeds skilfully and artistically to dissect the bait, with a view to clear up the mystery. It is no uncommon thing for the tyro to have the bait taken from the hook for hours without intermission. There cannot be a rational doubt that the fish, when this is the case, fully comprehends the situation. Worms, when well scoured and presented lively and fresh, are good baits. These, however, are to be used at the bottom, ledger fashion, only instead of the usual large lead a couple of perforated swan shot should be strung upon the line, and confined to within two-thirds of a yard above the hook and bait, by a small-sized shot attached to the line at the requisite place; or a double knot of the gut may be made to answer the same purpose. Potatoes, when part boiled, we have always found a more killing bait than any other for these fish; they may be used with ledger tackle as above.

Our method of using the above is to rig up 3½ yards of medium gut – a strongish fly-cast will answer this purpose – with three-dropper hooks – No. 6 Kendals are best – on eight- or ten-inch gut. These are placed two feet apart, a small shot being fixed to each yard of the main gut line. The whole of the hooks are then to be baited with the prepared potatoes, a piece the size of a cherry being used for each hook, the whole delivered out by a careful underhand cast. The bait is pitched well out to an open space on the water's surface. The prospects of sport are improved when the surface is covered with weeds, as the rodster's movements and person are thus obscured. When a bite is indicated, an interval of a few seconds, varying according to circumstances, must be given before striking; a safe signal is the attempt to carry away the bait; the fish has it then within his jaws, and a sharp strike may be given by the time it has progressed a couple of feet or so. In clear open standing water it is essential that the angler should keep as much out of sight, and as stationary upon the bank as possible; an intervening bush or tree trunk may serve as an admirable cover to operate from.

There is an endless variety of baits used for carp, particularly of pastes, which range from a compound of honey and sugar, to bread and bran. From our own personal experience, we cannot commend them as being generally efficient, though we have occasionally found them taking, but when a particular kind of bait has been much used, a change is often effective.

Tench are generally coupled with carp by fishermen, which may be owing to the similarity of disposition, both being, generally speaking, found together in the same water. Tench are, however, often the solitary tenants of some small pond, and when this is the case they, unlike the carp, very seldom show themselves, but are given to 'forage' in and about the mud bottom. The presence of these fish would scarcely ever be discovered, even in very confined waters, when the fact is not known. They are very capricious feeders, and may be fished for an extended period without success, from which the uninitiated are often led to doubt their presence. An infallible sign indicating the presence of fish, and more particularly tench, is *a disturbed or discoloured state of the still water*. When a portion of standing water, having a clear source, is seen to contain, when examined in a clear glass vessel, particles of earth, etc., it may be safely inferred that aquatic creatures of some size and strength are the direct cause. We have never known this rule to fail to indicate the presence of fish in stagnant water. When the tench *is* in feeding 'cue', he goes at it with grim vengeance, and an industrious rodster will often completely depopulate a small sheet of water in a few hours, if he is so minded. But though these fish may be 'lugged' out or skull-dragged at special times, almost as fast as they can be accommodated with a hook, they are 'higgerly, piggerly' biters; this may be partially owing to the smallness of their mouth, and the large size of hook usually employed. Even with the tench the employment of fairly fine tackle is found to answer. The baits most in repute are brandling worms, gentles and wasp grubs. The best part of the year to fish for them is July and August, early and late in the day. The bait should reach and lie upon the bottom; a float may be used if deemed necessary. The mouth of the fish is tough, like the remainder of the order.

With regard to its edible qualities, all we can say, if the successful angler, as a faithful follower of Old Father Izaak, has an intention of pleasuring some poor body, is *don't*, if your motive be honest and innocent, or the unsullied reputation of the fraternity will inevitably suffer. The haunts of the fish during life are decidedly *muddy*, and the flavour of his flesh after death cannot be correctly described by any other term. Its skin is most remarkably thick and tough, and when carefully taken off and preserved, will wear out, as uppers for dressing slippers, several soles of leather; indeed, it resembles, when dry, the shark's skin, so much used by cabinet-makers for polishing the surface of wood.

ॐ

Bream This fish is anything but gamesome. It also partakes a good deal of the general characteristics of its first cousin, the common carp, though not so subtle or so large. It is, however, more widely distributed in our rivers, in which it affects slow-running deeps and quiet whirls and corners, particularly where the bottom consists of a combination of clay and marl, or loam. The bream is to be taken by the ledger line, with a small lob or brandling as bait. Fine tackle we advocate as warmly for bream as for any more delicate fish, seeing that with uselessly coarse tackle it is a moral impossibility to fish for them artistically. With regard to lake-fishing for these fish, we may state that they afford no mean sport where they abound in profusion, as they do in many lakes, especially in the Sister Isle. Bream are to be taken by fly-fishing. We have experienced wondrous sport with the grayling grub baits, such as the artificial grasshopper, cabbage grubs, and gentles, etc., as we have also with the double-hooked palmer caterpillar when used as directed for perch, viz., upon a 3-yds fly-cast of moderate strength, two as droppers, in addition to the one at the point. These are cast like the fly, and then allowed to sink, a slight wrist motion giving them a lifelike appearance. Both in standing and running waters, lake-, pond- and river-fishing, this mode of fly-fishing for bream affords capital sport, and, not unfrequently, two fish are hooked at once. After the first impulsive plunge, the danger of breakage from this cause is diminished, if not entirely passed, the fish showing little 'fight' as a rule. It is not necessary to attach shot to the above arrangement of 'tack', as the fish, being a very portly one, with deep stomach, it feeds, whenever practicable, some little distance from the bottom, as to pick up food resting upon the bed of the waters he has to effect an almost perpendicular posture – to stand upon his head, in fact – therefore, when float-fishing, the bait need not range more than three inches or so from the bottom of the water. Whenever the bait is fished too low, the float is raised when a bite is experienced, so that it assumes a horizontal position.

The methods described for barbel fishing may be applied with success in the case of the bream, though a somewhat smaller hook should be employed, they having a smaller mouth. The different varieties of paste may be used with advantage, especially in the decline of the year, when the fish is in its best condition, being then fat and firm fleshed. In some localities the small lob and red worms are the favourite bait, in others wasp grubs and gentles. A change in the bait, contrary to the accepted rule of the district, we have always found to answer well, often surprisingly so. In river-fishing considerable caution should be exercised in bank movements, etc., as they are quick to take alarm, when they immediately retire to their holes, or stop feeding. When a boy, we often met with good sport bottom-fishing in the Trent. Our method of extracting them was to sink a live bluebottle, stone, or cinnamon fly some distance in the water upon a fine gut-hook, mounted with a very fine shot or scrap of lead wire entwined around the gut above a knot. This would be carefully let down in some deep quiet hole, whilst we would be rendered invisible by an intervening bush or bough, the bait being always within our ken, notwithstanding. The instant the lure was seized we would strike, and the capture be consummated quickly, to avoid a disturbance of the remainder of the family. By this process, takes of large fish, that were often numbered by the dozen, were secured in the autumn months.

Ground bait may be judiciously used in river-fishing, a hundred or two of cockspur or brandling worm thrown in for a day or two previous will amply answer to gather the fish together. In the early morning and late in the evening bream bite the best.

☙

Chub (*Genus leuciscus*) These fish may be fished for by an almost endless variety of baits. They will take a fly with as much avidity as they will swallow a worm. Bottom-fishers chiefly use pastes, graves or scratching, ox-brain and the worm when angling specially for these fish. But they are more often caught when angling for other fish, as for barbel, roach, bream, etc. Float-fishing is the best in the winter months, when surface and mid-water food is scarce. An old haunt for these fish will often yield great sport upon a sharp frosty day in midwinter. We once took six fish that scaled 27lbs from one hole on the Dove below Rocester. The scales of some of these were the size of a shilling. Chub are to be steadily headed from the hole when hooked, in order to avoid disturbing the remainder of the school. Ledgering is also a favourite style of angling for them in some waters, the gut and tackle being generally stouter than for other fish, as when a large fish is hooked it is a case of 'pull devil, pull baker'. A slender weak rod should especially be eschewed, as to keep the fish from the roots in the neighbourhood of their haunts, the best built and most evenly proportioned rod procurable is unequal to the occasion; a certain amount of pliant play is necessary to aid the tackle. The best wood to employ for a bottom rod for chub is ramshorn ash (English) for butt, hickory for middle joint, and a spliced treble cane top. We have had a rod of this description in use for the last forty years, and it is still as sound and useful as ever. Upon all bottom rods the rings should be upright, and the reel fittings, as in the case of the fly-rod, should be fixed to the bottom of the butt joint, so as to balance as much as possible. To place it a foot or so from the extremity of the joint is foolish, it being just in the way of the rodster's hand when using, and also highly inconvenient generally. In the early autumn months chub are to be taken by dibbing (surface-fishing) or daping (mid-water) with live insects, such as the larger of the flies and beetles, humble bees, grasshoppers, etc. Instructions as to the method of using these we have given in a separate chapter.

Upon the Thames and Trent of late young frogs have become the favourite bait for chub in their season. The average yield of a day's 'chubbing' with these lures is about eight to ten brace of heavy fish. This would often be larger were it not for the smaller fry biting so voraciously, and thereby causing loss of time to the angler, whose duty it is carefully to unhook and return them to the river. It is now no uncommon thing to meet an angler with his bait-kettle converted into a temporary prison for frogs, so popular has become this system of fishing for chub. The arrangement of tackle is simple: a No. 4 Kendal hook, at the end of two feet of tolerably strong round gut (slightly stained blue) with a scrap of lead wire wound round above the knot. The baby frog is then hooked by a bit of the tough skin at the back of the neck, and carefully lowered from the point of the rod, the weight of the bait taking out the line through the upstanding rings, when allowed, until it reaches the water's surface, the rod meanwhile being kept stationary. The struggling movements of the captive quickly attract the attention of the best and largest fish near, amongst whom the bait is often divided, and, when this is so, great diversion is afforded, as eventually the most voracious is the first to grace the creel.

The most artistic method of extracting chub is to fly-fish for them. The surface flies for these fish should be large and gaudy; if nature must be copied at all, bees, wasps and cock-chafers are the things to reproduce, the ordinary red, black and dun palmers, having plenty of tinsel upon them, are also killing. Lake or sea-trout fly size are very good, also old mayflies, and indeed anything that is sizeable and gaudy. A good strong cast should be used with these, especially when the water is a little turbid, or discoloured. The red-haired caterpillar, too, may be used for chub with marked effect, in the way we recommend for trout and other fish. The attractiveness of any fly or beetle, whether artificial or natural, is greatly enhanced in the eyes of a chub by the addition of a couple of maggots, wasp grub, or even a narrow strip of wash-leather or white kid upon the hook. Early-morning fishing is often more productive than midday or night in the autumn; why this is so we can scarcely say. The minnow is as easily taken by these fish as any other bait, and towards twilight in July, August and September, the chub will 'run' at either natural or artificial, so long as the bait is clear, bright and well spun.

CHAPTER FIVE

Bottom-Fishing – continued

Punt Fishing, Bank Fishing, Bottom Lines, Floats,
Silkworm Gut, Reels or Winches

In punt fishing, a much shorter rod should be employed than is necessary for fishing from the bank. The material should be cane. The East Indian variety is by far the best, both for durability and strength. This will be found to stand heavy punishment when other woods give way; indeed, we doubt as to whether the hardest and most solid wood that grows will surpass, or even equal it in these characteristics. Solid wooded rods are not only more apt to break, but to bend permanently, so as to necessitate the reversing of the rings to the opposite side of the joints periodically; but there is one thing we cannot omit calling attention to anent cane rods, and that is their liability to snap at the joints close to the ferrules. There is, of course, a stiff place where the parts meet in a non-spliced rod, and when an unusual strain is applied to it, the wood immediately, above or below, snaps off short. The nuisance of this may be effectually avoided by a small wooden plug, of some four or five inches long, being inserted in the hollow of the cane, which equalises the strength of the rod when correctly proportioned throughout. Solid upright rings are preferable to the ordinary loose ones; the most expensive rods are sometimes fitted up with agate-mounted rings and tips when intended for trolling purposes, which prevents the rings from being worn by the constant friction. Instead of the ordinary circular-shaped rings, we advise the use of dome or conical ones. These are not liable to entangle one's line, no convenient foothold being presented by their sloping sides. The limp loose line entwines around any projecting substance presented, and any removal of an habitual fouling place must of necessity be a step in the right direction. In boat or punt fishing, the method of procedure varies somewhat upon different waters, the custom in certain districts being to moor across stream, in others in a slanting direction. All we have to say upon this point is that the great consideration at all times should be how to disturb the water as *little* as possible. A constant surging against the stationary boat cannot fail to act detrimentally as regards sport in most circumstances.

In fishing from the bank, a tolerably stiff and strong tool should be employed, so as to have power over the quarry when it exhibits a strong and determined desire to retire into some thorny retreat in the bank beneath your feet. The novice quickly advances, upon a few experiences of this nature, in the piscatorial path of knowledge. The first impulse of the inexperienced is to extend the rod over the shoulder, and move backwards, so as to end matters speedily by extracting the hooked fish from his element. Matters take a sudden turn, however, the fish running in to inspect some festooned retreat. Here he speedily entwines the line in so effective a manner that all communication with his newly found acquaintance is cut off, and when matters stand thus the cutting process is generally applied to the reel line as a closing act in the scene. To land an extra-heavy fish with a limber rod would be well nigh an impossibility where the surroundings are unfavourable. The correct way to play a fish in a powerful current, or still deep from the bank, is to extend the rod over the water, whilst the line is drawn in as rapidly as circumstances will admit; and when a staunch tool is the sustaining medium, the fish cannot possibly, by anything short of a breakage, effect his object. The weapons not infrequently used in bank fishing are not only undesirably heavy and unwieldy, but unnecessarily so. A rod that may be handled deftly, may be used to much greater advantage than one a few feet more in length. A twenty-foot rod, whether it be a salmon- or merely a banking-bottom rod, is a cumbersome implement; that, for precision of casting and distance covering, as also for general utility, is easily surpassed by a modest weapon of 16 to 18 feet in the hands of a proficient rodster. Personally, we always use bottom-rods full two feet below the usual average length, no matter where we may be fishing.

The line is the next subject for consideration. For bottom-fishing generally, lines should invariably be as fine, and at the same as strong, as it is possible to obtain them. Raw unbleached silks are infinitely stronger than the ordinary bleached ones. The fine 'dram' silks are equal in strength, and occasionally superior, to the coarser, more bulky, and heavier. With the extra-fineness of texture, it is needless for us to add the scarcity of the article is found to range.

Plaited lines should always be preferred to twist, cable-laid though it be; the miseries of a line always twisting and curling being only equalled by the constant breaking of a tender one. A line of one-half the substance of another, if *dressed* in a proper manner, will be found to be much stiffer and less liable to 'kink'. With regard to colour, in habitually discoloured waters, green or sandy-brown should be used; in fine, clear and open waters, a pale grey or cloud colour is the best tint.

No more weights or sinkers must be employed than can possibly be avoided. The same observation also applies to the float. A cork should never be used when it may be effectually substituted by a quill. Lastly, never use even a quill when no float is really needed. We have oftentimes made a first-rate float of a moderate-sized leaf: a sycamore, chestnut, birch or oak tree, when so situate as to extend over the water, affords admirable facilities for this. A worm, fly, maggot or what-not is attached in the usual way upon a slightly weighted gut line. A leaf is then procured, the shank being split up the centre carefully until the middle of the leaf is reached. The 'tack' (just below a knot) is then inserted in the incision, which is now closed, and occasionally it may be, for better security, wrapped with a scrap of silk or waxed thread. The leaf is fitted and found not only to act well as a float, but also in the midst of a bright sunlit water to materially aid the guile, by shading the tackle. The least possible stir or movement is made manifest by the flat and flexible leaf. Porcupine quills are the best floats for all-round work. For heavy water and large fish it is sometimes necessary to have these mounted with a little cork, but no conspicuously bright colouring matter should be used in its finish. A speck of bright colour (say vermilion) certainly aids the eye *when placed upon the tip of the quill*, so as to project out of the water; indeed, this is a wrinkle that every float-fisher is not acquainted with. The new luminous floats are very useful for special purposes, though we cannot say we think it probable they will ever become generally used, float-fishing in the dark not being at present a popular pastime.

The runners appended to the float should be of rubber; these being flexible fit any ordinary-sized quill. The non-flexible runners are a nuisance, and should ever be avoided. They are always cracking when dry, and are highly inconvenient in more ways than one.

The best and strongest gut (silkworm for piscatorial purposes) is round and smooth, clear as window-glass, or as the limestone spring. The milky-white glaring gut, so often met with, should be studiously avoided. No fair means will take out the white glare from a batch of pearly gut. Boiling dye will effect the purpose, but the strength and sterling usefulness of the stuff will have so deteriorated as to render it practically worthless. The opaque silkworm gut is naturally found to be inferior in point of strength; four lengths of the transparent and clear variety are found to be equal to five of the white and brighter kind of similar thickness. Spanish gut is superior to that of either India or China. The most disreputable is the Sicilian. This is found to be flat and tender, as also so white and opaque as to be of little utility. The Indian variety is especially noted for its excessive length. This exceeds, usually, all its compeers. The colour is yellow, even when prepared and uncoated No dyeing will permanently alter the shade. As regards strength, it ranks below the Spanish and China gut. Good round and sound gut should stand a strain of from $2\frac{1}{2}$ to 5 lbs, according to the thickness, without parting. Before joinings are made the ends should be moistened between the lips, so as to admit of its bedding down, and to avoid splittings; otherwise, dry old gut will 'spilch', and break at the knots when forming.

When gut is imported, it is coated with a thin, brittle, yellow skin, which is easily removed. This is its raw or unbleached state. We may here observe that often too much doctoring is practised in baking, boiling, bleaching and unbarking the raw substance A large class are prejudiced in favour of what they term a beautiful white tint. This taste, unfortunately, the fish do not share; consequently, are not so easily to be duped through its medium.

In clear water the gut used should be either stained a faint sky-blue, so as to offer no lighter or darker contrast to its background, or be left a transparent tint undistinguishable in the water. Some rivers are habitually clear, others slightly this or that shade. The hue of the gut line should in each individual case tally. Our ancestors used sorrel, brown and white or even black hair; but when used under similar circumstances with gut prepared as above, the tender, hollow hair is found far behind the age. We have, however, dealt already fully with the relative virtues of gut and hair.

Bottom reels are made of almost every conceivable variety and substance. We are inclined to give preference to the Nottingham spring check. This check or 'click' action is put on at will by a moveable spring, something after the style of the old spring-stop reels. In the varying methods of angling now followed, a tool that can be regulated to any degree of action required is far preferable to a set contrivance, admitting of no alteration at will. These winches are now made with steel centres.

CHAPTER SIX

Pike Fishing

*Spinning; The Rod and Line; Artificial Baits and How to Use
Them; Fishing Story; Live-Bait-Fishing; Fly- and 'Frog'-Fishing*

The greedy, ferocious and excessively gluttonous nature of this, 'the
fell tyrant of the liquid plain', has been pointed out by angling authors
both ancient and modern. We shall, therefore, confine ourselves to the
most approved methods now in use for its capture. These may be
enumerated thus, viz.: spinning, live-bait- and dead-gorge-fishing
or trolling and fly-fishing. There is scarcely any limit to the
expedients adopted for killing pike: frogs, mice, worms, etc., in fact,
baits of every conceivable description meet with due appreciation
when these fish are on the run; toads, it would appear, are the only
creatures they reject, but a dab of yellow paint will make even these
presentable. The spinning art when skilfully practised is, beyond all
dispute, the most successful system for extracting these fish; we say
practised skilfully, not because skill is actually requisite to success, but
merely to point out the difference between the ancient and rude
hand trolling, and really scientific spinning, with rightly adapted
tools and tackle.

Spinning with the natural bait claims the precedence; it is practised
as follows: a small fish (dace, roach, etc.) of three or four ounces is
taken and placed upon a flight of hooks (the method of arrangement
varying according to the particular nature of the flight used); one of
the most simple and best we give upon Plate 3, Fig. 5. There are
other flights, consisting chiefly of a number of small triangles, the
use of which we cannot commend. Accidents are far too rife with
substantial hooks to make it worth one's while to risk anything by

the insufficiency of one's appointments. The complicated nature of most flights renders it extremely difficult for the novice to bait them properly, so as to enable them to describe the ordinary revolutions. In this tackle, no difficulty of this nature is encountered. The lip-hook is inserted through the upper and lower lips of the bait, so as to close the mouth, the most slender hook of the triangle pierces the side, leaving the larger span of hooks unencumbered; lastly, the tail of the bait is made to form a slight curve by inserting the end hook, so as to cause the bait to swim in a wobbling sort of way. At certain times this motion proves very effective in alluring the quarry. The statements bearing upon this point, given in another chapter (trout spinning), apply with equal significance to pike spinning. Pike flights may, however, be used perfectly straight, as by the use of a small F. G. spinner and swivel combined, which can be placed a yard or so above the bait, perfect action is secured, the lure revolving well, and in a direct line, a great desideratum in bait-spinning, especially in the case of the rapacious pike, as he is even more apt than other species to miss the whirling turn-tailed bait.

A diagram of this very useful metal appendage to the mid-water fisher is given on Plate 3, Fig 4.

The rod for pike is now made little more than one-half the former dimensions; the cumbersome tool of from fifteen to twenty feet is being rapidly discarded in favour of a more efficient implement of about nine or ten feet. The old *swing* movement for getting out the bait is quite surpassed by what may be termed the *spring* motion; the fisherman's right angle is reduced by this change, his general style and comfort vastly improved, and success rendered more sure. To the uninitiated, the idea of reducing the rod would imply a corresponding lessening of the power of the angler; but this is exactly the reverse of the actual result, for instead of *limiting* this power over general surroundings, it largely augments it. In the first instance, his casting powers are greatly increased, he being able to fish a much larger area from a given standing point, the precise limits varying according to the amount of practical skill shown by the operator. *Forty* yards, or thereabouts, was the possible limit with the old *long rods*, but since the introduction of the short ones, the cast that fails to exceed *fifty* yards is concluded nothing extraordinary. Secondly, the angler retains far greater command over the bait with a short rod; the large size of the upright rings, which are fewer in number, offer comparatively little resistance to the free passage of the line, thus causing the bait by leverage to carry out prodigious lengths of line, which would, under the traditional system, have been considered simply impossible. The style of using these modern pike rods is founded upon the fork stick principle of trolling; the weighted natural or heavy artificial is attached to a limp though strong plaited silk line, which is usually undressed, being simply waxed to take out 'kinks' and 'turns'. This is mounted upon a large Nottingham reel (see Trout Spinning, page 86), which is arranged to run freely. When these appliances are procured, the result sometimes exceeds the most sanguine anticipations. The very largest fish are held more under control, and are much more easily landed when a short and sturdy rod is employed; whilst as regards wear, our readers need not be told that the more timber used, and the more lanky the implement is, the less is its durability.

With regard to the artificial baits for pike, much might be said. Their variety is endless, ranging from the clumsy-looking spoon to the gaudy glass bait. Speaking of spoon baits reminds us that there has of late been an improvement of importance in their construction – we refer to the 'Colorado'. At the hollow side of the dished metal is placed a barrel-shaped lead upon a wire, around which lead and wire revolves the spoon itself, it having a pair of flanges at its upper or narrow end. The conspicuous triangle fixed at the extremity is partially hid by a tag or tassel of vermilion wool, secured by flat silver tinsel. Its action when in the water is really admirable, and great things are reported as having been accomplished since its comparatively recent introduction. We never did believe in 'spooning', but since the invention of the Colorado our sentiments have undergone somewhat of a change. For the capture of the very heaviest pike in river or lake this bait is particularly well adapted. Metal casts of fry mounted in various ways are now to be obtained. In many of these much ingenuity is displayed, as notably in the different makes of Gregory baits, some of which spin upon their own axes; these for rotary motion are perhaps unequalled, others being jointed and thus flexible, while others again are stationary, relying as per precedent upon the upper swivels for freedom in spinning. Many of the above are coloured with a view to the effect when in action. Other baits are representations of some distinct species of fish, as gudgeon, dace, etc. These are for the most part constructed from gutta-percha, rubber, etc. They are often much esteemed when stationary; they may please the human eye, but fail to meet with due appreciation from the fish when in action. The general curved shape of the body acts very detrimentally in causing the line to describe a spiral or corkscrew flight, which is calculated to miss what fish may deign to essay an acquaintance. The Phantom is another bait not well adapted for rough work, owing to its liability to sustain damage from the keen teeth of the pike.

The best 'artificials' to rely upon, when 'naturals' run short, we give as follows, viz., the Gregory, Clipper, Wheeldon, Windsor Bee and Excelsior. Most anglers have a marked partiality for heavy brass gimp, of thrice the necessary thickness. Gimp should be no thicker nor stronger than is absolutely requisite, and should be of the best quality, having the finest raw-silk centre. In common gimp, which is disposed of by the manufacturers by weight, the wire is much too thick, the proportion of silk being less accordingly.* The best gimp is usually made bright, and excessively fine in the wire. Before this is used it should be slightly stained with logwood and copperas, with just enough of the latter to darken the dye. This removes the glare, and effects a great improvement. Having advised as to the equipment of the pike spinners, we shall now proceed to lay down a few directions as to the most artistic and successful method of using them that is commonly followed upon the Thames. The line should not be worked from the reel nor yet from the feet, as commonly practised, but from the left hand, around the fourth finger and thumb,

---

* It is now made very fine and strong indeed, of very little more substance than stout lake gut.

off which it is wound rapidly crosswise. The motion thus conveyed to the bait works it well if rightly accomplished; some anglers simply haul in the line by instalments into the palm of the hand, but this is anything but sportsmanlike. The bait is delivered to the spot desired in the following manner: line to about half the length of the rod is let out with the bait ready fixed at its extremity, the length of line required for the proposed cast being first wound round the distended thumb and finger in the manner above described; this done, the bait must be put in motion, a backward and forward leverage is given which should be rapidly increased, and now an effective springing jerk of the rod, just as the bait reaches the extreme backward point, sends him out quickly, taking off the line from the disengaged hand in its flight. The point of the rod must be held so as to admit of the bait travelling as near as possible in mid-water. When the rodster experiences a tug at the extremity of his line he should strike instantly, but firmly; too heavy striking, it must be remembered, is highly dangerous, it imperils the safety of the tackle as well as the fish. A clumsy or too impetuous striker will frequently break away hooks and trace, or, failing that, the hold of the hooks from the mouth of the fish; it is therefore incumbent upon the tyro to exercise a little judicious care and calculation in driving home his steel into the bony jaws of the fish. Practice and experience are the mentors upon whom the young aspirant must rely for proficiency in these matters. Rare sport is sometimes afforded by well-conditioned fish when lightly hooked and handled, and many instances are on record of fierce fights; not that the pike is noted for gameness, rather the reverse, but in exceptional cases when an extraordinary fish is struck great sport is often afforded.

The largest pike we ever killed was taken upon a stout salmon spinning-trace, the flight being mounted upon the finest gimp. We were fishing in preserved water in a neighbouring western county, and had hooked a pickerel a few odd pounds weight; when we were about to land the young gent, the gleaming broadside of some larger relation of the family shone in the background, an instant, and then a heavy tug demonstrated the fact that our possession of the prey was disputed. Comprehending the situation, we let out line with the earnest hope that this considerate exhibition of feeling would meet with due appreciation; nor were we disappointed, for after the lapse of a few minutes, which, under the circumstances it must be admitted, seemed rather long ones, the fun began. We were in sole possession of a light punt upon an extensive sheet of water, and thus, having plenty of sea room, we were rather confident as to the result. At the first gentle touch of the rod, the fish ran out fully half a hundred yards of line, at one impetuous rush, despite the heavy strain placed upon the rod. A heavier reserve was now put on the remaining portion of line through the medium of the rod, but here we discovered our command over him to be considerably less than we calculated, for such was the determination of the hooked fish to explore the other side of the lake that the punt began to move in chase. To reserve the remainder of our line would tend to aggravate the nuisance, to let it run meant disaster. Whilst we hesitated we unconsciously stopped further supply of line, of which fact we were forcibly reminded by the rapid motion of the punt as it progressed across the water. Just as we had resolved to break away from him he suddenly doubled, making straight for the punt – we hauled in the loose line in coils at our feet as actively as was practicable under the circumstances – the next instant he dashed off with renewed vigour at right angles, and we again strained heavily upon every foot he stole, despite which our whole stock was all but spent before he again turned. For more than an hour was this operation of hauling in and paying out line repeated without ceasing, at the end of which time the final tragic end seemed as remote as ever. By this time several stable functionaries from the adjoining mansion arrived upon the scene, among whom a learned controversy ensued as to the probable weight and breed of a fish capable of towing a man and a boat with impunity. As the fish swerved along shore in their immediate proximity all dispute suddenly dropped, and we observed, what had previously escaped our notice, namely, a large stable fork in the possession of a bandy-legged individual who had stepped forward, fork in hand, ready for action. Before we could interfere a wild thrust was made, which, however, fell short of the mark, as may very easily be imagined; nevertheless it well nigh ended the fight, the terrified fish making for less dangerous quarters at a rate that eclipsed all previous exploits, the pressure upon the line availing little beyond keeping the snout of the fish above the water's surface. The winch 'whirred' loudly, notwithstanding the deeply curved sturdy rod. 'Hark how the devil squeals!' exclaimed the crooked individual in possession of the fork. Had that worthy chanced to have been in the punt at that particular moment, we felt an inward presentiment that he might have suddenly found himself *out* of it. After this final rush a reaction set in, the fish showing signs of fatigue for the first time, which speedily developed into complete exhaustion. To consummate the capture by gaffing and boarding was now a very easy matter, and successfully accomplished. The weight of the fish proved to be thirty-seven pounds and three-quarters. It was preserved and cased by the owner of the water, to whom it was presented, with the tail of the pickerel protruding from its extended jaw.

Live-baiting is another favourite method of fishing for pike. The tackle requisite for this style of angling is shown on Plate 2, Fig. 6. This is used with or without the barrel-lead. As the name implies, the bait is used alive, the small hook on the triangle is inserted carefully in the root of the back fin, the large span of hooks being loose at the side. The lure is then allowed to roam at will. It is necessary to employ none but the finest and best stained gimp. The reel line, too, should be both fine and strong, the lighter in weight the better. The line usually used in live-baiting for Thames trout is seldom much thicker than a piece of ordinary thread. The requisite substance and strength ever varies with the weight of the fish it is intended to hold. The line referred to in roach fishing would answer equally well for pike of 16 lbs and under, as it would for Thames trout. The actual dead-weight-sustaining powers range exactly double, when the substance is an animated body in water; thus, if a gut line will just raise 3 lbs from the dead level of the ground, it will hold a fish of 6 lbs in water, and this difference is still greater when a pliable rod is the sustaining medium, therefore it is the greatest folly to employ needlessly powerful tackle even for pike.

We, nevertheless, advise the use of tackle needful for the largest fish of the species you may be angling for that are known to be present in the length fished. To omit so doing would be to remove all prospects of landing a good fish; but exaggeration is rife in these matters, and the popular idea is that the most powerful tackle is essential for successful pike fishing, of whatever nature it may be. But to return, the movements of the roving bait must be carefully observed where practicable; and if, owing to the state of the water, this is not possible, the rodster must follow the movements of the bait by the feel conveyed by the line, and care must be taken not to distress the bait, or it will soon be exhausted. When a fish takes the bait, a minute or two should be allowed him to gorge it. In some localities the custom is to use a single gimp hook, which is attached to the upper lip of the bait; this, however, causes it to move in an unnatural way, with the tail uppermost, and cannot be said to equal the method previously described.

We now come to fly-fishing for pike. That these fish would take a natural fly is even less probable than in the case of salmon. A jack will come with evident gusto at a bird, just as he would at a rat, therefore it is essential that the artificial should be of very unusual proportions. Discarded salmon flies, of large size, render good account amongst pike; a regular pike-fly, generally speaking, is a clumsy combination of peacock-eye or sword feathers, cock pheasant's hackles, gaudy Berlin wool or worsted, gilt or silver tinsel, and glass beads; the peacock doing service for wings, pheasant for legs, beads for eyes, and the remainder forming the body.

The largest fish seem most partial to the fly; whether it is that they are hunger-bitten, or whether they rise in the spirit of wantonness, we cannot pretend to say. From the position of the eyes, situated as they are upon the top of the head, he naturally sees more directly above than around. In the northern lakes, pike are very often taken with the fly wherever they abound, whenever they are in the humour for rising, for like all other species, they have their off and on terms, even when in season.

In a work devoted solely to the more scientific methods of taking

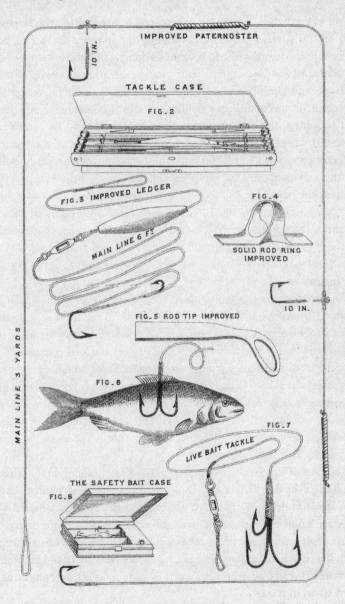

IMPROVED PATERNOSTER

10 IN.

TACKLE CASE

FIG. 2

FIG. 3 IMPROVED LEDGER

MAIN LINE 6 FT

FIG. 4

SOLID ROD RING
IMPROVED

10 IN.

FIG. 5 ROD TIP IMPROVED

FIG. 6

FIG. 7

LIVE BAIT TACKLE

THE SAFETY BAIT CASE

FIG. 8

MAIN LINE 3 YARDS

PLATE 2

fish, it may appear out of place to refer to what are sometimes deemed repulsive styles or systems. We would, however, crave the forbearance of those of our readers whose sentiments may savour of these, for a brief space, as we cannot omit a few remarks upon frog-fishing for pike, which is held so high in repute by veteran pike fishers. The style most in vogue is to work the frog as a live bait; the hook, which should be of special length, strength and size, should be passed through the bottom lip, and under the stomach, the bend being then secured to the thigh of one of the hind legs by a scrap of silk of the right shade. This is conveyed through an opening in the foliage on the banks of the water, a few odd feet only of the line being out. When through, a gentle swing motion is described by the line and the lure, a sudden lurch or spring being given to reach the spot desired, when at some distance; the line, as before stated, being wound round the distended thumb and finger. Another plan is to dape and sink alternately with this bait, which is also very deadly. Artificial frogs are now to be had that answer the purpose almost equally with the not always to be procured living ones. The legs upon these are so constructed as to admit of lifelike action when in the water.

CHAPTER SEVEN

Spinning for Trout

The Thames and Trent Style; Spinning in Discoloured and Clear Water; Minnow Flights and How to Use Them; Artificial Baits; The Rod, Line and Reel; Flight Cases

If it is important to know the haunts of the trout when fly-fishing, it is doubly so when trolling or spinning, as then no circling eddy betrays the habitual feeding grounds. In small streams and rapid brooks, however, this is not of nearly so great importance. Large fish generally locate in some secluded curl, not far from a deep hole, whither they return upon being disturbed or 'knocked off the feed'. The best and most likely places upon the whole river's length are sure to be tenanted by the largest fish, the second best fish are in the immediate vicinity, and take up the position of the extracted heavier one. When large trout are killed upon the open stream, it is a sign of their being out on the 'forage', and great execution ought then to be effected. There are quite as many grades of minnow-spinners as there are of fly-fishers, ranging from the old method of trawling or trolling with heavy primitive tackle in discoloured water, to the scientific Thames and Trent style, which is to stand at a weir or waterfall, and dexterously work the bait in the surging boil of water, near and far away, a fifty-yards cast being deemed nothing at all wonderful; but distance is not of so much importance as is a thorough command of the line, which should be gathered by the disengaged left hand, so that no slack hangs about anywhere. To acquire the art of casting should be the first care of the angler, whether he aspires to bait or fly. When able to pitch the bait fifteen or twenty yards, and from wrist motion to gently insert into water in a way that will not have the effect of disturbing the feeding fish, he may congratulate himself on having acquired the leading qualification requisite to become an adept in the spinning art.

The water that happens to be nearest the rodster should be fished first, afterwards the centre and opposite sides, and lastly, the obscure and more secluded spots to get at. There the best fish are to be taken. The parts usually to be preferred are the heads and tails of streams; the few yards of turbulent water at the head of the stream being generally the most productive.

The speed at which the bait is drawn should be graduated in accordance with the state and colour of the water. For instance, in the event of the water being thick and turbid, a much slower motion should be given to the bait, just sufficient to spin it, in fact. The bait, whether natural or artificial, should work freely at the slightest pull in slow running water; upon the other hand, in the clearest possible water, the lure should be brought round at a moderately steady sweep, not with a *jerking* motion. A sudden stoppage in clear water rather has the effect of alarming than appeasing the natural suspicions of the acute and well-schooled heavy fish; but, in highly discoloured water, the 'halting' or jerking motion is absolutely necessary to enable the fish both to see and seize the bait. Behind a projecting rock or bank, where the water is comparatively quiet, no matter whether shallow or deep, the fish congregate, as the thick, swollen streams cannot be stemmed and are therefore avoided. Here the fish fall an easy prey to the mid-water or minnow fisher, as what is known as minnow daping or dabbing (i.e., giving the bait the slow, whirling motion of a sickly fish) often produces exceptionally heavy takes, even when the water is bank-full, and, figuratively speaking, as thick as 'pea soup'. But this method of extracting fish at an undue advantage we detest, as being unsportsmanlike in the extreme. We have frequently observed individuals (we do not say fishermen) upon hooking a fish in such circumstances, with the strongest possible tackle, literally turn tail upon the water by shouldering the rod and walking away until the hooked fish 'flaps' high and dry on the bank. It is some consolation, however, that these gentlemen (?) occasionally catch a 'tartar' in the shape of a hidden stump, root or pile, in which case the diversion is pleasantly varied by a 'flap' or snap of the tackle, and total loss of bait. We do not hold personally with minnow fishing in temporarily discoloured water. It is too *sure* a way for real sport. Absolute certainty in the pursuit of game destroys the keenness, and takes off the edge, so to speak, of one's feeling of enjoyment when success is in no way dependent upon personal skill. With the finest tackle, in clear water and weather, there is more real satisfaction to be derived from the successful capture of a fine, well-fed fish than in forty such taken by unfair means. The minnow spinner, in clear and rapid streams, should always, where practicable, cast upstream, bringing the bait across and down by a judicious working of the rod from the wrist. As a rule, drawing against stream should be avoided. It is unnatural for a deformed or sickly fish to attempt any feat of the kind; and not only this, when spinning the *natural* minnow the force of the current causes the bait to assume a very *unnatural* attitude in the water, especially when the movable lip hook is used; therefore, uphill spinning should be avoided. The angler should ever remember that the secret of success lies mainly in the motion of the spinning bait. The theory of bait-spinning being founded upon the well-known propensities of the heavy fish for weakly fry accounts for the other-wise *unaccountable* fact of the well-spun bait being seized from the very midst of a shoal of living minnows. The peculiar forms of many substitutes for natural minnows act detrimentally as regards hooking fish. Take the old turn-tailed family of artificials for example. Watch the peculiar motions of a specimen as you slowly bring it through the clear water. You observe that it describes a kind of corkscrew motion. This, especially when accomplished rapidly, will entice fish far oftener than it will hook them; long practice dictates that *nine* 'runs' make one capture, through the instrumentality of these curved or turn-tailed 'artificials'. What is needed is a *perfectly straight* bait, when an artificial is employed, no matter whether the spinning propellers or Archimedean flies be at the head or the tail. So far as this is concerned it will then take a direct 'pigeon' flight through the water, moving an equal number of fish, whilst being more effective in hooking them. In natural minnow spinning this is not of so much importance, the fish that 'goes' for the natural bait without getting hooked, will more frequently come again, not meeting with so hard a substance. The minnow flight we have found preferable to those generally in use we give on Plate 3, Fig. 1. The minnow is placed upon the tackle in the following manner: first, the lead is inserted in the mouth of the fish, the lips being closed by the movable lip hook. This done the bait is pierced through from the one side to the other with the *large* hook, which should be so placed as to keep the lead well up in the minnow's back. Lastly, one of the pair of tail hooks should be made to slightly curl the tail of the minnow. When this arrangement of hooks is correctly inserted the bait is more secure, and will be found to last longer than when mounted in the older and general style.

The most objectionable 'flights' are those consisting of a number of small hooks, whether triangular or otherwise; the ease with which they are broken renders them an abomination when used amongst weighty fish. Another arrangement, which is also very good, whilst being very simple to fit up for use, is the old leaded-wire tackle, which, in lieu of the two side flanges, is fitted with a tiny *Fishing Gazette* spinner, Plate 3, Fig. 3. The bait is mounted merely by thrusting the weighted wire down the mouth, the position being rendered secure by means of the side hooks, which are to be partly hidden in the minnow. For strong currents this tackle is well adapted, its action in the water being perfectly straight and natural; for more open streams the first referred to is recommended, as being all that can be reasonably desired. In most waters the natural minnow is preferable, when procurable. In some streams the skilfully used artificial will, however, not only turn over as many fish, but will kill even more than the natural, the hooks upon it having greater play, while being hid in a measure by better spinning action. Amongst the many 'artificials' now in use, we may mention a few of those that are most distinguished for deadly qualities. The Devon or Totnes (improved pattern), the Derby Trout Killer, the Universal Killer and Foster's Excelsior. The first named is an old reliable bait, originally introduced by a clever Devonshire fisherman. Improvements have lately been made in its construction, which renders it perhaps one of the most effective baits for 'all round' fishing that has hitherto appeared. The bait is heavier metalled, German silver being substituted for the plated brass formerly used. The side flanges are larger and heavier, which materially increases the spinning powers, and altogether the changes effected have considerably added to its value, and are likely to enhance still more its already extensive reputation. The Derby Trout Killer was introduced in Derbyshire about the same period as the Totnes was in Devon. This bait is more especially adapted for fine waters. It is a capital bait for *scientific* fishing, as, for instance, in the middle of a hot day in July or August, when the flies, to avoid the sun's rays secrete themselves in the shades of the neighbouring foliage, and the fish refuse to rise in consequence; then does the Trout Killer distinguish himself in circumstances when spinning would appear the most *unlikely* style or system of fishing. So effective is this bait in some localities that it is there known as the 'Derby Kill-Devil'. The hooks and bait are delicately made, the better to adapt them for this method of fishing. The finest trace and swivel are essential to success in these circumstances.

The Universal Killer and the Excelsior are both metal baits (the latter solid) the former being an exceedingly 'natty' little thing, well suited for rough and turbulent brooklets, the tributaries of our main trouting streams. The spinning power is placed at the tail of this bait. This is considered an especial advantage by some anglers, as trout frequently 'come' at the head of the minnow.

The special advantage in the Excelsior is the extra weight – it being almost double that of any bait of the same size and dimensions – which enables the tyro to spin and cast with ease and success, with but little practice. Its *durability* adapts it for general use amongst pike, perch, chub, trout or salmon. The hooks are fixed in the bait without gut, being eyed triangles of heavy metal; the nuisance of hooks breaking away through faulty gut is thus obviated.

Upon the choice of colours much depends, as trout are partial to a change in this respect. Take an illustration. Upon a recent occasion, having been requested to test the killing qualities of a new artificial,

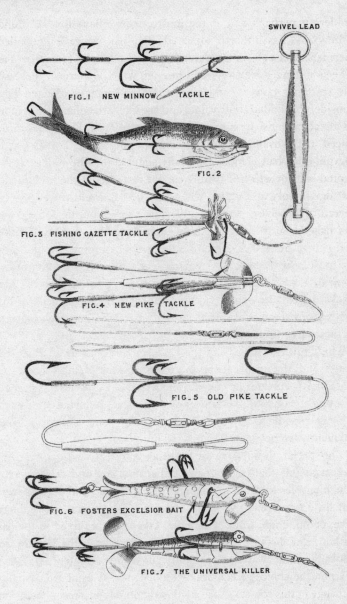

SWIVEL LEAD

FIG. 1   NEW MINNOW   TACKLE

FIG. 2

FIG. 3   FISHING GAZETTE TACKLE

FIG. 4   NEW PIKE   TACKLE

FIG. 5   OLD PIKE TACKLE

FIG. 6   FOSTERS EXCELSIOR BAIT

FIG. 7   THE UNIVERSAL KILLER

PLATE 3

we had repaired to a famous brooklet,* and had succeeded in creeling some four brace of good fish from a confined length of a hundred and fifty yards, which was the extent of our permit. All further dealings were ignored after this being accomplished, though we had moved many more fish than we had taken. Something like half an hour elapsed without our turning over a single fin. Upon this we put another bait of a totally different shade, *when in action*, upon the line, and commenced, and in the course of the next twenty minutes five more fish were landed, when the fish again turned stupid; but upon a bright metal bait, without colouring matter at all, being presented to them, two more brace were taken. Beyond doubt the fish's eye and palate are tickled by a change occasionally.

We invariably advocate the use of the very finest possible tackle for mid-water fishing in low and clear water. The popular belief would appear to be strongly in favour of the reverse; for bait-spinning under all circumstances, scarcely anything can be more erroneous. The accomplished scientific troller will catch fish where it is usually deemed almost an impossibility. And when an incredulous bungler fails to effect a single capture, and returns troutless and dispirited from the well-stocked stream, fair sport will often accompany the rodster who is really a master of the trolling art.

و

The Rod, to be suitable for spinning, should be bamboo or cane, light and stiff, and from twelve to fourteen feet in length for open water; but for small streams eleven or twelve feet is recommended as being quite long enough. The sixteen- and eighteen-feet double-handed rods, usually advocated, are now deemed much too cumbrous, and are rapidly being discarded. The greater utility of a single-handed light rod has long been obvious to a large class of anglers, and its admirers are yearly extending. East India cane is the best adapted for rods where stiffness and lightness are essential, it being extremely strong, though reasonably pliable. The rod we use ourselves for this

* Brailsford Brook

style of angling is but *ten* feet in length, the rings, however, are large
and stationary, and we find no difficulty in casting to eighty or ninety
feet with a tool of this description. The rings upon spinning rods
should all be upright and of fair size, so as to admit of a free and
unencumbered passage for the line when carried out by the weight of
the bait in casting. Where the fish do not run large, an ordinary fly-
rod answers admirably for spinning purposes, when a short stiff top-
piece is substituted for the slender fly-top joint, the only drawback
being the minute loose rings, which hinder the free passage of the
line.

ら

The Line should be plaited silk, waterproof, of about one half the
usual thickness of a dressed flyline; 40 or 50 yards are required for
any water more open than small brooklets, etc. Nothing is so trying to
a line as bait-spinning; and if it is desirable to keep the line sound for
a long period, it should never be worked undressed and unprotected,
or a very short time – when constantly used – will serve to rot and
fray it, so as to render it unfit for use. Twist or cable-laid lines are also
of little utility, as after a severe trial the reel frequently resembles a
ball of loose hemp or tow, the *turn* or twist having in part been taken
out by the spinning action of the bait. The new Acme wire lines are
now being used for all-round fishing, but they are best adapted for
the fly.

ら

The Reel, as in pike fishing, should be of the improved Nottingham
type. Some of these are made of metal, some of wood; the best of the
latter are metal-bound, these being greatly to be preferred to the
original all-wood patterns, no inconvenience being experienced from
the wood swelling. The free action of these Nottingham reels is their
great recommendation – practice will enable the angler to work
efficiently. A thorough command of both rod, reel and line is
necessary to comfort in fishing. In scientific spinning a slight touch
with the fourth finger of the hand holding the rod is sufficient to

regulate the supply of line and progress of bait. These reels are now made with a check, which is made to act at the will of the rodster by the action of a small movable spring. Some winches are made of ebonite * for spinning purposes; these are scarcely, we think, so desirable, as they are apt to break by a fall.

Artificial baits may be safely and conveniently carried in a small partitioned tin case,† as they are liable to be very troublesome if carelessly placed in the overcrowded fly-book; when brushing through a stile, or surmounting a gate or other obstacles, the fisher may perhaps have a personal and undeniably practical experience of the efficiency of his own steel, which will have anything but a soothing effect upon the feelings. August is the best month in the whole season for trout spinning in the smaller rivers and rapid brooks, and the novice will then do well to stay after sunset, and fish until twilight.

* An exceedingly light substance very much resembling ebony, but which is a simple composition.
† Flight cases are now extensively made to meet a growing demand. The 'Safety' case is one of the best, it being strong, very portable, and nicely finished. A sketch of this case is given on Plate 2, Fig 8.

CHAPTER EIGHT

Worm-Fishing for Trout

Antiquity of Worm-Fishing; Bush Fishing; Tackle Requisite;
'Trawling' for Trout; Scientific Worm-Fishing

The term worm-fishing, to many minds, conveys rather an obnoxious impression, anglers being as a class rather apt to ignore what has for ages been considered the most primitive bait for the simplest and most ancient method of fishing. As a lure for trout, until a recent period, the worm was but little used. We shall endeavour to show that this lure may be artistically and scientifically worked in clear and rapid trout streams, wherever situate.

Worm-fishing in discoloured water, it is well known, is practicable under circumstances when other experiments usually fail. Here the simplicity of the system pursued is exemplary of the art as practised by our forefathers: a cork float, leaded line, large hook and stout gut constituted the customary rig-out. In swollen streams fish congregate at the circulating side eddies, whether in or out of the usual watercourse. Here the fisherman inserts the bait, and as an undue advantage is extended to the rodster by the thickened state of the water, the largest and best fish by no means unfrequently meet with an untimely end. To this unsportsmanlike method we venture to assert that no true fisherman will devote himself. Let there be clear water, clear weather, and clear scope for observation, and man may with a clear conscience pit his superior intelligence against the animal instincts of the brute creation.

Bush fishing, in some localities more correctly termed bush fighting, is another type of worming for trout. This, as the appellation implies, is the plan adopted upon well-wooded streams or brooks which are practically inaccessible to the fly-fisher. Here the angler adroitly pitches his lure in every likely and unlikely looking nook, behind stones, by the roots of overhanging bushes, under shelving banks, etc. For the especial behoof of the novice we would observe that great caution should be exercised against uselessly scaring the fish from their customary locations. Indiscretion in this respect will spoil all chances of sport; therefore every interposing object, as bushes, etc., should be utilised, and the rodster should invariably fish *upstream*, as by that means not only will his bait act as herald in advance, but he has the additional advantage of being able carefully to take note of the particular position tenanted by the fish, and to regulate his cast accordingly. For bush fishing a short stiff rod is necessary, or it will be found next to impossible to keep the fish out of mischief when hooked. It is essentially necessary that the capture should be consummated as early as is consistent with the strength of the 'tack'. Of course there is no necessity for reviving early customs by attempting to extract one's fish in the earnest style of early youth, viz., at a strictly perpendicular angle. On the contrary, a judicious respite may be granted when circumstances permit.

The angler must never lose sight of the fact that in clear water his bait is very much more clearly on its merits than when that element is discoloured. It behoves him, therefore, not to disturb its natural progress, which is varied by the ever moving waters. Thus if the lure be gently dropped in a tiny eddy, its circulating motions are not to be hampered and foiled by the line creating a ripple and disturbance in the immediate proximity of the fish upon the lookout for food. It is seldom advisable to cast more than once in the same place; when neatly and carefully done, the bait will be readily seized if at all.

The tackle requisite for worm-fishing in clear water, differs considerably from that used in what is discoloured, no float being used, and except in rapid torrents, 'sinkers' of any description are not necessary. About a yard and a half of moderately thick gut is generally employed, at the extremity of which is placed one or more Kendal or Carlisle hooks (size 6 in single, 7 or 8 if double or treble). These should be attached to the gut with cerise or rose-coloured silk, so as to match the bait in point of colour. The hooks should be white, to prevent them from shining plainly through the bait, which latter should be small, lively and of good colour, no matter whether it be a brandling or cockspur, or even a small lob-worm, so long as it is lively and vigorous, instead of being limp, pale and apparently lifeless. An excellent way of making really durable bottom-tackle is to whip a minute scrap of roach, or any other fine line, upon the bare shank of the end hook, so as to form a small and well-nigh invisible loop, which will be found of great utility in general bottom-fishing. The very finest gut may be attached by means of a slip knot, without even a chance of its 'knocking off' at the head, as is the usual result of a small amount of heavy wear. When baiting, the worm should be carefully threaded up the gut, a small portion of each extremity of the bait being left free, to have as natural an effect as possible. Whenever a small or a solitary hook is employed, the rodster will allow a moment's breathing time ere he gently strikes. By this means it is more than probable that he will succeed in obtaining a safe anchorage amongst the side muscles of the fish's mouth; but a trio of hooks, the Stewart tackle, for instance, requires no such hesitation. We have frequently known young anglers miss every fish they have succeeded in moving during an extremely favourable period, during which they might have effected much had they displayed a moderate amount of discretion and aptness.

Another description of worm-fishing in rapid waters is to run out a long thin line, resembling the usual blow-line, in substance and weight, at the end of which a couple of yards of fine gut is attached, having a worm tackle fixed at its extremity. A stand is then made by some suitable swim, and the bait is allowed to travel with the stream. The line should be kept sufficiently straight to admit of a fish being instantly struck, as the length of line usually out allows amply (sometimes too long) for the proper seizure of the bait. This is a fairly good method upon tolerably open water. The chief feature, indeed we may say the secret of success in worm-fishing, in clear water, is keeping, as much as is possible, out of sight. When the attention of fish is attracted by surface food they are scarcely so keen as to the movements upon the banks and sides of their element; but when not preoccupied in this way, their organs of sight have ample scope and leisure for their full exercise.

And now we come to the more scientific style of using the worm. This is practised more particularly in the spring and early summer months. The bait is attached to the end of a treble extra-fine fly lash, by means of a worm tackle of three-hook power, when it is thrown as a fly, and worked upon the 'cast and draw' system of fly-fishing, with this difference, the bait is allowed to sink a few inches after each delivery upon the water. By this means, fish of the heaviest calibre are often taken. The produce of a single rod, when wielded by an adept, will often exceed the joint takes of several orthodox fly-fishers, more especially if the said rod be assiduously worked in early morn, during the first few hours of daylight. Just as the fish commence to move playfully, as though demonstrating pleasure at the advent of yet another day. Whenever the attention of the fish is absorbed by surface food, it is not advisable to fish with the worm after any method, modern or ancient; but when flies are scarce, and the fish are eagerly upon the lookout for what the stream may produce in the shape of mid-water food, or before the day's first instalment of winged insects put in an appearance, the worm will do great execution. This bait is inseparably connected with angling by all non-practitioners of the art, but it has been as much ignored in these fast-going times as it was adored by our ancestors. It will admit of the fly-fisher for trout pursuing his sport in the teeth of circumstances adverse to the more legitimate modes of angling.

The ordinary fly-rod and line are employed, we had forgotten to observe, in conjunction with the fly-cast. The most favourable spots to fish are in the surging waters of rivers and tiny cascades. A mountain trout stream, in which are combined a continuous and natural succession of turbulent rapids and pellucid pools in miniature, affords the very acme of perfection for the practice of this particular method of angling. Owing to the smallness of the (Kendal) hooks used (No. 10 being the size necessary), a small split shot should be attached half a yard or so from the bait, to give proper momentum in the boil of broken waters. The lure should be drawn briskly through even here, the strike of a fish being detected instanter in these circumstances by the feel, as in the various other styles of trouting in clear waters with the worm. As the use of living bait is not infrequently objected to on the ground of cruelty, we may state that even worms have of late been added to the immense category of effectual 'artificials', the identical rendering referred to having been found to answer in the last method of 'worming' described. The artificial here alluded to is constructed in part from india rubber.

CHAPTER NINE

Grub-Fishing for Grayling

*Grub Baits for Grayling; Methods of Using; Angling
Reminiscence; Camping Out; Maggot-Fishing*

This method of grayling fishing has now become so general that the
omission of a reference to it would render incomplete a work dealing
with this fish. The baits now commonly used consist of the green
(garden) caterpillar, and its artificial (which for some unaccountable
reason is designated the Grasshopper), gentles, wasp grubs, caddis-
bait, and the larvae of all the large water flies found in their sheaths
in the beds of streams; as also freshwater shrimps, and other aquatic
creatures. Of the larger of these grub-like forms, there are admirable
artificial renderings to be had; which, when used, as in the case of the
green caterpillar, or Grasshopper above alluded to, with a couple of
gentles upon the somewhat large hook, answer wondrously well, and
are often preferred to smaller naturals, owing to the sinking medium
being laid in the centre, instead of having it in the shape of shot,
sheet-lead or wire outside and in view. The system in vogue of using
these large artificial lures is to attach them, tipped with gentles or
wasp grubs, to the thicker half of a three-yard fly-cast, and throw out
upon either deep or shallow scours, frequented by the grayling,
according to the time of the year. The bait must be raised and
dropped rapidly and continually, after being duly delivered in the
required places, which should be the known haunts of these fish.
The line should not be raised more than some four or five inches
from the bottom, as the grayling, like barbel, are given to grope for
food of the description reproduced in the copy. In some parts a small
quill float is used, being attached with a wire loop at each extremity,

in lieu of the ordinary runner. By this arrangement a certain amount of freedom is allowed to the line, which admits of its sliding at various depths from the surface, whilst the bait has a roving commission. For our own part, we have always managed to use the bait comfortably without the aid of one of these articles. The use of a float in clear water, whilst fishing for so keen-eyed a fish as the grayling, is anything but artistic or sportsmanlike. When fish are repeatedly missed, it is advisable to secure a small brown twig to the line by wire, in the same way as the sliding float is arranged, as this will not, especially upon densely wood-lined streams, act detrimentally as regards sport.

The originator of the artificial grub system of grayling fishing (Hewett Wheatly) we are aware counselled the use of a float, but since the appearance of his *Rod and Line*, the fish have become so much more suspicious and wary that not even a *senior angler* can, with impunity, transgress accepted rules without paying the penalty in nett results. When the combination of artificial and natural lures is artistically worked by an adept, the slaughter amongst the heavy fish, which seldom or never rise, is immense. Although grayling are very partial to small baits, having a small mouth, they absorb a bunch of hooked threaded gentles, etc., with as much avidity as an eel will worsted-threaded worms. The best time for grub-fishing for grayling is from September to February, and the most severe weather is often the best for sport.

One of the brightest angling remembrances our memory retains was an excursion after the grayling-time of year, in December – Christmas Eve, in fact; water and locality, the Derbyshire Wye, near Ambergate. Our party consisted of three rods; the morning was frosty, dry, and clear, the air deliciously pure and exhilarating, the usually yielding turf was sufficiently hard considerably to increase our powers of locomotion. In the midst of the whitened landscape, the river flowed as tranquilly as on a long summer's day. We had arrived, fitted-out for grub- and hopper-fishing; and with a favourable prospect of sport we set to work. The fish proved in excellent condition, and in feeding humour, and our humour was, therefore, speedily equally excellent, notwithstanding several losses of unusually heavy or subtle quarry. The 'permit' being well-nigh boundless, we wandered far away from our starting point, and by the middle of the afternoon had left our quarters and luncheon miles behind, and when we assembled for a smoke and a chat, each creel was found to be quite respectably weighted. The fish, as is rarely the case when the water is below a certain temperature, had continued to feed throughout the fore- and afternoon, and as there had as yet been no indication of their 'knocking off', we resumed our diversion, and before long had filled our panniers.

As the winter's sun had long sunk to rest, we began to think of retracing our steps; but before having described a third of the distance that lay before us, one of the party, who was, by the way, a bit of an invalid, suddenly discovered himself to be remarkably hungry. The third rodster, being an American tourist, took upon himself the commissariat office. No human habitation appeared within reasonable distance, and how our weakly friend's languishing could be immediately satiated seemed a mystery. We were not long, however, to be left to speculate as to the nature of the expedient to be adopted. Upon the clear hard turf, under the spreading, though now stark branches of an ancient oak, the wood severed by the violence of late storms was arranged and ignited by pipe-lights; some of the choice medium-sized fish were split and cleaned in the silvery stream so shortly before their home, spitted upon a two-prong sapling and, in the glowing embers, were quickly done to a turn. The relish with which they were eaten was significant; the beautiful aroma imparted to the delicate fare by the oaken embers was simply delicious. Like the majority of anglers we seldom care for our takes, after having had the pleasure of extracting them; but we venture to assert that the most fastidious palate would, in similar circumstances, have found their quarry, so primitively yet so skilfully prepared, irresistible. Were we to state the precise quantity of fish so cooked and disposed of by the aid of pocket-knives upon that ever memorable Christmas Eve, we should scarce look for full credit for the statement. Let it suffice that the intervening miles rapidly disappeared under our reinvigorated footsteps, through the picturesque moonlit Wye valley, enlivened by the beautiful stream, and we arrived comparatively early at our comfortable quarters, and in a state of mind and body which made the pillow an elysium of repose.

Maggots and wasp grubs are often used by bottom-fishers for grayling, in a style somewhat similar to that adopted in worm-fishing for coarse fish. A quill float and very fine hook and tackle being, of course, substituted. Skilful roach fishers are proficients at grayling fishing with these appliances, though the fish are more frequently lost than when roach is the quarry. Ground-baiting prevails as a system, but is most certainly unnecessary, as, by an observant angler, the periodical haunts of these gregarious fish are easily discovered. A few hand sprinklings of gentles, etc., cast around the baited hook answers as efficiently as whole quarts of the same indiscreetly planted; indeed, these fish speedily become satiated, and the use of ground-bait is often highly detrimental to subsequent sport.

CHAPTER TEN

Piscatorial Entomology

To be a moderately successful wielder of the rod may be looked upon as a very desirable accomplishment, nay, more, a laudable ambition; but, beyond mere skill in casting a fly and killing and landing a fish, a little rudimentary knowledge of the truly scientific and, consequently, most attractive part of the art is essential in order to attain proficiency.

There are hundreds of tolerably good anglers who are such indifferent entomologists as to be unable to discern the difference between one species of common insect and well-known fly and another; and, lacking this rudimentary knowledge of the insect world, are apt to credit the fish with no greater powers of discernment than themselves – a great injustice to the natural instincts of the denizens of the streams. Such delusions are propounded by fourth-rate followers of every branch of the arts and sciences. That educated English trout can and do distinguish the most trivial difference in both attitude, size and colour is a truism well known and readily acknowledged by all fishermen of experience. The complicated, and ever-extending fly list of the leading authorities on fly-fishing tends rather to confuse and bewilder than to enlighten the youthful aspirant, leading him frequently to ignore the whole as unnecessary and superfluous.

In giving the following hints on entomology as applicable to fly-fishing, our aim is briefly and intelligibly to sketch the general 'standards', which are sufficiently numerous, generally speaking, to attract the attention of the fish when they put in an appearance. The numerical strength of the flies *out* at one time may be said invariably to determine the ardour with which the fish feed. Thus, when the Mayfly or March Brown are but scantily 'on', the Iron Blue Dun or

Black Gnat, if prevalent, will kill infinitely better, simply because the whole attention of the fish for the time being is centred upon them, owing to their greater abundance.

The flies that form food for fish may be divided into two classes, viz., the up-winged (*Ephemeridae*) and the flat-winged (*Phryganidae, Muscedae*, etc.). Of the latter there are many varieties, part being of the water, as are the whole of the first order, the *Ephemeridae* family. These water flies are of the greatest use to the angler, as they rise to the surface only to fulfil their natural functions, living but a few days, and ever delighting to sport on or near their native element. Not so the land flies. They do not habitually frequent the water, being seldom seen upon it, excepting when swept there by the force of the wind; hence it follows that they are rarely sufficiently numerous except upon cold and windy days, or after a boisterous storm.

In taking, first, the most important order of naturals (the *Ephemeridae* family), we deal with what has hitherto been made a most intricate and formidable list of insects, modern naturalists dividing and subdividing it into sections and subsections until the poet Pope's 'thousands of winged insects' threaten to descend from the ideal into stern reality. Personal observations, extending over a period of fifty years leads us to affirm the greater part of this extensive classification to be perfectly needless. There are, in fact, but four different species of up-winged insects, these forming the *Ephemeridae* family. The prevailing temperature of the atmosphere and the water at the time of the larva and pupa arriving at the stage of maturity is largely instrumental in influencing the colour, the body of the insect particularly being susceptible to change from these effects.

The four species here referred to are the ordinary Olive and Iron Blue Duns, the Large Browns and the Mayfly or Green Drake.

The Olive Dun makes its first appearance in February, when it is known as the Blue Dun or February Flapper. It then presents a dead lead colour, the inclement weather then seasonable causing the fly to assume so sombre a hue. A few weeks later, if the weather be more genial, it is a shade lighter upon the body, when it is styled the

1   *Blue Dun: Natural and Artificial*
2   *Cockwinged Dun: Natural and Artificial*
3   *Yellow Dun of April: Natural and Artificial*
4   *Rusty-Bodied Dun: Natural and Artificial*
5   *Pale Blue Dun: Natural and Artificial*

PLATE 4

Cockwinged Dun. By the beginning of April it is of a general olive colour, with yellow-ribbed body, upon which rests a bloom, like that of a ripe muscat grape, but upon dull days this is substituted by a rust-like fungus, which gives a ruddy appearance to the whole body at first sight. It is then known as the Yellow Dun of April, light and dark. In April, in the cold water near the springs or sources of streams, more especially in limestone districts, the fly appears of a light blue tint. This is designated the Pale Blue Dun. A few weeks later again, and the Blue Dun of February appears as the Yellow Dun of May, and, in ungenial weather, as the Hare's Ear Dun. This, like most of the multiplicity of appellations, takes its name from a part of the material used in the construction of the artificial, the former being a light and delicate olive, the latter several shades darker.

The 'Yellow Dun of May' continues plentiful through June on hot days, the action of the sun rendering it lighter on the body. In July it is designated the Pale Evening White, it being as white as a new shilling. The nymphae locating in shallow open water, where the sun's rays penetrate during the hot months, the fly appears excessively light and delicate. In June, unseasonable weather causes the body of the dun to assume a dirty yellow tinge, and it is then known as the Common Yellow Dun. It acquires a more pronounced yellow a little later, when the fly is termed the Golden Dun, being more partial to fine weather. There are still two other shades before the gradual tints of this interesting fly terminate, and a comprehensive glance may be given of them in an order of rotation as the season progresses.

The nympha of the Pale Evening Dun rises from deep still water, the colour very much resembling the common yellow shade of June. This, in common with all water flies, gradually assumes a lighter shade, even when exposed to the sun's rays for only an hour. Dull or inclement weather in July produces the July Dun, in which the old and more general olive shade is again visible, commingling with pale yellow. And now, with the declining months, the fish and fisherman are treated to a repetition of the various shades of the spring, though graduating in the contrary direction, i.e., growing darker as the months pass, instead of lighter. Thus, in August we have the exact shades of May, and in September those of April – the state of the weather and the water being similar to that in the corresponding earlier months of the year – until we again arrive at the Dull Blue Dun of February in November.

The whole of the foregoing are the natural progeny of the Common Red Spinner. All the duns, therefore, that live to maturity become spinners; they are, in consequence, very numerous. In the warmer months this becomes lighter in shade, assuming a golden tint on the body, when it is designated the Golden, instead of the Red Spinner. The limited period usually devoted to the study of the native water flies, which are designed for the sustenance of nonmigratory fish, both upon the surface and in the bed of the rivers, has led to erroneous and inaccurate inferences. During an unusually backward and dull season one particular shade of fly will be numerous, often for many weeks, and occasionally even months; and as no two or three successive years are exactly identical in this respect, it is essential that observations be assiduously carried on over an extended period, or misconceptions will be the inevitable result. Insects have been described in their first or imperfect stage minutely, whilst the greater part of their existence as flies and perfect insects has been ignored altogether. Other species have been honoured by a notice in their decrepit old age, when they are described as beings of a day or hour. This inconsistency is mainly due to the difficulty above noted of drawing correct inferences from limited investigation, and under the varying influences of the elements and seasons.

The next in importance to the angler, of the four different varieties of up-winged water flies, are the Large or Spring Browns, so called from their being more prevalent in the earlier parts of the season. The first appearance of this second species is the well-known March Brown of the northern and southern counties, and the Dun Drake of the midlands, the streams of which district produce this fly more freely than elsewhere. The term Dun Drake is applied owing to its bearing a conspicuous resemblance to the Mayfly or Drake in point of both size and attitude, being twice the size of an ordinary dun. When these flies first ascend from the watery depths they are eagerly

6   Yellow Dun of May: Natural and Artificial
7   Golden Dun: Natural and Artificial
8   Pale Evening Dun: Natural and Artificial
9   Pale Evening White Dun: Natural and Artificial
10   Red Spinner: Source of the foregoing range

PLATE 5

absorbed by the feeding fish. Though styled the March Brown, they are seldom *up* before the beginning of April on most streams. After a few weeks of genial weather, the fly becomes of lighter hue, as in the case of the Olive Dun, but with this difference, that it perceptibly decreases in size. A strange inaccuracy is credited in respect to the first change of this fly. It is supposed to be the female Brown, but that is perfectly erroneous, as the difference in sex cannot be distinguished until the final stage of existence, viz., that of spinners, in which they propagate their species. The spinners in this case are called the Great Reds, which are numerous, more or less, just in proportion as their predecessors, the Large Browns, have been prevalent; as is also the case with the ordinary Red Spinners of the Olive Duns. In May the March Brown is recognised as the Turkey Brown, light and dark, in accordance with the weather. This fly diminishes in size as the weather grows warmer. By August the fly is still a little smaller, and is known as the August Brown or Dun. These are seldom numerous, the nympha being generally in a state of torpor in the hot months as it is a hardy insect and partial to rough weather. A few Up-Winged Browns continue to haunt the surface of rivers and streams for the remainder of the season, but are seldom sufficiently numerous to merit attention.

The Iron Blue Dun ranks next in importance to the Up-Winged Browns. This is a distinct species, and is not to be confounded with the Olive Dun, which is double the size. The general prevailing colour of this insect is a beautiful deep blue, except upon the body, where there is a faint tinge of mauve, intermingled with blue. (For detailed description, see page 130.) It makes its first appearance in April; in May, however, it is infinitely more plentiful, but has then a mauve-coloured body, acquiring a lighter hue as the season advances, precisely similar to the other duns. The fly appears in June and July, but paler in wings and body, when it is recognised as the Little Sky Blue; and in the early part of September is called the Little Pale Blue. Later still it is very plentiful, but darker in shade, until in October it closely resembles the olive shade of the duns in April; indeed these are frequently taken for half-matured Olive Duns; but this cannot be, as all winged water insects attain full growth and dimensions immediately upon quitting the pupa case. The metamorphosis of this fly is the Jenny (or Jinney) Spinner. This is a beautiful and delicate fly, so delicate that it is a difficult matter to copy it successfully. The colour is pure milk-white upon legs, wings, and body, except a bright crimson band at each extremity of the last named.

Each of the three varieties of up-winged water flies live three days, after having ascended from the river's bed, and burst their 'swathings'. They then cast their skins, like stripping off a garment, reappearing as spinners. They live about five days in this, the concluding period of their life. We have several times taken for experimental purposes a number of Common Red Spinners, Jenny Spinners and Great Red Spinners (transformations of the Olive Dun, Iron Blue Dun and Up-Winged Browns). These we have deposited upon the water contained in a fish-hatching box, through which ran constantly a stream of freshwater, the whole being well and closely-fitted over. There they have deposited their eggs, each fly dropping several as it rose and fell upon the top of the water. After this last and most important function of their life had been performed, each having deposited its hundreds of eggs, every sign of vitality vanished, and they appeared lifeless, and merely a flimsy form inflated with air.

By the aid of a powerful microscope we were enabled minutely to investigate, from time to time, several points of special interest to us. By careful and oft-repeated researches we ascertained that from 36 to 40 days serve to hatch the eggs, when deposited in the summer months, but much longer if in spring; and almost immediately after this has happened, the larva or grub secretes itself amongst the sediment at the bottom of the water, instinct, doubtless, prompting this as security against the numerous enemies which prey upon it. The form of the larva is shown to be elongated, with six perfect legs, and whisked tail, also armed with a pair of formidable forceps, with which its food is seized. Along the sides there is a range of web-like appendages, which serve as fins; and by the aid of this propelling power the larva becomes exceedingly active. In the course of five or

11   *Iron Blue: Natural and Artificial*
12   *Iron Blue: lighter body: Natural and Artificial*
13   *Little Sky Blue: Natural and Artificial*
14   *Pale Blue: Natural and Artificial*
15   *Jenny Spinner: Natural and Artificial*

PLATE 6

six months the larva changes into a pupa, or nympha, by breaking through a filament or outward skin. Upon the shoulders there are now two small protuberances, which ultimately develop into wings. When in the larva and pupa states the insect is excessively voracious; like the small clothes-moth it feeds, not when fully developed, but when 'swathed' up in its tough pliable case. The larvae of both moth and fly devour many times their own weight in a single week, and this is the case with all water flies, whether *Ephemeridae* or *Phryganidae* (up-winged or flat-winged), which feed only when in the larva and pupa state, absorbing sufficient nutriment to sustain them during the short and final stages of their life. They afterwards appear in their new sphere, first as duns, secondly, as perfect imago or insects.

As the eggs of the *Ephemeridae* had been deposited in May, in the following February, whenever the state of the water permitted, the first flies emerged from their pupa case, rose to the top of the water, and bursting yet another shell-like skin unfolded their now perfect wings and appeared as early Blue Duns. A little more genial weather, and the Cockwing and the Olive, from which the fly takes its name, was predominant, the lighter shades appearing as the nympha gradually attained maturity, up to midsummer. April saw the first instalment of Iron Blue, also March or Spring Browns appeared, both being of a lighter shade, and the latter a little smaller in dimensions, after the lapse of a few weeks. Up to July the colour of the duns ranged in the precise ratio we have given, by which time the whole of the nymphae had attained maturity,* with the exception of a few of the Browns, which rose in August, smaller still in size. To have the whole season's supply of the *Ephemeridae* it is necessary to take spinners about May, and again in August. The latter produce first the delicate tints, ending with the lead-blue shades of November.

Such *casts* as are called the Apple-Green, Orange and Whirling Blue Duns do not occur anything like annually; they prevail only

---

* Sometimes freshwater shrimps and other water insects found their way into the hatching apparatus and made sad havoc; but this evil is evaded by placing a piece of the finest perforated zinc at the inlet.

during a spell of unseasonable weather. A dun of these pronounced shades may not be observed for several seasons, whilst for some weeks in the succeeding one it may be exceedingly prevalent. If the range of shades previously described are correctly asserted to be dependent upon the state of the elements, and therefore accidental, these latter are doubly so.

The Mayfly, Green Drake or Caddow concludes the order of up-winged insects. This fly is an annual one, appearing upon the majority of trout streams about the first week in June. Throughout Britain it may be said to be in season from the middle of May to the middle of June. These flies are often wondrously numerous. The first four days or so when they begin to come up, the fish seem rather afraid of them, but as they become more numerous they are greedily taken. These flies are common for twelve or fifteen days, when they entirely disappear till the next season. The fish so gorge themselves during the drake season that they lie dormant for some days before they are relieved from the effects of their excess. More has been written upon this than perhaps any other fly. It has been set up as an analogy for the lesser ephemeral orders, which is scarcely correct, as it appears but for a limited period annually; and in the second place the egg remains in the water two years before it grows sufficiently, and has arrived at a proper state of perfection to ascend. It is also longer lived as a fly. Swammerdam speaks of it as 'a being of a day, whose life in a perfect state is compassed in a few hours'. Another affirms that 'they lay about eight hundred eggs immediately upon the wings being developed, and the whole are deposited in a shorter time than another insect would consume in laying one'.

Our own experience tells us that they live from eleven to fourteen days – nine days as green, the remainder grey – and that they do *not* propagate their species until they reach the final or perfect state, viz., that of Grey Drakes. Nor do they lay eight hundred eggs. Our investigations go to prove three or four hundred to be the utmost possible limit; and, as to their depositing the whole instantly, the idea is absurd.

We have seen, more than once, Stone and Cinnamon Flies and

16 March Brown: Natural and Artificial
17 Turkey Brown: Dark: Natural and Artificial
18 Turkey Brown: Light: Natural and Artificial
19 August Dun: Natural and Artificial
20 Great Red Spinner: Natural and Artificial

PLATE 7

common moths lay eggs at the rate of sixty per minute – one per second; but with the up-winged insects the operation is much more leisurely achieved. Floods do *not* deter or retard the appearance of the water flies, further than what damage may be done in a sandy or loose-bottomed river by the larvae being crushed or swept away.

When the weather is seasonable, the Drake appears upon some waters literally in swarms, so thick that to fill the live-fly basket is often the work of but a few moments. The exact annual time to a few days when they come 'up' upon each river is slightly subservient to the weather.

The Grey or Black Drake is the metamorphosis or transformation of the Green. The colour is black and white, and the fly finely and minutely freckled in the wings. The body is milk-white, the ribs faintly touched with black, as also each extremity of the body. The legs and tail are black, the latter being double the length of the former. These flies are only prevalent as the season of the Drake begins to wane. They whirl in clouds in the shadows of trees near and overhanging the water, stragglers ever and anon dropping upon its surface to deposit eggs, which occurs particularly towards evening. In this act they are generally caught by the fish, which incessantly feed, so long as their prey is plentiful.

This fly is not nearly so much appreciated as the Green, being in its perfect state more active, for, in common with other ephemeral transformations, it improves more in outward form than inward substance; hence the preference of the wily fish. The Grey Drake generally takes shelter under the leaves of trees and bushes during midday in sultry weather, emerging in the evening in incredible numbers, and sporting in the air in every direction. When the fly is matured enough to lay eggs it is designated the Spent Black, owing to its gradually getting darker in colour towards the end of its existence. The operation of depositing the eggs so exhausts the fly that it dies immediately on the completion of this function, a hollow shell being all that remains.

This insect, when in its new-born aerial dress, flutters heavily, like the freshly-fledged song bird, and then appears devoid of all sense of feeling; but in its last stage it is too delicate for live fly-fishing; indeed, it is then so marvellously fragile that it may be said to be at the mercy of a breath of wind, the slightest touch ending its existence. In some instances this fly appears of a much brighter green, the metamorphosis being of a freckled red brown. This is commonly called the 'mackerel', light or dark. It frequents slow-running, thickly wooded streams, but is of little importance to the fisherman.

The flat-winged flies consist of a far greater variety of species; but, even taking them as a whole, they are of but secondary importance from a piscatorial point of view. We shall now, however, proceed to enumerate the two leading orders of the flat-winged insects which are requisite to a complete equipment.

The first of these claiming our attention are the water flat-wings, the leading species of which are the *Phryganidae* (consisting of the Red, Sand, Cinnamon and Bank Flies, also the Grannum or Green-Tail) and the *Perlidae* (which family includes the Stone Fly, Yellow Sally, Willow and Needle Fly or Tail-to-Tail). These flat-winged flies arise from the larva or grub which is found in small twigs, etc., these having been excavated to form a retreat.* The Red or Welsh Fly is a four-winged natural, its wings lying alongside the body, so as completely to envelop it except underneath, thus forming a roof-like ridge across the back. It is the earliest fly out in the spring, and may be seen upon the first tolerably open day in January, fluttering industriously as it is carried downstream. These are in some districts believed to be the March Brown, but there is, as has been elsewhere stated, a marked distinction between them. It is a very useful fly in the early months.

After the February Red, the next in this order is the Sand Fly, which is precisely similar as to size and attitude, but of a pronounced sandy hue universally. This fly usually makes its appearance in the latter half of April, continuing more or less prevalent during May,

---

* The small worm or grub found in the beds of streams, commonly termed the straw or cad bait, is the larva of the Stone and Cinnamon Flies.

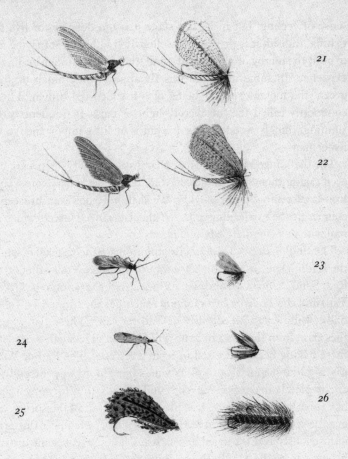

21   *Green Drake: Natural and Artificial*
22   *Grey Drake: Natural and Artificial*
23   *Red Fly: Natural and Artificial*
24   *Willow Fly: Natural and Artificial*
25   *Alexandra Fly: Artificial*
26   *Red Caterpillar: Artificial*

PLATE 8

and again in the autumn. Like the generality of four-winged flies, it is seldom on the wing, and when so is a solitary insect, but is a favourite with the fish, even when sparsely present.

The Fetid Brown, or Cinnamon, follows the Sand Fly. This is a much larger insect, being more than two-thirds of an inch in length, from the tip of the head to the tail. In general attitude it is precisely similar to those previously described, but it is of a darker and more ruddy brown than the Sand Fly; it is more plentiful in the autumn than at any other time of the year. Its name has originated from the fact of there being a faint odour of cinnamon emitted by it when handled. It is invaluable for live-fly-fishing, but it is seldom 'up' in sufficient strength on open water to make it equally valuable for casting. Being excessively heavy in its flights, its motions and flutterings are very awkward. In July and August it frequents the surface of the water under shelving banks and sheltered places, and is then styled the *Bank* Fly. In common with the Spring Browns it is considerably smaller in size during the hot months; but is more numerous on cold days.

The Green-Tail, or Grannum, completes this order of flies. It appears at first sight like a freckled Sand Fly, but upon a more minute inspection is found to differ considerably in several points. The body has a strange appendage of a conspicuous green colour at its extremity. This is its egg-pouch, and it is observed to drop its egg, like the spinners of the ephemeral order, as it rises and falls upon the top of the water.

The *Perlidae* order ranks next to the above. The most useful we have given as being the Stone, Willow and Needle Flies, also the Yellow Sally. The first named is a very large fly, and in some localities is termed the Mayfly, as it annually makes its first appearance in that month. There is, however, the same distinctive difference between this and the Mayfly, or Green Drake, that we have already described in the February Red and the March Brown, with this exception, that the wings of the Stone Fly are double the length of those of the Red Fly, and lie still more horizontally, being almost flat upon the back of the insect. Except upon blustering windy days, these flies are seldom 'on' in sufficient quantities to excite the attention of the fish; though as a luscious morsel, the large fish seldom ignore even the solitary specimen when it essays a paddling excursion across its native element. Its general haunts are amongst the gravel and pebbles by the sides of streams, hence the name; but when carried by a high breeze to mid-stream in any number, the artificial may be used with signal success. The larvae of these large water insects form food for fish some ten days or more before they are mature enough to 'rise', as the grub then becomes very active, and attracts the attention of the fish. The grub, when extracted from the case or twig which it inhabits, is used in a similar manner to the wasp bait and maggot for bottom-fishing.

The Willow Fly appears in August. This is a well-known insect, and on all our most frequented trout and grayling streams is one of the first flies that the latter fish feed ravenously upon, when coming into condition after the spawning period. The colour of its wings is a dark, ruddy, brown blue, with light coloured ribs, and legs a rusty black. Unlike most naturals, these flies, instead of taking their names from their own colour, are almost universally known by the term Willow, which appellation may have originated from the fact of their being generally most abundant in the immediate vicinity of willow trees, particularly while upon the wing, when they may be observed in whirling masses just above the surface of the water.

The Needle Fly, Needle-Brown or Tail-to-Tail as it is sometimes called, is a peculiar-looking insect; its wings are folded in a manner so neat and compact, and fit so closely to the body, as to give the observer the impression that it is devoid of them altogether. In the warmest hours of a September day, myriads of them are to be seen fluttering in clouds in the shade of trees, bridges, etc. They are of a dingy brown shade on the body, legs and wings, and unless seen in a certain light are almost indistinguishable when in action over the water. There are two sizes of these flies when full grown, the largest being fully half an inch in length, the other about two-thirds that size. This is one of the best of our grayling flies. The fish being partial to small insects, the lesser one is generally used by most fishermen. This fly frequents some streams in lieu of the Willow, and is equally killing. Needle Flies are numerous on warm mizzly days, throughout the fall of the year.

The Yellow Sally concludes the list of the *Perlidae* order deserving the notice of the angler. This fly is of a general primrose tint, and when once seen can never be mistaken. It rises about the middle of June, being more or less numerous during the hot months, but is not much appreciated by the fish. It is seldom really on the water, even when well out, being a stray flier, often descending from a great height to deposit eggs in the water, falling apparently lifeless, but immediately springing up to soar anew, and repeat the operation. The artificials of this fly fail to be effective, owing to their being dressed 'winged'; most flat-winged water flies should be dressed 'buzz' to kill well. The best chance of killing with this fly is during or soon after a passing storm, which beats them down upon the water.

We have now enumerated the three principal orders of winged water insects. A reproduction of one of each some accomplished fly-fishers place upon their casts for *all round* fishing; but we do not advise our readers to act up to any system, but would rather encourage them to use their own observation, to be quick to take note of existing influences and their general bearings on the occasion, and thus to adapt themselves to meet circumstances which would otherwise prove detrimental to sport. The real essence of the art lies in deceiving the fish *by a correct copy of any fly that may be at any time absorbing their attention*.

We have yet briefly to mention the casual killers amongst the numerous tribes of land insects, which may be summed up as follows: Cowdung Fly, small beetles (Marlow Buzz or Cock-y-Bondu), Oak Fly, Bluebottle, Wren-Tail, the Ants and Grey and Black Gnats. These flies pass their pupa stage in the earth, either in thickly wooded or meadow land; they, therefore, do not habitually frequent the water, but are driven upon it by rough weather.

The Cowdung Fly we have fully commented upon in 'Notes on the Months', pages 181-2. The term small beetles, includes the Lady-cow and Earwig, as well as the small members of the beetle tribe proper, which are prevalent more or less throughout the season.

The artificial is a simple hackled fly (elsewhere described) which effectually represents the numerous members of the above varieties.

The Oak Fly, or Downlooker, usually accompanies the Green Drake. This is another fly that is commonly used in its natural state, particularly upon thickly wooded streams; it is often seen upon the trunks of trees, etc., upon which it invariably rests with its head downwards, instantly assuming that position if alighting in any other. In cold or inclement weather, it secretes itself amongst the roots of luxuriant grass or thick moss, until more genial weather prevails. The fly is perfectly flat-winged, and in attitude resembles the House and Wood Flies. These three flies are, perhaps, the most commonly known of any British insects.

The Wood Fly resembles the domestic House Fly in all particulars except size, it being a trifle larger, and is especially numerous in the vicinity of cattle, to which it is very obnoxious, especially in wooded districts. In cold weather, in the fall of the year, the whole tribe of Wood and House Flies become blind, when they are swept upon the water in great quantities, to be picked off by both trout and grayling, especially the latter. The Grey Palmer efficiently represents these drowning insects, when vainly fluttering to extricate themselves from the foreign element.

The Bluebottle is most in request for live-fly-fishing in July and August. It is sometimes cast along with the Grey Palmer, and renders good account of its attractive powers, but cannot be said to be infallible. The Wren-Tail, or Frog-Hopper, forms one of the many varieties of winged insects numerous in July. In common with the small Blacks, it braves the heat of the noonday sun. The latter fortunately differ very materially in regard to their habits and movements, as they are incessantly hovering over the water, whilst the Frog-Hopper merely appears accidentally, and, therefore, unintentionally, upon its bosom. It is occasionally to be used with effect.

The Ants are only occasionally numerous, but in some localities the red species are common in sandy soils and amongst wild, broken ground. The black variety are found only in thickly wooded districts, where they build their hills to a considerable size of small twigs, leaf stems, etc. In sultry weather these little creatures will migrate to the nearest water to indulge in a cooling bath, and, when this happens to be a trout stream, both fish and fisherman experience lively times. Their eggs are much sought after for angling purposes, being excellent bait for almost every description of freshwater fish when prepared and used similar to trout and salmon roe.

The Grey and Black Gnats, and, indeed, the whole fraternity of 'smuts', arise from the soil of sheltered meadow banks; they are most obnoxious to the fly-fisher when out in any quantity.

Year after year, and century after century, a curious and interesting equilibrium is maintained by nature, with but few deviations, in regard to insect life in this temperate clime. Whilst various members of the beetle, ant and other orders increase, at intervals, to a really alarming extent in more southern latitudes, in this country a truly marvellous balance of insect existence is preserved by the restraining action of counter influences on the enormous procreative powers with which they are invested. When myriads of flies are observed depositing their eggs literally by millions, upon water or land, we are led to investigate the reason why their material increase is seldom rendered notable, and we find that the mass simply go to feed other creatures, whose sole mission would appear to be to counteract, regulate and hold in check their kindred species. All insects of the smaller kind, inhabiting the earth or water, feed upon the ova of the different orders of winged insects, the pupae of which retaliate in turn by preying continuously upon the minute insects, the enemies of their previous existence. Thus, by a wondrous scheme of providence, the perfect chain of animated nature and organised creation is accurately preserved.

When insects arrive at maturity, there is this signal and distinctive difference between the aerial and aquatic species. The former are voracious feeders when in their perfect state; the latter do not, as we have shown, feed at all when in the subimago and perfect stages of their existence, so that no devastating results issue from any multiplication of these. The same observation cannot be applied with equal truth to the case of the land insects, which, when plentiful, are the bane of man and beast. Reaumur makes mention of a swarm of Mayflies or Drakes on the Marne, which completely covered him two or three inches in depth, in the space of a few minutes. Most fishermen have experienced something similar, at long intervals, with regard to the water flies in certain localities: this is the result of a combination of circumstances favourable to them. Seasonable weather is always favourable to insect life.* A mild winter will tend to destroy the ensuing season's general supply, by causing premature activity, followed often by premature death, or at best by a relapse into a state of torpor. These changes invariably prove prejudicial to the existence of insects. Steady and severe cold, when seasonable, upon the other hand, is not only favourable to insect life, by causing a continued state of torpor, from which they emerge in due season, but also by indirectly preserving them from the attacks of their numerous enemies. It sometimes happens that, from a variety of causes, running water is of a higher temperature than the atmosphere, in dry frosty weather; and as the aquatic insect, prior to leaving its native element, is wholly influenced by it, an uprising of them when the air is too cold for them to live in it, is not by any means an infrequent occurrence. We have observed them rise to live but a few hours, and sometimes only minutes, in the event of there being no sun temporarily to counteract the effects of the keen air.

* We remember ourselves witnessing, one very hot summer, which had succeeded a hard winter, some forty years ago, a rising of Iron Blues upon the Dovedale length of the Dove that completely enveloped the summits of the surrounding rocks, which appeared to be clouded by a thick blue mist. There are instances on record of church spires being taken to be on fire from a similar phenomenon.

CHAPTER ELEVEN

On Fly-Making

*Flies for Trout and Grayling Fishing; The Advisability of Copying
Nature; Up-Winged and Flat-Winged Artificials; Dressings for the
Duns, Browns, Mayflies or Drakes; Flat-Winged Water Flies;
Land Flies; How to Dress a Hackle Fly, Palmer, etc.;
Salmon Flies*

Trout and Grayling Flies A really solid advantage the amateur fly-maker enjoys is his ever available ability to produce copies of any special insect the fish may just then be regaling themselves upon, when other lures fail to meet with due appreciation. Trout are often most tantalisingly fastidious; and though occasionally, at rare intervals, they are to be taken by almost anything in the shape of a fly, it is merely a reckless spirit of wantonness that is displayed, in which case *sport will prove but indifferent*, the fish in reality being merely playing and not feeding. Trout will take down almost anything when in this mood; bits of leaves, twigs and other floating atoms, we have repeatedly seen them close their teeth upon, when taking observations from the chinks of a wooden footbridge; but these floating substances we noted invariably rose to the surface almost immediately. But when, on the other hand, there are myriads of any particular fly out, the thorough earnestness displayed by the feeding fish, as they eagerly absorb the abundance of food thus presented upon the surface of their native element, bears a marked contrast to their former demeanour; and when the angler happens not to possess an imitation thereof to present, in nine hundred and ninety-nine instances out of a thousand, his lure will meet with an unflattering reception. It is then that the proficient fly-dresser, by a little display of patience and ingenuity, proves equal to the occasion, and by the prompt exercise of his art, rules the circumstances to which his less accomplished brother of the rod must bow.

Great disappointment is often experienced by the uninitiated (and we regret to have to admit there should exist grounds for honest complaints) in procuring flies dressed to any particular artificial or natural pattern. The prevailing custom would appear to be simply to choose the fly in stock, bearing the best resemblance to the pattern required in its various details; and as this is occasionally limited in its character, the credulity of the fisher is not infrequently imposed upon. These and other tests of patience, the angler, who has become an apt fly-dresser, spares himself. Upon the other hand, it is but fair to point out the little drawbacks it is necessary to surmount.

Firstly, then, time is essential, as a matter of course, for the practice of this pleasing art. We often hear it asserted 'that life is too brief to admit of fishermen making their own flies'; every art and pursuit demands a given amount of application, more especially until a thorough practical knowledge of it is acquired. To claim an exception in the case now before the reader, would certainly be unjustifiable; but in the particular circumstances to which we have made allusion, it cannot, we think, be denied that it is an advantageous accomplishment to the fly-fisher. Another fact, well known to all practitioners, whether amateur or professional, is that the creditable construction of well-known artificials requires a certain amount of studious application. Many dozens have frequently to be made and discarded before the hand acquires the accurate 'knack' for each different description of fly; therefore with well-known 'standards', the professor has unmistakably the advantage, large quantities of each of those most difficult to make being produced before another variety is taken in hand.

In fly-making, a natural specimen of the fly it is desired to imitate should always be placed before the artist. Man's greatest achievements in the fine arts are admired, and justly so, in proportion to their faithful accordance with the originals of nature. Mere reproductions of these are not nearly so much esteemed; for, though the original canvas may be valued at its weight in gold, even good copies are of small comparative worth. We have often deplored the perverseness of individuals who, misconceiving the object and aim in view, persist in reproducing old renderings, from books and other sources, and thus, instead of endeavouring to improve upon existing or old styles, *merely perpetuate them*, and are content. Many an old pattern of 'artificial' is considered irresistible in its season, owing to past exploits in which it may have figured favourably, when given the post of honour upon the fly-list. Their owners fail to comprehend that their vaunted virtues could and would have been eclipsed in the matter of conquests had a truer, and therefore better, copy been employed in equally favourable circumstances.

The natural insects, common to all pure running streams, are precisely similar upon all waters productive of them; nevertheless the immense diversity in the imitations (so called by courtesy) is simply astounding. To take the Drake, or Mayfly, as a case in point. Though, comparatively, this is a large and well-known fly, we venture to assert that if a copy of it be obtained from five hundred different fly-dressers, scarcely any two will be alike; and it may be that not many amongst the better renderings have much in common with the original. To the eye of the experienced fly-fisher, a glance at the handiwork of any fly-dresser proclaims the amount of practical knowledge and experience possessed by him. To distinguish an old style of fly from a more modern one, is a much easier matter; this is a problem, the solution of which need trouble no individual, as it certainly does not the fish. As we have before pointed out, nature is far too often imitated from memory, convention, and even tradition. Reproduction in art is a totally different matter from reproduction in nature. The first named means in reality degeneration. Through such a process, truth, ideality and efficiency are lost at each successive step down the ladder of routine. Let the aspiring student study and take his ideal and model from nature, and then progress in true worth and efficiency will be effected.

The first thing to note when a strange natural is taken in hand to copy is the position of the wings; if it be 'flat-winged', it may be dressed hackle- or palmer-wise, instead of being winged; whilst if it be up-winged, it should be dressed with wings nearly erect, and broad in proportion. The reason for this is obvious. The latter, when upon the water, float buoyantly along, over both broken and still water, which, however, is scarcely the case with the first named, as the majority of these insects being land flies, naturally fail to take to the water, like the 'up-winged' natives; therefore, to imitate their buzzing action the copies are usually made up hackled and wingless. The secondary point for consideration is the choice of colour.

⁓

The Choice of Colour, which, we would impress upon the mind of the tyro, requires the exercise of a certain amount of judgement; as what may appear to be the correct thing to look *down* upon, will in all probability be a glaring departure from the tint required when viewed from *underneath*. It must ever be remembered that the fish, from their position *below* the natural fly and the copy, see through them; when viewed thus they will appear, as a general rule, several shades lighter. To distinguish the correct colour of a fly as presented to the fish, we know of no better method than to place it in a clear glass of water, and hold it between the eye and the light in such a position as to be able to see underneath the insect. The precise shade of both legs, wings, and body will then be accurately ascertained.

⁓

How to Dress the Fly What we hereafter endeavour to expound may deviate somewhat from the general rules laid down by former writers; but when we state that the method of construction to be hereafter divulged has been to us as good as a patent since we originated the same, we trust our motive in finally making public the result of our researches in this by no means unimportant branch of our delightful art will not be misconstrued, as has, we fear, been already the case with more than one predecessor and originator of improvements in artificials,* whose works have been calumniated

* Blacker, of famed memory, to wit.

by individuals who, to hide their own incompetency, have adopted the plan of criticising the achievements of men of known merit. But we digress. It is customary to make all up-winged artificials with drooping wings. These, when wet, or when drawn through the water, lie perfectly *flat on the back of the hook*, and when this is the case with a dun or spinner, or other ephemeral, it is a glaring departure from the original. To dress up-winged flies so as to retain their all but erect attitude in the water, and that when subjected to hard and heavy use, we give the following: let us suppose for the time being that the intending operator has already fashioned the body, and has in readiness the material for its remaining appendages, viz., the legs and wings. Now, instead of next placing the legs, and lastly the wings, *he must reverse the operation* by attaching the wings first, the addition of the legs completing the process. To particularise, the wings should not be detached prior to being put upon the fly. The feather should also be ample in dimensions. A half-inch breadth of fibre from a small bird's quill feather, doubled so as to form the separate wings when attached, is about the amount requisite for the March Brown, two thirds of this quantity for the Olive Dun order, and one half for the Iron Blue Duns. After securing the wings, which should be about the length of the hook, thus a little longer than the body, they are placed in their correct position. The hackle, with which it is intended to form the legs, is then turned or wrapped into position *underneath the wings*, the whole being well supported by a few well-planted turns of the tying silk, which done, all that remains is for the silk to be knotted or looped off in the usual way, and your up-winged fly is complete. With reference to the first stage of its construction, much necessarily depends upon the precise nature of the material to be used and worked up. The best and most reliable way of reproducing the varying tinges of the bodies of the flies is by the use of raw silks and natural furs. The foundation of the body of the fly is formed as follows: the hook is taken in the forefinger and thumb of the left hand (point downwards), the tying silk in the right. A few turns of the silk are now given round the shank of the hook. Meanwhile, as a preliminary arrangement, the gut is slightly indented with the teeth at the extremity to be secured. This lessens the chances of drawing, especially in the hands of the tyro. The tying silk should now be *untwisted*,* so as to take all turn out of it, preparatory to wrapping on. This done, the artist works the textile round, leaving a fifth of the shank end of the hook bare to fit on the wings, the gut and hook, in so doing, straining the silk to its utmost tension. If whisks or tails are used, they should be secured by a couple of turns of the silk when the bend of the hook is reached, the fur (if any) to be in readiness. A minute portion is taken by the thumb and finger of the disengaged right hand, and twisted or rolled with the tying silk so as to adhere to that part of it near the hook, which done, the silk thus prepared may now carefully retrace the body, to form the ribs of the fly. These should be at a regular and natural distance apart. The surplus fur is then to be taken both from the silk left and the body of the 'artificial' (which is now complete) by an effective 'nip' or two of the finger and thumb, just leaving sufficient upon the hook's shank faithfully to represent the tinge required. When the ribs are of a contrasted hue, more carefulness still is necessary to give due effect. When the wings and legs are attached to the body, after the manner we have pointed out, a prim and neat rendering of an ephemeral is formed in faultless attitude.

The following are the various dressings for the Olive Dun shades:

The February and November Shade (commonly known as the Blue Dun) – Body, a small portion of blue fur, spun sparingly on yellow silk; wings, from the fieldfare's wing feather; legs, a light dun hackle.

March and October Shade (Cockwinged Dun) – Body, a small portion of water-rat's fur, spun sparingly on full yellow silk; wings, from an old starling's quill feather; legs, a bluish dun hackle, freckled with yellow, or a blue dun hackle, slightly stained yellow.

---

* The utility of the untwisting process will be conspicuously apparent in the making of fine-bodied artificials, as the substance of it is reduced by more than one-third.

Those of **April and September** (Olive or April Dun) – Body, small portion of pale blue fur, spun on yellow silk; wings, palest part of a young starling's wing feather; legs, a light dun hackle, freckled with or stained yellow.

Dark April Dun – Rust-coloured fur to be used in lieu of the pale blue for body. In September the rust-like shade of body here alluded to is yet more conspicuous. It is then termed in some localities the

Whirling Blue Dun, the body being formed by still more pronounced ruddy fur; legs, a dull ginger hackle. This latter is very difficult to procure. An ordinary ginger Cochin hen's preserved neck, steeped in copperas water, will be found to answer admirably.

Pale Blue Dun – Body to be dressed or formed with pale blue silk; legs, a pale dun hackle; wings, from a starling's short quill feather.

May and August Shades (Yellow Dun of May) – Body, palish yellow mohair, mixed with a little pale blue fur, spun upon palish yellow silk; wings, young starling's or fieldfare's quill; legs, a light dun hackle, freckled with yellow.

Hare's Ear Dun – Body, blue mole's fur, dressed with silk of a pronounced yellow; wings, from the redwing's quill; legs, hare's fur from behind the ear.

The name of this dressing is taken, for convenience sake, in common with the rest here given, from the nature of the material used in the copies of the graduated shades of the naturals, which periodically occur as the season advances and recedes.

In **June Shade** (Golden Dun), to be tied or dressed with deep yellow silk, neatly ribbed with fine gold wire; wings from a young starling's longer fiberia quill; legs, a palish dun hackle, freckled with yellow.

The common Yellow Dun is the same dressing, minus the gold tassel, the waxed tying silk being used for the formation of the body.

Those of **July** (Pale Evening White) – Body, a little white fur, spun on pale buff-coloured silk. Wings, the palest part of a young starling's wing feather; legs, a pale dun hackle.

Pale Evening Dun – Body, yellow martin's fur, spun sparingly on

yellow silk; wings, starling, slightly stained yellow; legs, a brassy dun
hackle. A pale blue hackle, stained in weak yellow dye, forms an
excellent substitute.

July Dun – Body, blue rabbit's fur, mixed with yellow mohair;
wings, the bluest part of a fieldfare's wing, stained slightly yellow;
legs, a darkish dun hackle. Tying silk, yellow.

The Iron–Blue Dun family or order may be dressed as under:

For **April and May**, also **September and October** (Iron-Blue Dun) –
Body, blue fur from the owl, spun around mulberry-coloured silk;
wings, from the male merlin hawk's wing; legs, a freckled blue dun
hackle, stained slightly by brown dye. Tying silk, mauve. For the
light shade, the body should be dressed with a strip of a quill feather,
stained the desired hue, or the tying silk only may serve for the
purpose.

August and September (Little Pale Blue) – Body, a small portion of
pale blue fur, mixed with a little yellow mohair, spun upon pale
yellow or primrose-coloured silk; wings, from the quill feather, or
from the small feathers upon the knob of the wing of the sea-swallow –
a pair of the latter to be used back to back; legs, a pale dun hackle.

October and November (October Dun) – To be dressed from same
material as the shades of the Olive Duns for April. The size the same
as the Iron Blue, and therefore one half that of the Olive order.

Spinners may be dressed thus:

Red Spinner – Body, copper-coloured silk, ribbed with round gold
thread; whisks, three strands from a red feather from the back saddle
of a game cock; legs, fiery brown hackle, from the neck of the same
bird; wings, from an old starling's end quill.

Dark Spinner same as the Red, but the floss silk for body, and
the hackle for legs, should be a shade or two darker, the latter
approaching a claret.

Golden Spinner – Body, gold-coloured silk, to be ribbed the same
as the Red Spinner; legs, sandy hen's hackle; wings, fieldfare quill.

Jenny Spinner – This is, perhaps, the most delicate fly to copy correctly of the whole species of aerial and aquatic insects that become food for fish. We find it kills best when dressed buzz or hacklewise. The body should be formed with floss silk of two shades, the ground-work being white, with a bright crimson band near the head and tail. It may also be tied with crimson silk, so as to form a head of that colour. The hackle may be a white hen's, or a small white feather from the knob of a pigeon's wing.

The first three shades of spinners are the transformation of the Olive Dun order. The last given is the metamorphosis of the Iron Blue.

For the Large Browns (ephemeral) the following are given:

For **March and April** (March Brown) – Body, fur from the back of a hare's neck, spun on reddish buff-coloured silk, ribbed with fine gold twist; tails, two strands of a feather from the back of a partridge; legs, a partridge's neck feather.

For **May and June** (light shade, commonly known as the Turkey Brown) – Body, light drab fur, ribbed with gold twist; wings, light partridge quill; legs, grisly dun.

For **August** (commonly termed August Dun) – Body, to be tied on or dressed with pale brown silk, ribbed with yellow silk; wings, from a cock pheasant's wing feather; legs, a pale dull brown cock's hackle.

We now come to the Mayfly, or Drake – the ephemeral series. The Green Drake, like all the smaller flies, requires copying accurately, in respect to the most minute detail. As we elsewhere pointed out, there exists no greater diversity amongst the imitations of any particular fly than is the case with this. That it is an extremely difficult one to dress, we readily admit, and that it is quite possible to copy effectually is also readily conceded. But to suppose that much more than one-third of the immense variety of patterns manufactured can be successful is an absurdity, hence it is they are so frequently discarded altogether, the live fly being substituted. But these are not always to be had, even upon the most prolific waters, therefore a good artificial proves a most desirable auxiliary, even to the live-fly-fisher. The main point to engage the attention of the artist is the *choice of material*. This should take the precedence of all and everything else in Mayfly-making; skill in construction is not nearly so much called for as in the smaller orders of the same species. Indeed it may be affirmed that the Drake, owing to its size, is comparatively easy, whilst the smallest ephemeral insects may be classed amongst the most difficult. The fly-dresser has to reproduce; but, as we have stated, the difficulty lies in procuring the material requisite for a good artificial. Dyed mallard feathers are for the most part used for wings, but of late years natural ones have been largely employed, notably those of the Egyptian goose, which present a decided brown tinge to the eye, but when held up to the light, bear a much nearer resemblance to the tint of the natural. For our part we may say that for several seasons we have used the breast and side feathers of the Canadian wood-duck, which, even when looked down upon, strikingly favours the peculiar green-yellow tinge of nature's original; and when viewed from beneath, and compared with the genuine thing, the beholder cannot fail to appreciate the similarity. The material to be employed in the construction of the body determines, more than anything else, the floating powers of the fly. Wheaten straw, when rightly tinted, is the best substance to be employed. This should be well secured at each extremity, and a hollow left in the middle of the body. Red-brown-coloured silk should be used to bind and form the ribs of this. The whisks should be three strands of a partridge's tail feather; the rabbit's whiskers usually used act very detrimentally as regards hooking the fish, which, as they essay to lay hold of the fly at the tail, are foiled in a measure by the undue stiffness of the head feelers of the animal, which cannot be said to have been designed to grace the tail of any-thing. As regards legs, these in a floating fly should be ample and full; a freckled breast feather of a ginger hue, entwined with a cock's honey dun hackle, is a combination that answers remarkably well. The fly above described we have found so successful and recommended it so strongly that it has been dubbed 'Foster's Favourite' by the many who now advocate its use. The grey or black transformation of the Green Drake may be rendered as follows: widgeon or dark mallard's feather, dyed pale slate colour; body, white straw put on as above, ribbed with dark mulberry-coloured silk; legs, two dun cock's hackles, these may be dressed from shoulders to tail; whisks, three strands of a black cock's saddle feather.

Green Drake – Body, straw-coloured mohair, ribbed with gold twist; wings, from a mallard's mottled feather, slightly dyed yellow; legs, honey-dun cock's hackle; the head of the fly to be formed with a peacock head or copper-coloured silk. To make this fly buzz, a mottled feather from a mallard, stained as above.

ॐ

For the grey copy, we give the following:

Grey Drake – Body, white floss silk, ribbed with silver twist, tied on with brown silk; tails may be made from hair from under the jaws of a brown horse; wings, mottled feather from the mallard; legs, a dark dun or black cock's hackle. To make this fly buzz, a dark mottled feather from the mallard. This fly may be used with success from six o'clock until twilight.

For the Dark Mackerel – Body, copper-coloured mohair, ribbed with gold twist; wings, from the brown mottled feather of a mallard; tails may be got from under the jaws of a brown horse; legs, a dark mulberry-coloured stained cock's hackle.

ॐ

To take the various species of flies in their proper order, we come next to the *Phryganidae* order, which ranges as follows:

February Red, or Red Fly – The body of this fly is dubbed with dark-brown mohair, mixed with claret-coloured mohair; wings, from the hen pheasant, or dotterel wing feather; legs, dark-brown feather from a pale partridge's neck, or a cock's hackle of the same colour.

Sand Fly – Body, fur from the back of a hare's neck spun sparingly on pale orange silk; legs, a pale dull-coloured ginger hackle; wing, from a landrail's wing feather.

Cinnamon Fly – Body, fur from a hare's neck, mixed with a small portion of sable fur, spun on pale dull orange-coloured silk; wings, from a brown hen's wing feather; legs, a pale dull ginger-coloured cock's hackle.

Grannum, or Green-Tail – Body, fur from the hare's neck, spun on fawn-coloured silk, with two laps of green floss-silk on the tail; legs, a pale ginger hackle; wings, the palest part of a hen pheasant's wing feather.

The above being what are usually termed flat-wings, should be dressed as in the old method, i.e., wings last, so as to resemble the naturals.

᠅

The *Perlidae* order ranks next. Some of these it is best not to wing at all, the dun hackle from the knobs of wings of various birds forming an excellent substitute for legs and wings when carefully wound on like an ordinary hackle.

Stone Fly – Body, dark-coloured fur, spun with full yellow silk, to be ribbed with some silk of same colour, unwaxed; wings, from the quill-wing feather of a cock pheasant, or may be cut from a sheet of gutta-percha (pure), dyed in cold blue dye;* legs, a black cock's hackle stained yellow; this, if rightly made will form an excellent artificial fly, not to be excelled by any combination of feathers and fur alone.

Willow Fly – Body, water rat's fur spun sparingly on yellow silk; legs and wings made buzz, from a dark dun hackle, with a brownish tint in it, or a small dark feather from the merlin hawk's wing.

Needle Fly – Body, sable fur spun upon yellow silk, dressed hackle with small brown feather from the knob of a fieldfare's wing. This fly

---

* Crayshaw's Crystal Aniline Dyes answer wonderfully well for staining feathers, etc., of delicate hues.

may be formed by a strip of the enamelled quill of a peacock's feather, which forms the alternate shades of ribs beautifully. This has been introduced by a clever southern angler.

Yellow Sally – This should never be dressed winged; it falls upon the water like a heavy beetle would be supposed to do, therefore the wings, not being extended, are not seen by the fish. The most killing way is to hackle it palmer-wise, with a white hen's hackle dyed light yellow, or by the small feather round a white pigeon's wing, stained as above; the body to be yellow mohair.

ॐ

The casual killers amongst the land flies may be dressed as follows:

The Cowdung Fly – To be dressed or tied on with pale dun orange-coloured silk; body, yellow lamb's wool, mixed with a little green mohair; wings, from a landrail's wing feather; legs, pale dull ginger-coloured hackle.

Oak Fly, or Downlooker – Body, pale orange floss silk, tied on with pale lead-coloured silk; wings from the wood-lark's wing feather; legs, a furnace hackle.

Marlow Buzz, Coch-y-Bondu, of Wales – Body, peacock herl, hackle with bright furnace feather. The Red Tag (fancy fly) is formed by the simple addition of a red tag, or tuft of wool or feather, at the tail.

Brown Palmer, Bracken's Clock – Body, black ostrich herl, ribbed with round gold twist, hackled with red cock's hackle stained.

Bluebottle, or Beef Eater – Body, light blue floss silk, ribbed over with black ostrich herl and silver twist, tied on with brown silk; wings, from an old starling's wing feather; legs, a black hackle.

Wren-Tail – Body, amber-coloured floss silk, or ginger-coloured fur from a hare's neck, ribbed with gold twist; legs and wings made buzz from a wren's tail feather.

Red Ant – To be tied or dressed with orange-coloured silk, which may be shown at the tail; body, copper-coloured peacock's herl; legs, a red cock's hackle; wings, from a redwing's feather.

Black Ant – To be tied on or dressed with pale dull fawn-coloured silk, which may be shown at the tail; body, black rabbit's fur, well mixed with copper-coloured mohair; legs, a dark-furnace hackle.

Black Gnat – Body, ostrich herl; wings, from a starling's wing feather; legs, a dark blue dun, or black hackle.

Grey Gnat – Body, grey mohair or wool hackle, with sea-swallow feather.

Red Palmer, or Caterpillar – Body, copper-coloured peacock's herl, tied with brown silk, ribbed with gold twist, a bright brown red-stained cock's hackle, having a gold-colour when held between the eye and the light.

The Alexandra Fly – Body, flat silver twist, hackled with bright feather of green or blue hue, from the neck of a peacock; wings (if any) from the turkey's wing.

෨

How to dress a simple Hackle Fly The first effort of the fly-making aspirant should be expended upon the wingless artificials; of these there are two kinds, the plain Hackle and the Palmer; the former is the best to commence with, it being the easiest to make;[*] but before attempting to describe the method, we would remind our readers that there is a vast distinction between practical and verbal teachings. Observation in these matters is superior, as a source for conveying knowledge, to reading; therefore, where available, a few lessons from a proficient will be found highly beneficial.

The process of forming the body for a Hackle Fly is not identical with the same operation in the winged one. In the construction of the latter, a small portion of the shank of the hook itself is left bare to fix the wings upon, thereby neatly to form the head. This, however, is formed, to begin in the case of the Buzzy or Hackle Fly, by a few turns of the silk at the extremity of the shank; a little blank is then left for the hackle to fit or fill in; the body is then to be

---

[*] Upon some waters these hackled flies are the local standard killers. This partiality is generally due to the source of supply, the local amateur reflecting the local maker's dogmas.

formed in the usual way. This completed, the hackle feather must be taken in hand, first having been stripped of its downy surplus fibres; the root of the stem is secured by a couple of turns of the tying silk at the shoulder of the fly. The hackle thus secured at its lower extremity, is ready for fitting in. Its point is then to be taken hold of with the tweezers, and two or more turns of the feather given; the end is then to be secured by a turn or two of the silk, the invisible knot formed, and the fly is made, wanting only the silk end to be cut carefully away to complete the thing. The Palmer is an artificial that is hackled from head to tail, such as the Bumbles, Caterpillars, etc. The process of body-making is identical, in this instance, with the Hackle Fly just detailed, except a little addition in the shape of herl, a strand of which is wound round the gut and silk, the feather being turned over this, and the bit of tinsel or silk, by way of ribbing, going over the whole, for the sake of both use and ornament, and the fly is made.

We append a few dressings for the various Bumbles and Palmers, which, though in some instances deemed fancy flies, are often good killers.

Bumble, ordinary – Hackle, white hen's, slightly stained blue; body, peacock herl, ribbed with orange and puce-coloured silk (floss); tying silk, brown.

Mulberry Bumble – Hackle, dun hen's; body, peacock herl, ribbed with mulberry-coloured floss silk; tying silk, claret.

Red Bumble, or Earwig – Hackle, red cock's, stained; body, peacock herl, ribbed with gold silk; tying silk, dark brown.

Honey Dun Bumble – Hackle, honey dun hen's; body, peacock herl, ribbed with orange floss silk; tying silk, yellow.

Furnace Bumble – Hackle, furnace cock's; body, peacock, or black herl, ribbed with dark orange silk; tying silk, red brown.

Black Palmer – Hackle, black cock's, ribbed with fine silver twist; tying silk, black.

Golden Palmer – Hackle, bright furnace; body, peacock herl, ribbed with gold twist.

Grey Palmer – Hackle, cock's, with black centre and whitish grey edge, ribbed with fine round silver tinsel; tying silk, black.

A variety of Palmers may be made by intermixing the materials here given for the different shades.

ॐ

Salmon Flies[*] In the construction of these there exists a grand distinction. The *taste* and fancy of the operator is called into request, and nothing in nature demands his study and attention more. A happy combination and contrast of various hues and colours, from sombre to brilliant, is the main object.

Salmon are extremely effeminate in the love of finery and tinsel, especially in the case of habitually discoloured waters. There are rivers upon which flies of a more sombre hue than the general run are used; but the bright and brilliant combination is found irresistible, more or less, wherever salmon are to be found, when they are in a mood for rising and gambolling. The great thing to keep in the mind's eye, when choosing or constructing a salmon fly, is the shine *through* the feathers, wool, mohair, etc., when held above the head, and thus viewed from beneath.

Some dressings are almost of one universal dull shade, or no shade at all, when held in the posture seen by the fish; others will have the colour rightly seen shining through in a few patches; but the correct thing is to get the whole of the legs, tail and body to shine brilliantly through, as well as when looked down upon, and the fault will be none of the fly's if it be refused by the fish. The materials used for salmon flies are especially picked with a view to their effect when seen from below; as for instance, the hard-to-be-procured pig's wool, which for transparency of shade stands well nigh unequalled; also mohair, which, though of finer texture, possesses the same characteristics. These, when well placed upon the hook shank, shine most effectively when wet, and viewed from below. Another feature in the

---

[*] The Compilers regret to have to withhold the lengthy and elaborate instructions left by the Author upon this branch of fly-making. In future editions they hope to be able to publish the whole.

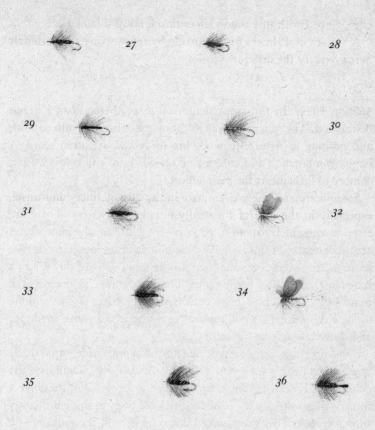

FANCY FLIES

27	Light or Blue Bumble		32	Little Chap
28	Mulberry Bumble		33	Grey Palmer
29	Honey Dun Bumble		34	Silver or Winter Dun
30	Furnace Bumble		35	Quill Gnat
31	Brown Bumble or Earwig		36	Red Tag

PLATE 9

arrangement of the salmon fly, the enormously large, and in many cases heavy hook, has to be floated as long as it is possible, and that in a right position. The old arrangement was best calculated to meet this difficulty, large wings being attached so as to preserve the side posture of the lure as it rested upon the water.

We give a few odd salmon flies for general use that are not at present generally known. Appended to these are a few of those most commonly in use: the Spanker, the Rob Roy, the Spartan, the Tam o' Shanter and the Mac Sporren.

Description of the Spanker – Tag, flat silver tinsel and cerise floss silk; tail, golden pheasant's topping; a few strands of scarlet flamingo's quill feather; body, orange, light and dark, and cerise floss silk bound over an old cock's hackle stained slightly sky-blue, the latter being palmered from the head to the tail, another of these forming legs; wings, turkey, with several side strands of argus-pheasant wing feathers, and red, yellow and puce-coloured feelers or strands.

The Rob Roy – Tag, gold (flat) and orange floss silk; body, orange mohair, graduating through full and dark orange to dull red; legs, guinea-fowl neck feather, stained yellow, and black cock's hackle, also stained yellow;* wings, black turkey feather; side feathers, jungle cock's hackle; streamers, yellow and red; head, black ostrich herl.

The Spartan – Tag, gold (round), white floss silk and peacock herl; tail, three strands from a green feather from the neck of a peacock, and a few strands of yellow and scarlet lucan breast and neck feathers; body, hackled with claret stained hackle, wound over with gold twist (heavy round) and bright-coloured silk; legs, dark blue hackle, and guinea-fowl feather over all; wings, golden pheasant's tail feather, ditto neck or tippet feathers for sides, blue chatterer's over all; head, peacock's herl.

The Tam o' Shanter – Tag, red silk silver twist (round); tail, a few yellow and red spires of macaw feathers, helped with a few strands of blue or green peacock's neck feather; body, pig's wool, navy blue, with broad flat silver twist; legs, rich fiery brown hackle; wings,

* This imparts a peculiar shine to the feather when held up to the light.

bustard feather; sides of ditto, American wood-duck feather; a few strands of argus pheasant's dark feather to be also added in larger flies.

The Mac Sporren – Tag, flat silver, and blue silk. Body, fiery brown pig's wool ribbed with round gold twist; legs, orange and purple, hackled (stained); wings, golden pheasant, red sides tail feathers; toppings, large strands of albatross wing feather; streamers, red and green over all, kingfisher's feathers, or blue chatterer.

The following are well-known dressings:

Jock Scott – Tag, gold twist; tail, one golden pheasant topping, and Indian crow feather; body in two parts; head, part black floss silk, with silver twist and palmered black hackle; tail ditto, gold coloured; at each joint is tied several toucan points, these being backed up by two turns of black herl. For wings, white-tipped turkey feather fibres of pintail bustard, brown mallard, with one long topping, and yellow, red and green streamers over all, a jungle cock on either side.

The Butcher – Tag, gold twist and orange floss; tail, a single topping of golden pheasant, with band of black ostrich herl; body, alternate turns of red and full blue, either mohair or pig's wool, broad silver tinsel, palmered with claret hackle; wing, mixture of brown mallard, bustard, peacock wing, wood-duck, golden pheasant tippet and rump feathers; streamers, blue and yellow over all; head, black ostrich herl.

The Doctor – Tag, scarlet silk and fine gold twist; tail, one topping; body, light blue floss silk, palmered with medium blue hackle, broad silver tinsel and twist; legs, blue hackle, with brown grouse or partridge over all; wing, argus pheasant's, brown turkey, and bustard; streamers, yellow, blue and claret; black herled head.

The Shannon – Tag, gold tinsel, and lemon coloured silk; tail, scarlet ibis or flamingo, two toppings, and blue macaw, black ostrich band; body, alternate coloured silks, beginning at the tail end, pale blue, full orange, violet and medium green, the alternate colours being set off by a hackle of the same shade, also ribbed with ostrich herl dyed same colour as alternate joints; wings, two yellow macaw feathers, black-centred (usually), a single strip of dark argus pheasant on either side, also a few fibres of golden pheasant tippet, two small

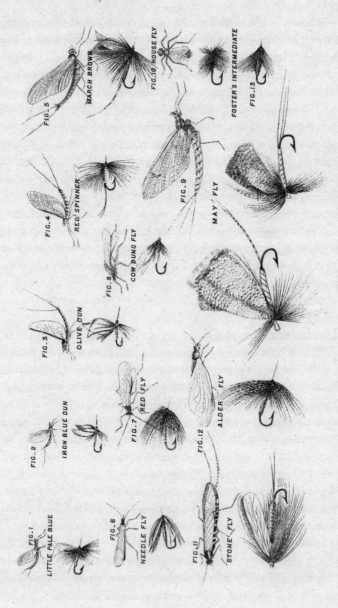

FIG. 5   MARCH BROWN   FIG. 10 HOUSE FLY   FOSTER'S INTERMEDIATE   FIG. 13

FIG. 4   RED SPINNER   FIG. 9   MAY FLY

FIG. 8   COW DUNG FLY

FIG. 3   OLIVE DUN

FIG. 2   IRON BLUE DUN   FIG. 7   RED FLY   FIG. 12   ALDER FLY

FIG. 1   LITTLE PALE BLUE   FIG. 6   NEEDLE FLY   FIG. 11   STONE FLY

PLATE 10

blue chatterer's feathers, and two large toppings over all; legs, fiery brown feather, black head.

Blacker's Gaudy Fly – Tail, two slips of brown mallard, and one topping or crest feather (golden pheasant); tag, gold orange floss and ostrich herl; body, one third crimson, palmered with black hackle, one third scarlet, with scarlet hackle, finish the body with crimson and scarlet hackle over it; wings, well mottled red and black turkey, feather off golden pheasant back under it; streamers, red and blue; legs, guinea-fowl feather; head, ostrich herl.

The Rainbow – Tail, light greenfeather, pheasant's topping, few fibres of bright green feathers; tag, flat, gold; body, pig's wool, graduating from bright yellow through orange, scarlet, to purple, and broad gold tinsel; wings, two toppings and two jungle cock's hackles, and two mottled feathers from under snipe's wing; streamers, crimson; legs, blue and brown hackles.

The Spey Dog – Black pig's wool body, sparingly ribbed with broad silver tinsel, to be palmered with black-cock saddle or side-tail feather, the thick end of hackle terminating at tail end of fly; in addition to the flat silver tinsel, gold of half the width is also run from head to tail; wings, golden pheasant tail; left bushy, and a few fibres of brown mallard, to be shouldered with a teal hackle.

The Parson – Tail, two toppings, and a few fibres of peacock's blue neck feathers; tag, silver tinsel and full red floss; body, a turn or two of golden floss, then orange pig's wool shading gradually darker up body, ribbed with silver twist, palmered with orange hackle; legs, hackle of dark shade; wings, two golden pheasant tippet feathers, two pairs of toppings, wood-duck and turkey on either side.

The Ranger – Tag, silver twist and gold-coloured floss silk; tail, red breast-feather of golden pheasant, and a topping footed with two turns of black ostrich; body, fiery brown pig's wool one half, remainder pale blue ditto, to be palmered with blue hackle; legs, wood-duck hackle from under wing; wings, two tippets, a couple of jungle cock's hackles, with a topping over all.

CHAPTER TWELVE

Fly-Fishing for Trout and Grayling

*Attractions of Surface-Fishing; The Rod, Line and Winch;
Casting, Striking, Playing and Landing; The Wet- and Dry-Fly
Systems; Brook Fishing; Meteorological Effects on Sport; Night
Fishing; The Dove*

The superiority of the art of fly-fishing over all other systems
of angling is universally acknowledged. The ever-exciting nature
of surface-fishing adds a zest to the sport, unknown to the other
branches of the art piscatorial. The high pitch of expectation
experienced as the rising fish daintily 'plop' off the insects around,
extends a highly exhilarating influence over both mind and body.
The whole of the faculties are thus concentrated in one focus, ever
stimulating to still greater earnestness and efficiency. It is owing to
these characteristics, this scope for science and skill, that this sport
is and has been the chosen recreation of men of the greatest celebrity
and the highest attainments of modern times. Since the time of
Walton the angler's skill has advanced wondrously, whilst keenness
of perception and wariness have developed amongst the denizens
of the liquid element in a degree quite proportionate. The well
educated inhabitants of the classic streams of the Midlands and of
the south, the former clear from the limestone district of the Peak,
and the latter pure from chalk districts, require no small proficiency
and tact to secure even moderate sport generally; nevertheless, the
accomplished fly-fisher can usually manage to bag a respectable dish,
even under circumstances adverse to sport. On the other hand we
have a multiplicity of trouting streams and brooks, especially those
north of the Tweed, whose fish are in a manner unsophisticated, and

comparatively unacquainted with the wiles of man. Amongst these the young student will do well to make a selection on commencing operations. The adept at flying for trout, when at work in real earnest upon the banks of a well-stocked stream, is a striking figure, exemplary of the true fisherman. The gracefully erect though expectant attitude, the latter assumed upon the delivery of the fly, the slender pliable rod, the long floating line and gossamer gut, combine to constitute an ideal angler. Before entering fully on the details of the subject, we would jot down a few brief instructions for the special benefit of the novice, who, aspiring to proficiency, must be prepared to acquire experience at some cost; and our object is to reduce that cost as much as possible.

The first consideration that should engage the attention of the tyro is throwing or casting; and after that has been well practised and a ten- or twelve-yards cast can be neatly made, he may essay striking and playing. Dace or perch in the summer months afford ample scope for the acquirement of these accomplishments. It is the determined will to succeed that attains its object; and when the resolve is once taken there is the immediate response of the will to the perceptive powers seen in the discernment of a rise, and at once, and without delay, the quarry is successfully struck. Well do we remember our first take with the fly; filled with the ardour natural to youth we were foolish enough to resolve to effect a capture prior to quitting the river's brim. All the day we flogged and fished, the result being simply nil; ten, twelve and thirteen hours passed away without so much as moving a fin. The summer twilight set in, shadowing the outlines of the surrounding landscape. Still our resolution was firm, and in keeping with a set purpose we presented the lure more gently, and with greater precision upon the edge of the shadows caused by the rising moon, where the heavy 'switching' sound, repeated at short intervals, proclaimed the daily dinner hour of an old veteran. After casting for some time directly over him, we finally hooked the old gent. As we had had the discretion to fit up a strong collar to carry the large fly employed, we had small difficulty in landing our quarry, which was afterwards found to measure 17 inches in length and 9½ inches in girth, scaling 2¾ lbs, a venerable monster in truth to our boyish eyes.

Care and patience in execution are required after the rudiments of the art have been acquired; a non-observer of these is sure materially to interfere with sport. *Perseverance* is all very well in its place, but when unaided by the exercise of due care and tact in presenting the lure, it will meet with small result. The tyro should therefore practise assiduously, ever bearing in mind that much as he may admire and aspire to a nearer acquaintance with the scaly beauties, they are coy and ungrateful. The instant they become aware of his paying them the least attention, they move contemptuously away; and no matter how lovingly he drops them a line, all further correspondence is thanklessly declined. It behoves him therefore to keep out of sight as much as possible, never allowing the sun to extend his shadow across the stream, always also avoiding conspicuously bright clothing; for, notwithstanding the naturalist's persistent assertions as to the dullness of the eyes of fish, owing, it is affirmed, to the skin of the head covering the pupil of the eye, the trout fisher knows very well that in their own element they habitually exercise the most keen and discriminating powers of vision, when the water is clear, and any moving or brightly coloured objects outside it attract their attention. In order to deal comprehensively with our subject, for the more especial edification of the tyro, we shall proceed to allude in detail to the leading items already referred to as being essential to success, viz.: Casting the Fly, Playing or Landing, and Killing a fish. Before doing so, however, the necessary appliances must engage our attention.

❧

The Rod, Reel and Line should be well adapted to act perfectly and in concert with each other. We have already pointed out the inconvenience and disaster arising from the common practice of employing implements totally incapable of working together evenly. The intending purchaser most frequently considers what is the strength, length or thickness of line required for some specified water or fish, and not for a particular rod. The rod forms the first subject for attention; the winch, or reel, and line being next chosen, with a view to the harmonious working of the whole, the reel to balance and the line to suit the 'play' of the tool. This is of the most vital importance. Fly-rods are made of many different woods and dimensions. It is a noteworthy fact, however, that during the two centuries that have elapsed since Cotton first wrote upon what afterwards developed into the most artistic and scientific branch of angling, the length of the fly-rod has diminished by more than one half. Notwithstanding this diminution of size, and we may also add of weight, the casting powers of the rodster have been so much augmented that almost double the distance may now be neatly covered by the adult adept than was effected with the unwieldy weapons of our forefathers. The propelling power of the fly-rod depends largely upon the material of which it is constructed. The fine-grained woods of the tropics exceed our own in point of strength, durability, and weight-sustaining powers.

The following are the materials and dimensions of a really service-able fly-rod for small-stream fishing:

Three joints or parts, each three feet six inches, the butt to consist of hickory or washaba, the middle joint of best washaba, green-heart or blue mahoo, the top of snake-wood or best jungle cane, the whole being ten feet six inches. The ferrule at the top of the butt should be $\frac{6}{16}$th of an inch inside; the one at the top of the middle joint $\frac{1}{4}$ inch. The actual weight of a rod of this description will be small.

The points to receive attention are strength and pliability; a combination of these forms the perfect casting-rod; and the more these qualities are exemplified in a rod, the greater the distance to be covered by it, and that with perfect precision. With a view to extend in the direction here indicated, we have made many experiments with metal and wood of every variety, as also with other substances of pliancy and strength. Metal, either hollow or solid, is too heavy and cumbersome; wood of greenheart, red locust, snake, and other descriptions, proves strong and pliant, and is so when spliced, like the mast of a ship, or similar to the glued-up American cane rods; but there is no especial advantage to commend them, seeing the weight is increased by something like one-third over the same substance solid and non-glued. The modern three-yards rod, as we have said, can be made to deliver more line, and that in a more elegant and sportsmanlike manner than a longer one.

But the question naturally arises, if the fly-rod has been diminished by one half during two centuries, of what dimensions is it likely to become in the immediate future? Our reply is that in the course of the next decade or so, still further reductions will take place. The length of a rod, as is now well known, has very little to do with the distance it can be made to cast the fly; the casting powers entirely depend on the pliancy and strength, hence it is that the very hardest, and we may also add, the most weighty (for one characteristic is almost inseparable from the other) woods are so far superior to open-grained northern timber. Bone, as is already known, is too heavy, buffalo horn is too limber when dressed in tops. The result of our investigations is that a combination of the best metal and the best wood would, if arranged correctly, and in right proportions, be an advance in a desirable direction. We therefore had a rod made of the very best of strong woods, with a *fine bevelled steel centre*, and this proved when, after some alterations, it was completed, to bear out the hopes conceived in respect to it. We had been enamoured of this idea theoretically and practically it gives every promise of ultimately meriting the pains and researches we bestowed upon it. The reel upon the new rod is made inside the butt, so to speak, thus all nuisance of the line entwining around the reel is entirely avoided. The general working of the implement proves this to be a decided advantage over the old side-fixing system.

ᔰ

The Line should be plaited of waterproof silk. The eight-plait waterproof fly lines have gradually, during the last forty years, superseded the old hair, as well as the hair-and-silk lines. As we have elsewhere stated, silk is the strongest textile, and, when duly protected from the action of the water, cannot be surpassed for surface-fishing. The new

Acme Line is a further improvement on the above. It contains a fine strand or thread of annealed and specially prepared copper wire, either in the plaiting or in the centre of the line, the whole being carefully waterproofed. The Acme is guaranteed to extend the angler's casting powers considerably.

᠁

The Reel should be of bronze, or brass, and the handle should be attached to a revolving plate, instead of a miniature windlass. This again is an improvement upon old-style abominations. Who has not experienced annoyance and loss from the entanglement of the line around the fancifully turned winch handle, just at some critical moment when line was imperatively wanted? And who can measure the amount of loss this one improvement alone, when generally adopted, will prevent?

Multiplying reels are now discarded in favour of a plain check reel without surplus and complicated cog wheels to clog and get out of order. The new reel shown upon the new fly rod is an ordinary reel, put upon the butt in the centre instead of at the side of the rod butt. These may be attached to any rod, when the socket is of a fitting diameter. A small screw or rivet will secure it permanently, or it may be temporarily screwed and used upon it, as well as the handy side-fitting reels, and can be put on any rod.

᠁

Throwing the Fly, contrasted with other branches of the angling art, has been little written upon, and seeing that this is the chief obstacle in the path of the beginner, and also the most important acquirement of the proficient practitioner, we think the omission a serious one. To this subject we have devoted much attention, particularly in the construction of new and improved implements for its more ready attainment and practice. It is a well-established axiom that in skilful casting lies the chief condition of success. 'He can throw a good line' is equivalent to asserting the proficiency of an angler, whether he be a fly-, mid-water- or bottom-fisher.

The ordinary routine cast is the first to be practised and acquired by the tyro. This is accomplished by bringing round the rod so as to describe a half-circle from over the left shoulder, and delivering it directly over the right, the action emanating from the wrist and elbow only. It is capital practice for the young student to cast upon a lawn or any closely cut turf. Line to the length of the rod should first be delivered efficiently and neatly, when a hat should be placed as the receptacle of the fly; after the distances have been lengthened at intervals a tumbler may be substituted, and finally a small wine glass. When these different exercises have been successfully accomplished, with a fair length of line, the rodster may safely try his hand upon the bosom of the watery element. Lightness and precision follow practice and experience. The exercise of casting into a floating walnut shell is a feat, the accomplishment of which, at a distance of not less than a dozen yards, betokens a fair degree of proficiency and precision in casting.

In fly-fishing the ever changing geological bearings, the varying meteorological influences, the position of trees and other impedi-ments, necessitate a constant change of tactics in order to reach the feeding fish, who, as they become more schooled, take up the more inaccessible and secluded positions. Although some streams are com-paratively narrow, it is not always incumbent upon or advisable for the fisherman to take up his stand upon the verge of the water. 'To fish fine and far off', as Cotton, the father of all fly-fishers expresses it, is infinitely better whenever practicable. Broken water should be chosen by the novice to commence upon, as while fish may be extracted by him from the rapids and purling streams, etc., the slower running and still waters may prove beyond his attainments.

After precision and lightness of execution are attained, the casting distance should next be extended, and upon this point we may briefly say that more depends upon the line and rod than, generally speaking, upon the rodster. With an unusually light line and stiff rod it is often a matter of great difficulty to get out properly a few odd yards over double the rod's length. The same result ensues when the reverse is the case, with a very pliable tool fitted with a stout heavy line. The rod in this case is in peril of parting in the middle, or 'breaking its back' so to speak, whilst the line, if unreeled to any extent, will constantly be in a state of entanglement. A great deal depends upon getting accustomed to the particular 'swing' of the rod, as when this is the case all other implements are generally rejected in favour of 'one like the last'. Hence it is that so great diversity exists, even amongst the oldest and best hands, upon every well-frequented water. Another consideration is the strength of the muscles. This has so important a bearing on the wielding of the rod, that it is yearly more and more taken into account by the gradual adoption of shorter and lighter rods. As we have previously stated, we have always paid considerable attention to the introduction of suitable appliances for casting, and that more especially upon fine and clear waters. The great difficulty experienced by young fly-fishers in acquiring the ability of getting out a good line we have attempted to remedy by the invention of an entirely new line, which, from its peculiar construction, combines weight and strength with excessive fineness. We allude to the now well-known Acme fly-line, which, since its introduction, has given such general satisfaction that the practical results now manifest warrant the conclusion that by the removal of the main stumbling block in the beginner's path, namely, the difficulty of a good delivery in casting, a great and important desideratum has been attained. From the testimony made public through the medium of the press, it has been proved that the throwing powers of both tyro and proficient have been augmented considerably by its use. We allude in detail to its construction, etc., elsewhere. All that is needful to be observed here is that through the medium of the Acme Wire Line the novice may with a few hours' practice, cast as effectually and efficiently as he might by the practice of as many months with the old-style lines. With reference to the degree of skill and proficiency in the delivery of the fly, the talent of the oldest and best fly-fishers varies. The real adept will adapt himself to surrounding circumstances, casting over intervening boughs and bushes, now over an impending rock or boulder, or around some partially submerged substance in midstream, or jutting portions of the river's bank, without regard to any orthodox principle or rule.

In short, a thorough command of the rod and line is as essential and important as the wielding of the whip in the case of a tandem or four-in-hand drive. We are reminded by this analogy that the most skilful cast we ever knew wielded the whip: we refer to the famous royal coachman, Tom Bosworth. Old Tom had, in the early part of his life, driven three successive British sovereigns, viz. – the Fourth George, the Fourth William, and finally, for a lengthened period, Her Majesty Queen Victoria. As a successful fisherman, Old Tom, when known to the writer, was unsurpassed. He would often fish in the wake of several rodsters, whose energy would exceed their skill, and would extract not infrequently three times over the weight of fish, by skilfully and carefully casting over the awkward and most unlikely looking spots, which the majority of anglers would rarely dream of trying. A favourite freak of his with the whip was to take the pipe from the teeth of a passing pedestrian by a carefully calculated whirl of the whip, and this aptitude was as remarkably exemplified, for a limited distance, in his use of the rod. Bosworth originated the Coachman Fly,* so much appreciated for night-fishing.

The cast most useful in boisterous weather is the Welsh or Spey Throw. This is more commonly known to fly-fishers for salmon. The line is whisked off the water by an upward and backward movement of the rod, but is delivered forward again, just as the last of the reel-line leaves the top of the water, by a rapid lower whisk of the rod's upper portion. This raises the line above all impediments and encumbrances in the shape of bushes, etc., fringing the river's bank. Personally we make our longest cast by it.† The usually-deemed-impregnable positions of the most choice and best fed fish are brought under fire by a resort to this cast, as indeed are all fish out of the reach of the usual run of rodsters. Some fly-fishers appear never to

---

* This artificial has recently been much used as a 'fancy' fly for day-fishing, and with considerable success.

† We never threw with a single-handed fly-rod more than 29½ yards, but with the Acme Wire Line we have been able to exceed this distance by some three yards.

aspire to a greater distance than the width of the stream or brook most fished by them. For mountain or moorland stream, Scottish beck and burn, and Welsh torrent this may answer amply, but upon the comparatively wide and open water something further and more extensive is needed. Every fly-fisher should be able to cast at least 20 yards of reel-line. The importance of artistically getting out the lure is fully recognised in districts where the natural surroundings render it a matter of vital importance, but as a general thing it is a point not so well practised or understood as could be wished.

ꜿ

Striking requires a keen eye and a quick wrist-effect to a greater extent than is easy to be conceived by the tyro. A really accomplished fly-fisher is not so frequently heard to complain of the fish rising short. A dilatory rodster, whenever the fish prove too quick by rejecting the steel-hearted lure, after giving him the customary 'pluck' falls back upon the old and convenient excuses, the tendency of which is to charge the effect of his own shortcomings to the fish. Many theories are expounded in reference to the matter of striking. Some anglers recommend an instantaneous 'knock', others advise a momentary pause after the lure has been closed upon as being the correct thing, and some affirm that, owing to the difficulty of acquiring the right 'knack' of driving home the delicate fly-hook, far more fish are lost by an unnecessarily heavy and spirited motion of the rod in a moment of excitement than if striking were not adopted at all. The late Mr James Ogden, an old friend of ours, never let slip an opportunity of declaiming against random striking, always affirming that young inexperienced anglers lose the major portion of the fish they raise through awkwardness in this matter. 'I have' – says he, in the columns of a leading sporting journal – 'in the course of my experience seen some of the best rods and tackle broken by this means, during a momentary excitement. I strongly recommend young fishermen not to strike at all.' We can fully endorse this statement; but to be more explicit, although it may be advisable for the youthful aspirant to avoid needless disaster, it is certainly advisable that he should acquire the right and ready 'knack' of hooking his rise in an effective and skilful manner. The result of our experience upon this subject is as follows:

First: It is an exceedingly difficult, if not impossible thing, success-fully to hook a fish that has risen at the end of sixteen to eighteen yards of line, in the event of his not hooking himself, as the impetus given to the line through the medium of the rod on the appearance of a rise reaches the scene of action too late to be of any utility. As a matter of course, when the feeding fish are near at hand, and the line is taut and straight, a small jerk from the wrist will have full chance of being effectual, and in this case the single moment's grace may be granted with safety in still water, as the trout are, generally speaking, more leisurely in their movements. It is essential that the details appended should be thoroughly mastered in order to attain proficiency. Our own private plan, after the delivery of the fly in the extending circle of the last rise, is to lookout for the gleaming side of the fish as it rises, in order to get which the eye should be centred within the circle, but some little distance nearer the rodster. When this habit is contracted, as it easily is with practice, wonderful accuracy will be attained in efficient striking, even at the longest distances.

Second: The action and amount of force required to hook the fish is an intricate matter to deal with definitely, as so much depends upon the bearings of the situation. That small fish require gentle usage, whilst comparatively large ones necessarily require more impulsive treatment, is an aphorism well known to all; but that the rodster should be cognisant to a nicety of the weight-sustaining power of the fine tackle, and should also be able to calculate accurately the probable result of a sanguine stroke of the hook upon the hard and bony part, or, upon the other hand, on the soft and impressible portion of the fish's body, is altogether another thing. Beyond this an accurate estimate of the elasticity of the line, etc., should be possessed, and the striking motion accelerated or modified accordingly. The action requisite is a short, quick, wrist-motion, commenced sharply, but ended almost instantly and abruptly, like a quick movement of the hand in bringing a foil in fencing from *tierce* to *carte*. The hand holding the rod is turned upwards and backwards whilst the arm is stationary when a short line is out, the movement being lengthened when the intervening line is either long or loose. One of the greatest charms of fly-fishing lies undoubtedly in the comparative absence of routine and sameness. The plier of the rod must adapt himself to ever-changing circumstances. It is a curious thing, and one that we have often been puzzled to account for satisfactorily, that it so frequently happens that precisely as the first trout is hooked so are all subsequent captures throughout the day.

This fact first forcibly impressed us many years since. We were fishing in company with Mr Ramsbottom, of Clitheroe, Lancashire, who wished to try salmon roe* as a bait for trout upon the Dove, suitable tackle for which had been baited by our friend for our personal use, we being then uninitiated in the mystic 'roe' fishing. Before rod no. 2 was equipped for action we had hooked a fish, which was ultimately landed. The hook proved to be embedded in the tongue, a somewhat unusual thing, as we then remarked. 'Every fish we take this day will be hooked similarly,' coolly prognosticated our friend. At the time we confess to having been rather sceptical as to the likelihood of this proving accurate, but the result verified the prediction, for every fish that fell to our steel upon that occasion was firmly hooked in the tongue. Had the hold of the hook been slight in the first instance, say near the external bordering of the mouth, we were assured that our take would have been diminished, as this would have indicated that the fish were not in a feeding mood, and would therefore close upon the bait in a faint-hearted manner. The same is exemplified in fly-fishing, though perhaps not in so conspicuously marked a degree. The first fish indicates, as a rule, the temporary state of the whole of his fellows, whether hunger-bitten and eager, or fastidious and indifferent.

In striking a grayling, it behoves the rodster to be extremely careful, as not only is the fish excessively delicate and tender-skinned about the mouth, but the tackle, being finer, is less calculated to sustain any sudden wrench. This is not the case with larger quarry;

* The use of roe for bait is now prohibited by the law of the realm.

a few weeks', or even days', lake-trouting will put out the hand for fine grayling fishing for some length of time. What we have always found a safe antidote in these cases is carefully to keep a taut line, and immediately a fish rises to give a forward motion of the rod a foot or so. The downward action of the line thus eased, has the effect of sending in the little delicate hook without the most remote chance of danger. This may appear incredible in theory, but we can answer for its efficiency in practice. In rapid-stream fishing a modification of the usual twist of the wrist may be given in the case of the grayling, where rapidity is the essential point; the twist here referred to should describe a downward direction, as when this is done the first action of the rod tip is directly upwards and opposite. The extent of the momentum ranges according to the pliability of the rod.

࿓

Playing a Fish comes next in order. The instant a fish is hooked the rod should be mounted at a proper angle, so as to *feel* the fish. The tactics to be employed vary in accordance with the lay of the water, as also with the conduct of the fish hooked, as when he descends immediately upon being struck, pulling heavily in the deep water, fighting hard for his hold, or neighbouring shelter, it may be certainly inferred that he is safely hooked; but when he exhibits a tendency to fight it out near the surface, occasionally attempting to clear the water altogether, he is, as a general rule, but lightly hooked, and if not carefully handled, will to a certainty be lost. The proper method of playing a fish in open water that is clear from weeds, sticks, etc. is to give him plenty of line, and play him till he is completely exhausted, cautiously keeping the rod on a regular bend; but in rapid and turbulent rivers playing a fish is almost certain to end, not only in the loss of the fish, but also of a portion of your tackle.

There are scarcely any rivers free from portions of trees lying concealed in the deep waters, the small holes being well stocked with branches. In the shallow waters there are plenty of piles placed regularly a few yards apart, which are generally laid to prevent depredations by nets, and are seldom unfurnished with branches of trees, etc. When a fish is surprised by being hooked, his next attempt is to dart upon the most convenient stick or pile, and with the rapidity of thought, he entwines your tackle two or three times round it, then he makes good his escape. If he darts into a bed of weeds he stays there, and the line is hopelessly entwined, and you are left to liberate it as you may. Notwithstanding these obstructions, the experienced fly-fisher seldom loses a single fish in the course of a day or two's fishing, though the gut tackle he uses is as fine as possible. When a fish is hooked in a stream, a moderately heavy bend should be immediately put upon the rod, the rodster keeping opposite his prey whenever the bank admits of it, and where this is impracticable line should be given and taken as occasion requires, and circumstances dictate. When the tackle is light and fine, and the quarry large, we commonly resort to this expedient, which seldom indeed fails. We suddenly stay all show of opposition and head the fish rather than otherwise a little in the direction he makes for so desperately. In open water, where this is more practicable, ninety-nine times out of a hundred he becomes utterly confounded at the sudden change, and will make a faint effort at a new departure in a side direction and widely different angle, but quickly shows broadside, and yields. This may appear incredible in theory; we are, however, speaking from our own experience, and can vouch for its practical result. Whenever a fish is safely hooked it is, as a rule, the fisher's own fault if he be ultimately lost. Personally, we never pass a feeding fish because of his locating in what is usually deemed an 'awkward spot'. 'Where's the use of trying for *that* fish?' queries a passing angler. 'It would be impossible to land him were you to get hold.'

It has always been our policy to get hold first, as a preliminary ceremony, which done, the landing question is an after consideration. The notion of the main mass of anglers would appear to be that if an unusually cunning fish takes up an impregnable-looking position he is to be religiously left unassailed. 'Breakers ahead' seem to be scented by the overcautious pliers of the rod, when the chances of conquest are really 'as even' as in less dangerous localities; and even supposing this were not so, the greater the difficulty the more exciting the sport, and the keener the pleasure. There is no necessity for lugging out instanter a hooked fish. In these circumstances a short line and a sturdy pliant rod will avert endless disaster, and by holding on like grim death at one end of the line, whilst the terrified fish holds on in a similar style at the other, the very largest and heaviest fish are to be generally exhausted, and that with small risk of failure.

Amongst the precepts to be impressed upon the mind of the novice are the following. Never play a fish against a stream, as by that means an additional weight is thrown upon the line and tackle, which in all cases is particularly undesirable, as in the event of the tackle holding to its tether, there is danger of the fish being forcibly torn away from the hook. A small fish drawn against the stream, strains the tackle inconceivably. Whenever a fish makes for weeds, roots or submerged timber at the rodster's side of the river, do not potter with the reel, but haul in the line by the left hand, allowing it to fall at the feet. The height of absurdity to the mind of the writer is the sight of a stalwart fisherman comfortably winding away at the miniature windlass, in an endeavour to hoist a hooked fish that has secreted himself amongst roots, sunken sticks, piles or other mischief, as though, seeing he had been observed to go in, there was not the least ground for doubts as to his being speedily got out again. Wherever weeds are most prevalent in a trout stream, there the best fish congregate. Like pike, they love to secrete themselves in the green shades of aquatic vegetation from whence they can dart upon their unexpecting prey. Whenever surface food is sufficiently tempting, they leave their cover, generally rising upon the less frequented side of the water, where they have still the full benefit of the weedbeds which intervene between them and their would-be captors. It is often most tantalising to lose one fish after another in a vain attempt to keep them from their weedy retreat; the position of this between the rodster and the fish, coupled with the circumstance of a long line being necessary to reach the rising fish, gives the latter every chance of escape, which, in fact, amply accounts for the presence of the best and finest fish in such quarters. In these cases an exceptional course of procedure may without complication be resorted to.

Immediately a fish is hooked, line and rod must be held in readiness for the first dash of the fish to the weeds. The interval, as a rule, is not long, as the moment they feel the hook's point, and recover from their consternation, instinct prompts them to make for the friendly shelter of the weeds, which, if entered, the chances are the fisher loses both fish and flies, with a portion of gut lash to boot. To avert this the line must be hauled in as rapidly as possible by the left and disengaged hand, whilst the rod's point must be brought back at right angles from the water, should the fish permit it. As a general rule upon all moderately large streams these combined tactics have the effect of bringing up the fish before the right angle is described, as in the case of a rod 12 feet long, for example, the line is shortened by 24 feet. When the head of the fish is thus brought to the surface he must be assiduously held there, line being gradually and carefully taken in as he flounders over the weedbeds. A freshly hooked fish will be found to force a passage by the stern or tail action, when firmly held by the head, infinitely better than the rodster unaided, in the case of an exhausted fish, could do it for him.

We well recollect once fishing upon the Wye (Derbyshire), at Bakewell, when the main incident of the day had a direct bearing upon the subject now before us, and may serve as an illustration of what we have endeavoured to point out. It was about the middle of April, the morning clear and keen; the night preceding had been dry and frosty. Before noon myriads of flies were out, whirling in ceaseless activity in the warm rays of the sun. We had been casting in a preoccupied sort of way up to this time, occasionally creeling a small fish and now and then imparting some little practical hint to a companion under our tuition. Now that the flies were numerous, the fish turned out to feed, and our lethargy was shaken off in the anticipation of a consequent change. During the half-hour ensuing, we had experienced exceptionally good sport, and whilst we were thus busily engaged the old keeper came downstream, opened conversation upon fish, fishing, etc., and seemed in no hurry to deprive us of the benefit of his attendance.

'Where do the best of your fish lie, keeper?' we enquired after a time.

'Oh, up by the bridge yonder, there's as nice a lot o' fish there as anywhere i' th' river.'

'How far is it upstream from here?' queries our companion.

'Better than two miles, sir; you can do it in twenty minutes or thereabouts.'

Having no special desire to test the accuracy of this statement, we ultimately agreed to fish up. After the lapse of about an hour or so, we arrived upon the spot indicated, in company with the keeper. Here, for about a stone's throw from the bridge, were dense masses of weeds, through which the water passed in narrow channels. The position was not of the most favourable, there being in the immediate background a display of evergreen shrubs, etc., which looked ill for the safety of the tackle. 'Well, here we are at last,' exclaims our pupil.

'Yes, gentlemen,' put in the old man, 'there's any amount o' fish in, but, plague tack um, nobody can get um out; the best fishermen we have canner manage um.'

'Ah! how do you account for that?' we enquired.

'Oh, them weeds bothers um; they loses the fish and tackle an' all;' and after delivering himself of this gratifying reflection, the old keeper calmly inserted his pipe between his teeth, and his hands in the pockets of his breeches, as a preliminary to seeing the fun. At the second or third cast we hooked a fish, and by a strict and prompt application of the tactics previously described, the fish wriggled through the breakers, in a style thoroughly earnest and effective. Once clear of the weeds we relaxed the pressure upon the rod, playing the fish at the extremity of a short line until exhausted.

'You've been very lucky with this un, sir.'

'We shall be equally as lucky you will find with the next,' was our reply. At the very next cast the game was repeated, with the same result, nor did we desist until we had sufficiently punished the cunning old fox by an extract sufficient to cram both creels with the lazy monsters, whose presence near the bridge we knew to be the keeper's pride.

ॐ

Landing – In trout fishing the landing-net should invariably be included in the necessary apparatus. The tackle is never constructed with a view to extract fish bodily out of their element, moreover it is anything but sportsmanlike to attempt it. When it is desired to net a fish, the usual rule is to head the capture to the nearest available place if it should be impracticable where hooked; and in all cases the net should be the medium by which the quarry is conveyed to land. It may appear a very simple matter to the unpractical mind to net an already hooked fish, but anglers of experience know well, too well, perhaps, that indiscretion and undue haste in landing or even presenting the net to a supposed exhausted fish will cause him to make yet another plunge, when least expected, for life and liberty. We always use the net with our disengaged hand, holding it edgeways, partly to enter the water readily, so as to get beneath the fish, and partly to meet the fish, which is so brought round as to enter the net forcibly. Bungling aid we have always found worse than no assistance; and when the practice of netting one's own fish is acquired we feel sure anglers generally will find it much more advantageous and satisfactory. Nothing is more common than for an awkward servant or attendant to hit the quarry by poking at him with the sharp rim of the net, instead of placing it under as he is brought near, thus knocking the fish off the hook, if not otherwise breaking the tackle. Who has not some painful remembrance of some deplorable loss of this kind? For our own part we have had quite sufficient lessons, not in trout alone, but in salmon and pike fishing, to cause us to refrain from trusting our net to any individual not thoroughly acquainted with the use and handling of it.

Grayling especially require delicate handling when about to be netted, for should the rod be unconsciously elevated, so as to cause the weight of the fish to rest upon the hook and tackle, the fish is in great danger of being lost by the hook breaking away under the strain. Fish should not be pulled even in part out of the water whilst the net is placed under them, as this always incurs danger of breakage, from the cause stated. The tail end of the fish, particularly of a large one, is to be inserted first in the net, except in special cases, as when, for instance, the quarry heads close by the rodster, up- or downstream, when the net may be used as a receptacle for him to head into when within reach.

The best times to fish, the seasonable flies and other information for the fly-fisher, we give in the Monthly Notes. We now purpose dealing more generally with the subject of fly-fishing in its various bearings. Fishing in rapid streams requires somewhat different tactics than those suitable for ordinary smooth running river, or still-water fishing. In these no humouring actions are required to be given to the fly. To draw against or even across stream in these circumstances is to extend to it an unnatural motion. The flies must be cast a few feet above the dimply indication of a rise, and then allowed to float over. This may be repeated several times before moving on, especially if casting over grayling, as these fish are given to take the proffered lure more often than not when passed over repeatedly. With regard to the vexed question of up- or downstream fishing, no strict rule need be observed, a continuous resort to either is not desirable. Adherents of the one deprecate the ever-recurring nuisance of the line becoming slack when cast upstream by the downward flow of water, thus lessening, after each delivery, the chances of a rise by the fly being brought again home to the feet. Upon the other side of the question we have arguments in plenty against downstream fishing, the most important being the habitual position of the fish heading upstream, and therefore in full ken of the operations instigated for his allurement.

Our method of fishing a strange stream is, after prospecting the length to be operated upon the night or early morn previous, to commence at its lower end, and casting, as we have attempted to describe previously, according to the lay of the land and water and general surroundings, now across, or slanting upwards, and occasionally, though rarely, downwards. Where a continuous succession of stream and pool are met with, each should be well and carefully fished. One of the best and most killing styles of still-water fishing with the fly is the sunk-fly system. This consists in drowning

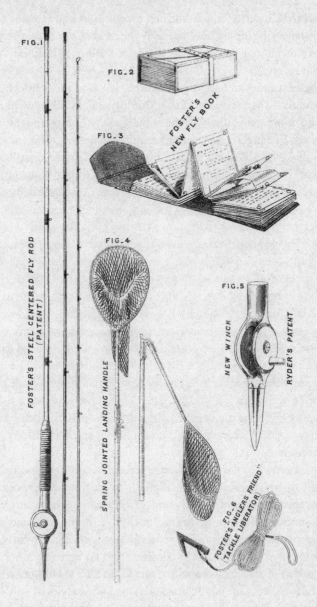

FIG. 1

FIG. 2

FOSTER'S
NEW FLY BOOK

FIG. 3

FIG. 4

FIG. 5

FOSTER'S STEEL CENTERED FLY ROD
(PATENT)

SPRING JOINTED LANDING HANDLE

NEW WINCH

RYDER'S PATENT

FIG. 6
FOSTER'S ANGLERS FRIEND
"TACKLE LIBERATOR"

PLATE II

the flies, so to speak, so that they will readily, though gradually descend, and working them very gently by a very minute movement of the rod tip. The very finest gut line is essential for the successful practice of this mode. The same method may be applied to the deep slower running streams, with deadly effect, when the fish refuse to rise to the surface. The dry-fly system is, however, by far the most scientific and artistic way of alluring either trout or grayling, and well-fished streams will yield more and heavier dishes of those fish to it than to any method or system of angling whatever. At twilight, and in the 'gloaming' of evening, as also in night-fishing, it is advisable to cast across and rather downstream, as the line cannot be kept so well under hand, the command over it being less according to the density of the gathering gloom. Sometimes the sunk-fly method is to be applied to the sharp running streams with signal success, as may also the dry-fly style to the quieter stills and pools. A change in this respect often proves advantageous, even upon well-whipped waters, the educated inhabitants of which so soon fight shy of the persistently applied lures. Whenever one side of a river or stream is habitually well lined with fishermen, the fish generally rise for the most part close to the opposite bank, in most cases close to the edge of the water. The plan to practise in these circumstances is to cast directly out upon the opposite bank, and allow the end to drop in a casual sort of way into the water, where it is generally seized instantly.

Fly-fishing for grayling and trout are not altogether identical, as we have elsewhere shown. Both are frequently found, however, in the same water, and are to be taken with the same cast of flies. Finer tackle, as a rule, is required in the case of the former, as also smaller and brighter flies. In most trout streams of note grayling are found in profusion in their lower portion, where the water flows more serenely. Here they locate near the bottom, even when surface feeding; therefore if the dry floating-fly is preferable in the case of the trout, it is doubly so in that of the grayling, which, though perhaps more expert as a fly-catcher habitually, rises a much greater distance to absorb it. We contend, therefore, that in the *surface* cast-and-draw method, the fish is scarcely allowed a chance to get within seizing distance. This once prevailing practice of trailing along the cast is now being discarded, and deservedly so. How it should have so long held sway we never could conceive. That fish are occasionally taken by it we know, and that they are more often abashed by it we understand as being a perfectly rational result; but how the fisherman who trails his lines across, or slantways over a stream, at so rapid a pace as to leave a trail similar to that of a passing rat or water-hen, can imagine he is extending to the flies a natural and seductive action, we confess is entirely beyond us. The whole of the land flies appear naturally out of their element upon the water, and are at the mercy of wind and wave, especially upon broken water; upon the stills they certainly have a little more power, so as to enable them to essay a paddling excursion with a view to escape impending perils; but even here, either the floating or the sunk or drowned fly is found preferable to the insane system of trailing. The native water insects, as every fly-fisher worthy of the name knows, are quite 'at home' upon the element, floating downstream with their wings erect in the case of the ephemerals, like the minute craft upon a marine engraving. To meet the case of the fluttering land flies, wingless or buzzy artificials answer amply. With the duns the wings must be both full and erect, or 'cock-up' as it is sometimes designated, so as to admit of the fly being kept comparatively dry for some little time, when, becoming saturated, a few backwards and forwards whisks of the line and rod should be given before the delivery of the cast again. This is repeated whenever the flies become saturated, as by so doing the trouble of repeatedly changing the lure is greatly lessened.

Fly-fishing in brooks is practised much the same as in large and more open waters. Where the banks of narrow water are clear of encumbrances, the rodster should fish some distance away, so as to avoid needlessly exposing the person and purpose. The flies for brooks and tributaries of good 'trouting' streams should be some-what larger than those used for the main streams, to enable the fisherman to land his prey safely and quickly as, where the water is turbulent and confined, the fish have greater chances of breaking away. Often the least leniency will be rewarded by an entanglement

with sticks or roots of trees; playing in these circumstances is, therefore, not to be considered for an instant. The flies here alluded to are
suitable for discoloured waters generally, the hook, hackle and wing
being somewhat larger to withstand rough usage. The same order of
land and water insects appear upon all running waters containing
trout or grayling, no matter where situated; nevertheless, some anglers
will persist in presenting upon all and every occasion a wonderful
fly or two which is said to kill upon that river only. For our part, we
may state that we never make any distinction in our list of flies, no
matter what river we may cast over. We have often heard the phrase –
'Your flies are too large for this water,' or – 'Your flies are too small
to kill here, sir.' Upon some Welsh and Scottish streams, the fly-
fishers use unduly large flies, whilst upon clear spring waters, the
local flies are excessively small, and in this case invariably hackled.
Both large and small flies are objectionable when they do not correspond with the 'naturals' frequenting the water. We can testify from
our own experience that the flies, irrespective of locality, are the
same as regards size upon every river in England, Wales or Scotland;
even those upon mountain lakes, situated in some cases at great
elevation, are similar, in their season, both as regards size and colour,
to those upon low-lying rivers.

Fancy flies, when used judiciously at the right time, may answer
just as well for trout, and especially for grayling, as they do for
salmon; indeed the two last named have many characteristics in
common: both display an effeminate appreciation of gaudy glitter
and happy combination of colours, whilst the more circumspect
and subtle trout often ignores the unnatural 'artificials', though
presented temptingly. The most important of nondescript 'artificials'
are, beyond doubt, the bumble tribes. These in their various shades
seldom fail to kill when no rising of naturals has occurred during
the day, or when there is a miscellaneous host of 'oddlings' about
the water, under which latter circumstances the palmered 'artificials'
are undoubtedly taken for some one of the flies about. Another
useful 'child of fancy' is the flat gold-bodied Whistler Fly. This is
hackled with red-brown pigeon's breast feather, or with that of the

whistling plover, from which it takes its name. This fly is really valuable for discoloured, and even thick rising water. Many are the times we have, instead of having a futile journey, and leaving the rapidly rising river in disgust as have companion rodsters, killed a good dish of fish through its sole agency. Upon the Wharfe we, upon a late occasion, took trout sufficient to fill our creel some five times, had they been all retained, whilst several anglers who had repaired to the same length returned to the hotel, under the impression that the water was too thick for the worm.

When the fish are basking, during the midday hours in the hot summer months, they are not always to be drawn to the surface by small flies. The Red Caterpillar, elsewhere described, we believe to be unsurpassed for trout and large grayling at midday; and when cast as a night-fly in the 'gloaming' of evening. Browns and gaudily-dressed Lake Flies, too, when cast and played like a minnow, just below the surface of the water, are good. But the combination more suitable for this method is the dressing known as the 'Alexandra Fly'. This is as large as a full-sized Sewin Fly, the hook employed being a Limerick, the shank carefully wrapped with broad silver tinsel, to represent the body; the wings, if any, consist of a dozen strands or so of brown turkey feather; hackles, blue feather from the peacock's neck. This fly was originally introduced by Dr Hobbs, some fifteen years ago. Upon well-wooded, swift-running waters it is most useful; the line is allowed to run out with the current, being then drawn back upstream by a series of short jerks that serve to open and shut the fibres of the hackle, thus exposing the white body only at intervals, at measured distances. It is surprising how the fish will follow and take this fly when in the 'running' mood. It is, most certainly, far superior to the minnow from the fly-fisher's point of view.

In angling there are various influences that affect the fish, and which are as yet but little understood. Not only are their habits and movements most important to the angler, but, for the better pursuit of sport, meteorological changes and influences should also be noted by the observant student. To some it is not known that the temperature of the water is most frequently responsible for bad 'taking' days; we habitually carry a small instrument, by no means generally used by the fisherman – we refer to a small pocket thermometer. This proves most useful in ascertaining the temperature of the water, either at the surface or at the bottom. By the use of such an instrument the observant angler soon learns that when the water is of unusually low temperature, the moving fish will be rare, notwithstanding the favourable atmospheric temperature. When the air is cold and the water proves at a higher degree than common, the fish will be certain to be more or less on the feed; but when both atmosphere and water are genial, every description of fish will be found to be upon the 'forage' for prey, if not satiated by some proper food supply. The observant fisherman upon any particular water soon finds out much more to guide him in his choice of fishing. The water of different rivers and streams, as a matter of course, varies, and the fisher in any particular water should ascertain precisely, not only the prevailing temperature of the water, but that in which the fish feed most eagerly, as also when it is useless trying to tempt them to 'rise' or 'run'. The old nostrums anent weather wisdom are mainly inaccuracies. In the coldest eastern or north-eastern wind we have killed repeatedly many a fine basket of fish, owing to the temperature of the water being high and unusually genial from some cause or other.

The ancient belief in the stoppage of sport during a thunderstorm is not strictly true. Some little time before the breaking of the storm atmospheric influence appears to act detrimentally, almost invariably through the warmer months, but during the storm itself the fish will rise more often than not most eagerly at the numerous insects drowned during the downpour, and this too, whilst the electric fluid gleams and the thunder roars immediately overhead, all without visible effect upon the fish. As regards the fisherman we fear the same observations do not apply with equal truth. The nearest sycamore tree or honeysuckle hedge is sought, and the angler is seldom to be convinced, save by practical arguments, that the time for taking fish is while the rain falls, just as the time for making hay is whilst the sun shines, as the old adage has it.

Between the tyro and the proficient grayling fisher there exists a wider gulf than is the case with the experienced and inexperienced in any other branch in the whole art of fishing. Practical skill and general artistic bearing are more fully exemplified in fishing for grayling than for trout and salmon, whilst upon the same ground the unskilled efforts of the bungler stand at a yet more glaring contrast. Mark the long sweeping casts of the adept across and upstream, ever true to the circulating eddy, the centre of which forms the 'bull's-eye' at which to aim. See the gradually whirled line, how lightly and efficiently it is cast, the obstructive force of the air and the flowing water being all taken into consideration when that measured swing is given. Observe the varying tactics resorted to when called for in varying circumstances, and yet above all the efficient mode of handling the hooked fish while it makes determined efforts to free itself from the tiny thread so recently ignored, and to avoid the necessity of a premature move to other parts of the stream through undue disturbance of the water. Upon the other hand, the inexperienced grayling fisher's awkwardly managed line is planted splashingly upon the bosom of some tranquil pool or still deep – the collar, which owing to its dryness, and left to its own wayward course, dancing and dangling in its aerial flight, becoming hope-lessly entangled (as it inevitably must) the instant it nears the water, causing a break larger than the bold rise of a heavy fish; all these signs make the presence of their owner known and appreciated, both upon the banks and beneath the surface of the water.

Fly-fishing at twilight and afterwards is prohibited, and justly so, in some districts. The deadly nature of the practice presents no recommendations to the true sportsman; nevertheless, where the water is overrun with excessively large fish, whose acquired wariness prohibits them from surface feeding during the day, they may with perfect honesty of purpose be legitimately extracted at such times as they may deign to dine. The cast for night-fishing should not exceed two yards, the gut being of medium thickness, though round and without flaw or blemish. One fly is ample to fish with, though upon a moonlight night the usual trio may be used with the three-yards lash. When the evening shades gather and deepen, the fish will be found to rise more upon the verge of the shadow thrown upon the water by high banks or foliage situated near. We do not commend the use of salmon casts and swivelled monster moths, etc. This may be all very well in peculiar surroundings, when the night is densely dark and the water well lined with sticks and piles, but under these circumstances we must confess to seeing sport only in name. In point of sport and true diversion, there is certainly more in the gloaming of evening when the moonbeams 'silver the landscape o'er', rendering the surrounding objects almost as bright as when under the orb of day. Then may the fly-fisher conscientiously ply his art upon fair vantage ground and with a clear conscience.

The flies to be used are the largest and heaviest of the day flies, such as the Large Browns, Cinnamon and Stone Flies. The first named form admirable copies of the small grass moths, so prevalent late in the summer's evening. The usual night lures, such as the large moths of the customary shades, the Coachman and the Caterpillar, may be used with success in the way alluded to. With regard to the best size of moths to use, we do not advise them to be too heavy. It has become the practice recently upon some waters to use lures well-nigh as weighty as the American half-ounce; the size should average that of a live Mayfly. An artificial dressed by us to imitate the fluttering action of the moth when upon the water is much used in the Midlands, since its recent introduction – we refer to the 'Dun Cut'. This dressing has proved itself to more than equal the usual reproductions of the moths. It is a double-hackled artificial, the feathers being dun and brown hen's breast feathers (usually used for wings), the outside feather being dun; body, drab fur ribbed with silver twist; hook, long shanked Limerick or Kendal – Mayfly size.

Before the subject of trout and grayling fishing (which has been dealt with more in detail elsewhere) is concluded, we feel it incumbent upon us to make some allusion to the Dove, upon whose banks resided the first writer upon this, the highest branch of the art piscatorial, in our land. This is classic ground to every follower of Walton. Here have assembled all noted fishermen since the days in which the common sire of us all trod its banks and wielded the rod;

and they still come, though many a famous rod that was wont to whip these waters is laid away for ever. Every rock and pool seems to imbue one with

> Meek Walton's heavenly memory.

The ancient and original fishing-house, too, standing as it does, scarcely impaired by the ravages of time, seems to impress the mind with familiar associations. It requires no great stretch of imagination to call up the venerable and benevolent features and stalwart form of the 'Modern Patriarch Izaak', and his adopted son, discoursing pleasantly whilst making flies, or rigging up the tackle for the evening's rise.

> Cheerful, sage, and mild,
>   Walton's discourse was like the honey balm,
> Distilled along these waters wild.
>   Smit with the love of angling he beguiled,
> With his adopted son, the hours away,
>   Whilst Cotton owned the fondness of a child
> For him, in whose glad company to stay,
> Had made the whole year pass like one sweet month of May.

Yes, the structure and general appurtenances are still the same; time has dealt most kindly with the erection; over the portal the immortal inscription '*Piscatoribus Sacrum*' remains still unobliterated; every disciple of the rod may with veneration read

> His title clear to enter here.

The Dove is noted for its blue transparency, hence the name. Centuries since other waters were polluted in comparison with the crystal stream of the Dove. The renowned Cotton, the Minstrel of the Vale, thus sweetly sings:

> Such streams Rome's Yellow Tiber cannot show;
> The Iberian Tagus, or Ligurian Po,
> The Maese, the Danube, and the Rhine,

> Are puddle-water all compared to thine;
> And Loire's pure streams yet too polluted are
> With thine much purer to compare;
> The rapid Garonne and the winding Seine,
>> Are both too mean,
>> Beloved Dove, with thee
>> To vie priority;
>> Tame and Isis, when conjoined submit,
>> And lay their trophies at thy silver feet.

About Beresford, the scenery through which the stream flows resembles much that of Dovedale; Beresforddale being a sort of miniature representation of it. In the first named, the volume of water is, of course, greater, it being situate several miles lower downstream. Trout and grayling are the only fish here found, with the exception of a few eels. The trout predominate largely from Dovedale upstream; here the best efforts of the rodster are to be brought into play in order to achieve even moderate success. The water contains a fair stock of fish, but for education and attainments, Dove trout, and especially Dovedale trout, vie successfully with those of the Wandle, Itchen, Test, or any other stream wherever situate; and the adept upon the Dove may, with perfect safety, consider himself sufficiently accomplished to rank amongst the first fly-fishers of his day.

> Oh, Dove, thou art so clear, so bright and sweet,
> Men's choicest lures with scant approval meet;
> Did not the beauteous Dale such charms reveal,
> The pilgrim rodster oft regret would feel.
> Romantic vale, renowned for varied scene,
> Sylvan abode, meet for a fairy queen;
> Rare gems of nature deck the scenes around,
> With wooded heights the lofty rocks are crowned;
> Cascades impetuous fall with arrow flight;
> Rainbows presented glisten in the light;
> The waters, purling at the angler's feet,
> In crystal streams and sparkling eddies meet.

Soft strains of music borne upon the breeze,
Resound from warbling choirs amidst the trees.
Fair scenes, adieu. Alas! charmed stream, farewell,
Where speckled trout and grayling dwell.

W. S.

NOTE – Below the renowned Dale, downstream, the grayling gradually gain the ascendency, until for the last 25 miles of the river's length they predominate over the trout as eight or ten to one. This may be owing to the fact of the water being of less rapid fall, and of a slightly higher temperature. Of the two open lengths of the upper portion of the Dove, Dovedale is five miles northwards from the nearest station, viz., Ashbourne, upon the N. S. R. line; Hartington is about ten miles from each of the following stations, Bakewell, Cheadle, Buxton and Ashbourne. The guests staying at the hotels in the neighbourhood of the Dale are entitled to daily tickets, free of charge. Tickets for the Hartington or Beresford length are issued at the Charles Cotton, price 2s. 6d. *per diem*. No fishing is allowed in June upon this reach. There are over three miles of good fishing upon the Dovedale length. Except at general holiday times, this length of water is but little fished, as compared with other and less desirable streams of the Midlands. Excellent accommodation is afforded by the host and hostess of that ancient and renowned hostelry, the Isaak Walton, proprietor, Mr W. Prince. This hotel is conveniently near the river, which is but a stone's throw from its windows. A goodly number of guests also find accommodation at the Peveril, which has been recently enlarged.

The Hartington length is upstream, in a northern direction from the Dale. Accommodation is afforded to anglers fishing this length at the Cotton (host, Mr J. F. Wardle). Private lodgings are also obtained in the village. There are many private lengths accessible to respectable applicants, notably below Rocester. There for some miles the freeholders or tenants grant permission to fish for a day occasionally to the legitimate angler. In this part the tenants of the river are more varied than upstream. Almost every species of freshwater fish abounds, and that in many instances to profusion. Upon the Manifold and Hamps, and many other tributaries noted for their trout, tolerably good fishing may be had, the landed proprietors and holders giving permission in many instances upon application. There are two Club lengths upon the Dove, viz., the Norbury and Okeover lengths. The number of members in the first named are ten, the annual subscription being £5; those of the latter number five, the annual subscription £12 12s.

COMPLIUS

CHAPTER THIRTEEN

Live-Fly- and Beetle-Fishing

Dibbing or daping with the natural fly is an easy art, and is, more-over, a very productive and, we may add, a very seductive one, when reasonably practised upon a densely wooded stream. It is often useful as a means of weeding out old fish, whose cannibal propen-sities go far to exterminate their own species, as well as their immediate neighbours and relatives. There is small scope for skill in the use of the live fly, as employed under the above circumstances, as the foliage lining the banks shields the rodster's person from view, whilst the struggling lure accomplishes the rest. The rod and line must necessarily be both short and stout for the general comfort of fishing. An ordinary fly rod with short top answers admirably for the purpose, whilst the three or four feet of gut bottom line should be strong, round, and clear, without a faulty place or blemish. Deplorable loss often ensues from carelessness in looking over the tackle before commencing operations. It needs ever to be remembered that the weakest place in a line, be it of what substance it may, decides its precise degree of strength throughout, as when the testing time arrives, the thing breaks at that point, despite its strength elsewhere. A flat or unduly thin place in gut should always be taken out before loss and damage are experienced from its presence.

The systems of using the natural fly for the allurement of fish in use at the present day are three in number and may be described as follows – 1st: throwing or casting in open water; 2nd: mid-water fishing or daping with the sunken fly; 3rd: surface-fishing and dibbing. The first enumerated is fully dealt with in the Monthly Notes. The method of procedure to be adopted in the case of the sunken fly varies but little from that of worm-fishing without a float.

The fly is attached to the hook between the wings, the bend of the hook to project towards the tail, and two small shots are fixed a foot or so above the hook. Thus equipped the angler carefully introduces the lure to the notice of the fish which lurk under roots or projecting banks, etc., always endeavouring to keep an eye upon the bait, as the moment to strike is when the fish has closed upon it, and leisurely turns away. By the moment's grace thus given, the rodster is enabled to hook his quarry in the corner of the mouth, which is always a desideratum in the case of large fish, trout especially, their mouths being excessively hard, grisly or bony. The movements of a large trout are always leisurely, and as the bait is genuine no fear need be entertained as to the possibility of his rejecting it, during the moment's respite given.

Surface dibbing, as the name implies, consists in working in a natural way the live flies upon the top of the water. In order to do this effectually, the impaled fly is made to float and flutter by the action given to the line, occasionally settling upon the water for a brief interval. Just before twilight, upon a summer's evening, this system of angling is very deadly, and more especially so on small brooks. Here the fish are then wide-awake, and upon the forage for moths, minnows and other legitimate food which approaches within grabbing distance; and any other larger insects prevalent that may be placed before their notice are extremely likely to be absorbed. The large white grass moths are capital lures for this purpose. The flies most in repute for daping and dibbing purposes, are the mayfly, stone and cinnamon flies, the bluebottle, the alder and oak flies, as also the common house fly. The first of these is usually carried in a small basket, specially made for the purpose, which is strung upon the creel strap. The remainder, being flat-winged flies, may be kept in a glass bottle, the cork having a small, gradually widening nick made in one side, to allow the passage of one fly only when partially drawn and also to admit air. A fly will always frequent the opening, no matter how quickly they may be extracted. The size of the hook usually employed is a No. 7 Kendal, with shortened shank. Sometimes two flies are placed upon the hook at once, with the smaller of them next the point. This is often found to answer, as the hooks are more obscured and the bait more significant and tempting to a large fish. Always fish over the eddy of a rise, and whenever the bank of wood of any description admits, keep well back from the river side; even the still pools may be found productive. In this case the nearest bank must be fished first, afterwards the middle and opposite side, and then the open water. The instant the fish rises at your fly you must strike as in artificial-fly-fishing, and play as is usual in that branch of the art. For this open dibbing, a full length of fly-cast is necessary, and that too of fine substance. The artistic method of fly-fishing with the blow-line, as referred to in the Notes on the Months, is much practised in Scotland and Ireland, upon the lochs containing trout, more especially when the mayfly is up.

Beetles of every kind form admirable baits for trout, as also for chub and other fish. These are to be had 'artificial', and when a maggot or wasp grub is fixed upon the hook, they are found quite as killing as the 'naturals'. Cockchafers, cockroaches and clockers are all deemed acceptable to the hungering fish during the season of low waters and scant food.

When either daping or dibbing, care should be taken to keep a taut and straight line, as intervening slack line renders it a moral impossibility to handle the bait and strike effectually, more especially when angling through a small opening in the bushes bordering a brook. In small places, the small ladycow (the fisherman's Marlow Buzz or Coch-y-Bondu) is used as a live lure in fine water. These hardy little insects do not leave the hook so readily as the more slender and frail flies. A capital plan of using them is to fit up a fine four-yard gut collar, or lash, with four of the insects, three as droppers and one at the point, the former being attached to fine gut-hooks (No. 8 or 9 Kendal), when they may be cast as 'artificials' when trout are shy; and when there is a scarcity of ephemeral and other water order of flies this method often proves extremely killing.

CHAPTER FOURTEEN

Notes on the Months for Fly-Fishing

February The angler, as a rule, commences to angle for trout and grayling upon St David's Day, the first of March, when, according to the calendar, 'fly-fishing begins'; but we would recommend the tyro to try his hand about the middle of February, when he will be sure to effect captures that will give him a relish to follow the pursuit, and exhilarate him to become an adept in the 'flying' art. We note that the majority of youthful beginners take their trial trip in July or August, flogging assiduously when the sun shines powerfully, and leaving dispirited with their ill-success, just as the fish begin to feed at sunset. The angler should be at the waterside from eleven to three o'clock – it is little use starting earlier, as the fish do not rise freely except in the middle of the day. Slow-running streams and still deeps are the most likely places on which to cast. We recommend the Red Fly, the Blue Dun, or February Flapper, and the ordinary Rough Bumble to make up the cast, as being the most likely trio for early spring-fishing. The last named is only a fancy fly, but is an excellent killer in spring and autumn. To the experienced fly-fisher, it is a well-known fact that few flies rise to the surface of their liquid element while the river is impregnated with snow 'broth'. This cold stimulant is no inducement for the little insect to quit its sheath in the bed of the river, but when the genial influence exercised by the rays of the sun pierces into its retreat, then the small fly quits its abode, rises to the surface, spreads its wings, and commences life's voyage, which probably ere long is cut short by the appearance of the

> Pearl-tipped snout
> Of the speckled trout.

The Red Fly first makes its appearance in this month. Its wings and body are of an olive colour, but after two or three sunny days its legs and body assume a russet-brown, and as the weather becomes warmer its colour changes until it attains a deep ruddy hue. The prevailing shade in March and April of both legs and body resembles that of a coffee bean, though slightly claret-coloured towards the tail. The Red Fly, we believe, is common to all waters containing trout or grayling. The Welsh anglers consider it one of the best flies that can be used, indeed, it is sometimes called the 'Welsh Fly'. In some districts in this country its local appellation is 'Old Joe', in others the 'Early Spring Red', and the 'Spring Brown', and another local name is the 'March Brown'. The Red Fly's wings lie nearly flat on its back, the wings of the March Brown are almost upright, after the manner of the duns and other ephemerals. Many a neatly folded packet finds its way into our hands containing naturals for identification, and as the March Brown proper, like the Mayfly, does not frequent all waters, this fly, acting in a manner as a substitute, causes endless misconceptions; and vast numbers of the Red Fly come to hand which are invariably mistaken for the March Brown. The Blue Dun, or February Flapper, so called because of its fluttering on the water more than any other dun, is of a smoky-blue hue all over, and when once seen can never be mistaken.

For further particulars of these flies see pages 128-45.

ॐ

March The angler should be at the waterside from eleven to four o'clock. The fish, not yet having recovered their full vigour after the winter season, are to be found on the slow-running streams and still deeps. The Red Fly, Blue and Cockwinged Duns, Cowdung Fly and March Brown are the most abundant flies on the water, and therefore are the best to be used. A description of the Red Fly has been given under February. For particulars of the Blue and Cockwinged Duns, see page 128. The Cowdung Fly is a common insect, the appearance of which is well known to all. It is in boisterous weather plentiful on the water. This is a land fly, and is found in profusion on rich meadowland where cows have been pastured. These insects rise from the earth with the first days of spring. On cold windy days, or in a sharp wind succeeding a few hours of bright open weather, when the inclement season has terminated, these flies are carried by the wind upon the water, the surface of which being thus quickly besprinkled with struggling atoms of life, the attention of the hunger-bitten trout is speedily arrested, and under these circumstances they seldom fail to shake off their lethargy to feed freely upon them. It is the best fly that can be used early and late in the day through the whole of this month, and occasionally in April.

The March Brown is a general favourite with both fish and fishermen throughout Britain. In Wales it is termed the Cob Fly. In the northern counties of England it is known as the Brown or Dun Drake; but, though in different localities the name varies, the insect itself is characteristically the same everywhere. The wings are nearly erect, after the manner of all the duns, the colour being a beautiful freckled brown, and the legs the same shade. The body varies, but is generally a decided rusty hue, with yellow ribs protruding, and it resembles the Green Drake or Mayfly more closely than any other species. It is two-thirds the size, and goes through similar changes. As the weather gets a little warmer these flies appear a shade smaller in size, and lighter in colour. This is called the Turkey Brown, though exactly the same ephemeral. It is often erroneously supposed to be the female March Brown. This Large Brown, with its metamorphosis, the Great Red Spinner, lasts until May, and even June, and appears again in August, but smaller still in size. In the Scotch Highlands it is used as a general fly throughout the summer, and is a capital killer. Many a weighty pannier have we had the pleasure of creeling through its agency, for when once really well on the water, which it annually is on most streams, better sport is not afforded by any fly. The Great Red Spinner referred to is an elegant fly, and is sometimes a good killer, but as in this stage it lays the eggs that propagate its species, like all the other spinners, it is scarcely more than a film or shell after having fulfilled its natural functions, and it is no matter of surprise that the lusty fresh Browns are more appreciated by the fish.

It is the last Sunday in March. Nature is again assuming her green garb, and the birds are joyously carolling their overflowing meed of earthly bliss at the return of ever welcome spring. Tempted by the promise thus held out of an enjoyable commune with nature, you, after the morning's devotions are over, indulge in a quiet stroll by the neighbouring trout stream. After a time you observe what mayhap had previously escaped your notice, namely, that there are quite a number of up-winged 'browns' about. You approach for a nearer inspection. A glance at the water proves the fish to be equally curious. Dexterously capturing a specimen in your hat, you pronounce it a March Brown. The fish, too, seem to have made a similar discovery, as all the way downstream you are treated to a constant repetition of the sweetest sound in the whole range of music to the angler, 'the plump little swish of a rising fish', and you console yourself with the reflection that as the March Brown is well on today there will be murder tomorrow. By ten the next morning you are therefore upon the scene of action. As the slanting rays of Old Sol penetrate the murky clouds the flies commence to rise from the bed of the river, sweeping in battalions up- and downstream, or buoyantly breasting the miniature rippling waves. Having hastily put together your rod, and rigged up your cast with a trio of March Browns, you approach the stream; first wetting your line by way of prelude, and carefully measuring your distance, you cast in the midst of the perpetuated eddies. 'There!' you hook, almost at the same instant, two fish, one on the bob and the other on the stretcher, which immediately dash counter to each other, smashing up your delicately fine cast. The lesson here experienced teaches that the extra-fine grayling lash of the previous autumn is not equally adapted for heavy trout. But lose no time. Quick! Look out something more substantial. Ah, to be sure! this looks more like it. Pull out the coils by drawing the gut slowly through your fingers. We must now 'rig up' again with fairly substantial artificials; which done, we move on a little ahead. Now, very carefully by the foot of yonder old alder. There, splendid! You have him. Gently! Mind the weeds and hold the point of the rod well up. Be careful! He exhibits a strong desire to embrace that old stump.

Ah! keep his head well up, and take in line with your left hand. Look
out! There is some spurt in him still; show him due courtesy by
paying away line with due reserve nevertheless. Now he wearies, and
lies athwart the glistening surface of the water, as pretty a contrast to
its silvery ripples as can well be imagined. Here we are at last, with a
splendid one-and-a-half pounder, which ultimately proves but a type
of a dozen or more which grace your basket at sundown. The only
rivers of the north that the March Brown does not frequent are the
Tay and Tweed. Upon every mountain burn and moorland stream
this fly is a standard killer. The Rough Bumble is also an excellent
lure.

৵

April This is the best month in the year for fly-fishing. The proverbial
showers which characterise the month have the double effect of
drowning the flies and stripping the water of its transparency; indeed,
the more inclement the weather, the greater chance of sport. The flies
are more sturdy than in the summer months, getting more delicate as
the season advances.

   The flies recommended for last month will be found equally service-
able in this, especially if the season is rather backward, the weather
retarding the progress of the little insects in proportion to its severity.
There are the Yellow Dun of April (two shades), Pale Blue Dun (see
page 129), Red Spinner, Sand Fly, Stone Fly, and Foster's Intermediate. The Iron Blue Dun comes on in this month, but is much
more numerous in the next, for which see description.

   The Yellow Duns of April (two shades) and the Pale-Blue Dun,
being April specimens of the Olive Dun (ephemerals) are of great
importance; indeed, I look upon this fly in its various stages as
being the most useful to the angler through the whole season. This
fly, after living three days, casts its coat, and then appears as the Red
Spinner. These flies whirl in clouds a distance above the water,
frequently alighting on the surface; every time they do so they
deposit an egg, which, as we have observed elsewhere, produce
duns of the olive family, ranging in shade from the Blue Dun to the

Pale Evening White, according to the temperature of the water and weather, when the larva attains its maturity. The Red Spinner is a delicately transparent fly, the legs are fiery brown, the tail double the length of the dun's, the body a ruddy yellow. In consequence of the tails being long, it is necessary to put them on the artificials, though not requisite in the case of the duns. As the fish generally rise at the tail-end of the fly we have found it detrimental in hooking, especially when rabbit's whiskers are used, as is generally the case. When we do attach the tails, we use three fibres of a large cock's hackle. Towards evening is the best time to use these flies, as in the heat of the day they take refuge in the foliage of bushes and small trees on the banks of the stream, but at sunset appear in great numbers. The duns are principally used at midday, the Light April Dun and Pale Blue Dun on light genial days, the Dark April Dun on dull cloudy days. It may be as well to remark that if the water be clear, with a bright sun, it will be useless to fish on the still deeps and slow-running streams; but eddies, small holes and rapid-running streams are the best places to fish. Should, however, a strong breeze of wind disturb the surface of the water, the angler may pursue his sport on the smoother reaches. Foster's Intermediate will be found very effective when duns are on the water. This is a copy of all the duns prior to their reappearance as spinners. It is well-known that fish invariably seize sickly or maimed insects, or small fry, etc., from the midst of their more lively companions. The Sand Fly, as its name implies, is the colour of reddish sand; it is a flat-winged fly, and is very plentiful in this month and the next, and is a good killer when there is no quantity of any particular flies on the water.

The Stone Fly is a flat-winged fly; the wings and body are of a dark stone colour, the latter is strongly marked with yellow ribs; the legs are of a greenish brown, and these it uses with extreme activity. When not on the water it frequents stones and pebbles by the sides of streams, on the rapid parts of which the artificial should be used. Many fish are taken by dibbing with the natural fly near the roots of overhanging bushes. It resembles a beetle in its flight, falls very heavy on the water, and is a substantial bait for large fish. On some streams it is known as the Mayfly, as the Green Drake does not appear on those waters. It is a water fly, and lasts from the beginning of April to the middle of June.

The Grannum, or Green-Tail, makes its appearance in this month. This is a flat-winged fly, of the size and shape of the Sand Fly, with the addition of a green appendage at the end of the body, which is its egg-pouch. This fly is quite a favourite with fishermen in April, but we confess we have seldom done much with it till the latter part of summer.

ᘓ

May At this season of the year the fish leave the deep water; and sport on small streams is now good. The best flies for this month are the Hare's Ear, Yellow Dun of May, Iron Blue and its transformation the Jenny Spinner, the Alder Fly, and the Yellow Sally. The Green Drake, or Mayfly, seldom appears on any stream before the last week in May or the beginning of June, under which month we give a descriptive account of the various methods of using it. The title Iron Blue will now be found very abundant upon most waters, especially in the Midland and Southern counties. Its local appellations are numerous, but being precisely the colour of a piece of new iron, the very appropriate and descriptive term Iron Blue is more generally adopted. The fly appears a shade lighter upon the body in this month, a mauve colour prevailing. This fly assumes no other name upon undergoing this change of colour in the body, but is universally recognised as being one and the same fly. Were this the case with the larger species of duns, much complication would be avoided. To the entomological student, the habits of this little insect form an interesting and amusing study. It is extremely hardy, being a lover of inclement weather. Its water nympha frequents the cold spring heads during the whole summer, rising to the surface in clouds whenever the weather happens to be dull, with obscure sun. A cloudy morning will entice myriads from the watery depths, the fish being in turn allured from their accustomed haunts in the bed of the river to the surface of the water, where they regale themselves upon these prim little yacht-like insects. Great execution may often be effected through the medium of a good copy of this especial favourite of the fish, even in the hands of an indifferent rodster, though it is not to be inferred that any artificial, or even a bad rendering of the Iron Blue, will be equally effective as when the light-coloured 'blues' are absorbing the attention of the fish. The dark shade will, in clear water, often fail to accomplish much; in these circumstances, no matter how well the fish may be rising, other 'artificials', infallible as they may be in their seasons, will prove utterly useless.

Whilst we were fishing the Kennet upon one occasion, not very long ago, a rather striking instance of this came before our notice. Out of a round half-dozen of fishermen upon the length we were about to fish, there were two northern anglers, spider theorists. These gentlemen, being strongly prejudiced against the southern regimen, had very eloquently declaimed, prior to our setting forth, against the absurdity of attempting to copy any special fly, maintaining that when fish are inclined to feed, one fly is as good as another, so long as the size is somewhere near the mark, adding that when fish were not inclined for feeding 'every conceivable object in the fly-book would fail to tempt them'.

Finding verbal arguments ineffective, we had adjourned to the river's brim to try the effect of practical ones. The day opened bright and clear, with no flies on the water, and no fish on the rise, in which circumstances our Scotch friends wisely, in their own opinion, declined to fish. The remainder of the party, upon the other hand, rigged up with double-hooked Palmers, and commenced. These are cast on the water the same as the fly, and are then allowed to sink and move with the current, see page 200. After a few fish had been allured from unseen haunts in this manner, to the amazement of the north-countrymen, they protested that alluring ointment must have been used, which imputation was indignantly resented by several of the company, who affirmed that the sense of sight in fish was all they attempted to deceive; that no modern fisherman believed in the efficiency of obnoxious ointments, and other pigments, and that the whole reason that Walton and Cotton shone above their numerous contemporaries so conspicuously was owing to the fact of their having proved themselves to be half a century ahead of their times by ignoring suchlike trash. About noon a smart breeze sprang up, the sun being occasionally obscured by drifting clouds, and an odd fish or two now began to rise. The prim little Iron Blues quickly appeared, as though by magic, on the water's surface, jauntily riding the tiny billows in quaint style. Now all set to with right good will. The party separated for business, and during the ensuing hour and a half we had taken as many fish as could conveniently be creeled, as had also a neighbouring rodster, when one of the Scotchmen hove in sight round a sudden turn. 'Now for an exemplification of the relative virtues of spider and flies,' observes our neighbour. 'Science versus ignorance and presumption,' was our response.

'The fish are really playing and not feeding; I have risen dozens, but have not hooked a single fish,' remarked the Scotchman.

'Indeed,' was the reply, 'but then you see you do not use alluring ointments!'

At this moment our acquaintance of the morning hooked a good fish, which, judging from the unceremonious way in which it was landed over some weeds, must have been hooked very well indeed.

'They would seem to be feeding a little better hereabouts.'

'Rather,' sagely observes our friend, as he opened his well-filled creel to squeeze in his late capture.

'By heavens!' ejaculates the disciple of typical delusion, 'you don't mean to say you have taken that basket of fish this afternoon?'

'That's precisely what I do mean to say, nevertheless; and what is more, I will wager the price of a dinner that each of our fly-fishers have accomplished something similar.'

'Oh, you may take my word for it there has not been a fish killed down below; but I tell you what, I am going in for one or two here;' saying which, he assiduously set himself to work. Our offers of the taking fly were declined by him, although the tongue of every fish taken was seen to be covered with one particular fly, and that fly the Iron Blue. Obstinacy and prejudice still held rampant sway, obstructing the path to success, and damping the spirits of the inner man as effectually as the proverbial Scotch mist does the external one. Some fish were still to be seen rising.

'I thought I had that fish, he rose within two inches of me at something else; it's very strange they will not take it.'

'It would be strange indeed if they *did*,' was the reply.

After witnessing more futile efforts on the part of the angler with the infallible artificials, we landed a small fish or two, evidently to his no small discomfort, and then wound up for the day. By the time all had met at the hotel, every creel was found to contain fish, with the exception of those of the free-thinkers, who returned in company, troubled and dispirited. It is needless for us to add that next morning saw them on board an early train bound for other latitudes, where it is hoped they will benefit by the lesson taught by experience.

The Jenny Spinner is the metamorphosis of the Iron Blue. It is of a universal milk-white colour, with the exception of two crimson bands, one at each extremity of the body. In this new dress, the insect after the manner of all other spinners, is prevalent at sunset, whenever the Iron Blue has been well on in the course of the day, which generally is the case on all cloudy days, between April and October, though the colour of this fly changes somewhat during this period. In August the Iron Blue assumes a more olive cast upon the body; in September and October the precise shade and colour in wing, leg and body is the same as the Olive Dun of the same period, having a rusty shade upon the body precisely similar, the only difference being in point of size. These little duns are sometimes erroneously supposed to be half-matured Olive Duns; but flies do not grow or expand gradually, they are full sized when they quit their sheaths, as in the larva and pupa state they feed voraciously, laying up an internal store which lasts them the remainder of their existence, as we have elsewhere observed. The Jenny Spinner is a good killer, even when the water is extremely fine. The Yellow Dun of May is very prevalent on fine days, when it should be on the cast. The Alder Fly is very abundant from about the last week in May to the middle of June. It is a flat-winged fly, and comes from a water nympha. The wings are of a dull brown, veined, the body being a dark claret, and the legs of a rusty black shade. It is a great favourite with trout and chub, particularly towards evening. The natural insect may be used for dibbing, it being a large fly, though slightly varied in different localities. The Black Gnat is a very small fly, which is a great favourite with trout and grayling, when fully on the water. The fisherman's Black Gnat is a small winged fly, and is not to be confounded with the angler's plagues or pests, so prevalent at the latter part of the season; indeed, the naturalists aver that it is not a gnat in reality, that term being correct only in the case of the minute black smuts referred to, which resemble nothing better than a fine speck of soot. The copies, however, of the Black Gnat, generally speaking, are much too large, being nearer the size of a Bluebottle. The same observation also applies to the Iron Blue, the Jenny Spinner, and other small flies. Just when the Mayfly (the Drake) begins to appear the gnats generally come on in clouds, they being the fore-runners of this celebrated fly.

᎒

June As this month opens, the nymphae of the Drake, as a general rule, arrive at a sufficient state of maturity to essay a change of element. They become active prior to the impending change, and by their movements in the bed of the water attract the attention of the trout, which feed upon them for some week or ten days before the great and continued rising. Just as the aquatic insect begins to change into the aerial being, the attention of the fish is not attracted by them. Fish appreciate the quantity as well as the quality of their edibles, therefore as long as the majority of the insects remain undeveloped in the water, their attention is monopolised by them. When, however, the surface is plenteously laden with feathery atoms of life, they speedily become as bold as the angler could desire.

Before fully entering on the subject of Drake fishing, it would be as well, perhaps, to enumerate the small flies that are killers, more especially early and late in the day, before the Mayflies or Drakes appear. These we give as under: Little Chap, Black Gnat, Oak Fly, Alder Fly and the Spinners. These naturals often in part accompany the Drake upon the water, before and after its appearance. The fish feed upon them when prevalent, before ten a.m. and after six p.m. being the most likely times for their proving useful; though it is by no means uncommon to find the fish taking the small flies at midday, when the Drake has been on for awhile. We have often watched a heavy trout eagerly skim the surface of the water in chase of a small gnat, which fish has ultimately proved, on being brought to land by this minute insect, to be fairly gorged with the Mayfly. The only explanation we can suggest is that Master Speckle was anxious for a change of diet.

The Green Drake appears upon the lower portions of the streams first, often being four days or a week later in rising near the source, where the water, being colder from the springs, retards its maturity. The season of these flies varies in different localities. There are three lakes at varying altitudes at Mullingar, in Ireland. The Mayfly first makes its appearance upon the lower lake and is plentiful, and the fishing here is good so long as these flies remain on the water. They usually last ten or twelve days, and when all is over on the bottom lake they commence upon the next in elevation, where they also last about the same period. Then the angler must travel a little higher, to number three lake, and here the Mayfly will just be found coming out, and the fishing is quite as good as on the lower waters. The fish run large in these lakes, not infrequently a four- or six-pound trout is taken in the day, and sometimes much larger fish are killed. Throughout Ireland the mayfly comes out in abundance on many lakes. In Scotland, on the other hand, there is very little Drake fishing. Upon a few odd lochs, the Awe, Lomond and others, a few of these flies make their appearance, but sport is not good. Upon the other hand the mayflies are extremely abundant upon almost every stream that produces trout, no matter in what latitude or clime; and with regard to the exception referred to, the Stone Fly forms an admirable substitute, being equally abundant at the precise time the Drakes should appear. The fishy feast of St Mayfly is annually looked forward to by the major portion of fishermen as the 'good time coming'. Many an old timid fish that at other times only ventures abroad by night, or at twilight, now boldly makes its appearance at midday; and a long, thin, underfed fish, with disproportionate head, will in a few days become vigorously healthful and plump, and of nearly double the strength it possessed previous to feeding on the Green Drake.

We have had the pleasure of wetting our line upon all trout streams of note in the three kingdoms, but nowhere have we had such sport with this fly as on the Dove. Centuries ago this river was considered the best stream for trout fishing in England, and it still bears the palm for Drake fishing. In this renowned dale, which not only takes its name, but whose sylvan scenery derives an indescribable charm from the river, the flies are far more numerous than on any other stream. This may be due to various causes, the sheltering of rocks and foliage, or the geological formation of the bed of the river. This, however, we pass over; suffice it that the Green Drake, when scarce and almost a failure elsewhere, is to be found in clouds in Dovedale. Here fishermen of all grades throng the banks of bonny Dove with almost every conceivable equipment; long men with short rods, small men with large ones, from the youthful novice to the venerable old fly-fisher of seventy years.

And now, with our reader's kind permission, we will conduct him to a favourite length some distance upstream, keeping a lookout meanwhile in our progress as to what is doing. The first object that strikes our notice as we walk leisurely along is an old man, who sits rod in hand under the friendly shade of some rather overgrown bushes, quietly and contentedly blowing his weed, his eye intently fixed on some object on the water near.

'Why, he's certainly float-fishing,' you observe.

'Not so,' we reply; 'it is the hale old miller from above, who has been tempted by the morning's bright promise of this being a good day with the Drake, with one of which he is dibbing or daping upon the water's surface, near the roots of the hawthorns.'

'But surely he cannot hope to do much in that way?' you ask.

'The very largest fish are taken in this manner. You observe he is perfectly still and easy; he has evidently seen the rise of a feeding fish below there, and he is content patiently to watch. Ah! there, he has missed that fish; the fly is gone and so is the fish; he has taken his "hook" and left the miller's.'

'Any fault of the angler's?'

'Oh no, none whatever. The fish has simply taken hold of the living fly by the tail, and so stripped it from the hook, which was placed between the wings; he is rather fastidious in feeding. The flies are merely out as stragglers yet; if two naturals be put upon the hook, he will, ten chances to one, get him the next time. The strongest tackle is used in this primitive style of angling; the shadow of the thick foliage, and the actions of the impaled insect, aiding materially in effecting the deception.' Every minute now the sun shines brighter, and more flies appear. We now move onwards, passing several more fishermen of the daping school. And now, directly preceding us, a fisherman is observed with a conspicuously long stiff rod, attached to which is a very inconsistently fine line, which is out a great length. The rodster is as motionless as though the least action would upset his equilibrium, and seriously imperil the safety of his person and property, the twenty-foot rod in question.

'Gracious goodness! Whatever kind of fishing do you call this, pray?'

'This is in general use upon the lochs frequented by the Mayfly, and is sometimes very successful here. The line consists of the finest possible substance, of the very strongest textile procurable, viz., that of pure raw China silk, which, though not perceptibly thicker than the gut lash, is infinitely stronger. At the extremity of this is a live fly, which, if you watch very closely, you will see is made by the almost invisible action of the tip to frisk and flutter gently in the most natural manner possible upon the top of the water, exactly like a lusty insect in the full enjoyment of perfect liberty. This is a much more scientific way of dibbing than the one recently noticed. The gut is generally used three yards long, and is as fine as it is possible to draw it. The hook is small and is a cropped short shank; this is usually inserted between the wings, as in the other style of daping. Occasionally two hooks are placed back to back, in which case two flies are used, this more particularly on cold windy days.'

'How about the wind? I should imagine the whole thing impracticable without wind.'

'A slight breeze is certainly essential to the successful working of the method; but, when too strong, a small-sized split shot, attached near the foot line, acts admirably as ballast.'

'See yonder! we have still another type of a Drake fisherman. His method is more difficult to practise, but it is more scientific, and is generally more successful. Mark how carefully he measures the distance requisite to reach the rising fish, which now forms the focus upon which his entire attention is fixed. He is evidently a more than ordinarily skilful fly-rodster. Observe how carefully he keeps away from the river's edge, casting dexterously within an inch or two of the rising fish.'

'Is he not rather circumspect in his use of the rod?'

'He is casting the live fly, and that careful swing round from the left to the right is absolutely requisite to retain the fly upon the hook. Were not due care and caution paid to this the fly would continually be flipped off, and nothing but bare hooks presented to the fish. It must not be forgotten that

> Though gudgeons strike
> At the bare hook and bait alike,
> The wily trout regardless lie,
> Till art like nature sends the fly.

The rodster before us is an adept at this particular branch of the art of fly-fishing. His rod is very pliable, as is necessary; and providing his gut and tackle are of the finest description, he will do some execution before nightfall.'

Whilst we have been taking observations the fish have turned out from their hidden haunts and sheltered nooks, attracted by the ever-increasing show of mayflies, which flutter upon the surface of the water. Without waiting to see the luck of our ideal rodster, we hasten onwards until our favourite swim is reached. Here the tackle is speedily arranged, fine double hooks mounted back to back upon the finest stained gut, being attached to the extremity of our treble-X fine lashes. A live Drake is now placed upon the larger or uppermost of the two hooks, the hook being inserted in one side of the haunch forming the shoulder, which will admit of its maintaining a natural position when thrown into the water. And now we commence. But stay! your rod, being not made specially for the purpose, will be found too stiff and difficult to use successfully. We must first remedy this little, though serious matter. This small piece of fine lead wire will work the oracle if rolled round the tip of the top. 'There, how does that feel? Rather limpy? Take an inch or so of wire off then. Now it is all right, everything that could be wished, in fact. Now let's at it! Bring round the rod over the left shoulder, taking especial care not to whisk or whip off the fly. Now that was done very nicely indeed, and if it only had reached that fish over there, it would doubtless have been appreciated, as it in all justice deserved. Again, "up he comes". Strike! Right! You have him this time; "handle him gently, treat him with care" – slightly parodying Tom Hood. Take him a little below there to the shallow and land him or he will damage our sport hereabouts. That was very prettily done; sharp for another fly; here, you have it upon your coat; the very air is getting thick with flies. Ah! the sun is now obscured by passing vapours; stay your hand; now for the artificial. Art before nature, when there is a lively chance of its being successful. Here we have our floating favourite, the Canadian wood-duck-winged Drake, with hollow wheaten straw body, let's have him on. Now for business. Away surges the line, the further extremity of which no sooner touches the water than it is seized, and you have an antagonist who, in the tug which immediately ensues, proves worthy of your steel. The first terrific wrench he gives the rod and tackle as he dashes majestically away, shows him to be the tyrant of the length hereabouts. Did you not courteously *give* to his wild and indignant rush with faint reserve, the fight would be brought to an abrupt conclusion, for had your tackle thrice the strength it has in reality, grim force would be utterly futile. Play upon him by placing a heavy strain upon the rod, allow him to steal his lengths heavily, and more heavily, in his frantic efforts to escape, ever keeping a lookout for mischief, such as sunken timber, roots and sticks, to avoid which the heaviest strain the line is capable of standing must be put upon him, or he will prove victor, and will vanish with his spoils, which, though they may desperately encumber him, are not to be recovered; consisting of several yards of choice gut, and perhaps your last artificial. Exercise, therefore, your judgement and ingenuity, and his natural cunning will be put to rout. Time is no especial object in a fight of this description; every waning minute is a minute gained; the heavier the fish the longer the time to be expended over him. According to the poundage of a trout, as a rule, the sport he gives extends over an equal number of minutes, though, in a case like this, each seems an hour.' These disjointed sentences escape us as the scene is prolonged. Now, however, our captive's spirit is broken, his golden broadside lies athwart the silvery stream; and as he is 'limp as a log', you slowly tug him ashore. 'Don't present arms with that net, but keep it out of sight until his tail end can be got at first. Capital! There! Safe at last, a three-and-a-half-pounder if an ounce; small danger of your eclipsing this if you fish for a week. But now is the prime time of the whole season, the fish are all out and feeding, therefore it is the time for the angler to weed out heavy fish, whose cannibal propensities are exemplified the more weekly, monthly and yearly, until the water near their haunt is entirely depopulated. Let us see how's the enemy? 2.15 p.m. You will extract a heavy pannier before dinner if you labour against time; though the fun may furiously thicken, don't retain more than your fill.'

Personally speaking we make a practice of drawing the line at the lid of the creel, all conquests afterwards being relinquished as soon as effected. This rule, humane reader, we would commend to your acceptance in all exceptionally favourable circumstances, whenever practicable.

Should the weather prove fine, and favoured with warm sun, the flies will appear a few days earlier in each locality, but will terminate a week or so before their wonted time. The genial weather and warm temperature of the water admit of their attaining maturity almost simultaneously; and in these circumstances, it naturally follows that their stay will be more limited. Chub are bold risers at the mayfly, and after the close time, that is about the last week of the Drake, much diversion may be derived from Mr Leatherhead. Grayling and all coarse fish come in season on the 16th of June. The small flies, when numerous, tempt them from the slow-running deeps to the rapids or shallows, where they congregate in shoals, being a gregarious fish. The Little Chap and Black Gnat – both very small flies – are usually picked off by them in preference to the Duns, Spinners, Oak Fly, or what not, that may be plentiful. We have frequently counted eight or ten fine fellows rising within the compass of a few yards, while at the same time there has not been another fish rising up- or downstream. Under these circumstances, it will be obvious to all that great care is necessary in 'playing' the fish, for should the rodster land his fish in a reckless or clumsy manner, his chances of hooking a second will be exceedingly small. The best way to land a grayling, under the above circumstances, is to keep a gentle pull on the rod, and let the fish bolt down to the bottom of the water for some distance below where he rose, where he may be safely bagged. Grayling may be taken in the latter part of June with the Honey-Dun and Mulberry Bumble, Little Chap and small Midges. The rod, like the line and gut, should be fine; an ordinary one-handed fly rod, in good play, is decidedly the best, as with it you will often feel the fish in time to hook him; whereas with a less pliable tool you will feel nothing, save perchance a stake or a root. An hour or so at daybreak will, at this season of the year, seldom fail to yield capital remuneration in the way of sport, as, during the warmer weather, numbers of insects fall upon the water in the dark hours, and are taken by the fish as soon as they are discernible each morning. This is a wrinkle.

For a week or ten days after the Green Drake has disappeared the trout lie dormant in the deeps; until again hunger-bitten they disdain small food, but after the lapse of this time, they leave the stills and return to the shallows and rapids.

The Oak Fly is really invaluable to the fly-fisher in June, after the Drake season. This fly has the form somewhat of a Bluebottle, and the colour of the Sand Fly, the body being more slender than that of

the former, and ribbed with black. This is a good fly to dib with in a
style similar to the Mayfly (see page 192). Towards evening, after
sundown, the Red and Golden Spinners are generally on the water in
great force, at intervals here and there, mostly near weirs, bridges or
overhanging trees and bushes, where they may be seen whirling in
clouds. The trout are in better condition at the latter part of the
month than at any other part of the year, a small half-pound fish
proving as strong and vigorous as a fish double the weight a month
or two earlier or later. The extraordinary fattening qualities of the
heavy ephemera are mainly instrumental in effecting the change.

ᘐ

July The fish are now to be found in the small eddies and small
streams behind large stones, sunken rocks, or any other impediment,
in and by the sides of rapid streams. The Golden, July and Pale
Evening Duns and the Pale Evening White (shades of the Ephemera
Olive) will predominate. The Spinners, especially the Golden, are
very numerous, as are also the Midges and the Grass Moths.

This month is perhaps the most difficult to fish successfully during
the whole season. We often meet with young inexperienced anglers
during a long sultry July day, who flog industriously from 'early
morn till dewy eve', meeting with but faint encouragement. Fine
weather would seem to act as a magnet to draw the uninitiated to the
waterside. For the special guidance of such, we append a few brief
instructions as to the plan of procedure. To commence at daybreak, a
cast of flies similar to the dead ones seen upon the water beneath the
overhanging boughs of bushes, trees, etc., should be used over the
moving fish before breakfast, when it is no uncommon thing to find
the fish rise until the dead flies are picked off. During midday it is
of small use whipping the waters, unless the day be windy, wet or
cloudy; in these circumstances a cast of 'artificials' corresponding
with the 'naturals' then upon the water will be found to take. In the
event of the weather being hot and oppressive, use the Red Palmer
Caterpillar, of which more anon. At sunset small flies may again be
resorted to. The evening rise after a seasonable day at this period is a

sight worth seeing upon any well-stocked water. During and after twilight the Caterpillar, Dun Cut, Moths, Coachman, and any of the large trout flies contained in the fly-book, will be found most deadly. In concluding, we may state that, provided with suitable tackle, the fault lies with the rodster if no sport is obtained.

In the middle of the day, during the whole of this month, small blacks are frequently numerous; both trout and grayling feed upon them when on in sufficient strength. These tribes of blacks are almost invisible in most lights, and especially so when on the water. Whenever the fish are rising at these minute specks of life, it is almost vain to present anything else to their notice. The tantalising effects of this insect upon the temper of the fisherman has caused it to be stigmatised as the 'angler's plague', the pests themselves being little larger than a grain of mustard seed, closely resembling the appearance of a minute ball of soot, the wings so filmy as to be almost indistinguishable to the naked eye. This is the black gnat of the naturalist; the gnat of the fisherman is a much larger insect. The term gnat is usually associated with the troublesome insect whose habitual tendency would appear to be to plague and annoy the human race. The fly-dresser's gnat is usually of quite a different species, being of wondrously increased dimensions, more often resembling the common house-fly rather than the gnat. The fisherman's Black Gnat proper is a fly a little less than the Iron Blue, and should never be dressed larger. The artificial 'plague' is ingeniously contrived by a fine-point strand of black ostrich herl; but the hook used being too small to be effective for anything except grayling or small trout, we can scarcely commend their use. It may be an artistic feat to land a fish through the instrumentality of an artificial of this description, when attached to gut collars as fine as human hair, but the predominating chance of breakages, and the uncertainties, over which the fly-fisher exercises little or no control, of unsafely hooking, etc., cause us to ignore these, adopting in preference a safe-sized hook and fly, viz., the Little Chap. This is somewhat less than the angler's Black Gnat, and is dressed buzzy, and with this the fish's chance of hooking and holding are largely increased. There are some fly-fishers who care less about landing fish than hooking and turning them; to such as these, as a matter of course, a more correct copy is preferred.

About the middle of this month the Wren Tail appears, and on hot days often in large numbers. Being a land insect it is of much consequence to the angler in calm weather. There are always, through the season, a variety of 'oddlings' about, which, as a rule, affect neither fish nor fisherman, especially when seasonable flies prevail. Favourable weather at this part of the year for the fly implies brisk breezes, dull cloudy skies or sharp showers. The evening rise after a hot, dry, sultry day is nevertheless a famous time for sport, the fish usually rising vigorously until after twilight. The flies that have risen and hidden in the foliage fringing the river's bank during the day, turn out immediately the power of the sun begins to wane. From the natural position of the fish in clear water, they have every advantage of position, and faculty for distinguishing differences the most trivial between one fly and another; and often is the angler nonplussed in his endeavours to arrive at the precise thing absorbing their attention. A valuable aid at these times we have always found in the use of a small glass-bottomed drinking horn, as in the froth and foam that is found in quiet corners, at points where the water eddies round, drowned specimens of what are monopolising the attention of the fish are sure to be discovered. Whenever the trout are not to be drawn to the surface, owing to the scarcity of surface food, there is for the fly-fisher a rarely failing method of procuring sport by means of the Red Palmer Caterpillar. The way we use it is to cast it precisely the same as the fly, at the extremity of a nine-feet gut lash, in which fineness and strength are combined. This done, and all being in readiness, the mounted cast is delivered with more than ordinary care, a couple of yards or so above any fish that may be on the lookout for what the stream brings forth. In comparatively still and clear water, this style of angling excels most from a genuine sportsman's point of view, as each movement of the fish is plainly visible to the angler. The lure should be slightly worked by a wrist movement, just sufficient to open and shut the feather fibres. When the artificial has passed the fish the operation must be repeated; and fish, especially large ones, are more often than not killed after a certain amount of attention in this matter. We have often creeled a trout, grayling, salmon or chub after casting twelve, fifteen and even twenty times, the bait being subjected to an all round inspection each time of its appearance. It is thought by some that by this repetition of casts and workings the fish finally becomes eager, under the impression that from the constant succession of baits they are becoming numerous. Be this as it may, that the fish do take this bait not only in these, but in a variety of other circumstances, is now an established fact, placed beyond all dispute. We have personally used this lure for more than forty years, and can fully testify as to its killing powers when properly presented. By its use the fly-fisher is enabled to pursue his sport at any time of the day (or night) when the fish are not rising, and all ordinary means fail. This bait was originated by a famous Dove angler some half-century or so ago. This worthy, however, assiduously kept the thing private, and it was finally divulged in a purely accidental manner. Mr Professor having, during a fly-fishing match, through a laxity of vigilance, left a type of the unknown mystic lure upon a twig on the opposite bank, his rival, upon whom the action had not been lost, being in the vicinity, took the opportunity of solving a problem that had perplexed him and other fishermen for several seasons as to the nature of an artificial capable of killing almost unfailingly, and that, too, when all ordinary artificials were all but useless. The discoverer referred to was the writer from whom the author of the *Fly-Fisher's Entomology*, and the general public, obtained the secret of the mid-water fly. As Mr Ronalds points out, the artificial in question is a copy of the *Arctia caja*, or Tiger Moth.[*] In Scotch and Irish waters it is equally killing when dressed somewhat larger as it is in the well-whipped streams of England. To both the salmon and trout fisher it forms a sort of auxiliary in reserve, convenient in otherwise trying circumstances.

ॐ

---

[*] more commonly known as the Woolly Bear

August During this month the most favourable days for fly-fishing are when the weather is cloudy and the water's surface is slightly ruffled by a breeze of wind. As the weather usually prevailing is similar to that of the month preceding, the instructions there given apply equally to the present month. Upon clear sunny days the fish will be found under the shade of the bushes, on the sides of the banks. The Caterpillar, both as a midday and night fly, may be used with success, seasonable weather prevailing. The best evening flies are the Green-Tail or Grannum, Golden Dun, the Spinners, and the Intermediate. The last is a representation of the fluttering attitude of a dun during the transformation scene, when it slips from its old covering, or skin, and reappears more delicately graceful and fragile than before. The fish are especially partial to the up-winged naturals when in this temporary transitory stage, for which there may be many reasons, the most important being that the metamorphosis always, or nearly so, takes place upon the top of the water, and therefore within reach of the feeding fish, which, it is well known, show a marked partiality for deformed or distressed prey, inasmuch that they will seize the sickly little fish, or a copy of one, from amongst a shoal of perfect fish, almost any one of which was in their power.

The Red and Black Ants, Grey Gnat and Wren-Tail are to be seen upon the water on bright days, the small flies being then abundant. These are essentially midday flies, the larger species being numerous towards evening. When the fish are feeding upon small 'naturals', the contents of the stomach of the fish taken should be examined, so as to ascertain correctly the taking fly. Sometimes this is discerned by an inspection of the tongue only, especially when the fish are feeding well.

About the 10th of this month, the August shade of the Large Browns (August Dun) comes upon the water; north of the Midlands it is much later. This fly, in common with the duns, seeks the shelter of the neighbouring foliage immediately upon rising from the bed of the river, venturing forth about sunset. This, and the light Turkey Brown shade, are to be used with signal success until the fisherman can no longer see to manage his line. The March Brown, dressed a size or so larger than those usually used this side the border, is the best trouting fly throughout Scotland, being a standard killer upon all its waters, excepting the Tay and Tweed, for which rivers the ordinary southern flies are adapted. In 1864, Lord Erskine took the heaviest take of trout of the season upon the Tweed, with the small Black Gnat.

A heavy shower often has a very beneficial effect upon the rodster's sport. We have frequently seen young anglers, at the preliminary drops of an impending shower, rush for the nearest shelter, whilst the descending raindrops, beating down myriads of insects upon the water, allured the fish from their customary haunts to the surface, where in these circumstances they are to be readily taken by the persevering angler. Directly the favourable and friendly rain has ceased to fall, Mr Novice assiduously recommences to flog the stream, inwardly congratulating himself, doubtless, at having been so fortunate in evading an unpleasant experience.

Amongst the flies numerous in the evening of sultry days, the spinners figure conspicuously, from the Great Red of the heavy browns to the prim little creatures of the Iron Blue order. The fish are usually all life from sunset till dark, and after this, too, when the moon rises; thus, if the angler is not busy too, in all probability the fault lies with himself. This month is the best in the whole season for minnow fishing in brooks and rapid-running waters. For information upon this subject we refer our readers to 'Spinning for Trout' (Chapter Seven). The largest trout are generally found feeding at some distance from very deep water encumbered by tree roots or large stones; sometimes the bank is hollowed under an old tree root for yards, by the constant washing of the water. When disturbed, the trout will make for these retreats at a rapid pace, and should the unfortunate angler allow the fish once to get to his hold when hooked, he will to a certainty lose his capture and imperil his tackle. Much is to be learned, therefore, *when the water is fine and low*, as then observations may be taken as to the lay of the river's bed, etc.

September Grayling are now rapidly coming into condition. Seasonable weather prevailing, good sport is afforded by these fish wherever prevalent. Trout and grayling take the fly in an entirely different way; the former, as a rule, comes up boldly to meet the fly as it floats downstream, whilst the grayling seldom rises at a fly until it has passed over or close by him. This is owing to the singular formation of the mouth of this fish, the upper part of which, projecting over the bottom lip, incapacitates it from closing upon the fly when before it, as is habitual with the trout. The grayling being gregarious, it is of the utmost importance that each fish should be landed quietly and carefully, with the least possible disturbance of the water. In order to accomplish this satisfactorily, the hooked fish should be headed downstream, whenever practicable, to the nearest available spot for landing. The angler who has been accustomed to whip for trout upon the waters of a small lake or pool will know perfectly well how to accomplish this. To be a successful grayling fisher, it is essential to have a thorough command of the rod, to have a sensitive touch, a quick eye and a gentle hand. The secret of success, in fact, as in other branches of the art, lies in the acquirement of certain details, which together constitute proficiency. First, the art of throwing should be thoroughly understood and acquired. This rule is imperative, as the least awkward movement will 'knock the fish off the feed'. It should ever be remembered that the eye of the grayling is even quicker and keener than that of the trout, though his cupidity is greater.

Next in importance ranks 'striking'. This requires a quick hand and eye; and if either one or the other be in any way defective, the angler should not strike at all, but should let the fish hook himself. Striking forms one of the most fertile sources of loss and disaster that exists in the modern method of fly-fishing. This is particularly exemplified in the case of grayling, they being, as an old writer quaintly expresses it, 'excessively tender about the chaps', and a very slight motion of the wrist is ample to drive home the small hook. It is here that quickness of sight and tenderness of touch are called into play, in the absence of which requisites the delicate tackle, or the hold of the hook, and sometimes even a portion of the jaw of the hooked fish, will be broken away by an impetuous rodster. Great care is therefore essential in this matter.

Whenever the grayling are not rising, unlike the trout, they congregate in considerable numbers at the bottom of deep holes; but when there is a good number of flies upon the water, they quickly leave the deeps, and will be found in the slo-running streams, more especially where the water averages a depth of three to four feet. Here they rise freely, so long as the supply of flies is unfailing; but upon these quitting the surface of the water, the fish gradually retire again to the still deeps. The best flies to use for grayling are the Grey Palmer, Willow and Needle Fly, the Little Pale Blue and seasonable shades of the Olive Dun order, which are all more or less numerous at this time, if seasonable weather prevails. The first named is taken freely when the common Wood and House Flies are stricken with cold, and are carried upon the water by every gust of wind. Every naturalist knows that these flies go blind in this and the following month, but they don't all know that they furnish food for fish. Father Izaak used to make this fly from grey badger's hair: he terms it the Hearth Fly; but there is every reason for believing it to be the common House Fly. The inexperienced would naturally suppose that a copy of the insect at rest, in correct attitude, would be the thing to fish with; but owing to the incessant struggles of the 'natural' when on the water, this would practically prove a great mistake. Most land flies flutter conspicuously when upon the water, causing a ripple which is not infrequently taken for the rise of a fish. The Willow and Needle Flies are also great favourites with these fish, and when sufficiently prevalent are the centre of attraction for the time being. The Little Pale Blue (September shade of the Iron Blue), like all little ephemerals, is fully appreciated throughout the autumn. These flies appear upon bright days, and are general flies upon every trout and grayling stream. The temperature of the weather and water being now similar to that of May, the shades of duns common to that month are again prevalent and are useful for the capture of trout and grayling. The whole of the foregoing flies are seasonable 'naturals'. There may be days, however, upon which none of these may be out, when the fly-fisher has to fall back upon what are designated 'fancy' flies, the chief and foremost of which are the palmered-dressings, known as the Tassel Fly or Bumble. These are constructed in many shades, ranging from the blue-white ordinary dressing to the dark-furnace or black-red one. The Honey Dun, the Red and the Common Bumble are the best for autumn fishing. Tag-tailed artificials are also used to tempt the fastidious fish, being hackled flies with a tuft of wool or feather at the tail, after the fashion of a salmon fly; but fly-fishing for grayling cannot be said to be usually lucrative when the fish are not on the rise. The food of the grayling consists of aerial and aquatic insects and their larvae, small worms, grubs, etc. Amongst the contents of their stomachs are also small shells and pebbles; these latter, we doubt not, are taken up, as in the case of gallinaceous birds, to serve some digestive function.

In most rivers containing these fish they are not found in the higher portions; they seem to prefer the deeper waters, at the bottom of which they lie in the hot months, to avoid the effects of the high temperature of the atmosphere. Whenever the water is a little dis-coloured the fish will be on the move for food; a little inclement weather often does wonders in preparing the water and its inhabitants for the pursuit of sport; and the most favourable time for the tyro in fly-fishing for grayling is to repair to the river's bank when the water and weather are thus favourable. Grayling will frequently take a sunken fly upon the stills, ofttimes even when some considerable distance below the surface; but this method need never be resorted to when they care for surface feeding. Upon windy days the Cinnamon Fly is often found useful amongst the trout, which are as partial to the larger naturals as the grayling to the smaller ones. In genial weather it is of little use employing it, as although there may be thousands upon the grassy bank near the river, a smart breeze is needful to carry them upon the water within the reach of the fish. Clear, frosty nights tend to improve autumn fishing. They invigorate the grayling, causing them to fight gamely when hooked, which is the case with other fish seasonable in the colder season.

ॐ

October This month may be said to be the best in the year in which to fish for grayling, which are now in prime condition. These fish have acquired a reputation for being less wily, and therefore more easily deluded than trout. This may have originated from the fact of their being at times given, like the salmon, to take some gaudy combination resembling no living insect in creation. The angler who contemplates an excursion to the haunts of these fish, fully expecting to do much execution by such unnatural lures, will, nine hundred and ninety-nine chances to a thousand, be grievously disappointed; an odd brace, indeed, may be considered the average yield *per diem* of the nondescript artificials.

Our earnest endeavours have always been to put the novice in the way for thorough sport; and having this object in our mind's eye, we would impress upon the mind of such an one that, although in an exceptional way a fish now and again at rare intervals may be turned over by almost anything in the shape of an artificial, usually they are found to be more expert in discerning the points of difference between a natural and its copy than any trout that ever evaded hook. Their visual organs we believe to be superior to those of any other fish; for, although they habitually lie at the bottom of the water, they are not only greater adepts at fly-catching, but can discern the most trivial deficiency in colour of any imitation of what may be so monopolising their attention. Prodigious takes of these fish are often secured,* when fully upon the rise at the flies with which the water's surface is laden; but these are effected by an exercise of considerable proficiency and caution on the part of the rodster. The October shade of the Iron Blue Dun order, the April shade of the Olive Duns, together with the Willow and Needle Flies (small) and Grey Palmer, are the flies that

---

* Since the introduction of artificially hatched trout in well-nigh unlimited quantities in our rivers and their tributaries, these delicate fish appear to have become more local than was the case before. We see no reason why the artificial propagation of the grayling should not be followed more assiduously in conjunction with that of the trout.

will be found in this month. In unseasonable weather there are often a multiplicity of winged insects about, each species having but few representatives; in these circumstances the sunk-fly system may be practised with success. This is more particularly resorted to upon still deeps, when the cast of flies, after being thoroughly saturated, are allowed to sink some five inches beneath the water's surface. Here the rodster has to discern by the feel when a fish touches the lure. Grayling will often examine the fly in a very leisurely sort of manner before essaying finally to absorb it. A gentle hitch should always be given before taking the line from the water, as by that means fish are often killed that would otherwise be broken from and lost. It is also necessary to cast direct across stream, a few feet above the rising fish, instead of directly upstream, as in the case of the trout; as with a slack line the grayling are apt to reject the fly without being hooked, when under water especially. A gradual drawing motion, when not tempting the fish upon the surface, may be described, until the gut collar reaches the rodster's side of the river. The very largest fish take the fly in a remarkably quiet manner, therefore it is essential to give a slight feeling motion of the wrist at the least possible indication of a rise. A marked characteristic of the grayling is that he will often un-concernedly permit the lure to go by many times before closing upon it. This is exemplified in a very marked degree in grub-fishing,* when, after the bait has passed say nineteen times out of twenty, the twentieth by no means infrequently proves successful. The accredited theory is that the constant passage of the lure acts as a sort of ground bait in exciting the attention of the fish. Be it so or no, the fact remains that grayling are thus to be taken when not exactly upon the feed, and more especially the larger fish. Frosty nights and genial days bring the flies upon the water, and the delicately fastidious grayling upon the rise in a thoroughly healthful style; and if the angler fails then to do considerable execution, the fault most assuredly lies at home. One of the best day's grayling fishing we ever experienced was on the Dove, a few miles above Uttoxeter. The water's surface was plentifully

---

* Of this a separate description has been given on pages 93–6.

besprinkled with the October shades of the Iron Blue, every grayling upon the length seemed to have left its accustomed haunt in the bed of the water to feed upon them, and as these fish, in the lower portions of the river, predominate largely over the trout, the few rods that happened to be out were doing heavy work when once furnished with presentable 'artificials'. Two fish were now and again taken at the same cast. This scene was prolonged for several hours; a sudden atmospheric change, however, finally caused the almost instantaneous retreat of the flies from the water's surface, the repast of the fish and our sport being as suddenly brought to an abrupt conclusion. The produce of a couple of neighbouring rods were to be enumerated by the dozen; not only their basket, but their empty provision receptacles were filled with silvery grayling of all sizes upwards of half a pound. For our own part, we had captured at an early part of the day sufficient to fill the vacuum in our pannier, and for the remainder and greater part of the time had returned all subsequent captures. Such days as these are ever to be looked back upon as memorable reminiscences, and at the end of a long life of activity, cannot fail to form food for pleasing reflection.

꒜

November As the season advances, the grayling will be found a few yards above and below the deep holes, where they will rise when the flies are on the water, even in severe weather; indeed it is by no means an uncommon thing to find grayling taking well during a severe frost, when the line resembles an extended icicle, for like Jack, the grayling are in the very zenith of healthful vigour in the cold season of the year. When the world of vegetation is lifeless, and the whole landscape is submerged by an arctic wave, no sport can possibly be more exhilarating, or more conducive to health than grayling fishing in these circumstances. The rodster uses grass-hoppers or hoppers of another shade before and after midday, filling up the interval with the fly, say from twelve noon to two p.m. A pleasing variety is thus afforded, which seldom fails to meet with due appreciation on the part of the fish. The flies to use, even in midwinter, should be chosen from those last 'on' in the latter part of the fall, as when old Sol makes a feeble effort to rise in the heavens, a few insects are almost invariably induced to leave their retreat to meet death, either in the jaws of the fish or by the nipping wind of nightfall. A capital fancy fly throughout the grayling season is an artificial we term the Winter Dun. The body of this is formed of flat gold or silver, neatly laid on; legs, light blue hen's hackle; wings fieldfare. This fly should be fished point. We can commend this before all the fancy fly species for the allurement of grayling in either clear or discoloured water. In the early winter season the flies prevalent in February will be out; the sombre-hued dun of that month and, on fine days, the Cockwinged Dun will be seen about; and as flies appear merely in nominal numbers, the grayling exhibit great eagerness in taking what comes within their ken. Should the day prove cloudy, with wind or showers of rain, the Light Bumble will be found deadly, as will also the Grey Palmer. Upon these occasions the Cinnamon Fly is often to be observed on and about the water, and when this is so a copy may be placed as dropper[*] with advantage, as, though grayling as a rule prefer small flies, the big fish will often rise to larger lures. In clear water the fish will sometimes be observed to double back, after cautiously rising to the surface, without closing on the fly presented. This is often owing to the tackle being too strong and coarse. We would impress upon the tyro in the art of 'flying' for grayling the absolute necessity of the very finest bottom-tackle, ere he can pursue his sport with any degree of satisfaction. As in trout fishing, whenever the water is slightly discoloured the chances of sport with the grayling are enhanced, as then the fish are on the move. In these circumstances the novice, providing he can put out a moderate line, will achieve wonders; but upon the other hand, when the day is calm and clear,

---

[*] The reasons for employing this fly as 'bob' are simple. It being a full-winged fly, a good sized hook may be used, which, being well feathered, is more buoyant on the water, and more natural, and you can make almost certain of hooking every fish that rises at it.

with no friendly breeze to detract from the transparency of the stills of the limpid deeps, the proficient's best exertions and most accomplished skill is called as much into request in November as with trout in July.

By way of conclusion we would observe that whenever mist is observed to rise from the surface of the water, either at nightfall in the warmer months, or at any part of the day in late autumn, all prospects of sport are to be considered annulled. However much a descending or descended cloud may enhance sport, certain it is that an *ascending* one infallibly indicates to the observant mind that further attempts at allurement would be futile, the fish being off the feed for the time being.

CHAPTER FIFTEEN

Salmon and Sea-Trout Fishing

The Salmon; Sea and Bull Trout; Sewin; Salmon Fishing as a
Sport; The Rod, Line and Reel; How to Use them; Jiggering and
Sulky Fish; Salmon Flies; Spinning, etc.

Before entering into the practical part of this ponderous subject, we think a few remarks as to the varieties of salmon, sea or white trout, and other andamorous fish, may not only be necessary, but may also serve to supply a deficiency hitherto conspicuous in angling works.

In the ichthyological classification of migratory Salmonidae much difference exists, the ordinary method followed by naturalists in determining species proving inadequate. So innumerable are the variations, that the sub-generic group (Salmones) are for the most part named after the water they inhabit, as Galway sea trout, Tay salmon, Shannon salmon, etc., etc. The differences between these consist both in size, form and colour and are due to the following amongst other causes: first, the varying properties of the water in different localities; second, the complications implied by inter-breeding – an extremely fertile source of difficulty, producing, as it does, endless changes in detail amongst the Salmonoids; and thirdly, the varieties dependent upon age and sexual development.

Salmon proper attain much greater weight and dimensions than the sewin, sea or white types, and when in condition are also distinguished by outward form and colour, in both of which we deem it unequalled by any other order, family or species of fish. The sea and bull trout – the former shorter and broader than salmon proper – are distinctively marked by a quantity of black spots, which, when the fish is cooked, become more vivid. There is also a marked absence of that beautiful fiery bronze natural to the well-conditioned salmon; and lastly, we may state that, if not distinguishable from the genuine species in its outward aspect, its inferior edible qualities should render it easily discernible. In the north the sea trout is equally abundant with the salmon, and large quantities find their way to the southern towns, where they are retailed by the fish dealers, whose boisterous cry of 'Salmon without any gammon!' is heard whenever a fresh instalment arrives. In many cases these people have been unwittingly 'gammoned' themselves, their customers, nevertheless, being the ultimate dupes. From the fisherman's point of view, the sea trout is equal to the finest grilse that ever ascended Tay or Tweed, exceeding, as he does, for gameness and pertinacity every other British fish. The bull trout ascend their native rivers in April and May, their first appearance at any distance from salt water being immediately after an early spring flood. These are for the most part young fish, ranging from three to five, and occasionally six pounds. The oldest and best fish ascend in great numbers in November and December, ranging from six to twenty pounds in weight. In some localities the term bull trout is erroneously applied to the sea or white trout; nor is the error confined to the illiterate, some authors of eminence having endorsed this inaccuracy. Mr Frank Buckland was convinced of the fallacy of this when he penned the following: 'It is supposed by some that the sea trout and bull trout are identical. I know the bull trout very well; indeed, I could pick him out amongst a thousand other Salmonidae. I am certain, therefore, that there is a difference between the ordinary sea trout and bull trout.' From our own observations we are led to think that the bull species are hybrids between the salmon and sea trout (*S. trutta*). The external difference between the salmon and bull trout is much less than between salmon and sea trout, both in point of colour and size, thirteen to fifteen pounds being the average weight. The sea or salmon trout, upon the other hand, seldom attain more than six or seven pounds weight. They abound in nearly every beck and burn, loch and river of Scotland and Ireland, and are readily taken with the fly. We have already adverted to their gameness: the bold dash, wild leap and game fight are more or less exemplified wherever they may be found. The rivers most noted for these fish are the Spey, Don, Tay and Tweed. The peal, or salmon peal, as it is termed, is the grilse stage of these fish, as it is also of the Sewin.

∽

Sewin (*S. Cambricus*) though chiefly found in Wales is also abundant in several southern rivers of England. This fish is closely allied to the sea, white or salmon trout. It has the delicate colouring of the salmon parr, the prevailing hue being a pale slate blue, which graduates from the dull black upon the back to the pure chaste white of the breast, the broad expanse of the side being profusely spotted with black, and occasionally red; the latter about the lateral line. Sewin, in common with the whole species, are subject to great variety of tint, the action of freshwater causing them, after a protracted stay, to assume somewhat the colour of the ordinary brown trout. Commercially the sewin is not nearly so important a fish as the salmon trout. Its flesh is generally preferred as an article of diet, but it is not so plentiful as its northern relative. The whole migratory body of the Salmonidae family flourish infinitely better in the more northern than in temperate regions. The salmon of Norway, and even so far north as Iceland, attain much greater dimensions than the natives of more southern latitudes. The sewin is far less vigorous than other members of the same family, and when its instincts prompt it to ascend the rivers to attain the requisite medium temperature of water and atmosphere to insure the vitality of its eggs, is more easily obstructed in its passage.

∽

Bull Trout have the most hardy temperament, being more vigorous than the salmon, and owing to this, generally succeed in reaching and occupying the best and most favourable spawning beds before the salmon put in an appearance.

∽

With the **Salmon** we have dealt under the heading of 'Habits and Haunts of Fish' (Chapter One). From a piscatory point of view, it is a truly noble fish, and affords splendid sport, as every angler will corroborate who has had the pleasure of landing a good lively fish after a hard and heavy fight. Upon salmon fishing as a sport much might be written: the salmon fisher is a sportsman of an almost distinct species from ordinary anglers. The superiority of this game fascinates its followers, and prompts them to ignore, not only all other and inferior branches of the gentle craft, but by no means infrequently other field sports and national diversions for the pursuit of the salmon when in season. The true sportsman, however, pursues his peculiar vocation arduously, zealously and spiritedly, and whether it be Nimrod, ramrod or fishrod, for the time being his whole soul is thrown into the pursuit. Salmon fishers now wander far afield for pastures new; some enthusiastic sportsmen make the pursuit of the salmon their one object in life, roaming over the vast area of the European and American continents, and of late years the boundaries of these have been overstepped, since the virgin waters of the antipodes have proved so fertile. The popularity of salmon fishing has increased something like a hundred per cent during the last half-century. Since the opening up of the Scotch Highlands by the royal steam route, branch extensions have rendered districts, once remote, comparatively easy of access, and a part of the brief vacation of the most eminent statesmen and professional men and others, forming the brain power and intellect of the nation, is spent annually in the northern wilds, the royal emporium for the sportsman. Here in the

> Land of brown heath and shaggy wood,
> Land of the mountain and the flood,

the roving disciple of the rod wanders up to the head of the river, into the heart of the mountains, sometimes cheered by the pleasant converse of a few true men and honest anglers like himself, often alone with nature in her fairest or wildest loveliness. Solitary or social, his appreciation of all the sweet charms of wild nature is ever keen and lively. Ubiquitous even as the *Murray*-bearing British tourist is now the rod-carrying British angler. For his enthusiasm Scotland's most extortionate hotels have no terrors, nor do Norway's ruggedest solitudes and coarsest fare deter him from seeking the lordly salmon by many a 'fjord' and 'foss'.

Before passing on to the practical part of the art, it will be necessary to enumerate the chief articles requisite to a tolerable equipment.

ᔑ

The **Rod** first claims our attention. The remarks anent the choice of a rod for fly-fishing – as also winch and line for small-stream fishing – apply equally to salmon fishing. The lake and large-river implement is of necessity of greater dimensions. The Castle Connell style of rod is tolerably good for some waters, but the small 'grip' or hand-hold afforded by the slender stock has a very cramping effect when the rod is wielded industriously for a lengthened period. The six-feet joints, with the delicate spliced extremities, are very liable to damage whilst travelling. Greenheart is undoubtedly the best wood for heavy work. There are, however, good and bad varieties of every description of wood without exception. Thus we have indifferent Greenheart, Wahaba, Maho and Locust, just as often, and perhaps more so than not, made up into both salmon and trout rods; but the most deplorable error, and the one to be most assiduously avoided, is *cross-grained joints*. There are individuals careless and unprincipled enough to make up short or cross-grained wood in most rods made by them. This defect is most noticeable in coloured or japanned articles. The steel-centred salmon rod is a weapon several feet shorter than the usual old-style lengths, a rod of fourteen being quite equal to an all-wood tool of sixteen and a half feet.

ᔑ

The **Line** and **Reel** need but little comment. The former should be from one hundred to one hundred and twenty yards in length for all round lake and river work. Salmon lines, as well as trout, are plaited taper, both double and single. Personally, we prefer a straight line, no matter of what material it may consist. The fine ends are worn and frayed by the constant friction, becoming soft, limp and waterlogged, whilst the thicker parts of the line, not coming in for a fair share of the work, remain sound and good. The weakest part of a line, always in constant casting or spinning, gets the twist and turn, and is thus the more readily frayed away. The hair-and-silk, cotton-cord and plaited-hemp lines are inferior both in point of strength and durability to silk, plaited and prepared to resist the action of the water and friction. The new Acme line, as we have already pointed out, is an advance on the waterproof silk lines. The nuisance of a bad or defective line can only be equalled by a defective reel. The salmon reel should be bronzed, and when made with check, this action should be of steel. Brass cogs are a delusion, being simply useless for heavy wear. It is no uncommon thing for an ordinary reel of this description to get completely deranged, through the non-durability of the centre parts. This is particularly noticeable in Indian Mahseer fishing, in which the wear of the winch is heavier still. The advantage of the centre stock reel is yet more exemplified in the larger tools. The convenient catching place for the loose line, always afforded by the side-fitting winches, is removed; indeed, we have equal confidence in the centre butt winch doing away with a fertile source of annoyance and loss, as we previously had in respect to the revolving plate, when we perfected that improvement, as compared with the old windlass handle, which is now being discarded in favour of our improvement. A small hole should be pierced in the revolving plates of large reels to admit of oil being inserted when needed.

کی

How to use Rod, Reel and Line This is a difficult matter to deal with on paper. Observation and practical instruction are so superior as means for conveying knowledge, as compared with mere verbal instruction, that we recommend the novice to make a combination of the two, by placing himself under the guidance of an experienced salmon fisher, if his circle of acquaintance embraces one.

Long-casting ranks amongst the foremost of the attributes to success and proficiency; and when some twenty-five yards can be put out tolerably straight the rodster may congratulate himself upon his having overcome the leading difficulty in the beginner's path. When a cast can be made fairly well, the knack of striking, etc., follows as a natural consequence. This is readily acquired from that best of tutors – experience. We have invariably found that if the loss of fish and tackle does not instil knowledge and suggest improvement, other expedients will be equally futile. The rules already laid down for casting in the case of trout and grayling hold good for salmon fishing, though with this difference, that the implements and tackle being of heavier calibre, a greater distance is to be attained by the action and impetus given to the rod and line. Precision is also of equal consequence, as the rodster has to cast when the fish are in a sportive humour, within the 'ring' of a rise, just the same as when in quest of smaller quarry. This requires a considerable amount of application to accomplish at a good distance; but just as the experienced cricketer handles the bat with tact and skill, so must the salmon fisher wield the rod; proficiency in both is the reward of constant practice, and of that only.

Some anglers acquire a certain right-, and in some instances left-hand cast, and acting up to an orthodox system, swing without deviation upon all occasions. The thing to do is, as we have elsewhere stated, to adapt oneself to the situation at all times, and learn to handle the tools so as to cast in any direction requisite to reach the fish. It is an endless source of pleasure to the adept to test his powers of casting under more than ordinarily difficult circumstances. He well knows that assiduous application to this matter is repaid by exceptional sport, and that too when but little is doing in the well-thrashed open.

When a fish is hooked, the variety of expedients resorted to is frequently considerable, one of the most common being that of 'jiggering'. In this a side-to-side motion is described by the line in the water. This is caused by the fish endeavouring to *rake or rub out the hook in the bed of the water* or upon a flag or submerged stone. It is believed by some to be caused by the mere shaking of the fish's head in mid-water, but this is pure nonsense. We have watched the action of jiggering fish in clear water often, at almost every angle, and have generally found that a continued 'jigger' bodes ill for the consummation of the capture. During a late visit to the Hebrides we experienced a rather striking instance of this. Upon the occasion in question we had hooked a good salmon, but at the expiration of two-thirds of an hour had not succeeded in landing, owing to our peculiar position. We had hooked our fish whilst bank fishing upon a perpendicular rock, some six or eight feet above the surface of the water. During the greater part of this time the salmon had been active, so much so, that more than once our fine gear was in imminent danger of being severed. After these plunges and wild determined rushes to and fro had subsided, our quarry finally settled, in deep water, near the rock upon which we stood. There an unpleasant jiggering motion was described by the line. In this instance, the water being comparatively clear, the movements of the fish were plainly discernible some ten feet or so from its surface he was energetically rubbing his snout upon a jutting part of the rock, from right to left and left to right, without a moment's cessation. We ran paper down the line in the usual way, to no purpose, the exasperating 'rub-rub' still continuing. Donald, the keeper, had meanwhile set off to explore for pebbles, but even this chance was denied, and he returned, as he went, empty-handed. As a last desperate venture, our pocket key-ring was fixed on the line (it being split steel) and run down. No sooner was this accomplished than the fish dashed away towards the open. Now for the first time the thought struck us that if the fish was not taken our keys were irrecoverably lost. Regretting our impetuosity, we cautiously gave and took line as occasion required. The presence of the nose ring and jingling appendages, meanwhile, kept the fish in action. This, however, speedily told upon him, and finally he was safely gaffed in a more accessible situation. Since this occurred, we have had a number of small bright metal rings made, which we have found most useful for both sulky and jiggering fish.

Another frequent freak of the fish is to make for underneath the boat, when the angler occupies one; there the tackle is in danger of damage from the rough keel, even if the fisherman is quick enough to pass the rod's point around the stem or stern in time to avoid a dead wrench upon, and probable smash of, the tackle. The sulking propensities of salmon when hooked and wearied by futile efforts to escape are well-known traits of their character. It is very tantalising to await the pleasure of a stubborn fish of this description. There are instances upon record of anglers staying through the dark hours with a sulky fish. All that we would say further upon this subject is that the necessity of such a thing is entirely obviated by the use of any small metal contrivance that will serve to drop down the line to arouse the fish from its lethargy or persistent doggedness of disposition.

In river-fishing for salmon, every stream, pool and likely eddy should be well and carefully fished. When the gleam of a fish is discerned below the fly, and no rise ensues, a change of flies should be made. Salmon for fastidiousness stand unequalled. Upon certain days they take with avidity a certain kind of fly, whilst for some time afterwards it may be refused for another of totally different description. Upon the most frequented salmon waters peculiar flies are used of local notoriety. We do not believe, ourselves, in the hard and fast rules given as to this or that special dressing being infallibly successful upon any specified water, and on its uselessness upon another adjoining lake or river. The salmon fly is but a fanciful combination, arranged with a view to the general artistic effect; and as nature presents no model for man to imitate, the fanciful amalgamations of feathers, tinsel, fur and wool are closed upon by the sportive and capricious fish in a mere spirit of wantonness or because of its being novel. We have often (and we doubt not that a few of our readers have had similar experiences) surprised native rodsters by the effect of a *non*-observance of their given rules of procedure. A strange fly, whether it happens to be sombre or gay, frequently does wonders amongst these fickle fish. Change, in this respect, is far more effective in influencing the nett yield than can easily be credited.

Salmon flies exist in myriads of varieties, and to attempt to enumerate the whole of those in general esteem would be a needless task. The following are a few of the standard killers of universal repute:

the Jock Scot	the Wasp
the Black Dose	the Doctor
the Spey Dog	the Rainbow
the Butcher	the Captain
the Shannon	the Lightning
the Parson	the Blacker's Patterns
the Ranger	etc., etc.

In addition to the above, we commend the following: the Spanker, the Rob Roy, the Spartan, the Tam o' Shanter and the Mac Sporran, for a description of which see Salmon Fly-Making (pages 138-45). The impartiality of this fish towards any particular lure or class of artificials for all seasons and occasions is at a marked contrast with the pedantic partiality of many anglers, who pin their faith upon an odd fly or so that has happened to do something exceptional in their hands, it may be; but it is of small use trying to convince these of their error. Prejudice and obstinacy satisfy them that they are infallibly right. Whilst fishing some few years ago on Loch Nell, we took an exceptionally large salmon, whose habitual haunt was in one particular spot, near a submerged rock. Upon our return to the inn, the landlord eagerly enquired as to what part of the water he had been extracted from; and our capture proved to be an old acquaintance of his, a fish that had nevertheless cut his acquaintance very frequently according to his account. Though the form and dimensions of the fish greatly interested our worthy host, the fly that had been instrumental in his capture monopolised his chief attention. Ever after this event the landlord played the 'Spanker' without cessation or intermission. Subsequently, whenever the man was seen with a fish, the query, 'What fly?' was certain to elicit the reply, 'Spanker, sir!'; indeed, among the visitors, the virtues of the Spanker was so well worn a topic that the subject was finally suppressed at first scent.

Next in importance to the fly is undoubtedly the gut cast. Personally, we invariably use single gut of the strongest and best description, with a yard and a half of the same double and treble cable laid (i.e. twisted like the cable of a ship, which method ensures greater permanency in water), or plaited in taper form to serve as connecting foot line, between the reel line and gut lash. Round and sound single salmon gut, new and strong, we believe to be transcendently superior to anything hitherto discovered or applied to the piscatory purpose. Long and careful experimental experience upon well-fished waters – under conditions as far removed from those described by the eminent votary of modern science, Sir H. Davy, in his *Salmonidae*, as can be well imagined – has led to this conclusion; indeed, as with other and less important styles of angling, so with salmon fishing, needlessly strong tackle is open to deprecatory attack. It is unworthy the accomplished fisherman, and will with time be regarded with increasing discredit. For, though the advance achieved in the manipulation and skill in the use of salmon tackle has not for the latter half-century been significant, still its scope has been such as to inspire what may be termed the more scientific portion of the angling fraternity with bright hopes for the ultimate progress in refinement and utility of the implements employed by them, a progress which is assuredly already inaugurating. As anglers multiply, the laws of merit will assert their exacting influence gradually and surely, the force and combination of circumstances and changed conditions of sport will increasingly deter the habitually or preferentially indifferent angler from consummating the end in view. Artistic skill and exactitude of execution have yet more and more to exhibit their claims in practical issues and results to priority, and as in succeeding generations waters frequented by the Salmonidae family are more heavily and constantly whipped, the results indicated will be the more apparent. To return.

The rules given under another heading as regards the colour of gut under different conditions are equally applicable to salmon fishing. Under no circumstances should it be strongly stained, a faint and permanent dye should be employed, no matter what shade may be desired. Good gut is transparent, so should be the stain. We have seen casts black as ink (they frequently having been stewed in that commodity), stretched over the haunt of a salmon vainly, and because so vainly, persistently for a protracted period. Purblind fishermen but seldom meet with purblind fish; therefore, when a fish is seen to be hooked, fought and it may be safely gaffed by the next rod on the length, the temporary baffled disciple of the rod strolls or steers for the scene of slaughter to be in at the death. Arrived here he plies the usual query, What fly? which elicits a courteous reply, together with perchance a fly of the kind killing. The black lash is again whirled away, and is allowed to stretch its full length over all the most likely places, till finally the nonplussed and unsuspecting victim grows irritable. The mood intensifies until, in a fit of exasperation, the climax is reached, the deleterious lash is snapped through its having caught away back in the rear in making an exceptionally and recklessly long throw. Another and less objectionable one is now installed in its stead, and a consequent change in the sport prospects forthwith ensues. A fast sky-blue hue is the shade best adapted for the generality of waters. From the position of the fish beneath, the medium connecting the fly and the reel line should show small contrast with either the blue haze of the firmament or the transparency customary to the liquid element. Broken and fallen water shows plainly and unmistakably the true tint prevailing on the river about to be fished. Appearances are liable to be deceptive when viewed tranquil, owing to disparity in the geological formation, as also in the variety of substance forming its bed. For habitually discoloured waters, a light brown or a delicate olive may be advantageously employed. The former may be had from either fustain chips, barberry bark or the coffee bean, when pulverised and made into a solution by the application of boiling water. The gut not, however, being inserted until the liquid has cooled down to a few degrees above blood heat. Gut is often irretrievably ruined by being scalded in the process of staining; gut damaged in this manner loses strength and stiffness, and is thus rendered weak and limp, with a marked tendency to rub rough with slight friction. To boil, in short, is to surely spoil the best and strongest gut ever obtained from the worm. Gut, indeed, of any description will fail to withstand the process, though the product of the invaluable little silkworm in its compactness and strength will stand successfully more tampering with than others. An olive may be had from logwood and fustian chips, with a mere atom of copperas or sulphate of iron, no more of the latter substance than is needed to give the shade requisite to the solution when boiled.*

Upon a two-and-a-half to a three-yards lash, one or more droppers may be used. Upon lakes or broad open rivers they should be habitually employed as in the case of trout fishing. 'Tippets' are used to connect the looped flies to the gut line, these are simply stout gut lengths with a tight knot at one end and a wrapped or knotted loop at the other; the latter is attached to the line by being 'linked' around it, the tag end is then attached to the fly by means of the knot known as the 'Carrick' bend, which is formed in the following manner. The knotted tag threads the loop of the fly, then goes round and through the single gut loop thus formed, again it goes round the middle strand, but backwards, and the tag is threaded through this last formed loop, and then all is tightened; the knotted tag being bedded or nestled up near the knot for greater security. An ordinary slip knot or running noose is commonly used by some anglers, others again eschew both, preferring to loop both fly and cast in the traditional style, or otherwise adapting some one of the endless variety of knots for their purpose. Droppers should hang five inches or so from the cast when attached, the 'tippets' used being of first quality to ensure the needful amount of stiffness which is essential to avoid entanglements and obnoxious twistings. In river-fishing, the angler accustomed to the single-hand trout rod will find but little difficulty in his path in the pursuit of the salmon. His former ideas and conceptions need expansion, though, as regards call for skill, certainly not elevation; his gossamer gut is exchanged for the opposite extreme and the lightly made, well-balanced, single-handed rod is exchanged for a double-handed weapon double the weight and dimension, with which double the distance must be covered in casting. If he couples with the foregoing a like advance in regard to manual exertion, in short, with his entire physical and emotional organism, the trout fisher will have

* For further information on gut staining, see recipes on page 254.

comprehended the nature of the distinctive elements of the two highest branches in piscatory art. Entomology, it should not be forgotten, is marked from the lists in the trout fisher's new regime as salmon fisher, a knowledge of meteorological changes *only* so far as they affect the fish being needful. A study of the nomenclature of the migratory and non-migratory orders of Salmonidae leads the observer to this conclusion, that their advancement in educational attainments, acquired wiliness and keenness of demeanour, is *not identical*. The location of the one permanently in freshwater causes a continuous development of the ocular and optical faculties; whilst, upon the other hand, the marine trips to fresh feeding grounds are so strikingly beneficial to the constitutional functions of the fish that the recollections of former experiences are apparently dulled, if not entirely erased. With the conditions of life so at variance, there exists small grounds for surprise at the issue.

It may be as well here, prior to plunging into generalities, to append an outline of the mode of procedure in two-hand casting, which is due to the tyro, for whom we venture to assume upon the indulgence of proficients. Sea- or white-trout fishing forms a sort of intermediate stage between trout and salmon fishing proper, therefore may, with advantage, be tackled prior to the latter. The essentials are: (first) lake rod of fourteen or fifteen feet, strong and moderately supple; (second) winch, three inches or more in diameter, metal; (third) seventy to ninety yards of line, medium thickness and strength. These, with the usual accessories for fly-fishing in the shape of a fly-book, replete with flies, and gaff, of which latter article – by the way – there are well nigh endless varieties, portable and otherwise. Individually we prefer a good plain article, though a full-sized strongly made telescope metal is fairly good for use, and highly convenient for travelling. A very useful implement, especially for boating and loch-fishing, is a large, rough and plain landing-net, consisting of an iron hoop, say three feet in diameter, which is connected by means of two straightened and strengthened ends of the circle of metal which are turned outwards at right angles; when flattened, these admit of the hoop being lashed to a handle or shaft, temporary or otherwise (a hazel sapling answers well for the purpose). The net should be four if not five feet in depth, with an inch-and-a-half mesh. A landing-net of this description is more useful than can easily be conceived. In both loch- and river-fishing, a large tanned canvas bag, nicely partitioned and lined with india rubber, will be found convenient when stocked as a 'possibility bag' for general purposes. And now, supposing the young student to be equipped with these requisites, we transfer ourselves to the ground, or rather the water, for operations.

Here, not at the brim, but out upon its bosom to avoid troublesome objects of obstruction, seated in any posture most convenient on the cross-boards of the boat, line is unreeled, and, as a novice, you make your first essay at double-handed casting. The rod and line at first scarce would seem to act in concert, so varied are the twists of the former and the curls and capers of the latter. A small amount of handling will enable the adept angler for smaller fry to feel his way to the accomplishment of a respectable output of line, and even the genuine tyro, a perfect stranger to the rod, will encounter but comparatively few difficulties in his path. A strict determined application to the course of the essential three Ps, viz., Practice, Patience and Perseverance, will thoroughly indicate the first principles of the art, and, if aided and supplemented by an intelligent application to the several studies which, while outside the immediate operation of fishing, are yet so connected as to be the very heart and soul of it, the progressing path to proficiency will open right rapidly. But to our casting.

The amount of force to employ with a light two-handed rod is one of the principal points needing thorough comprehension, but first we would endeavour to initiate as to the motions described by, and the mode of wielding the rod in, orthodox throwing, etc. The hands grasp the butt some distance apart, the winch between; in *right*-shoulder casting, the left hand is placed below the reel or winch, and the right hand some distance above. In *left*-shoulder casting, these positions are exactly reversed: and now in extending motion to the rod and unreeled line, work gently, allowing sufficient time (the length of which must graduate in obedience to the length of line out) for the back line to extend into position for the forward impetus; by means of the customary side swing (by which a sort of horseshoe sweep is described in hurling back and paying forward again the line), control may be still exercised as it straightens out and falls to the water by action extended to the rod tip; the character of this interposition varies, as a matter of course, with circumstances, but the usual action is to raise backwards and upwards the rod's point a foot or so to each dozen yards of line out; this, if accurately performed, ensures greater precision and lightness in delivery.

The right- and left-shoulder casts tried, and a knowledge of them as performed with the two-handed rod acquired, the Welsh whisk or cast is next to be tried. This we have already alluded to;[*] the longest distances are attained by it. The motions of the rod and line are precisely the same as in the case of trout and grayling fishing. You raise your length of line from the water upward and backward in the usual way, but deliver forward in a direct line, a little under the back line, ere the fly quits the water. This cast may be effected either from the right or left sides – it is as well to acquire both methods – the same individual is seldom equally proficient in the two, but it has an easing effect on the muscles to exchange and exercise in different postures, which is a consideration often important. The usual dexterity called for in fishing a clear, well-fished southern trout stream may be of use here in salmon and sea-trout fishing. The many magnified conditions of sport may render more strength necessary, but mere blustering and purposeless whizzing and whirling of the tools is scarcely exemplary of the artistic proficient in any branch of angling, not excepting salmon fishing. The experienced skater glides gracefully, rapidly and well-nigh silently over the frozen surface of the water, whilst the awkward 'scuttler' flusters and flounders in his energetic wayward course, clumsily cutting up the smooth surface of the ice to the general detriment; so with fly- and bait-casting, *as a rule*, the more successful fisherman will expend less muscular power

---

[*] See Throwing the Fly, pages 151–5.

in delivering a long line than will the less experienced a much shorter one. This qualification and degree of proficiency should ever be held in the mind's eye for ultimate attainment. Casting has, after precepts and rules have been assiduously and carefully instilled in the mind and thoughts of the angling aspirant, still to be *learned*. The exercise of judgement in calculation of the bearings of surroundings, and the influence of the atmosphere in its ever changing moods, have to be taken into account at all times. Therefore, the mere routine cast is but the first step of necessary knowledge. To pursue this path more deeply is the self-imposed and cheerfully assumed task of every disciple of the rod; some are given to loiter at the earlier stage of the journey, many press onward until the pathway is difficult to tread – finally, when difficulties thicken, and the track is lost in the unexplored maze, few, how few, are then the wayfarers eager for progress and advancement. This is but a type, however, of what exists in every pursuit; the large capacity for endurance, natural perseverance and play of intellect demanded in successful pioneering science debars the main mass of minds from attempting the efforts necessary for investigating the great maze of unknown knowledge.

Before concluding the subject of casting, we would add an extra purchase method or two. The first is this – when a long distance is desired to be reached, and the longest line that can be rightly held under control is out, a few additional yards may be got out by unreeling and allowing the line to fall at the feet; this is allowed to run through the rings when the forward impetus is given. If rightly achieved, this will carry out the line loosed (without interfering with the precision of the cast), thus reaching a greater distance than could be attained in the usual way. Another and perhaps a still more successful way in which additional distance can be covered, we here append. Loop down the line from between the rings of the second joint in one or more links; these can be held by a finger of the hand uppermost on the rod's butt; let go as before, when the line is surging forward, prior to it straightening out and descending over the liquid expanse. Greater facility is afforded by this resource for the passage of the reserve line through the rod rings.

In taking a long line from the water, the strain upon the rod is much more marked than is that borne in its delivery. It is, in fact, the constant lifting of lengths of line partly submerged that permanently warps and bows the rod to the side occupied by the rings. This is often so marked a tendency that the periodic reversal of the rings is rendered necessary. In the case of a really good rod this weakening is seldom exemplified, but as all rods do not come under the category here implied, it will be perhaps as well for us here to notice a simple though effective method of obviating this necessity of ring changing, i.e., when whisking out and back the line, the rings may be brought uppermost by a twist of the wrist; this utilises the strain and counterbalances the effect when the joints are beginning to give and curve. Many an old prized implement has closed its chequered career in a vain attempt to whirl backwards a length of sunken line. A defective new rod will frequently collapse under a similar trial. The nature of wood expends itself after a number of years' straining service; this is more rapidly effected in woods worked persistently one way, hence it may be perceived that a little consideration is amply repaid in these matters.

In plying the fly over salmon, much divergency of method is evinced by different anglers whose individual modes are contracted under different conditions. The plan of the old school, which is still largely followed, is to 'dribble and jerk' and otherwise 'humour', or, as they express it, work, the guile in a tempting and seductive manner. The action thus employed consists of a series of 'shakes' and 'draws' against the current. This 'humouring' action is conceived to be giving a lifelike and natural motion calculated to entice capricious fish. That it is occasionally successful we cannot deny, as our thoughts recall instances of its having proved irresistible when other means have been futile. Unfortunately, however, the humouring in this method of salmon fly-fishing is not always on one side; mostly we have found a very little 'humouring' edify and enlighten a sportive fish to an extent sufficient to stay all trivial tendencies, instilling at once desire for food and reflection in quiet retirement. But, as we have said, it is sometimes successful, and these times are generally when the beclouded sky and the ruffling breeze ripples in gentle wavelets the surface of the element of the fish, thus aiding the guile. Upon some waters it 'pays' better than upon others. The straight drawing or trailing system over moving sportive or poised fish we have ever found most worthy allegiance for all-round salmon and sea-trout fishing. When a fish shows himself and is cast over, and fails or refuses to take when the fly has been neatly put out to him, it may be steadily drawn over his home or haunt, then slantwise and by him in side directions, should he be still indifferent, finally – humour. Our method of so doing is generally to let him alone for a season; his fit of coyness most frequently vanishes ere long. A heavily plagued fish is often to be got when a passing mass of vapour in the form of a threatening cloud looms between the earth and the sun's beams, or a ruffly 'choppy' breeze befriends by obscuring the too apparent deception. Rest assured, too sanguine impetuosity is not rewarded. Many fishermen are given to wield the rod and ply the fly for hours after being honoured with an offer from a fish seen on the move. Long hours are by no means infrequently expended in working the tackle as industriously and laboriously as though the motive power was a piece of mechanism propelled by steam. Rest assured, friend student, *few fish are to be bullied into biting*; this is a truism fit to be recognised as a proverb; therefore, the true angler's virtue – 'patience', the virtue undeniable of the fraternity it follows, is the best policy. This, with skill and tact, precision in delivery and perseverance, is the most important constituent of proficiency in salmon fishing. These it is incumbent upon every angling aspirant to possess in some degree. Upon different waters widely different methods are in vogue as to striking, playing and gaffing. Impetuosity is bad for sport, as we have endeavoured to point out, in well-nigh every branch of angling, no matter in what way it is displayed. In striking, however, it is in the majority of instances absolutely fatal to the end and aim in view. In the case of the inexperienced – who, failing to put out a good line, strike at the least resemblance to a rise – this, at the end of a comparatively short line, has the totally unintended effect of frustrating the intentions of the fish. To try to treat with a rise after the proficient's style, at the extremity of thirty to thirty-five yards of line, is to commit an error;

the conditions are widely diversified, and so are the results. We have devoted some space to the subject of striking in another chapter, and from what is there advanced it may be inferred that it is impossible to pay too much attention to this important point, no matter what may be the conditions of sport.

When a salmon rises to the fly, it is either with the intention of seizing or merely to inspect – at the dictum of aroused curiosity, and if the latter, as it by no means unfrequently is, especially in still and slowly flowing water, it is purely suicidal to jerk back the line and lure; the fish, rest assured, will close upon it if *permitted* when so minded. Should the appearance of the fish or the evidence of a rise be accompanied by a tug of the line, you may then safely strike, speedily and with moderate force. The measured stroke varies mainly with the distance, as when this is short, the stroke should be short too; but a small tug of the rod's upper portion with a taut line will serve to send the hook well home into the fish. The mouth of a salmon, it should ever be remembered, partakes more of the delicate outline – whether internal or external – of the adult grayling upon an enlarged scale, rather than that of the trout, and is therefore still less to be confounded with the heavily armed pike. With a bold rising salmon every chance of good vantage ground is afforded the fisherman at the onset, and he assuredly has very seldom ulterior causes for complaint or blame in the event of miscarriage in the course of treatment imposed. Occasionally it may be that in the rapid dash for the fly he misses, turns or doubles, and takes in thorough style at the next offer. This is more exemplified in rapid running water, or where the fly is 'worked' somewhat energetically over the fish's lair. Even here, keenness of perception, a quick hand and eye, with an exercise of prudential patience, will more surely yield success. The amount of force to be employed, as we have said, depends wholly upon circumstances, such as the intervening distance, the loose state or otherwise of the line, and the characteristics of the rod. Each of these several points materially bear upon the case, and have to be calculated upon at the moment of action.

To exercise command over the perceptive faculties, so as to adapt oneself to the necessities of the case when the pulse quickens and the nerves thrill with sudden excitement, this proclaims the adept. The great precept to be impressed upon the mind of the tyro, and one which is applicable to every branch of angling, is this: *never cast without expecting a fish*. How often is the rise taken out of the indifferent angler of sanguine temperament and excitable disposition by the plunge of a speculative fish, whose demonstrative turning has the effect of a galvanic battery, recalling the absent-minded one to things present, of personal import and bearing – the pipe has fallen from the partially distended jaws, the hat, too, is raised somewhat by the suddenly manifested upward tendency of the hair. These things are readjusted, the tangled line put straight and in trim, and now how industriously and ardently is the fly whirled over the waving ringlets widening from the point of disturbance. Praiseworthy perseverance is expended, the greatest nicety of delivery put forth in presenting the lure, but to no purpose; your steel has been felt, and an opportunity for reopening negotiations is denied for the time being. Every pursuit, without exception, has a sure Nemesis following upon indolence and half-heartedness, hence it is that thorough application achieves the heavier feats, and claims, thus, our ungrudging allegiance.

The weight of a salmon rod, reel and line, when out in action, is often a source of complaint on the part of some habitual salmon fishers; many eschew the sport solely on the grounds indicated. Veteran fishermen, too, find their physical organism fail before the perceptible decline of the mental, and it is with grievous regrets the old favourite rod is laid aside for the last time. Many, very many, are the instances we have known of the time-honoured heroes of many fishy fights, anglers sterling and true, whose piscatory pleasures have been abruptly closed by the stern mandate of declining strength and feeble health. When man is touched by the first frosts of the approaching wintery period, and his habitual physical powers are felt to be on the wane, how tenaciously and persistently for a time does he cling to his customary pursuits; but, alas! his determination is short-lived – nature is not to be overruled. Who can describe, or, in fact, conceive the reflections of such an one? None, surely none, but they who have experienced them can truly sympathise.

Expedients, practical in their bearings, might be suggested, by way of neutralising, at least for a season, these effects. The only feasible plan that would appear to commend itself is to tone down somewhat the heavy tools employed; first, the winch, weighty and cumbersome, may be reduced much more than a third in substance of metal by constructing it from a *skeleton design*. We have made and used large and small reels constructed on this principle for some time, and find it a genuine improvement to have the solid plates of the winch hollowed and cut out in such a manner as to retain the real actual strength, while much surplus weight is avoided. The flat circular plates are cut away to some approved design, leaving intervening bars to support the axis, or, in other words, crossbars are left to connect the centre with the outside edge (a Roman cross design answers the purpose as well as any). The bobbin, too, may be made with perpendicular sides which may be reduced in fine strips so as not to admit of the line protruding; the revolving plate and flat bar may also be skeletoned in like manner. The centre-fitting winches equally with the side-fitting ones are improved by the reduction, and if diminished weight is a desideratum, there cannot be a doubt but that the idea given is an advance in the right direction, and that it is applicable to reels of metal generally. With reference to the rod, we have already alluded to one great change, implying less material and weight for strength, as also a decrease of the length of the salmon rod – we refer to the steel-centred principle. The old thick-butted tool contrasts very badly with the Castle Connel style of rod, but both are improved on by the combination of the fine yet strong metal core in the hardest pliant wood procurable for the purpose, viz., greenheart. Durability in the first quality of this wood is combined with pliability; this to an extent other woods have failed to equal, when tested in conjunction. Another plan to resort to in order to allow ease in casting moderate distances, more especially from a boat, is this: a strong leathern band or belt is affixed around the body, upon which has been secured safely a small round receptacle for the button, or 'mushroom' as it is sometimes called, at the termination of the rod; this termination of the rod should be of india rubber which works in the small round socket thus provided.

This arrangement lightens the weight incredibly, transferring sustaining power to a more convenient quarter. This method of easing the muscles of the arms and hands is useful in very many styles of fishing, though more especially, as we have said before, in boating. The line if tapered single or double is considerably lightened, and when the latter object is the premier consideration, tapering is to be commended as efficient. The wire lines are much reduced both in substance and actual weight. Thus equipped, the ease and comfort of fishing and casting powers are enhanced.

For salmon and sea-trout fishing, the employment of German silver wire ensures still greater strength and casting power; this metal being a combination of zinc and brass, is hard and durable, and increases the springing tendencies of the line.

The distinctive issues of real artistic angling – *scientific fishing* – and mere thoughtless blundering wielding of the rod cannot be shown too vividly; there exist small grounds for apprehension of exaggeration in the matter; we are too apt to ignore the teachings and dictates of experience to be in danger of erring on the side here implied.

All things worthy the earnest application of human intelligence, demand the concentration of the whole of the faculties, both physical and mental. The gradual development of scientific knowledge grants us further instalments and extensions of power, which necessitate an increasing application and attention rightly to develop. Each and every pursuit, no matter whether recreative or industrial, ranks without distinction under this general rule. Salmon fishing can therefore offer no exception. Some few years since there were methods in common everyday use for the capture of the *Salmo salar*, then looked upon as being perfectly legitimate, but that are now branded as illegal by national statute.[*] Primitive and unsportsmanlike methods of taking fish have been more and more discarded, as years roll on, in every branch of the 'gentle art'. The more general impression of the popular mind is that these semi-poaching methods are the more successful

---

[*] 'Otter' trailing, salmon-roe-fishing and other roe-fishing have recently been added to the prohibited lists.

ones from a pot-hunting standpoint. A supposition true in the abstract only, as we will proceed to instance. The medley of modes of taking fish by means other than legitimate angling for and thus attracting and beguiling fish are not included in the scope of observations advanced here or elsewhere through this book. The instance we have promised to relate transpired upon one of the Black Lakes more years since than we would care to count, and the point in the incident was repeatedly confirmed upon Lochs Awe, Nell, Ness, Kalliper and others. The eye brightens, and life's citadel pulsates at a heightened rate, as the mind in magic thought lives in and wanders through the pleasurable adventures of the past. As we write we once again see the broad expanse of slightly heaving water, bordered and bound by the huge heather-clothed hills through which ever and anon the primeval moss-clad rocks are seen to peep in clusters, adding nobility and grandeur to the scene. From the green-garbed slopes, rich in verdure, upon which the shaggy wild-looking north-country cattle are grazing peacefully, to the shining waters that reflect the rising sun in his refreshing splendour, our mental gaze wanders. All nature seems serene, save when the crack of a distant gun or the splash of an oar betray the presence of man. Now and then a sportive fish, fresh-run salmon or bull trout, causing a quiet boil, shows his broad tail above the rippling water's surface in his playful friskings or wilful plunges after real or fancied food. Dotted at long intervals are several boats, occupied by fishermen. One of these moves rapidly in response to the heavily worked oars, leaving, as it progresses, an extended line of curls and bubbles in its trail. This is tenanted by an angling visitor who, with his attendant or gillie, is plying the 'otter'.* This boat is observed to work

---

* This engine consists of a strong cord, from fifty to seventy yards in length, to which is affixed a miscellaneous assortment of baited or tin-garnished triangles, veritable meat hooks in coarseness, mounted on gimp; these are attached to one end of the cord at intervals, together with a large-sized single hook or two, wrapped on strands of gut, these being disguised with scarlet wool, and a strip of white goose feather higher up the cord; a large lead of about 1¼ lbs weight is fixed to serve as sinker. The whole is used upon a reel, formed by a square framework of wood with a loose peg to turn upon.

an isolated portion of the loch, by incessant repetitions of long roving flights, intercepted only when nearing either shore, or when about to turn. The trailing 'otter' then is relieved of its captures, if any. The way in which this operation is effected sufficiently initiates as to the unsportsmanlike nature of this mackerel-line style of taking fish. The line is hauled in rapidly, hand over hand, the string of lures is with small show of ceremony banged aboard with but meagre regard for consequences; a sort of certainty of success seems responsible for the rude and ready way in which the whole apparatus is plied. The natural issue is that the larger fish hooked are more often than not lost by bungling treatment when nearing the boat; indeed, it was a common practice to strike and thus stun the larger fish (after the fashion followed still upon the St Lawrence and other American rivers), preparatory to unhooking them, line or rather rope being loosed immediately in case the blow should fail of the desired effect. Personal interest had invited our attention as to the mode of procedure in 'otter' fishing, on the occasion in question. We had consented to make an effort to out-bag the product of this appliance preparatory to our setting out, the owner thereof having a breadth of water set apart for his use, whilst we individually had a roving commission.

The earlier hours of the day had yielded us but meagre sport; brown trout, with the exception of a solitary sea trout, were our only acquisitions up to midday, whilst the 'otter' boat had been busily engaged, and to all appearance, had been much more successful. After noon, however, the prospect speedily brightened as the brilliancy of the sun's reflections were temporised by passing clouds brought up by a smart breeze. Now we turned our attention to the known haunt of a good fish, whose habitual resting-place we were well acquainted with. On our way we rose and hooked into a grilse by a random cast; this was picked up safely. The 'good' fish, however, was good enough to inspect and reject the sombre-hued lure proffered. We, therefore, presented a more attractively dressed fly, but to no purpose; bright and gay, dark and dim, were severally ignored; we thereupon left with the inward resolve of an attempt to reopen negotiations later on. The boat is now steered in the direction of a fish seen moving in the vicinity, this is ultimately moved and missed. At Sandy the water-keeper's suggestion (he is in charge of the boat) we now visit the adopted home of a wondrous fish he described as having acquired a reputation for eluding the gaff, though not so vigilant, it would appear, in evading the hook. The hollow side of a sunk boulder, the top of which was just discernible above the water, was pointed out as being his usual position, and after having elicited what further information we could get as to the way he lay, we selected and fitted the best and most reliable single-gut lash from the book, furnishing with a monster red-sterned Humble Bee, for which we were informed he had already displayed a weakness. This was cast over and worked repeatedly across in a variety of ways, but the 'bee' had evidently lost his fascinating attractions. The hidden sting was not outshone this time, at least, by the brightly bedecked nether end. After half an hour's attention to the *Salmo fario*, we approached the 'invincible' once more. The Parson is awarded the post of honour this time; he, however, fails to meet with due appreciation, and we try the Doctor, but with no more success. Just, however, as we are about to substitute the Captain, the azure lure is closed upon, and the necessity of plunging further into the professions is obviated. We drive home our steel instantly. The play that ensues is of a lively description; a considerate and careful use of the line, rod and boat wards off the effects that appeared impending from the boisterous determined plunges. After these have somewhat subsided, the salmon ring prohibits an inconvenient show of sulkiness or jiggering, and two-thirds of an hour from the time of hooking sees the fish, an exceptionally fine salmon, safely gaffed and boarded.

During this lapse of time the 'otter' boat has been industriously propelled well-nigh without cessation, but with what result we cannot surmise. In casting over one or two more fish showing themselves as the day wears away, the plan of persistent plaguing is ignored still as far as it is possible, strict and unflagging attention being devoted to the ulterior bearings. These, more frequently regarded as outside issues, we would emphasise by repeating are inseparable in their connection with the end held in view by the devoted angler. It is simple trifles, insignificant in themselves, that *combined* form results. The shadow thrown by a towering rocky cliff, and the shelter afforded by sedges grouped near a moving salmon, aided us in rising and hooking two fish which were brought within reach of Sandy's ready clip. The first of these being a kipper was returned, the second proved a 14 lbs clean fish. By this time the sun was sinking rapidly behind the western heights. During the remaining hour or so of daylight we took a fine fish with the Mac Sporren, and subsequently lost a white trout from the same fly after a few minutes' play. This terminated the day's proceedings so far as sport was concerned. In crossing for the usual rendezvous for landing, we encountered a squall which, beating dead against our cockleshell craft, necessitated the united and utmost efforts of its occupants to keep her head to the wind, and it was only after a row of a couple of hours in darkness and danger that we effected a safe landing. The 'otter' boat we subsequently ascertained had put in but a short time prior to our appearance.

The analysis of our take was reported as follows: four salmon, weight 34½ lbs, 22 lbs, 14 lbs and 7¼ lbs, and white trout 4¼ lbs, total 82 lbs, together with our nineteen dozen brown trout.

The contents of the 'otter' boat proved to be very much under the *Salmo salar* yield, but slightly in excess of the smaller fry; the five largest fish scaled from 11 lbs downwards; their combined take being under two-thirds of the yield of the rod and line.

Spinning and Trolling continues still a common practice upon most waters in fishing for the higher orders of Salmonidae. Upon lochs, as also the estuaries of salmon waters, a boat is propelled with the bait trailing at a distance of fifty yards or so in its rear. Whenever the fish refuse to rise, spinning may with advantage be resorted to; indeed, mid-water fishing may, under these circumstances, often be practised with signal success, though as a general thing it yields not the sport of surface-fishing. Small fish of almost any description, when from four to six inches in length, may be used. The best artificial baits are the metal ones, the Universal,

Excelsior, Devon, etc. The Derby Killer is also good, salmon size.

The Red Caterpillar is as killing a lure for salmon and sea trout, *when they are not rising*, as it is for common brown trout, etc. It is used in precisely the same way, but is constructed, as a matter of course, much larger; the loop, too, at the head, should be of double salmon gut. Black Palmers, with silver twist, are also good, but not to be compared with the Red, as the habitual users of both can testify. If there is anything objectionable in the use of the Caterpillar for sea trout and salmon, it is the partiality of the smaller fry for them; they, especially the brown trout, are really boring in their incessant attentions. At the end of a day upon the Awe in Argyleshire, when we had been more than usually pestered in this manner, the following colloquy ensued with Gibby, the gillie in charge of the boat.

'Weel, noo, dun yer ken what fysshe wa'en ta'en the day, wath the hairy worrem?'

'No!'

'Wal, twanty-four dozen sma' throut jest – an they twa white fysshe – sure, it's a fearsome baste, an' a regular kill deil.'

To those anglers who habitually smoke whilst fishing, and their name is legion, we would tender a word of advice. Never carry vesuvians loose in any of your coat pockets, or you may perchance be troubled with a touch of heartburn externally, as was the experience of the writer on one occasion whilst playing a fish from the banks of the Tweed. We had unconsciously given the receptacle of the pipe lights a touch with the butt end of the rod, when the whole ignited, the result of the conflagration being loss of the fish, and the spoliation of certain garments.

We may here also observe that when landing a fish with a short-handled gaff upon a high bank over deep water it is *not* always safe to be backed with a well-filled creel, for should the creel happen suddenly and unexpectedly to find its way to the front, why you may feel as we did once, viz., that a cold-water plunge is inevitable under the circumstances.

In salmon as in trout fishing, the location of a fish poised for feeding or perhaps rising requires often a little reconnoitring. The course of the water in his immediate vicinity should be noted, and the lure presented accordingly. In order to circumvent exceptionally large fish more particularly, it is by no means advisable to cast haphazard in the vicinity of the fish before the distance is rightly calculated, or the course of the water appreciated. If it is your earnest desire to take the fish seen rising, like an efficient general you must take in the bearing of the situation, with a view to so presenting the lure as to leave nothing wanting in skill and judgement upon the part of the angler.

CHAPTER SIXTEEN

Amateur Tackle-Making, etc., with Recipes

Utility of Knowledge in Emergency; Choice of Materials for Rods;
Rod-Making; An All-Round Tool; Splicing under Difficulties;
Accidents and Expedients; Hook-Dressing; Flight- and
Cast-Making; Knots; Useful Recipes

One of the most fertile sources of pleasure to the fisherman is undoubtedly that of alluring fish with baits, etc., fashioned by his own hand and ingenuity. In having made the medium of allurement, he experiences an extra spice of genuine enjoyment when his skill is crowned with success. Making and working combine in the causes for self-congratulation; not only this, the mere power and tact exercised in so altering a rejected lure as to render it successful subsequently, tends to a similar result. For example, J— makes the discovery, after vainly trying to raise fish seen feeding, that his copy of the fly prevalent is defective in colour in its most important point, viz., the body, this showing a pronounced departure from that of the natural. A strand of the needful shade of silk supplied by an obscure recess of the fly-book forms the requisite material, and the next moment sees the necessary transformation accomplished; the silk, having been wound round and over the existing body, is finally knotted off in the usual way, and now fishy favour and sedate finny wisdom succumb readily to the faithfully portrayed fly.

Again, as each gust of wind upon a rough autumn day scatters leaves, twigs and insects upon the water's surface, a copy of the fly most plentiful is temptingly presented at the extremity of the customary fine cast, and the gleaming side of a moving fish is seen as it advances to take – ah! no; he turns, doubles down, and is gone. This is the effect;

the cause needs investigation. A contrast of artificial and natural reveals nothing definite; the eye finally falls upon the stream, the vast majority of insects there are seen to be *drowned*, and are borne along at the wild will of wind and wave. On this becoming apparent, the hackle of the copy is thinned out or cut away to two-thirds its original bulk, which extracts from its buoyancy and materially changes its appearance. It is again whirled on its diplomatic mission repeatedly, and proves its success in the net yield during the subsequent hour or two. Herein is exemplified the veracity of the philosophical assertion, 'In knowledge reposeth power.'

   The followers of every given pursuit, whether recreative or industrial, are ever liable to be thwarted and frustrated by unlooked for contingencies, accidents or breakages in the varied requisite appliances, and the ability to rise in the case of urgent emergency, to adopt oneself to an occasion of pressing necessity when thrown entirely upon our own resources, is commendable in all circumstances, hence our object in writing under the heading here given. The accomplishment of being able creditably to dress our flies may be, and doubtless is, a pretty general one; but anglers capable of splicing efficiently a broken reel line, a smashed middle joint or rod-top, when in a position remote from competent aid, are certainly not so plentiful. How much annoyance, irritating waste of time and opportunity is often occasioned by a single mishap occurring when least expected; but upon the other hand, what is gained by a little aptness in rising to the level of the emergency, the individual practitioner alone knows.

   We are here reminded of an instance, bearing upon the points indicated, in which also was implicated the late Professor F— (the well-known lecturer on the natural sciences), who had happened to be fishing the same water with us, whilst wandering solitary at will among the then open and freely accessible waters of Norway, then, as now, a veritable Eden to the piscator; a paradise not wholly devoid of penalties, nevertheless, as for a recognised monument of patience to discover his stock of mild Honeydew or Birdseye run out, when three days to a week from a source of supply, invariably proves the force of the compact between patience and tobacco, and that disunion means a mutual collapse.

The particular predicament to which our mind recurs, however, partook much more of the tragic element. A native nondescript craft had capsized in shooting a sharp rapid, distributing rods, gaffs, lines, and the whole paraphernalia of oddments necessary to the equipment of fishermen on a walking tour in isolated regions, far and away, necessitating a new departure in piscatory operations, viz., fishing for tackle. The boil of the foam-beaten and falling waters obscured the whereabouts of the varied appliances dispersed through the mishap. The movements of two forming the trio (the third person of which was a native piece of animated nature, to whose stock of stupidity we owed the ducking and disaster) were greatly hampered by the watertight fish bags which, filled with the gushing liquid, stood from the back like eastern leather bottles. Thus laden, after gathering whatever was visible in the shape of tackle, we struck out for *terra firma*, which, safely attained, our first act was to disburden ourselves of the heavy fish receptacles; our next, at the suggestion of the professor, to probe a hole in their bottoms to prohibit a possible repetition of their water-bagging proclivities, thus adopting the quaint Highland custom of providing ample exit for the liquid element in the shape of gimlet holes in the soles of boating and shooting boots. On our comparing notes, it was found that rods and their immediate accessories, in the shape of lines, winches and gaffs, had been secured almost without an exception, *but the fly-books* were gone.

Keen search for signs of their presence in the whirl of waters revealed nothing, and it soon became evident they were lost beyond recall. Thrown upon our own resources, we hastened to the apology for an inn, the primitive comforts of which never appeared so favourably to us as when, in changed apparel, we prepared to make a fly or two for immediate use, in the genial warmth of a glowing pine-wood fire, the logs of which, rich in resinous matter, burnt brilliantly, brightening and bathing in cheerful light each primitive object within the four or more (here we cannot be precise) angles of the room. In the collection of material, the first essential, i.e., hooks, were not to be found, and after a time we recollected having put them in a missing case. Upon this stern fact becoming evident, something bordering on dismay threatened to enthral our spirits. A packet of small dun hooks was all we had to rely upon for a period indefinite, far too long for us to regard with feelings of serenity, and it was speedily arranged that we should severally prepare some plan of solving the perplexing problem of the moment. Minus flies and minus hooks, save such as were suitable for the Iron Blue, how were we to reopen negotiations with salmon? At this we mutually and severally set to work. The result of an hour or so's ardent application being three ideas in practical shape, which may be briefly described as under:

The first consisted of a needle, two inches or more in length, softened by fire, and transformed into a hook, heated again, and hardened by sudden immersion in water; upon this foundation was fixed the ordinary materials used in the composition of a Butcher.

Second was a very natural representation of a monster Humble Bee, it being dressed upon an eyed spinning lead, the yellow-and-red rear end being garnished with a battery of six small dun hooks, in a band or circle.

Third was the combination known as the Black Dose (a famous Norwegian fly), which presented a strikingly original appearance, the long and neatly proportioned body terminating with nothing more prominent than one of the insignificant minute hooks previously referred to, but in lieu of the hackles for legs, stained gut had been used, each of the numerous strands being tipped with a fine hook.

Practical testing proved the first to be of indifferent worth. The notion was no doubt good, and ample for the purpose, but the difficulty of tampering with already tempered metal was not got over successfully before the supply of these very necessary domestic implements failed.

The second answered very well, but the plan was not equally

applicable to the generality of salmon flies, and as the Humble Bee was no more *infallible* in its death-dealing qualifications than any of the thousand and one reputed never-failing guiles, our mainstay was the 'centipede' salmon lure, which answered most admirably the necessary end and purpose during the eight or ten days intervening the arrival of a supply of Limericks.

We purpose, firstly, to give simple directions for amateur rod-making, to be followed by a few brief suggestions as to repairs, temporary or otherwise; secondly, to deal briefly with cast- and flight-constructing, hook-mounting, etc. *Re* rod, the size and dimensions are first to be decided upon; this settled, the wood must be chosen to suit the particular description of rod desired.

For fly-fishing, the material of which a rod is composed is of the greatest possible importance. The scope for selection, too, is so extensive as to be perplexing to the inexperienced. Each clime and country contributes woods of a specific class. Some are so compact in substance, and fine in grain, as to be equal to metal, both as regards weight and solidity. Others, again, are porous and open-grained, light and lithesome, and are *talkative*, so to speak, when handled; indeed, it is an infallible rule that if a dry scrap of timber sounds in echo to the friction of the fingers, or when struck lightly with some hard substance, it is unstable, and is unworthy for any particular purpose. There is a happy medium, however, to all this. Outside the tropics, and yet within the influence of a genial sun and climate, there are many varieties of woods that, whilst being slightly porous, yet retain so much strength as to be tough and stiff, pliant and comparatively light. The best of such are greenheart (Australian), washaba, snakewood, blue mahoe, red locust, partridge wood, white hickory, logwood, Brazilian lance, etc., etc. It is never advisable to make all the parts of a rod from the same wood. They should be graduated according to strength, nature and quality. There is invariably great divergency in the nature of the same species of wood when grown under different conditions. Thus Cuban lance is below the yellow variety found in South America in general utility. The distinction in quality, in one and the same variety of wood, is not generally so strikingly marked as to enable the manipulator to cut the butt from the same log as the top. An amalgamation is, therefore, mostly adopted, the lighter woods of fair strength being used for the butt, medium for the middle joint, and the very best and most select for the tops; but we would commend a still closer application of this rule, by the adoption of the same routine in the tops, good wood being used at foot, better up to second splice, and the *very best* it is possible to procure for the tip of the top. This may appear superfluous perhaps to some; the bean-stick epoch in the career of many anglers appears to leave primitive longings for unpermissible things. We would remind such that perfection is *only* to be attained by trifles in construction; it is purely by keen application to these that sterling and permanent improvement is achieved.

The length and number of joints decided upon, the wood and sizes of ferrule chosen, the first step is to take off the four corners (presuming the wood to be square) of the butt with a 'jack plane'; there are then eight smaller ones to be taken off in like manner. This done, the joint will be found to be fairly round, and now the shape must be determined upon, as, if the rod is intended to be light, limber and small, it should be shouldered or 'bottle necked' a little above the usual handhold, thus imparting a feature of the balance handle to the joint. The alternative is to leave a gradual slope or taper up to the ferrule. And now for fixing on the metal. In fixing ferrules, one great blunder and cause of disaster should ever be assiduously avoided, viz., *cutting foundations for their accommodation*. The metal should be made to fit the wood, and not vice versa, as is, we fear, the more general custom. To rob the wood to accommodate the metal, is to sacrifice future convenience for a little present effort and legitimate commonsense precaution. Each ferrule should be so tapered as to fit over the wood; this tapering process is easy enough to accomplish: a 'mandrill', i.e., an iron or steel rod is procured, and the ferrule threaded upon it and beaten with a smooth-faced hammer, and thus swelled to the requisite extent. The next joint should follow in process precisely similar, which done, the top is put together in the following manner: the pieces of wood chosen are cut to meet each other evenly at the joinings or splices, which are then charged with best joiner's glue, and bound tightly at each splice with a scrap of waxed hemp; the whole must now be straightened before leaving to harden. It is a common practice to employ quick-drying spirit varnish to avoid the waiting time necessary in using glue, but this again is false economy, for shaky joinings and weak splices are almost invariably the result, and then one hears the well-worn expression: 'My top has given way; it is quite weak at the wrappings; there, see, I shall most certainly have to get a duplicate.' When reason dictates the splice should be the *stronger* part of the whole piece, we comprehend the evil arising from this cause.

Directly the ferrules are mounted, and the tongues cut upon the foot of the top and second piece, and the holes bored at the top of the last named and butt, the whole may be put together to ascertain the power and play. A little taken off here and there, evenly, adjusts and perfects, which done satisfactorily, polishing with fine emery cloth or shark's skin follows; it then remains for the rings and similar furniture to be fixed upon it by the usual silk bindings. The ferrules are to be set on permanently, with thick oil varnish, and finally riveted; the whole is then ready for coating, first with French polish, then with copal or some other equally good waterproof varnish, and your rod is done, though by no means ready for immediate use, as many days are often required for its 'coat' thoroughly to harden; indeed, the better the quality of the varnish, the longer time necessary for hardening. Spirit varnishes, dissolved shellac, and other gums, dry in a few minutes, or hours at most, but they are comparatively of small value as waterproof protections against wear and weather. An additional short top converts the foregoing into a good stiff spinning rod, whilst an extra short butt of say from 18 inches to 2 feet makes a general implement for all-round use, as with the long top and short butt the result is a whippy small-stream rod; but the long top and the *long butt* make a powerful rod for heavier waters, while if you have a short top and butt too an excellent pike rod is the result.

How to make a splice *Localities* are highly important here, as splicing a broken joint at home and at leisure is an operation depending upon widely different issues than when at the waterside, with but a pocket knife and twine as repairing agents. With the former we must deal first as a sort of ideal at which to aim in less advantageous circumstances. The mode of procedure is briefly thus: the two portions are each marked some *three inches or more* from the broken ends (short joinings are unsubstantial), and now, after seeing to the row of rings being in a direct line, the taper-cutting is to be done carefully by means of a keen wood chisel; this carefully effected, the splice must next be fitted with the greatest possible exactitude with a file. The glue having meanwhile been prepared, the splice is effected and secured firmly by stout cord, and when the glue is dry any remaining uneveness is erased by the file, and the whole is then carefully wrapped and strengthened with strong silk, which is again protected with wax and varnish in the usual way.

Temporary splicing at the waterside may be done both quickly and effectually by the observance of the following simple directions: first, the length of the intended splice is to be decided upon, and pencil marked on each of the detached pieces, then care must be taken ere you ply the knife that the rings will be in a direct line on the top when finished. In order to get at this the cutting upon the one half of the top must be directly opposite to the other, i.e., if you pare away from the ring side of the one broken and detached piece of the top, it is imperative the corresponding paring should be made upon the *side opposite the rings*. As soon as the detached parts are fairly even, cut to fit, they should be rubbed with fly-maker's wax; finally, by means of a few feet of strong twist, or a scrap of fine line, the splice may be 'whipped', or bound up, which is the better accomplished when wound transversely, as by wrapping rapidly from end to end greater security is allowed for a temporary purpose.

Perhaps the most deplorable accident that can happen to a rod is a breakage where the ferrule joins the wood. All the joints of a rod improperly fitted at this point are liable to breakages when strained more heavily than common, as we have elsewhere pointed out. The only practical way of rendering a rod again capable of casting for the remainder of the day, in the case of an accident of this kind, is to ignite a few dry twigs, and thus burn the wood from the ferrule socket, which done, it may again be fitted upon the joint, with small difficulty. Should the ferrule be broken from the top of the butt, the second or, in the case of a four-part rod, the third joint, a socket for the tongues of the next upper joint may be bored by means of the pyramid piece, upon an ordinary pocket penknife, providing the wood to be operated upon be first wound about with a bit of twine or other substance equal to the purpose, as this operation is a guard against splitting.

Often upon a showery day the tongues or pegs at the foot of the joints will stick in their sockets, owing to their having expanded somewhat by the presence of moisture within the fittings. An ignited vesuvian, or a scrap of paper in a blaze, will, on being applied in a way effective enough to cause the steam to leave the ferrule, render the joints readily detachable.

Winches and reel lines cannot well be constructed without the necessary appliances, in the shape of machinery. When the former consisted of a simple arrangement of wood and wire (the latter forming the handle, centre pillar and side pillars too, whilst the wood was employed for the circular terminations), the article was easy to construct, but now that the various parts are made detachable, and are cast and dressed up superbly, endless tools and skill in lathe turning are requisite to construct a metal winch of an improved pattern. Our object we conceive to be purely to initiate and interest, as much as possible, the amateur in the construction of his own tackle, so far as is practicable. Plait lines, casted and turned winches we pass over, as articles as yet beyond the ordinary amateur's attainment and capacity. We resume with flight-making, etc. The first essential step in tackle-constructing is undoubtedly that of hook-dressing. To attach gut or gimp to a hook may appear a very simple operation at first sight, but to secure it firmly, in a style eligible for the best and most particular purposes, the novice finds to be by no means so easy as it would first be assumed to be; indeed, many angling writers, up to comparatively recent times, recommend a knot to be tied at the end of the substance it is intended to attach to the hook, 'to aid', as they assert, 'in preventing a slip'. Another practice in vogue, even now, is to twist the gut or gimp around the shank of the hook in the process of tying, to avert the same catastrophe. That hooks often do slip when the moment of trial arrives no one can attempt to confute; but that they can be securely dressed, without knot or similar artifice, is known by the major portion of accomplished fishermen. All that is really needed to ensure security and solidity in whipping on a hook is to hold both silk and hook firm, and to extend a strain to the tying silk as great as it is capable of bearing; this done evenly and well, it will be found (providing the tying silk is not tender) inseparably secure. To tie on a hook, three whisks or wraps may be given on the bare shank, then the substance it is desired to connect may be placed alongside, when the wrapping silk may be carefully wound around, the utmost tension (as we have said) being extended to the tying silk, which should be bedded closely and evenly, until almost opposite the barb, when it may be knotted off by means of the ordinary invisible knot or slip noose.

In flight-making an arrangement has first to be decided upon, and the materials procured; this settled, the hooks are to be lashed in the positions needed, to work out the pattern selected. A pike flight is the best to commence upon, the coarser materials are the more readily united. In wrapping gimp it is often advisable to unwind the end of the gimp for a distance equal to one-half of the hook's shank, as this ensures a desirable taper. In wrapping on a triangle or treble hook, the same thing is needful to aid in security, the flossed end of the gimp being in this case brought tightly round the back of one of the hooks' bend and then lashed alongside with the wired portion of the gimp. A precaution advisable in the case of large fish is to wind a strand of the fine wire taken from the gimp over the silk wrapping, this protects the latter in a measure from the raking jaws of the fish.

For trout spinning-traces, fine flat tinsel, gilt or silver, answers the same end, whilst it adds to the attraction of the bait it adorns. A flight of hooks protected thus will wear a much greater length of time than a non-protected one; varnish, of course, is added, to give finish and solidity to the whole.

Barrel and dropper leads are moulded in metal moulds made for the purpose, but from lead wire of the requisite thickness both may be fashioned. For the first named the wire, after being cut the length required, needs tapering towards each extremity, which done, it may be partially split from end to end with a knife, the gut or gimp untwisted, and then closed in the same way as a split shot. A minnow tackle dropper may be fashioned in the same way, but in lieu of the splitting, a small hole is drilled at one end, from which the whole should gradually taper. Two-thirds of an inch is the usual length of a lead of this description. It should, in the case of being bored, be attached to the trace by means of a loop, to admit of freedom. Movable lip hooks are also looped on. The hook in this case is tied on to a separate scrap of gut, the ends of which are turned back on the hook's shank, and secured with the tying silk, thus forming two tiny loops through which the main line or trace may be threaded; a twist of this around the middle of the shank, after being threaded through one loop, and before going through the next, is often done, to ensure a necessary degree of stiffness to the movable hook.

Cast-making is a task of easy accomplishment, *when the knots are known*, as after the most useful of these are acquired, care in tapering the cast, in utilising the gut by the least possible expenditure of material, in waste ends from knots, is readily attained. The knot most indispensable is the one known as the fisherman's. It is formed as follows: place the two ends (one in each hand) it is desired to unite horizontally side by side, take one of them and turn it back so as to form a loop; now bring the tag end of this loop round under the straight end of the gut hitherto untouched, and then through the loop. It is merely forming a couple of Staffordshire knots, the one being knotted on to the other. This knot is invaluable in cast-making, as it may be opened without loss of time (by drawing the two knots apart) when it is desired to exchange the fly. A little practice with a piece of twine soon leads to the acquirement of the knots most commonly in use amongst inland anglers. The 'bowline' knot forms a loop which never draws; it is sometimes used for attaching the droppers to a cast not made with the opening knot above described. The 'bowline' is also formed on the lines of the well-known Staffordshire knot, as one end of the gut, or other substance forming the knot alluded to, is brought back and re-inserted in the open bow of the knot and the other end is then threaded through the second loop thus formed; the dropper – if knotted to prevent slipping – is inserted in any part of the knot prior to its being tightened up. If no knot is used upon the gut of the dropper, it is threaded through twice or thrice, and is tightened as before, and all is secure with very little show of a splicing place.

The ordinary 'slip-link', or catch, is another useful knot by which the 'bob' flies may be secured. It is most convenient, owing to its simplicity, and the rapidity with which the operation may be accomplished, *without severing the cast*. It merely consists of a bowed loop or link, threaded by yet another link; the first being drawn tight, leaves the second loop open for the knotted dropper, which is inserted, the cast being pulled at each side of the knot to bed the whole securely. By this method the 'bob' flies may be fixed on in a moment or two at any time, and when it is desired to exchange them for others, by cutting away the knot *on the dropper*, the cast knot will straighten out on being pulled, thus rendering it intact, both in the operation of attaching and releasing the 'bobs'. As a matter of course, the knots of the cast are avoided in fixing the dropper appendages by means of the two last methods given.

For spinning-traces, the double-looped knot is useful. It simply consists of two well-knotted or well-wrapped loops threaded together, the one loop passing through the other being threaded so as to form a detachable looped knot; for instance, loop A is put through loop B, and the opposite end of loop B is then passed through loop A, which completes the connection; this forms an easy detachable joining, most convenient in salmon and pike fishing, and for spinning purposes generally.

We have now dealt with the construction of the more important items in the angler's equipage, including rod-making, fly-making (the latter in an earlier portion of the work), flight-making, etc., etc.; we shall, therefore, now append, by way of conclusion, a few recipes likely to prove of value to the fraternity of fishermen who find pleasure in manipulating their own tackle, as also to anglers generally.

Recipes

Gut Dye Take a handful of logwood chips * to a pint of cold hard water, place in an earthenware vessel and gently heat it near a slow fire or in an oven until a few degrees off boiling point, then add a small portion of copperas or sulphate of iron – say of the size of a no. 4 shot. The whole should be well stirred after the addition of the copperas. This done, and the colour deemed correct, the gut may be inserted in a loose coil. No tightness should be permitted to exist about it, as it may cause a divergency of shade in the places tightly bound or in any way compressed. A small piece of white cotton may with safety be loosely wound around, to hold the hank together.

There are numbers of stains for gut in use, but none are so well adapted to take off the surplus glaze as the one given above.

A very strong solution of green tea will tint drawn gut, but for the enamelled it is not sufficiently permanent or pronounced. Ink is largely used by amateur fishermen for gut staining. From the nature of some of the usual ingredients the deleterious effects are often deplorable. Inks are so variously made that it is at best a haphazard venture – one that too often proves deceptive and delusive. The tendency of an excess of this substance is to rot the gut and unduly to darken it for proper use, as we have already stated. The light-brown shades needed for some habitually discoloured waters are yielded by fustic chips, barberry bark and the best coffee beans (well roasted), these in equal quantities.

---

* It is often as well to use exclusively the larger pieces, as with the very small, other substances are frequently mixed up designedly or accidentally.

ঔ

To keep Moths from Feathers There are many receipts for this purpose, but practically they are but partially successful. Powders of various kinds are useful. Arsenic mixed with pepper (black or white) is good, as is also ammonia, but a more efficacious mode of keeping valuable feathers is the following: place in well-made or closely-fitting boxes of wood, tin or other material the feathers it is intended to preserve, and keep an uncorked bottle of spirit of mineral naptha inside. So long as it is so kept, no moth can exist in such a case or box. With very valuable feathers, it is an unfailing plan of evading the devastating moth to place in india-rubber bags,* tightly tying up the entrance afterwards, and charging the same with a weak solution of india rubber, dissolved in naptha or methylated spirit. This, of course, is infallible as a preventative, as is easily conceivable. Though prevention is undoubtedly the best policy, still it may be advisable to say what can be done with a stock of feathers or flies once infested and damaged but not totally destroyed by the larva of moths. The first thing to do is to place the package so infested in an oven heated by a slow fire, and when the grub-like forms to be seen in the midst of the work of damage are found to be dried, the parcel may be rummaged over, the good being carefully picked from the worthless, which latter should be burned or otherwise effectually destroyed.

ঔ

To make the best Transparent Wax For fly-making purposes, take of best resin 2 oz, ¾ oz of ordinary white wax, simmer them together in an earthenware vessel from five to seven minutes and pour into cold water; then work the whole by pulling it until white and pliable, it may then be scissored up into small pieces for convenience in use. The above freshens up the colour of the silk, rendering it in a degree waterproof and lasting; these advantages are due to the absence of

---

* Old rubber cushions, etc., answer well for this purpose, or sheet mackintosh may be made into bags with the dissolved rubber.

tallow, suet or other fatty substance. The practice of employing Burgundy pitch is deprecatory on the score of discoloration. The presence of grease in wax is bad for the same cause, as we have already pointed out.

᠉

Waterproof Varnish   The best 'Copal' is preferable for wear and protective qualities. It forms a sheet like glass over an article coated with it, and will retain it for many years, but the length of time needed for drying is so great (from two to three weeks) that save for the most choice articles it is eschewed. The variety known as 'Oak' varnish is good, it quickly dries hard, and is durable. Carriage varnish is more generally useful for rods, etc., as elegance in appearance is combined with sterling utility and wear-resisting qualities. Cheap varnish is false economy. The best qualities of oil varnish are seen to be *light* and clear, and free from impurities when held up to the light. Prior to varnishing an old rod, it is advisable to rub it down (especially about the handle), with turpentine or powdered pumice stone, in order to make an even foundation upon which the *oil* varnish can harden, or a coat of spirit varnish will answer the same purpose.

᠉

Spirit Varnishes for General Tackle   These differ very widely from those previously alluded to. They will dry upon any foundation whatever in from a few minutes to a few hours. Some are resinous, but these the angler should avoid, as they are not adapted to resist exposure to the action of the weather. Others consist of dissolved gums, and some of these are good for hook wrappings, bindings, etc., being fairly waterproof. The most useful may be had from the following: gum shellac dissolved in methylated spirits or vegetable naptha; 2 oz of the gum will be sufficient for about half a pint of the spirit. Place the vessel containing the admixture in the influence of warm air – but if a bottle, take care the cork is not tight down, or an explosion is inevitable. The above is most useful as a dressing for hook wrappings, and exposed silk bindings of any and every description that may occur in the angler's tackle. When applied with a soft linen rag the above forms an admirable and durable polish for rods and all wood work.

◦ᡒ

Line Dressing India rubber, dissolved, acts as a very good dressing for reel lines. It wears well, and preserves the silk from the action of the air and water. In a preparation of this kind the greatest caution is needful in choice of materials, as to employ inferior or adulterated rubber, or weak diluted spirit, would be but to anticipate defeat in the object sought after at the onset. *Pure* rubber must therefore be obtained, and placed in contact with a pure spirit, whether of wine, turpentine, naptha (vegetable) or methylated, it matters not, strength and purity are the primary points. The silk line may be steeped in the preparation when ready, and when thoroughly saturated through may be well shaken or lightly rubbed down, and then subjected to the drying influence of a warm room. Some days or even weeks in a low temperature must elapse ere the drying is near being hard. Air of a uniform temperature of about 100° will materially quicken the process. The numerous oil dressings are generally bad in their after effects, rotting the fibre of the line upon which they are applied to protect; but when oils are boiled, and silks and similar textiles are introduced to a seething mess, the deleterious effects are more speedily and pronouncedly shown. If a line be first charged with sugar of lead, dissolved in lukewarm water (the former to be of sufficient strength to make the water milk white), and then allowed to dry *thoroughly*, a dressing of cold boiled oil and gold size will have very little indeed of the deplorable effects. One of the most frequent defects in dressed lines is outside coatings. This is certain to shell away with friction, no matter what the dressing may consist of. In some receipts paste and starch are used wherewith to charge the line *before* waterproofing, with the ostentatious purpose of preventing the protective dressing penetrating to the centre. The object in view is to keep the preparation upon the surface to form a body smooth and sleek to the eye, to save the necessity of more dressings needed to combine a pleasing appearance with durability. As the originators of the system of waterproofing and plaiting silk lines, it is purely with the best of motives that we point out existing sources of discredit, when widespread and growing in extent, as is most certainly the case with the points alluded to. As a renovating dressing for old lines the following admixture is good: take of fly-maker's wax, sugar of lead and solid paraffin, one-third each, and dissolve by heat; then pour into a shallow vessel and cut into cakes convenient for use. This preparation is also most useful as a stiffening dressing for limp spinning- or trolling-lines. A rub down will render an awkwardly kinking and curling line comparatively pleasant to use.

ॐ

Feather-Staining To attempt to enumerate the whole range of the shades of colour would require far more space than could be wisely accorded in a general work of the present character; therefore, we shall merely append a hint or two applicable to feather-staining generally, to be followed by a few natural dyes, useful more particularly to the trout fisher. Gay colours, and all pronounced shades needful in hackle- and streamer-staining for salmon-fly-making may be got from the new aniline dyes. These are prepared from coal tar, and may be obtained either in crystalline form or dissolved. The former is more generally to be preferred, owing to greater strength.

Stains useful for the materials for small-fly-making are of another and totally different order. They must be of sterling value, be permanent, sombre and harmless in their effects upon the delicate feather fibres to be operated upon. In preparing a batch of feathers for staining, the uniform size required should be selected; these should be first soaked in warm water in which has been placed a scrap of common soap or soda, this removes the oil natural to the feather, and enables the dye to strike evenly throughout; when drained they are ready for the dye. In the case of large feathers it may be as well, in order to strike a delicate hue, to steep first in a solution of sulphuric acid; but generally speaking this is uncalled for. We now append a few useful receipts for natural dyes:

Fiery Brown – Camwood, logwood or partridge wood chips in equal parts, boiled in pure water.

Olive – Fustic and camwood, or logwood in equal parts, with a very small portion of copperas added when at the boiling point; the last named determines the shade. The outside of large onions boiled also are good.

Green – An infusion of fustic chips, to which must be added oil of vitriol, in a quantity sufficient to gain the shade required.

Light Yellow – Barberry bark in solution.

Dark Yellow – Walnut chunks.

Dun – Longwood and copperas (see gut dyeing).

Brown – Take of fustic chips two-thirds and of logwood chips one-third and boil in rainwater.

Black – Take half a pound of logwood chips and boil in a pint and a half of water; this done, put in one ounce of copperas and stir up.

୬

To Stain Gimp Take of camwood chips four ounces, and boil in a vessel, and drop into it (after cooling a little) oil of vitriol sufficient for the precise shade of colour desired. Fine white gimp may be stained admirably by the blue gut dye.

୬

Waterproof Dressing for Boots Take mineral naptha and black japan, equal parts, add together a small quantity, mix into a liquid, and apply with a brush. Another dressing: sperm oil, beeswax, solid paraffin and sugar of lead; melt together into a paste, colour with lamp black, and apply warm before a fire.[*]

୬

Hints for the Preservation of Gut, etc. Never expose the delicate materials used for fly-making to the action of the sun and air more

---

[*] Strawson's boot dressing is also very good. We have found it act most admirably in the most trying circumstances.

than can possibly be avoided. Gut and silk lose their strength and colour. Tinsels and furs and the usual body materials lose their brilliancy and become entirely worthless on being exposed for a protracted period. A gut cast is quickly covered with bright silvery specks, on being submitted to the action of the hot sun whilst coiled around the crown of the hat. The waxed silk in the body of an artificial fly works loose, and is soon whipped to shreds, or is drawn by a fish. Exposure is the baneful source of many ills – a source too often overlooked and unsuspected.

The exercise of care in properly casing not only casts but flies and fine bottom-tackle generally, when not required for use, it will be obvious is of the utmost importance.* Upon the other hand, reel lines and nets of every description require a given amount of exposure to dry thoroughly, as, if put up in a heap wet, they will, even in the case of waterproof articles, decay in time. A valuable trammel, sheet or other description of net will become so tender in a short time as to be utterly worthless if thrown aside immediately after use without spreading and drying. Lines of all kinds should be coiled from the reel and hung upon a peg, wound upon the back of a chair or placed elsewhere for a short time until dry.

✧

To Test Old Gut First soak for ten minutes in tepid water, *then allow to dry before testing*. Even new gut, when wet from the warm dye, is temporarily tender. Warm water would appear to strike to the core of the gut under its influence, detracting from its strength. It is necessary in the case of the old gut, as the humid nature has perished and needs reviving.

✧

---

* A small compact circular box is most useful for carrying, not only casts and loose flies, but spinning-flights, worm-tackles, etc., circular partitions effectually preventing entanglements.

To Pack Fish Fresh fish may be safely packed in wheaten straw alone, a straight bundle being fairly tied at one end with twine and the fish inserted in the middle of the straw, which is evenly spread around; the twine is now wound around the whole until the end opposite is reached, when it is securely fastened off, the straw cut level at each extremity, and all is complete for the label. When a long journey is intended, the fish should be rubbed dry, and some preservative should be used. A lump of salt, sugar or charcoal placed inside each fish, or even in the mouth, will suffice for any ordinary journey.*

---

* Glycerine and liquid gum arabic, when applied to the external surface, will tend to retain the colour of fish it is wished to preserve and case.

CHAPTER SEVENTEEN

About Hooks

Crippled Hooks; The Over-Barbed Hook; Defects in Temper, etc.;
The Limerick, Kendal-Sneck, Carlisle, Kirby and the 'Swan'
Bend; The New Eyed Hooks

In a country which takes the lead in piscatorial pursuits, and whose
improvements serve as the type and pattern for other nations, constant progress should at least be made, and improvements achieved
in order to retain the position gained. If there is one thing more
than another in this branch of industry that we excel in it is the
manufacture of our hooks. These are in general use upon the
continent, in the colonies, and everywhere where the angling art is
practised.* It will, therefore, be readily conceded by all who have
devoted attention to the subject that *more* attention is due to this
important item in the angler's equipage and in our national commerce
than has, of late years, been bestowed upon it. Previous to our
suggesting any improvements in detail, we intend calling attention to
a few very common defects in hooks, as generally constructed, to
which may be directly traced much unnecessary loss and disaster.

The excessively bony nature of the mouth of most fish has
frequently a very trying effect upon the hook, therefore any little
deficiency in its make, or manner of construction, leads to untold
evils. In order to render ourselves intelligible to the reader we shall
first describe the usual system of making the hook. First, then, the

* There is scarcely a single hook manufactory anywhere outside England, and
  what few there are in the United States do not meet a tithe of the home
  demand.

wire is struck off in given lengths, in accordance with the size of the hook required; next, the point is formed and the shank reduced by a few strokes of the file; and next, the barb is cut by means of a large knife. All is now ready for bending, which is one of the most particular items in the construction, as the operation decides the *shape*, and, consequently, the particular species of hook to be produced. This is quickly done by means of a small steel block around which the wire is bent, the shape of the block varying according to the particular bend required. Now comes the final operation, viz., that of tempering. This is done in a large pan over a slow furnace. Millions of hooks are frequently tempered in one operation, therefore the greatest care should be bestowed upon this important point; but of this more anon.

The most fertile source of complaint is, we believe, the undue weakness of the majority of hooks at the barb (see Plate 12, Fig. 2). A deeply barbed hook may be safely discarded as being too dangerous to use. There is no earthly necessity for it. Not only is the wire half cut through by the operation, but the point of the hook is forced quite out of the straight line, thus not only requiring heavier striking properly to hook a fish, but being more liable to snap by the sudden strain. The very action of inserting the bearding knife too deeply causes the point to project outwards inadvertently (see Plate 12, Fig. 2), giving it a 'scratch and let go' appearance, and no less effect; indeed, there are but two alternatives for a hook of this description when a fish is caught upon the gristly or bony part of the mouth – (1) to scratch as described, or (2) to break clean off at the barb near the point of the hook. We have seen hooks fitted with costly salmon flies, nine-tenths of them being quite useless, having broken at this identical point. A batch was shown to us by (the late) Mr Frank Buckland, H. M. Inspector of Inland Fisheries, numbering one hundred and twenty-seven, all broken. The original value ranged from five shillings to one guinea each. Nine of these were broken at the sharp bend of the Limerick hook, the whole of the remainder at the barb. The loss incurred at this rate is considerable, and when we take the fish into account, it is simply monstrous.

This defect is by no means confined to the Limerick bend of hook;

it is frequently more conspicuous in the Sneck or Kendal bent hooks, so universally used in trout fishing: *vide* the experience of everybody. Another point of paramount importance is the tempering, as when this is done in a defective manner, by being left too high or too low in temperament, another source of disappointment and loss ensues as the inevitable result. Amongst *non*-japanned hooks uselessly soft ones may sometimes be distinguished by the colour, as when steel is left a very light blue, it is invariably soft and pliable. The best tempered hooks are left a purple-blue colour. In japanned hooks the only reliable way of detecting faulty ones is to test them by sticking the point in a piece of porous wood or cork, and applying a heavy though steady strain to the shank. Our idea of a perfect Limerick salmon hook we give upon the Plate 12, Fig. 3. The distance from the *bend* to the *point* is greatly diminished; the barb and point being short and sharp are well adapted to take good and firm hold upon a hard or soft substance. The main strength of metal, too, is just where most needed, namely, at the sudden turn of the bend, which, it may be observed, is not nearly so sharp or decisive as in the old-style Limerick. Experience teaches, so says the maxim. Experience long since taught us that changes in this respect were absolutely necessary, and for an equally long period experience, the self-same teacher, has proved the hook now submitted to be perfectly exempt from the evils previously pointed out. The Kendal Sneck, to which we have already made some allusion, is the bend generally adopted for trout flies. It is often made from very fine wire, which renders it useless for a heavy fish. This is the hook most generally used for dry-fly-fishing. A judiciously tapered *shank* will reduce the weight whilst retaining the full strength requisite for an emergency round the bend. This, as we have already pointed out, is of the most vital importance; an exhibition of false economy in this matter will cause the angler's skill to avail nothing. We know of no more tantalising thing than to lose the heaviest fish of the day, month or season through a defective hook. When once a fish is well hooked upon sound 'tack', it is the rodster's own fault if he fails to land it. A spell at the salmon will frequently put out the delicacy of the trout fisher's touch, and he, by

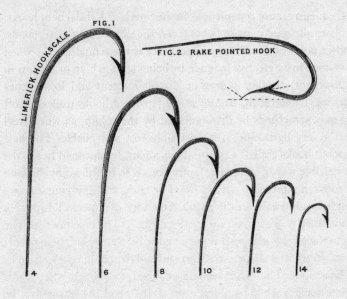

FIG.1

LIMERICK HOOKSCALE

FIG.2 RAKE POINTED HOOK

4 6 8 10 12 14

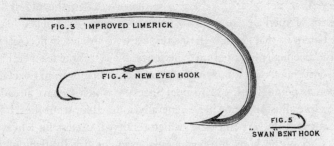

FIG.3 IMPROVED LIMERICK

FIG.4 NEW EYED HOOK

FIG.5 "SWAN BENT HOOK"

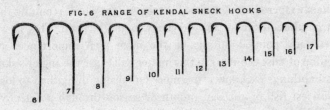

FIG.6 RANGE OF KENDAL SNECK HOOKS

6 7 8 9 10 11 12 13 14 15 16 17

PLATE 12

too sanguine striking, will lose every fish he hooks, either by breaking away the hold, or otherwise the hook. The range of Kendal hooks, given upon the Plate, shows the relative strength and sizes of what we have used for trouting flies for many years. The Kendal hook should be slightly crooked or twisted in the bend, as the body and the hackle standing out will, to some extent, serve to guard the point. A great many of the short rises one experiences sometimes are due to the non-observance of this rule, the fish taking the fly with the skin of his teeth, so to speak, the point fails to take any hold whatever. The wide 'span' of the salmon hook obviates the necessity of this. The trout hook then, for the same reason, should have reasonable scope in this respect, so as to be capable of taking broad hold and retaining it. The point and barb should be anything but 'proud'; the evils of this are far more objectionable, whilst being quite as prevalent, in smaller and lighter hooks than has been shown in the case of the heavy Limerick. The relative weight-sustaining powers of straight-pointed and 'rake-pointed' hooks may be exemplified in the following manner. Take a 'rake' pointed, deeply barbed Limerick, Kendal, or any other bend, and take also a 'straight' pointed hook of the same size and strength of metal. Secure a length of gut to the shank of each hook, and stick the points slightly into a deal board, and now attach a spring-balance to each piece of gut, and pull. The staying powers of the 'straight point' will be found to be almost double that of the others.

Up to a recent date eyed hooks have been looked upon as associated only with the most primitively uncouth styles of angling. The recent development above implied is known as 'Hall's Eyed Hook', it having been invented and introduced by Mr H. S. Hall (Clifton, Bristol), who, with several of his friends, has devoted much time and trouble to its perfection.

The hook is refined to an extent difficult to conceive from description. The advantages claimed are its adaptability for dry-fly-fishing (this, owing to delicacy of make and quality of metal), the economy incurred by the loop shank in lieu of the attached gut, and the convenience common to all looped flies, which are sufficiently well understood to obviate a detailed allusion here. We have used the new eyed hook and find in it elements of merit sufficient to warrant mention in these pages. The advantages claimed are fully borne out by its use. It will be seen that the loop projects upwards (see Plate 12, Fig. 4). This in a manner casts the weight upon the wings, and preserves the equilibrium of the 'artificial'. The gut may be attached to the loop, as in the case of salmon flies, by means of the slip knot, known as the 'Carrick bend', with this difference, that the gut is passed through the underside of the loop first.

Hooks used for spinning purposes are required to be very heavily ironed, more especially for pike; weak triangles are the rule rather than the exception. Weight here is no detriment but rather an advantage. In selecting hooks, the weight they are required to bear should always be taken into consideration, and the thickness of the wire chosen accordingly. Treble hooks for salmon and pike fishing, in particular, are much too delicate, generally speaking. We have seen several triangles broken at the strike of a heavy fish. The temper of many triangles or brazed hooks sold has been affected during the brazing operation. The plan generally adopted over-tempers them, thus causing them to be hard and brittle; and as two or sometimes three and more hooks have frequently to be driven home, the odds are that if the fish does not break them the rodster often does. Breakages are so rife in the case of brazed hooks, owing mainly to the causes above named, that many anglers have been led to eschew them altogether; but the fault lies largely with the angler who selects them too fine and delicate in the metal.

The hooks requisite for successful roach fishing should be moderately long-shanked. We prefer the 'Sneck' to the 'round' or Carlisle bend, the latter being frequently too short in the shank, and having much too exaggerated a 'span' in the bend to work with a short shank properly. The remarks anent weak wire apply equally to round-bend roach hooks; and if we combine with the above the usual fault of a turned-out, rakish-looking point, no room is left for surprise at the many disasters incurred by their use. The greater utility of a well-proportioned hook may be easily ascertained by the following simple experiment. Take two hooks – a moderately long-shanked one nicely tapered, with a straight point, and a short-shanked hook with a turned-out point. Attach gut to each. Now procure a small piece of parchment or thin cardboard, upon which take good hold with both hooks and endeavour to penetrate this by applying equal pressure to each. If this is done at all evenly the long-shanked hook will quickly pierce the substance, making a clean incision; meanwhile the attitude of the remaining hook scarcely admits of any impression being made at all, a perfectly flat surface being presented from the tip of the point to the end of the barb, which effectually prevents any incision.

Most of the various forms or bends of the hooks now in use were introduced before the advent of the present century. Of these, however, there have since been many modifications and variations. One of the oldest bends is the 'Kirby', the originator, Charles Kirby, having lived and flourished in the seventeenth century. In the third edition of an old book on angling, published in 1700, entitled *The Angler's Vade Mecum* – a copy of which we are pleased to be able to say we have in our possession – the following quaint advertisement appears appended to the preface:

At the Sign of the Fish, in *Black Horse Alley* near *Fleet Bridge*, liveth *Will Browne*, who maketh all sorts of *Fishing Rods*, and selleth all sorts of Fishing Tackle; also *Charlie Kirby's* Hooks, with Worms, Gentles and Fly's; and also the *East India Weed*, which is the only thing for Trout, Carp, and Bottom-fishing, first being well soaked for half-an-hour before you use it in water, being of a brittle nature, if not moistened before used, and then proves so strong and fine, of a water-colour, that it deceives the Fish, much more than Hair or Silk. Note – That *Kirby's* Hooks are known by the fineness of the Wyer and Strength, and many Shops sell Counterfeit for his, which prove prejudicial to the User. The true *Kirby's* are to be sold by *Will Browne* and nowhere Else.

Kirby's hooks, however, have long since been discarded, except in perch and suchlike fishing. Another hook that used to be greatly in vogue was the 'Staple-bend'. Sproat's, too, have now about gone out.

Those in general use at the present day are the Sneck or Kendal, the Limerick and Carlisle, or round bend; for eels, the bend known as the 'Shepherd's Crook' is greatly used.

For fine grayling fishing, perhaps, a really strong and *delicate* hook is more essential than in any other style or system of angling. The grayling is a much more fastidious fish than the trout, and is moreover the most tender-mouthed fish that swims. It is no uncommon thing for the angler, when fishing for grayling, to find a portion of the jaw of an escaped fish remaining upon his hook; more especially when rough bottom-tackle is used. The hook useful for trout is, generally speaking, too large and heavy for grayling, the excessively small flies he usually prefers being difficult to copy when a clumsy and heavy hook is employed. There has long been a want felt of a suitable hook for grayling, to be at once light, durable, and effective in shape and make. Many experiments we have tried in years past with the view of surmounting this difficulty, but failure was the characteristic feature of each, until we accidentally hit upon a peculiar bend (Plate 12, Fig. 5), which was found to work with unusual success. Conjointly with several friends of the rod, we have tested this hook thoroughly, and with perfectly satisfactory results.

This hook has been designated the 'Swan'-bend, and as such it is known amongst the few anglers who have hitherto kept it a secret. It may be gathered from what has been previously stated that the faults and deficiencies, as well as the merits, of hooks rest to a great extent with the manufacturer; and we would observe that Messrs Allcock & Co., from the large extent of their productions, are enabled to devote every attention to the all-important details to which we have alluded. This firm have always assiduously and carefully carried out any suggestion submitted to them, never failing to give the most complete satisfaction.

CHAPTER EIGHTEEN

Trout Culture

*Origin of the Art of Pisciculture; Its Great Importance and
Utility; Method of Procedure; Spawning; Hatching; Time
Requisite for Vivifying and Rearing; The Wet and Dry Process of
Spawning; Hatching Apparatus*

The immense progress yearly achieved both at home and abroad in
the artificial cultivation of well-nigh every variety of fish, cannot fail
to be noted with pleasure by fishermen generally. It would be difficult
to say who really originated the system of artificially propagating fish:
certain is it that it was unknown and unpractised by the ancients.
Perhaps the earliest writer upon it was Jacobe, a German, who lived
in the last century, a translation from whose book is given by Yarrell.*
His proposals would not, however, seem to have been followed out, as
until within the last forty years nothing further appears to have been
written upon the subject. About this time two French fishermen,
Gehin and Remy, of La Bresse, in the Department of the Vosges, first
practically developed what had been previously known to eminent
men of science as a scientific curiosity, and not as of practical utility. A
few years saw the whole of the rivers and streams of the Vosges,
Moselle and Bas-Rhin, which had previously been almost depopulated, well stocked with fish. The Government, on its part, saw
that the application of artificial propagation to the rivers and streams
of the whole country would not only afford employment to a vast
number of persons, but would enable an immense addition to be

* Vol. 2, pp. 87–96

made, at scarcely any expense, to the food supply of the nation. The lakes and rivers of France were therefore replenished with not only trout and salmon, but with divers other species of freshwater fish. The United States have since adopted this method of replenishing their somewhat exhausted waters, and with still greater success.

Though we in the narrow boundaries of our sea-girt isle, do not look upon our inland fisheries as being so much the auxiliary of our national bread-basket as a field for a time-honoured national pastime and recreation, still, as the popularity of this sport widens yearly, the artificial propagation of our best kinds of migratory and non-migratory fish ought to, and must, be cultivated in corresponding degree. Long and patient study of the habits of male and female fish at spawning time proves that scarcely one in a hundred of the eggs deposited by the female in the beds of rivers, and duly fecundated, come to maturity, the rest being devoured by other fish, washed away, or destroyed by the shifting bed of the water. It is also found that of this small percentage of successfully hatched fry, the major part again is devoured by the larger fish of the same or different species. The incalculable utility, therefore, of fertilising artificially at a rate of from *eighty* to *ninety* per cent, which can easily and simply be done, as we shall proceed to show, will be obvious to all.

Apart from this, fish-culture forms in itself a really interesting amusement, as instructive as it is pleasing, being free from all cruelty, and affording indeed a perfect fund of interest and enjoyment to the lover of nature and her beauties. Very many proprietors of trouting streams, known to the writer, annually hatch thousands of trout, which are used for restocking brooks and streams far and near. The spawning and hatching of trout takes place in winter, when cold weather sets in, sooner or later according to the locality of the stream and the weather. The trout run up into small side streams or tributaries to spawn. The spawning lasts three weeks or so usually. The period greatly depends on the temperature of the water and atmosphere. When stock fish are required the overgrown weeds and other debris should be removed from a rivulet or branch stream they are known to frequent, and the pebbly gravel raked level over upon a tempting shallow. This done, some inviting shelter should be provided for them in the stream to lie under, such as moored boards, sunken hollow tile or drain pipes. When the fish are well up upon the beds, which may be seen, as the cock trout or milter works the gravel about, they may be caught.

Trammel nets must be used for this purpose, fixing one at each end of the beds. The fish will rush into the nets when the shelters are removed. When caught, the sexes should be separated. They are easily distinguished, as at spawning time the eggs can be felt in the female fish, whilst in the male the milt, being a liquid, is easily recognised. Unless a fish is thoroughly ripe it should be kept until it is, in a box or can used for that purpose, as unripe eggs are of no use for hatching purposes. The following is the most approved method of procedure.

⟳

Spawning All being ready for the process, the pan or vessel to be used is laid upon the ground, tilted to one side, quite dry, and a hen fish is taken from the tub and allowed to kick about a short time to induce it to lay its eggs more freely. The fish is carefully held with a piece of woollen fabric in the left hand, an assistant holding the tail. The fish is held sideways, and the spawner with his right hand strips the fish, beginning at the upper end of the ovary, which extends nearly to the pectoral fin, and carrying the pressure gently but quickly to the vent; only using the thumb and fourth finger. When one or two hens are stripped, the milter is held over the eggs, which are then fecundated, the milt being abstracted in the same way.

Each fish should be carefully returned to the shallow water. The pan should be tilted a little, so as to mix the milt with the eggs, and then allowed to stand for a few minutes, after which a little water must be added, just enough to cover the eggs, and the pan set aside until these have completely separated. They may then be washed with clean water and transferred to the receptacle prepared for them. This should be filled with water, and the eggs poured into it. The eggs of two hens are sufficient for one pan, although the eggs of three or even four hens may be fecundated by a full-sized milter. The eggs are then distributed in troughs by a quill, or, better still, a glass tube; covers are then to be placed upon the troughs, and a good supply of water turned on. In arranging eggs in troughs, begin at the lowest, so that the shells from the first hatched do not interfere with those hatched later on; one square foot of trough should be allowed to a thousand or fifteen hundred eggs. A small quill feather may be used in arranging the eggs, but should be handled lightly, so that no two may touch each other. They will hatch out much better for this, as when the eggs are heaped pell-mell their fertility is in a measure frustrated.

࿚

Hatching When the eggs are once placed in the hatching trough they must remain there until they are hatched. They require to be daily examined, and dead eggs carefully removed by means of a pair of forceps or nippers, great care being exercised not to injure the living. A dead egg is opaque, and when once seen can scarcely be mistaken. A species of alga grows upon the dead eggs if left in the water, which spreads speedily over the healthy ones in the vicinity, and would in time seriously imperil the wellbeing of the brood. In the event of a casualty of this nature being threatened, frequent washings through a finely perforated watering pot may avert the unfortunate result of neglect. These discoloured eggs may in some cases hatch, but can never be reared, the fry dying prematurely.

Seasons vary, and in precisely the same ratio do the times of spawning and hatching. The latter operation does not always occur at a stated time after incubation. Late eggs hatch much sooner than early ones, the temperature of the air and water gradually accelerating the operation. The longer the time consumed in attaining maturity for hatching, the more vigorous will be the brood. From numerous experiments we gather that, with a maximum temperature of water of about fifty-five degrees, both salmon and trout ova may be hatched in from ninety-two to one hundred and six days; but in the case of the salmon, if the temperature be under forty degrees, the hatch will not take place under one hundred and thirty-five to one hundred and forty days. As the eggs ripen they swell considerably, and assume a beautiful yellow colour.

The general hatching period is heralded by the appearance of several moving atoms, more forward than the rest, which have already burst the membrane. This, the first stage of the trout's life, is called the 'alevin' stage. The body consists of a fine elongated substance, with a conspicuous pair of optics; this is sustained, horizontally, like the trembling needle of the compass, by a much larger body, which closely resembles a yellow ball of butter, or congealed oil, in appearance. When viewed through the medium of a microscope this yolk-like substance is seen to be part and parcel of the aquatic being itself; blood veins traversing and retracing it both inside and out. This is nature's provision, which serves as proper sustenance for the first month or six weeks, being an internal store of food by which all the animal's needs are supplied. It rests quiet for the first few days, wriggling but at intervals, but after the fifth day or so a great desire to hide is shown, and this is seen to be the case for about a fortnight. Ere this length of time has elapsed the little creatures will have gained much in size and vigour, the fins and tail not only being fully developed, but in full and perfect use. The alevins will now be very desirous of emigrating, more especially during the night, and if great care is not taken in grating over the outlet of the water, serious loss is certain to be sustained. No food need be supplied yet, and all that it is necessary to do is to inspect the brood carefully once *per diem* to remove all bad eggs.

Rearing Immediately the vesicle has quite disappeared, the fish are seen to be very active in their movements; then it is time food should be given them. The fry, when hungering, invariably dart at tiny insects or other objects upon the water's surface. Their first course should be hard-boiled yolk of egg, which should be pressed through the fine gratings of a delicate strainer, and, if merely to test their hunger, some small gnats should be thrown to them. It is best at this stage to test the most forward lot daily. Gnats, together with small blood worms, should be supplied them for five or six weeks or so, and finely chopped or minced liver may be substituted by way of change: three meals are ample during this period. Plenty of room is requisite for the wellbeing of trout fry, therefore a month or thereabouts after hatching, part of the young fish should be removed to cisterns or large tanks, through which runs briskly a constant supply of water, the outlets being properly capped by perforated zinc to prevent their exit. When a suitable rivulet is available, and the natural aquatic and aerial enemies of the young fry are comparatively scarce, the best course to pursue is to confine the whole brood in a part of the stream by the aid of wire or zinc screens at given points. They should have plenty of shelter, as a resort; indeed we have always found it best to cover quite half of the water with boards, which enables them to shelter from the hot rays of the sun. All obnoxious weeds should be removed before the introduction of the fry. If a few falls can be easily made they will have an advantageous influence. It is generally the wisest policy to keep up the fry until April or March following the spring in which they are hatched; but this is simply a precaution. They should be fed well once or twice a day as long as they are confined. Some take out the larger fry periodically, and turn them adrift where required. This, however, is a matter quite at the rearer's discretion; his object is attained as soon as the trout can feed eagerly. As grayling spawn in the hot months, it proves a comparatively easy matter to hatch and rear them. We have hatched grayling in an ordinary square box, the bottom being formed by a sheet of finely pierced zinc; the eggs are placed upon this without any covering, and the wood lid secured, a rope being then attached to a staple fixed at one end of the box near the bottom, and the box then moored in mid-stream so that the water can flow intermittently through the bottom, which acts so well upon the ova as to vivify and cause it to hatch in a comparatively limited time.

To vivify salmon and trout ova when impregnated by the milt, the combined influence of running water of a given temperature and of solar and atmospheric action is required. The fish themselves, it must not be forgotten, often ascend the stream to the very source in order to gain a lower temperature, and the maximum heat of the water should be about 55° to produce a vigorous and healthy brood of fish, as we have already stated.

Andamorous or migratory fish, it is well known, invariably return to their native river after their marine trip for breeding purposes, therefore the rearer of these has ultimately the full benefit of his enterprise; and if only the water is adapted to the natural requirements and wellbeing of *non-migratory* fish, they, especially, will locate permanently wherever placed. Considering the many thousands of eggs carried by a female trout, it will be found an easy matter to hatch and rear – if our instructions are followed out – any quantity of fish. By the older systems fifty to sixty per cent of vitalised eggs was considered excellent; by the dry process of spawning, and the use of more suitable hatching appurtenances, a percentage of eighty-five to ninety is now considered quite ordinary. Hatching frames or tanks are constructed in almost every conceivable way, and of a great variety of material, including slate slabs, earthenware, iron (galvanised and otherwise), wood and perforated zinc. We ourselves find the last named material to answer the best, as by its use gravel beds are rendered unnecessary, the finely pierced metal admitting of each egg, when properly spread out and arranged, being perfectly surrounded by water. Fungus is also avoided and easily checked, as its spreading is a moral impossibility if carefully looked over daily. The French, it would appear, were the first to discover that the use of gravel was not requisite in artificial hatching. As regards concealing the eggs, which concealment engenders the spread of fungus, animal parasites and fin disease in more open water, the instinct of the parent fish, it is presumed, prompts them to conceal their progeny in a degree by the aid of the gravel; but though gravel be thus objectionable, it is necessary that the eggs should be subjected to the action of the water upon their whole surface as far as practicable. M. Coste, the originator of the new system, placed the eggs on or between the edges of slips of glass, systematically arranged across the bottom of the hatching apparatus so as to admit of the water operating upon all with the least possible expanse of surface. The advantages claimed for the system are numerous. We are told that greater facility is afforded for counting the eggs; that detection and expulsion of blind or unfertilised eggs is made easy; and that the rough edges of the glass will enable the little strangers to extricate themselves more readily from the egg membrane; but all these advantages are possessed by the perforated zinc troughs, which have the additional recommendation of being much simpler to manage.[*]

Judging from the increasing interest that has of late years been exhibited in this subject, we confidently predict that the time is not far distant when angling clubs, leaseholders and proprietors of private waters generally will sow the seed, as well as reap the harvest, by practising pisciculture as well as piscicapture.

IN MEMORIAM.
DAVID FOSTER.
BORN SEP. 22ND 1816.
DIED APRIL 4TH 1881.

THE SWEET REMEMBRANCE OF THE JUST
SHALL FLOURISH WHEN HE SLEEPS IN DUST.

[*] These and other requisites for the amateur pisciculturist are supplied by the Cray Fishery Co., Foot's Cray, Kent; from whom the eggs also, as well as hatched fry and yearling fish, may be obtained.

Index

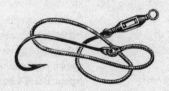